My Best Friend, Marty

M. Jandreau

To Mallory,
Thanks for helping me raise a great little girl!
With Gratitude,
M. Jandreau

Copyright © 2024 by M. Jandreau

All rights reserved.

No portion of this book may be reproduced in any form without written permission from the publisher or author except as permitted by U.S. copyright law.

My Best Friend, Marty is a work of fiction. Names, characters, places, and incidents are the products of the author's imagination or are used fictitiously. Any resemblance to actual events, locales, or persons, living or dead, is entirely coincidental.

To Jill.
For twenty-four plus years of friendship.
For a lifetime of laughter.
For always reading my books.
For putting up with every single ounce of my bullshit over the years.
And for a million affectionately delivered insults.

For more information, updates, and signed copies, visit mjandreau.com
Scan the QR code below to be taken there.

2003

Meeting Marty

Some moments in your life happen, and you never forget them. They stick with you. Through ups and downs, good times and bad, some memories are permanent. Occasionally, they're silly things. Sometimes, they're small, mostly insignificant memories with no value, but they stick with you anyway.

My memory is odd. I tend to remember primarily unimportant things. Directions to a friend's house I haven't been to in 30 years. A phone number someone once told me to remember so we could call it back later. What shirt someone was wearing at my 16th birthday party. The lyrics to Snow's "Informer" that I painstakingly learned in eighth grade to impress my friends (while I simultaneously got an F in Science class). The memories seem to make no sense, but they're in there. Locked away for all time. For some reason or another.

So many people have come and gone in my life over the years. They've been so important to me, and then, for whatever reason, they're gone. Sometimes, there are reasons why a friendship stops. Sometimes, it's organic, and you grow apart as people. Especially when you're younger. As you grow up and become an adult, sometimes the adult version of you doesn't like the adult version of who your best friends became. That's fine. That's not the point here, really.

One of my most vivid memories of my entire life was the day I met Marty.

It was October of 2003. It seems like forever ago. So many important things happened to me that year. I met my wife in March of that year. I met the girl I'd marry, my first wife, if you'd like to be specific. And while I remember the gist of those events, they're not quite as vivid as the moment I met Marty.

It was unusually warm in New England at the beginning of October. Warm enough that, on my drive home from Boston, I had the windows in the car open. Music blasting, as usual. Enjoying having just left the dorm room of the girl who'd become my first wife in a handful of years. I was high on happiness.

Like every other night, I pulled into the driveway of my childhood home, parked the car, and sat listening to the remainder of the song I'd been listening to on the local rock radio station, WAAF. Though I've outgrown the habit, I used not to be able to get out of the car before the currently playing track finished. Perhaps it's because, nowadays, you can pause what you were listening to on Spotify or Apple Music or whatever, get out of the car, and pick it right back up when you get inside. Technology has changed a lot of how someone my age lives their life.

I got out of the car when the song was over, closing the door quietly not to disturb my mom's sleep. I knew she'd be asleep already because it was late. I always did my best to be quiet when coming home, no matter what time, not for fear of getting in trouble but just out of courtesy.

We lived on a quiet street. The adjacent streets to ours formed a U-shaped neighborhood, with our house sitting at the exact middle of the bottom of the U. Therefore, not many cars drove by our house, even in the middle of the day. So, when someone came walking down the street in the middle of the night, it caught me by surprise.

It's more common now, with the people who live in my mom's neighborhood, to see people walking their dogs at all hours of the day. So, today, I wouldn't be surprised by this. But twenty-plus years ago, it was a bit of a shock.

I froze, not knowing who this person was, barely able to see them on the mostly dark street. The streetlight on the corner about a hundred or more feet away didn't help illuminate the person.

He must have been startled at seeing me as much as I was shocked at the sight of him. He froze as well.

Neither of us moved for a beat, trying to size each other up.

In hindsight, he probably figured, based on where I was standing—right up against the car door—that I was breaking into the car. Standing there in the middle of the night, in a pitch-dark driveway, only illuminated by the half-moon in the cloudless sky above, I probably looked like a criminal.

And I, in my state of panic, initially thought the same. He was in our neighborhood for something nefarious.

Why'd my brain go immediately to something negative? I'm not sure. Maybe it was the twenty-something mentality of knowing what I'd probably be doing if I walked around in someone's neighborhood in the middle of the night.

"Oh," he said after a moment. "Hello there."

Still frozen, it took me a moment to respond. Likely furthering his thought that I was doing something illegal to the car in front of me.

I turned to my right to face him. "Hi," I said. "What are you doing here?"

He stepped closer to our driveway from the far side of the street he'd been walking along. "I'm new here," he said. "I'm just getting the lay of the land."

"At night?" I asked quickly.

"There are fewer automobiles after dark," he replied equally quickly.

"Huh," I thought out loud. "I guess you're not wrong."

There was another moment of awkward pause between us. Both of us were partially still frozen.

"I'm Matt," I said.

He nodded. "Hello Matt, it's nice to meet you."

He didn't give me his name, which I found odd. I still find it odd to this day. I never questioned him about it, which was odd of me.

I stepped toward him. "Are you lost? Do you know how to get home?"

"I am not lost," he replied. "Home is just there," he said, pointing down toward the end of the street, in the general direction of where my childhood friends Josh and Sarah lived.

"Oh," I said. "Okay."

The lights by our garage came on, which I knew meant my mother had either woken up and heard me outside or heard me outside and woken up from it. In either case, she'd turned the lights on for me, allowing me to see him a little more brightly. With him now standing at the end of our driveway, I was able to make out his facial features and clothing.

He wore jeans, normal-looking sneakers, a plain white t-shirt, and a non-descript baseball hat covering his short brown hair.

His blue eyes reflected the light from the garage vividly. Even from twenty feet away, I could see their clarity and color.

When he realized I could now see him, he smiled.

"I better get going," he said, stepping back and turning to his right to face the road ahead of him.

"Good night," I said, watching him walk toward the streetlight.

I don't know why I stood by the car for so long that night. Like some sort of creep, I watched him walk to the end of my street and make the right on the adjoining road. I watched him until he disappeared behind the fence at the house on the corner.

When I went inside, my mom stood in the kitchen, the fridge open, rummaging through its contents.

"Who were you talking to?" she asked.

"There was a guy out in the road, walking."

"At this hour?"

I looked at the clock on the microwave. It was just after 12:30 a.m. It was not an uncommon time for me to get home from wherever I was, but it was very unusual for my mom to be awake at that hour. Wrapped in the same bathrobe, I'm convinced she'd had since before I was born, I figured she must have gone to bed and gotten back up to get a snack or a drink.

"Yeah," I said. "It was weird. He said he was 'new here,' so maybe he just moved to the neighborhood."

My mom, ever the gossip, immediately responded. "There haven't been any houses sold in the neighborhood lately."

As was typical of me when not knowing what to say, I gave a big shrug and slithered past her toward the stairs up to my bedroom.

"Night," I heard her call from the kitchen as I was halfway up the stairs.

"Night," I called back down.

Introductions

It wasn't long before I started seeing him more often. Usually at night, generally walking along the same side of my street that he'd been on that first night.

I'd get home from wherever I was, and there he'd be.

The fourth time I'd seen him, we talked closer, physically, to one another.

That was the first time I had heard the slight accent in his voice. I couldn't place where it was, though. It wasn't American, not a southern accent or mid-west. Not anything obvious, like England, Australia, or France. Just this every so slight, tiny little accent to his voice.

"What's your name?" I finally asked.

"Oh," he said, fumbling. "Did I not introduce myself before?"

"No," I said. "I don't know your name or where you're from."

"Oh," he said again. "I'm from all over. Papa travels a lot for work, so we've lived in lots of places. We are originally from Belgium."

It was the first time he'd referenced any other people. I suppose I had assumed he had a family up to that point, but the reference to "Papa" seemed to solidify he was living with at least one other person.

"Ok. So what's your name?"

"I am Michel," he said.

"Michel?"

"Yes, that is correct."

"Do you have a nickname?" I asked.

"Yes, I do."

I waited a solid ten seconds. "Well? What is it?"

"Oh, yes. You'd like me to tell you. When we first came to America, I chose an American version of my name. I chose Marty."

"Marty? Why not Mike? That's closer to Michel, isn't it? Well, anyway, nice to officially meet you, Marty." I walked to the end of the driveway, hoping he'd meet me there to shake my hand. He didn't budge from his spot and seemed a little frightened that I'd gotten so close to him.

"I must be going," he said.

"All right then, Marty. Have a good night. Get home safe."

Like the other nights we'd talked, I, again, watched him walk to the end of my road and make the right, eventually disappearing behind the fence at the house on the corner.

Part of me wanted to follow him, to see where he lived or where he was going. My mom's voice echoed in my head, reminding me there had been no house sales in the neighborhood recently. It made me wonder if he lived in our neighborhood or not.

A Gift

The next morning, I ran into Marty on my way to work. Somehow, as I'd left the house door and made my way to the car, I'd heard his footsteps coming down the street.

He was coming from the same direction he'd always come from previously, though I'd never seen him during the day before. Our encounters had always been at night.

"Hey, Marty," I said, waving as I unlocked my car.

"Hello, Matt," he said, waving back. "It is a beautiful morning, isn't it?"

It was a beautiful morning. Something I hadn't, and didn't normally, notice. I was usually so focused on jumping in my car, finding a good song on the radio, and getting off work to stop and see what the world was doing.

"It is," I said. "Great morning. I'm off to work."

"Before you go," he said. "I've brought you something."

"Oh, huh?" I fumbled for words, half jogging to the end of the driveway to meet him.

"It's a gift," he started. "From the last place I have lived."

From his pocket, he pulled out what looked to be a small rag or towel. Dirty and tattered, it looked like junk someone had picked up from the street.

I stared down at it, confused.

"My apologies, this seems odd," he said. "This is not the gift."

He opened the rag slowly, one corner at a time, as if intentionally trying to be dramatic.

As the corners were removed, I saw a small stone, shiny on all sides that I could see, with a hollowed-out center. A completely round hole, all the way through the stone. The stone looked like a six-inch-long oval with a perfectly circular hole in the center around an inch.

"I've kept it with me for a while. When I found it, I felt something special about it. Something that felt unusual but gave me comfort."

"And you want to give it to me?" I asked.

"You've shown me kindness," he replied. "And I've been taught that kindness deserves reward and appreciation."

"This is..." I fumbled for the right words. "This is so incredibly kind of you. To give me, a virtual stranger, something that's meant so much to you and been important to you is really nice."

"I thank you for chatting with me these handfuls of nights and now this morning, Matt. You have been a very nice man."

I was still unsure of what to say. No one had ever given me something like that before. Certainly, no one that I'd just met. Definitely, no one that'd been walking down my street in the middle of the night.

"You must go," he said. "You don't want to be late."

And then, like always, he sauntered off down the road, making the right and passing the fence into non-existence.

I got in the car, found a song I wanted to listen to, and off I went to work. My new stone was sitting next to me on the passenger seat, still partially covered by the tattered cloth it was wrapped up with in his pocket.

The stone is still with me to this day. It's become one of my most sentimentally valued items, which I will never get rid of.

My Big Secret

By the time I got home from work that day, I'd half expected Marty to be walking by as if some magic would get the timing right so that I'd pull into the driveway just as he happened to be walking by the house.

It didn't work out that way. So, I did what any completely sane and normal person would do. I got two lawn chairs from the backyard, set them up at the end of the driveway, and plopped down in one of them, waiting.

From my vantage point, I could see where Marty was coming from for the first time. Rather than just being surprised when he passed the small side street next to our house and appeared in front of our driveway, I saw him at the far end of my road, making the right from the adjacent street.

I'm not sure if he saw me right away, but as he got closer, he definitely saw me sitting there.

"Matt!" he said, "What are you doing?"

"Waiting for you," I said with a smile. "Grab a seat."

"Thank you," he said, always so polite.

The sun had begun setting, casting a shadow from behind my house, inching its way down the driveway, eventually covering us from behind.

"Tell me about yourself," he asked.

"What do you want to know?"

"Tell me something no one else knows," he said.

"No one? Oh man, let me think."

As I pondered what fact to come up with about my life, we both sat, staring across the street. The house across from us was off to the right, so their side yard separated us from the house's backyard on the next street over. Paul and Pete lived there. Paul was my age, and Pete was two years older. Nothing extraordinary ever happened in those two yards, though years later, Paul and Pete's parents put in a pool, so we'd see them swimming from time to time.

"When I was seven, I was at a friend's house. Not someone I was really close with. I think, if my memory is right, my mom had to go somewhere for an appointment and couldn't bring me with her, so she dropped me at this kid's house in the neighborhood we used to live in, around the corner from us. I forget the kid's name now. Anyway, I'm over there for a while and suddenly have to poop. For whatever reason, I'm embarrassed by this. The fact that I, like every other person, needed to poop should have been no big deal, right?"

"Right," he confirmed.

"But there I am, seven years old, fully potty trained for years by this point. And I'm scared to poop in this kid's house for some reason. I just don't want to. So, I do what any kid would do, right? I hold it in. I squeeze my tiny ass cheeks together as hard as possible for as long as possible."

"I know where this is going," he said.

"Oh, that's right," I laughed. "Eventually, I can't hold it anymore, so I poop my pants. It's November or December, so it's cold enough I'm wearing pants. I was thankful I didn't have shorts on and had it fall out of my underwear."

Marty started laughing, not at me, but with me. I had a hard time getting the rest of the story out.

"But that's not the worst part," I said. "It was another hour before my mom came to pick me up. So, there I was, in this kid's house that I'd never been to before—and never went to again—with poop in my pants, playing games, and running around outside, doing my absolute best not to let on that I had a load in my underwear."

Tears were flowing from my eyes. The memory of myself at such a young age trying to be nonchalant about the whole thing was so funny, in retrospect.

"So what happened when your mom came?" Marty asked.

"I flee the house. As soon as I hear the horn, I go running from the house to the car. I jump in the passenger seat as fast as I can. But I'm not dumb, right? I don't want to sit *on* the poop. I don't want to squish it into myself."

Marty was having a hard time hearing me over the sound of his laughter by this point.

"I... I can't..." he said, huffing and puffing for air.

"So I stand up on the seat," I said. "I squatted on the seat and buckled myself in. My mom looks over at me and says, 'What are you doing?' I burst out into this big confession about how I was too scared and embarrassed to go to the bathroom in a stranger's house. How I felt so uncomfortable with the whole thing and that I'd pooped my pants."

"Did she burst out laughing?"

"No," I said. "But I imagine they laughed when she ran through the story with my dad later that night."

The two of us sat in total darkness, now laughing hysterically at this story from decades ago. This embarrassing story that I'd never told anyone before. Come to think of it, I've never told anyone else that story. So now, in addition to my mom and Marty, you know as well, dear reader.

"That is a wonderful story," he said.

"I haven't laughed that hard in a long time," I said. "And I've never told anyone that story, either."

I chuckled to myself as the hysterics died down.

"I value our time together, Matt," Marty said, suddenly getting very serious.

"Me too, man," I said. "I really like hanging out with you."

He paused momentarily as if he wanted to tell me something or say something he had on his mind, but he didn't.

It was the first of many nights we'd sit in those lawn chairs at the end of my driveway, laughing.

As time passed, we'd plan what time to meet, order dinner, get drinks, whatever. We'd hang out at the end of the driveway like it was the hottest club in the city.

Lil' Peach

It was late one night when we'd agreed to meet up rolled around. Something that always stood out about my friendship with Marty was that we always made plans. With my other friends, one of us would call the other and ask what we were doing. If we were free, we'd get together. Go to the mall. See a movie. Whatever. It was always spur of the moment.

But with Marty, we'd make plans before parting for the evening. I'd jokingly say, "Same time tomorrow?" and he'd agree. Or, if I had other plans, I'd say, "Day after tomorrow?"

We always made the plans in person. We never called each other. We never sent emails or texts. We made plans in person. And, honestly, I loved it. It was not only so great to have this new friend who I felt really understood me, who I got along with famously, but was someone who I could count on. Someone I could know would show up when he said he would.

Every time we met, we met in my driveway. I still didn't know where he lived and hadn't brought it up. Whenever we'd talk about where he lived or what he did for work, he'd brush it off. It seemed like he was embarrassed about his living situation, so I didn't press it.

"I have to run to the store," I said toward the end of the evening. "My mom needs me to get milk."

"All right," he said, as he said every other night as we were getting tired and ready to wrap up.

"You want to come with me?" I asked. "It's just up the road. You know where Lil' Peach is?"

"I am not familiar," he said. "But I would love to come with you."

I ran inside the house to grab my car keys and noted that the clock on the stove said 12:15 a.m. Lil' Peach was open twenty-four hours a day, so I wasn't concerned with the time, but I knew if I had forgotten to get milk, my mom would be mad by morning time.

"Let's go," I called out, seeing Marty folding the lawn chairs and leaning them up against the mailbox, where we'd always left them.

He speed walked, almost comically, to the passenger side of the car and waited for me to unlock the door.

"This is very nice," he said after hopping in.

I paused for a minute and turned sideways to face him. "That's not funny."

"It was not meant to be funny," he said. "This is a very nice car."

It was the first time he'd said anything truly sarcastic to me, even if he didn't mean it as such.

I knew it wasn't a nice car. It was a 1997 Saturn that was falling apart. The lining of the roof was coming off, often blocking the view out the back window; the sunroof leaked any time it rained, so there was always a faint, musty smell to the car, and the passenger window didn't go down unless you pushed it down with your free hand, probably from the water damage on that side of the sunroof leak.

Something about the way he insisted he was not joking made me chortle. He was trying to be sincere, but I knew it was, on some level, sarcasm.

The car eased out of the driveway, heading out of the neighborhood through the road that Marty often left my house walking toward.

As we made the right, he looked out the passenger window, staring at the houses, yards, and cars that adorned the road up to Main Street.

It was as if he'd never seen some of the houses before. It felt off to me, but I didn't mention anything then.

"I like this song," he said. "Very much."

We hadn't previously discussed music, which was strange given how big a part of my life it is. So I was surprised when he came out and said he liked the song we were listening to. As I mentioned about random memories sticking with you, I recall the song was Linkin Park's

"Somewhere I Belong." I still get chills a little when it comes on, partially because of the memory of hearing it with Marty that first time, but also because years later, one of the vocalists from Linkin Park would take his own life.

"It's a good one," I said, having heard it non-stop on the radio for months.

The night air had gotten chilly, so I put my window up. Marty reached for the window control on his side, but the window didn't move.

"You have to hit it," I said.

"Hit it?"

"Yeah. You have to hit the control really hard, or it won't go up or down."

I looked over, trying not to take my eyes off the road, as he smashed his right hand against the door handle, making sure to make contact with the window control.

When he tried moving the window again, it went up all the way and closed, blocking out the cool night air and making the music seem much louder.

By the time we'd gotten to Lil' Peach, we heard two other songs on WAAF. Both of which Marty said he really enjoyed.

It seemed like, somehow, they didn't have rock music where he used to live. It felt so strange to me, like he was hearing it for the first time.

We both jumped out of the car once I'd parked and ran into the store. The bright lights of the neon signs in the window felt blinding against the nighttime darkness.

Dave, the same night cashier who had worked there for as long as I could remember, was there. The door chime faded slowly after we entered. Dave gave me a small nod, as he always did, as the door closed behind Marty, who followed me in.

His eyes lit up in wonderment. "Wow!" He exclaimed.

"Wow, what?" I asked. "It's just Lil' Peach."

"Wow, this is amazing."

"You're so weird," I said. "Have you never been here before?"

"No. I have not. I only got here a week before I met you. I have not been able to walk this far from the house."

He walked out in front of me, passing through the line of people waiting to either check out, buy lottery tickets, re-up their supply of

Marlboro Lights, or collect their winnings from the Keno game that ran in the corner of the store. At half past midnight, an astounding number of people stood in line. Though thinking back, that wasn't an uncommon thing. Lil' Peach was always busy, probably because it was the only twenty-four-hour store anywhere in our small town.

I watched him walk up and down the various aisles, grabbing an item, looking over the front and back of the package, and then putting it back. A bag of Lay's chips. A can of Pringles. Some Devil Dogs. He seemed fascinated by all of it.

"Hey," I said. "Milk's at the back."

He pointed as if to say, "Over here?"

I walked past him, grabbing the same handle to the same fridge I'd opened every time I needed milk at Lil' Peach because I'd forgotten to get it from any other store during daylight hours. I knew my mom's boyfriend—who lived with us and is now her husband—needed milk for his coffee in the morning. He got up early, so he wouldn't be able to get any before work, so it usually fell to me.

Marty grabbed the first half-gallon of milk he could reach and handed it to me, still standing in the open door to the fridge that I'd opened.

"It's cold in there," he said.

"Well, yeah, doofus. It's a fridge."

"So it is," he said. "Our stores in Belgium did not have fridges in them. And they did not have the selection of snacks your store here has."

"Hey, Dave," I said, popping the milk on the counter.

"Hey," he said. "New friend?"

Dave seemed to know everyone in town who'd possibly go into Lil' Peach after dark. He was there almost every night I needed to go there, from when I could drive to when I moved away to another town. He either owned the place or he lived in the back. He was a staple. So it wasn't surprising that he recognized I was with someone I hadn't been in there with before.

"Yeah, this is Marty," I said.

"Hey, Marty," he said, grabbing the five-dollar bill from my hand.

"Hello," Marty replied, picking up the milk as Dave handed me back a dollar fifty-three. I was there to buy that same milk once a week and never once thought to bring exact change.

As we jumped back in my dilapidated Saturn to head back to my house, I toyed with asking him if he wanted me to drop him at home. Ultimately, I decided to at least offer. "Do you want me to drop you at home?"

"At my home?" he asked.

"Yeah, since it's late. There's no need to walk home from my house."

"That is kind," he said. "That would be great."

He held onto the milk like it was a small child the entire way back to the neighborhood.

As we made the left down to the street I'd known him to walk toward, he gestured to the right. The road that ran parallel to mine went straight across the adjacent streets, making almost a cross shape through the U that the neighborhood was.

The end of that road was a cul-de-sac. Wooded on most sides, but three houses on the right side of the street, all with long driveways leading back to the houses.

Each house was dark, being almost one in the morning at that time.

"That's ours," he said, again referencing other people. "That one there." He pointed to the last house on the right.

I pulled up at the end of the driveway, partially turning around in the cul-de-sac, and he hopped out of the car, leaving the milk behind on the passenger seat.

"See you tomorrow?" I asked.

"I'll be there. Thank you for such a fun evening," he said.

I waited a moment before driving off to ensure he got inside safely. But it was too dark at the back of the driveway, and I lost sight of him in the darkness after a few seconds.

Like every other night, I parked the car on the right-hand side of the driveway, gently closed the door, went into the house, popped the milk in the fridge, and went up to my room, passing out within minutes. I still don't know how I did it all these decades later. I stayed up until one or two in the morning almost every night, slept for six or maybe seven hours, and then got up and went to work. Nowadays, if I don't get a solid eight hours, I'm as useless as an oar on a battleship.

Office Depot

The more time I spent with him, the more I looked forward to seeing him. Something about him made me feel so comfortable, like a familiar pair of socks. Something that you could, proverbially, slip on and feel at home. Feel supported and safe. I know comparing a person to a pair of socks is a weird analogy, but it suits how meeting Marty felt.

We had planned to meet at eight one evening, which was when we'd usually get together in the lawn chairs and hang out. But Marty arrived early.

"Hello?" I heard a voice from outside. My spot on the couch was right by the window adjacent to the side door of our house, so he was literally just behind me, on the other side of the window.

Although I was confident I recognized his voice, I still did the same thing I always did: I popped up, slyly turned around, and looked out the window. I always did that to make sure that the person outside was someone I wanted to see. The last thing I wanted in my twenties—well, I guess even now, too—was opening the door to someone trying to sell me something or convert me to their religion.

I tapped on the window to get his attention and gave him the universal "be right there" index finger pointing upward signal.

He nodded as I turned back to head out of the living room, through the kitchen to the door.

"Hey," I said as I opened the door, pushing the screen door open and motioning for him to come in out of the unusually cold October day.

"Hello," he said.

"I thought we were meeting tonight?" I asked.

"That was the plan, yes." He looked away, down to his right.

"Everything okay?" I asked, trying to get him to look back up at me.

"I need your help," he said. "My Papa needs me to go to the store, and I fear it's far to walk to."

"Oh, you need a ride?"

He still hadn't made eye contact. It seemed he thought the ask was much more inconvenient than it was.

"Would it be too much trouble?"

I laughed. "Unless the store you need to go to is in Maine, I think it'll be fine."

He smiled and looked back up at me. "It is in Burlington. Are you familiar with Burlington?"

I was. It was only a fifteen to twenty-minute drive, depending on traffic. "I know the place, yes. Where do we need to go?"

Marty pulled a small piece of paper from his pocket and carefully looked it over. "I need to go to Office Depot. It is a store for offices."

I laughed. "For offices? You mean for office supplies?"

"Is that not the same?"

"Close enough," I laughed. "Let me grab my stuff."

My usual ritual of "I'm leaving the house" began. I grabbed some socks and my wallet from my room, popped my Red Sox hat on my head on the way down the stairs, grabbed my keys from the end of the kitchen counter, where I'd always left them, and pulled my still-tied shoes on. "Ok, let's roll."

"Thank you, Matt. You are most helpful."

"That's what friends are for, right?" I asked.

"It is. This is the first time you've referred to me as your friend."

"Is it?" I smiled. "I guess it is."

"You are my friend, as well," he said. "That brings me joy."

Marty followed me out and pulled the door to the house closed behind him, gently letting the screen door close. He waited at the passenger side door while I walked around to unlock the aging Saturn. The remote to unlock the door from afar had long since stopped working; please take a look at the aforementioned water damage from the leaky sunroof.

We both plopped down simultaneously and buckled in. He seemed to struggle with the seatbelt momentarily before getting it to click in.

"Do you want to pick the song?" I asked him.

"You would let me?"

"Why not? You seem to like the same type of music I do."

"I enjoy all kinds," he said. "Music makes me feel wonderful."

Although I felt it was weird to phrase it, I understood what he meant. Music was an escape for most folks, myself included. It is a way to live through the song, through someone else's eyes, and experience the story they were telling through their lyrics.

He clicked on the radio, which I'd thankfully turned down when I got out of the car the previous evening. He toggled through my presets and landed on a soft rock station, Magic 106.7. I'd listened to that station every night I was home before midnight. The "Bedtime Magic with David Allan Boucher" show was so soothing. The DJ had the most calming voice. My aunt played a part in the show for me when I was 11 or 12, and it just stuck.

"At This Moment" by Billy Vera and the Beaters was on.

"I like this one," Marty said.

"This is one of my all-time favorite songs," I said. "I love songs that tell stories, and this one tells a great love story."

"I, too, enjoy stories," he said.

I backed us out of the driveway and headed out of the neighborhood, knowing exactly where we were heading. I'd worked in Burlington a few times over the years and was familiar with where Office Depot was.

"What does your dad need?" I asked.

"Papa needs me to get some specific-size paper for the printer."

I made a mental note that it was the second time he'd referred to what I figured was his dad as 'papa.'

"Got it. We should be there in just a bit."

The rest of the drive we spent talking about the songs that came onto the various radio stations that Marty would change to. We'd bounce from Magic 106.7, to WAAF 107.3, to WBCN 104.1, and countless others.

We discussed the songs, the lyrics, their meaning, and how they made us feel.

It was a very normal and very friendly ride to Office Depot. The first of many trips where I'd take Marty somewhere he needed to go.

• • • ● • • ● • • •

"I appreciate you taking me here," Marty said as we returned to the car.

"Of course," I said. "That's what friends are for, right?"

I saw him smile out of the corner of my eye.

"It's just all so fascinating to me," he said. "Being able to go to a place and get something you need without walking there."

Much like the trip to Lil' Peach, Marty was fascinated with everything in Office Depot. Eventually, he found the exact paper size his father had sent him to get.

"You're so weird, Marty," I said.

"I know," he replied. "It's just that the last place we lived, we didn't have stores like this."

"You didn't have office supply stores?"

"No. We didn't have anything like this."

"That's weird. Where was that, again?" I tried pretending he'd already told me where he last lived, just that he was originally from Belgium.

"All over," he deflected. "Here and there and everywhere."

I turned the key, and the engine fired up.

"That's kind of weird," I said, shifting to reverse. "Have you ever driven a car before?"

"Just once, when I first was old enough," he said.

"Only once?"

"Just the once."

"So you don't know how to drive?"

"No, I don't know how to drive. I never needed to learn. Papa drove everywhere we needed to go."

We left the parking lot and headed down Middlesex Turnpike toward the Burlington Mall. I made the right onto the ramp down to the parking lot as we approached the entrance.

"You're going to learn today," I said.

"Today? No. I couldn't possibly," he said, seeming nervous.

"Why not? Today's as good a day as any other."

"I am scared," he confessed. "I'm not sure I know how."

"I'll teach you," I said. "Don't worry!"

I pulled into the farthest part of the parking lot, away from the mall. Other than Christmas time, hardly any cars were parked back there, so the lot was wide open and enormous—the perfect place for someone to take their first steps at learning how to drive.

"You ready?" I asked, looking over at him.

"Do I have a choice?" he asked, avoiding eye contact.

"It's not scary. You're going to love it!" I was trying to reassure him. But also, on some level, myself. I'd never taught someone to drive, so it felt a little out of my comfort zone.

My door clanged shut behind me before he even opened his. As I walked around the car to the passenger door, I had to tap on the window three times to get his attention. Once he realized I was standing there, he opened the door and hopped out, standing next to me for a few moments.

"What do I do now?" he asked.

"Go around to the other side and get into the driver's seat."

He followed my instructions, and we were both sitting in the car after a moment of him fumbling with the driver's side door handle, which often felt locked but wasn't. This is the part where I'd tell you to avoid buying a Saturn because they're so poorly made. But they don't make them anymore, so you're safe.

Once seated, he turned his body to me. "What now?"

"The first thing you want to do is adjust the mirrors. There are three of them," I said, pointing to each of the mirrors.

"How do I know it's right?" he asked.

"The big one up here should let you see out of the entire back window."

"Okay. Got it," he said, twisting the mirror a bit to his left.

"And the two on the sides should show you most of what's behind you but also a little of the car itself."

"How do I..." he trailed off.

"Oh. Right. There's a little button on the armrest to your left."

He found the adjustment knob and fiddled with both mirrors for a minute before claiming he was satisfied. He was roughly my height and build, so he shouldn't have had to adjust them all that much. But, in hindsight, I suppose just getting familiar with the functionality of how it worked was good for him to know.

"What now?"

"Now we turn the key to start the engine..." he immediately did, and the car made a horrible cranking sound. "Ha. You didn't let me finish," I laughed. "We don't need to do that this time because the car is already running."

"Oh no. Did I break it?"

"I'm sure it's fine," I said. I knew very little about cars, so he could have caused irreparable damage for all I knew.

"I remember now you would grab this handle thingy and move it to D. What does D mean?"

"D means drive, which we use when we want to go forward. Sometimes, we use the R, too, which means reverse. For when we want to go backward."

He grabbed the gear shift, pressing the button, but it wouldn't budge.

"Look down by your feet," I said. "See the two pedals?"

"Yes," he replied.

There wasn't a time I was ever more thankful that I owned an automatic. Trying to explain a stick shift and the clutch to someone for the first time would have made my head explode.

"Press the one on the left. That's the brake. It's what'll make us stop when we're moving."

"And the other one makes us go?"

"Correct."

I saw him put his foot down on the brake and try the gear shift again. This time, it moved down from P to R to N to D easily.

"Now, let your foot off the brake. But don't hit the other pedal yet. Just let the car roll and get a feel for it."

He did as instructed, and the car began to roll along the pavement ever so slowly.

"I'm doing it!" He was so excited I could feel it.

"You are!" I was equally excited. It made me so happy to be able to help him learn something new.

"Here we go," he said. "I'm going to press the other pedal."

I unconsciously grabbed the armrest and door handle to brace myself, but he barely tapped the gas pedal.

Then he immediately hit the brake again.

"How was that?"

"A little more of the pedal on the right and a little less of the pedal on the left," I said.

He again tapped the gas, then hit the brake. Then he repeated the process, creating a stop-and-go effect that I can only equate to the world's worst roller coaster. We jolted forward, then stopped completely again and again.

"Ok, okay. Let's not touch the one on the left unless we need to stop," I said, clutching my stomach.

"Is it wrong?"

"Not wrong, really. Just not as smooth as it should be."

It took him another ten or so tries before he got the smoothness down. Before we knew it, we were driving across the massive parking lot from one end toward the other.

"This seems easy," he said.

"Well, sure. It is, mostly. Let's try turning."

"To do that, I just spin this wheel?" he asked, pointing to the steering wheel.

I nodded. He was a quick study. He'd only been in the car with me a couple of times, and based on his past not having been in a car very often, he seemed to understand the mechanics of it pretty well.

We turned to our left, almost in a full circle, then back to our right. Again, almost in a full circle.

"Weeee," he exclaimed. "This is great!"

I couldn't help but smile. My friend was a big weirdo, but he sure seemed to love the simpler things in life.

"I think that's enough for today," I said. "Let's park over there." I pointed back toward the end of the lot where we'd started.

"Got it," he said, half saluting me, laughing at himself.

We pulled into a spot—well, mostly into a spot he hadn't yet learned to park—and switched seats back to where we'd started.

"You did great," I said, giving him a high five when we were both seated and buckled in.

"I had a good teacher," he replied. "Thank you, my friend."

As we drove back to the neighborhood, I tried to explain what I was doing so he'd understand not just the mechanics of driving but the psychology of it. Where to look at another car to see if it would pull out in front of you, what the traffic lights meant, what it meant if someone flashed their lights at you. All the tips and tricks that I'd learned but wasn't actually taught in driving school.

"Can we go to your house?" he asked.

"Sure. You want to hang out?"

"Yes. Maybe we can order a pizza?"

"You like pizza?" I don't know why I was surprised. But seeing as he was unfamiliar with many things, I wasn't sure he'd ever had pizza.

"Yes, very much. We had it when we first moved here."

"Sure thing. We can get one."

I knew Papa Gino's phone number by heart, so I called and placed a delivery order as soon as we got back to my house. Growing up, we ordered from there at least once a week, so I didn't even need to give them the address. They knew the house just by the phone number on their screen.

"It'll be here in twenty minutes," I told him as I went back outside.

He was sitting at the end of the driveway, in the same lawn chair he always sat in, on the right-hand side, looking up at the sky.

The sky was perfectly blue, except for one small white cloud floating just overhead—a beautiful day. The air was crisp but not too cold. The breeze was more comforting than chilling.

"What are you looking at?" I asked as I approached.

"Nothing," he said. "Sometimes, I just like to gaze up and see what I can see."

"I do that, too," I said. "Sometimes I just stare for hours. Especially at night. I love to see the stars."

He let out a big sigh. "Me, too."

We both sat side by side, as we'd done so many times before, waiting for the pizza to arrive, just staring up at the sky. We watched the sole cloud float from over our heads, toward the end of the neighborhood, where Marty lived, and eventually disappear over the line of trees on the horizon, just as the sun started heading down.

Papa Gino's & The Internet

The time had gone by quickly as we looked at the sky with wonderment. The pizza guy came turning down the street to our right. Given the lack of usual traffic on the street and our line of sight, we could immediately see the Papa Gino's sign on the top of the car.

I hadn't realized it until that moment, but I was starving.

The driver didn't even bother pulling into the driveway. He just pulled up in front of us and stopped.

"Waiting for me?"

"You know it," I said, smiling and getting out of my chair.

I handed him the money for the pizza and a tip. He reached over to his right and grabbed our pizza from the warming bag on the passenger seat.

"Here you go, guys," he said, handing it out the window to me.

"Thanks, man," I said.

"Thank you," Marty added.

He drove off, heading down the street toward Marty's, and was gone before I got back outside with paper plates.

We each took a slice of pizza onto our plates, and I put the box down on my lap, not wanting to rest it on the ground.

"Have you had Papa Gino's before?" I asked him.

"I'm not sure," he said. "Do you like this Papa Gino?"

"Yes. That's where we usually order from. But sometimes we get Domino's or House of Pizza. It depends on our mood."

He took a big bite and smiled. "Oh, me. This is very good pizza."

"It's one of my favorites."

"Thank you for today," Marty said. "For teaching me to drive and for taking me to the store."

"You're welcome."

Halfway through our first slice, Marty turned to me. "I know I've said it already, but I appreciate your friendship."

"Same, buddy." At that point, Marty was one of my only close friends. All the friends I'd made as a teenager had all moved on. We got older and went our separate ways by that point. Not due to anyone's fault; we just grew apart. Aside from casual friends I had online, Marty was the only person I spent a lot of time with. Other than Brooke, my new girlfriend and eventual ex-wife. More on that later.

"It is nice to just spend time with you," he said.

It made me smile.

I had briefly told him about Brooke at that point. He never really asked for specifics. I wasn't sure if he was being polite or just wasn't interested. But, out of the blue, he asked about her.

"How did you meet Brooke?"

"We met online." The truth is, I met almost everyone at that point in my life online. Even going back a handful of years to the late '90s. It was easier for me to make friends electronically. I don't know why; perhaps it was how shy I was growing up. Or that it just came more naturally to me to be able to think about what I was going to say—usually as I typed it out—before I said it.

"I'm not familiar. What is online?"

"On the internet. The World Wide Web."

"Oh, yes. The internet. I wasn't allowed to use that growing up," he said. "Papa's job is very secretive, so I couldn't risk doing the wrong thing online."

"Do you want to try it after we're done eating? I won't let you do anything you shouldn't."

"That would be wonderful. Thank you. I love to learn from you."

"Great," I said. "So, we met online, and then I went into the city to meet her one night last month. We've been seeing each other a lot since then."

"Do you know lots of people online?"

"I do," I said. "I've met a ton of people and spent time with a bunch of them. There are some good people out there. It's not as scary as they might want you to believe."

He smiled. "Nothing is scary when you examine it close enough."

"That's a good way to look at it," I said. "I think you're right. Nothing's scary when you take the time to figure it out, or try it, or whatever."

Before I knew it, we'd eaten the whole pizza and finished the Cokes I'd brought out with the plates.

"So you like Brooke?"

"I do," I said, blushing a little. I knew it was too early to see if it would be anything serious.

He smiled as he wiped his mouth with his shirt sleeve, making me realize I'd forgotten to get napkins when I entered the house earlier.

"I'm done when you're done," I said.

"Yes!" he shouted. "I can't wait to get online!"

The way he said online was adorable. He was so excited to try it for the first time.

• • • • • • • • • •

After discarding the empty pizza box and soda cans in the recycling, we went into the house and upstairs to my room, where the only computer was. The rest of my family didn't care about computers or the internet until much later. My dad did, but he'd already left by then.

My desk was next to my bed, so it was easy for him to see the screen while I sat in the computer chair.

"Is this online?" he asked, pointing to the monitor.

"No," I laughed. "This is just the computer. It's how we *get* online."

"I've never used one for anything other than schoolwork."

In all its glory, complete with a big boxy monitor and giant computer tower, that computer had served me well. It wasn't the newest or fastest computer in the world, but it did its job. Which, until that point, was very basic web surfing, downloading music from Napster and Kazaa, and building simple web pages that no one but me knew about or visited.

I popped open AOL and clicked the connect button, triggering that dial-up connection sound. I don't need to explain because you can likely already hear it in your head.

"This is online," I said, pointing to the screen.

"This is... it?"

"It is. Well, there's more to it that we can do now, but this is online."

"What can we do?"

I showed him the basics: chatting, searching, and email. He was most interested in, and immediately infatuated with, searching the web. Although Google hadn't been around very long then, it was still the best search engine out there. It was always accurate and informational.

An instant message from Brooke popped up via AOL Instant Messenger, or as it became known, AIM, as soon as I got online, but I closed it out and set a quick away message.

"May I?" Marty asked after a moment of showing him how to look up silly things, like sports scores, history, or a specific person.

"Of course," I said, sliding myself back from the desk and letting him take over the chair.

"I just spell out the thing I want to look for? I've never done this before."

I nodded, gesturing to the keyboard. "It's that simple."

He began hunting and pecking for letters, clearly unfamiliar with the keyboard.

As he searched for the history of humanity, nature, animals, and friends, I walked over to the stereo and put on the CD player on random. It shuffled through its six discs, picking tracks as it saw fit. I kept the volume low, figuring he would have questions as he clicked through search results.

But he didn't. He kept quiet for quite some time. Minutes turned into hours, and hours seemed to stretch for eternity. He just kept looking up new things, clicking on a few results, then going back to Google. He was fascinated.

"Matt," he said. "This is astonishing. Amazing. I cannot believe this. I've seen computers before, but Papa's was never connected online."

"It's pretty great, right?"

The computer dinged. A small window popped up from the bottom right corner, another message from Brooke.

Hey

"What is that?" he asked, noticing the message this time.

"That's a chat. It's a one-on-one conversation between two people online."

"Is that her?" he asked, pointing to the screen name at the top of the window. Musicagal84.

"That's her," I said.

"Do you want to respond?"

"You can do it," I told him. "Just tell her it's you. She knows who you are."

"I can tell her? How?"

"Just click in the window and type out the message."

He did. *Hi Brooke. It is Marty. Matt says hello.*

It took him five solid minutes to type out those sentences.

Hi Marty. Is Matt coming here tonight?

I'd forgotten I had a date with her that night.

"Tell her yes and ask her what time."

Yes. What time?

9?

"She asked if nine o'clock was good."

"Yes. Tell her okay." It was only seven-thirty, so I had plenty of time to get ready, get Marty home, and get down to the city. I knew it was about ten minutes to park in the underground parking and walk across Boston Common to her dorm, but still plenty of time.

Okay. Bye, Marty!

Bye

He seemed so proud of himself. "I did an online chat!"

"You did," I said, almost congratulating him.

"You need to get ready," he said. "I'll go."

"You can hang out if you want," I said. "Keep playing online."

He didn't even respond. He just turned back to the computer and popped open the browser to continue searching for anything and everything he wanted to learn more about.

I lost track of what he searched for while getting dressed but casually joked with him. "Don't search for anything that'll get me in trouble. Who knows who's watching."

He laughed. "Okay."

Once I was ready, I showed him how to disconnect from AOL but told him I usually never shut down the computer. It took forever for them to boot, so it just made sense to leave it on all the time.

"Have a good night," he said, heading out of my room toward the stairs.

"See you tomorrow?" I called out louder than necessary, not knowing how far down the stairs he'd gotten.

"I'll be here," he said. "I'll move the chairs out of the way when I go out."

"Thanks," I said, remembering we'd not put the chairs back against the mailbox.

• • • ● • ● • • •

Seemingly full of knowledge for the day, Marty spoke up in the typical way he'd say he was leaving. "I should go."

"It's raining," I said, having recently looked out the window when I heard my mom get home from work. It wasn't too late, but it was starting to get dark.

"I hear it," he said, pointing his nose to the ceiling as if looking upward would help him to be able to hear the rain better.

"Why don't I drive you home?" I asked.

"That's not necessary," he said. "I don't mind walking in the rain."

"It's really coming down," I said, looking out the window. "Are you sure?"

He rose from the chair at my desk and walked over to the other window in my room, pulling back the shade. Struggling momentarily, I assumed he was waiting to formulate an opinion about whether it was too rainy to walk the block and a half home.

"I appreciate the offer," he said.

"Then take it," I cut him off. "Let me drive you. It's not like it's far."

"If it's not too much of an inconvenience," he said, looking back toward me but still standing at the window.

"It's not," I said. "Let's head out."

He followed me down the stairs, stopping by the side door to the house to put our shoes on. My mom said hello before scurrying back to the living room with her now-filled glass of Pepsi.

"It's really coming down," I said. "Let's run."

I high-tailed it from the door to the car, doing my best not to let the screen door hit him as it swung closed. My key had just made it into the lock, allowing me to jump inside right as Marty made it to the car. I'd already unlocked the other doors from the driver's side armrest before he grabbed the handle to pull it open.

"You are right, like usual," he said. "I'd have gotten very wet walking home."

"See?" I said, half joking. "I told you!"

The rain flew in all directions as the wipers turned on, the reverse lights barely cutting through the torrential downpour, barely illuminating the driveway behind us. I turned my head in all directions, ensuring no one was walking by.

As we made the left down Marty's street, the rain let up—just a tiny bit, for just a moment or two.

We cruised past the houses lining both sides of the street, now dark enough to see inside lit-up windows, watching people saunter around their houses, getting ready for dinner or what have you.

Once we pulled up to the end of his long driveway, I saw a light come on. The last time I'd driven him home was pitch black, so I couldn't see him make it safely to the house. The light came on this time, and it was just past dusk.

Marty leaned forward and looked out the windshield up at the sky. "It'd sure be nice if the rain would stop now," he said, under his breath but loud enough that I could hear him.

"Wouldn't that be nice?" I asked jovially.

"Thank you for letting me use the computer again," he said. "It gives me such happiness to learn the things I never learned as a young person."

"Any time, buddy. My things are your things." I noticed my voice trailing off. The need to talk a little louder than usual had subconsciously disappeared. I was talking in my normal voice again, not quasi-shouting over the sound of the rain. As odd as it seemed, at the time, it seemed like Marty had made the rain stop just by saying it out loud.

"Well, look at that," he said, opening the door. "Better get going before the rain starts again."

"See you tomorrow?" I asked.

"I'll see you then," he said, closing the door and jogging halfway up the driveway.

The faint light from the house cast a silhouette of Marty, allowing me to see him as he approached. The silhouette grew with every step he took.

For a brief moment, he paused. I could see the silhouette's arm rise and a small blur of a hand waving.

The light turned off once it seemed Marty had made it inside.

Once the light went out, it was as if someone had flipped a switch, and the rain started again.

I chuckled and drove myself toward the highway to head to see Brooke, not giving it a second thought.

Marty Opens Up

I couldn't help but think there was something amiss with Marty. Although we were becoming so close, I knew so little about him. He seemed so withholding about his past or home life. The only things I knew about him, I was able to glean from the time we'd spent together, not from anything he'd actually told me.

When he showed up at my house the next night, I was waiting for him at the end of the driveway. His chair was set up to my right, covered with a big quilt my mom had made when I was a kid. It was the middle of October then, and the nights were starting to get a little cold, to the point where it wasn't comfortable to sit out there for any extended period without a blanket. Eventually, when it got even colder, we'd move into the garage, always leaving the door open to look out at the road or sky or whatever we felt like looking at.

"Hey," Marty said as he approached. He always came from the right, as if he'd walked down his street, across from mine, past my house, and doubled back to get to my driveway. Or he was always off doing something at the other end of the neighborhood before he came to my house.

"Hey, buddy," I said, handing him a Coke.

"How was your day?" he asked.

"It was fine. How about you?"

"My day was wonderful," he said. "I went to the center of town to explore."

"Explore what?" I asked.

"Nothing in particular. I just went and walked around."

"What did you see? How did you even get there? It's too far to walk."

"I spent a good amount of time walking there," he said, seeming a little off.

"You walked there? It's pretty far."

"Yes, it was a nice walk."

"What did you see there?"

"I saw the library. It was magnificent."

"I have a question for you. Where did you live most recently?" I asked him. "You mentioned you lived all over, and were from Belgium. But where did you live before coming to America?"

"I told you," he said, avoiding eye contact. "I'm from all over." He gestured broadly from his left to his right, a swooping motion indicating he'd lived all over the place.

"But where are you from?"

"I doubt you've heard of it," he replied very quickly.

"Try me."

"In my native language, it is called Crupet."

"Crupet? You just made that up."

"I told you that you likely hadn't heard of it."

"Where is it?" I asked.

"In Belgium," he said, pointing off toward the little of the horizon we could see through the tree line in front of us. "I told you this was where I was from."

I adjusted my chair to face him and pulled my blanket over my shoulders. It was getting colder the later it got. "Belgium. Right." I asked, trying to make eye contact, though he avoided me.

"That's right."

"What is it like there?"

"It's nothing like here," he said. "It's quiet and peaceful. My nearest neighbor lived so far away that you couldn't get to them without transportation."

"So you lived in the middle of nowhere?"

"Quite, yes."

"Were there stores or schools or anything? Any civilization?"

"It was just Papa and I," he said. He seemed a bit sad by this revelation.

"How did you end up here?" I asked.

"Papa found a way for us to get out. He got a promotion at his job, which meant we could move to wherever we wanted. We decided to come here, to this place."

"But why?" I asked. "If you could go anywhere, why this little town in Massachusetts? You had the whole world to pick from, and this is where he picked?"

"I do not know," he said. "I just know that this is where he picked. This is where his promotion lead him."

"What's his job?"

"I don't think I'm allowed to say," he said, slyly looking at me out of the corner of his eye as he still faced forward, not having turned to face me.

"Is it a secret?"

"I believe so," he said. "I believe part of the job is not telling people you're doing the job."

"Like some sort of security?"

"I think that's the translation of it, yes."

"I never see my dad much anymore since he left. Maybe once or twice a year."

"Is it sad for you?"

"Well, sure," I said. "It's no fun not to see your dad, right?"

"It is not," he replied. "I do not enjoy being away from him for so much time."

"Does he have to travel a lot for work?"

"He does," Marty said. "He's gone quite often, sometimes for weeks at a time."

"Oh, man. I didn't know that. If I had known, I'd have had you stay with us for a while. We could have had epic backyard camp-outs or stayed up late in the basement goofing off. I'm sure my mom wouldn't have minded."

"Perhaps next time he goes," he said. "Perhaps then I could take you up on the offer."

"I think that's a good idea," I said. "Tell me more about Crupet."

"There isn't much to tell. It was a small rural town where people had much land and didn't see their neighbors much."

It previously hadn't crossed my mind, but it suddenly did. "How did you get to the airport without a neighbor or car?"

"A friend of Papa's from his job drove us. What else would you like to know?"

"Did you have any close friends?" I asked.

"No," he said, still looking away but side-eyeing me. "There were no other people close enough to be friends with. It wasn't as easy as going to a friend's home like it is here. I couldn't just decide one day to pop over and see if my friend was sitting outside, waiting for me. It wasn't the same."

"So what did you do?" I asked.

"For what?"

"For anything."

"Papa spent much time working, much like he does here. So I stayed inside. I'd read the books Papa would buy for me on his trips."

"Do you miss it?"

"Miss it? You mean Crupet?"

"Yeah, Crupet."

"I miss it, but only sometimes. We had this amazing delicacy there. It's hard to explain what it is in English, but it was my most favorite thing to eat. It was sweet and salty but warm and gooey at the same time. It always made me feel so happy to get to eat it, though it wasn't an everyday meal, just a special treat. Papa usually brought it home with him after he'd gone out for a long travel."

"Sounds like he might have been trying to bribe you to forgive him for being gone for so long."

"Perhaps," he said, finally turning to face me. "Is that something your father did to you?"

"Sometimes. After he first left, maybe seven years ago. He'd bring gifts when he'd come to see me. It wasn't very often, but occasionally, he'd bring me something."

"Did it make you forgive him?"

"No," I laughed. "I don't think I've ever forgiven him for leaving us. It's just my mom and I. We've been closer since he left than ever before, always looking out for one another and having each other's back. I am an adult, for lack of a better word, but still her child. She treats me like a peer rather than always trying to parent me. Especially since my dad left, that really helped us bond."

"I'm glad you have her," he said. "It sounds like she means a lot to you."

"She does," I said. "Where's your mom?"

"She..." he looked away for a brief second. "She's been gone since I was first born. She did not survive my birthing."

"Oh. I'm so sorry, Marty," I said. "I can't even imagine how hard it must have been growing up without a mother."

"It was quite difficult, especially with Papa gone so often."

"Did he travel for work a lot when you were little?"

"Oh yes. My birth did not stop his work. So his friend would come and take care of me. I suppose you'd refer to her as an aunt, right? A good friend of one of your parents?"

"I have a bunch of those. My mom's good friends."

"She helped me grow. Taught me so many things. Helped me learn to take care of myself."

"Do you still keep in touch with her?"

"Not since we left," he said. "We've lost touch since we left Crupet all those years ago."

"That's too bad," I said. "Does your dad keep in touch with her?"

"I don't believe so. He hasn't mentioned it."

"How long ago did you leave your home?"

"I was just a small child when we left. I think you could compare it to when you went to junior high school."

"Wow, so you were about twelve or thirteen?"

"Give or take," he said. "I was very young when we left my home."

"Where did you go from there?"

"I'm not sure," he said. "It's all a blur of moving from home to home, place to place. It was so foreign to me as a small child; it felt like completely different worlds."

"But you remember Crupet the most?"

"I do," he looked off into the distance. "I spent the most time there out of anywhere, so I remember it vividly. I remember all of it as if it were yesterday."

"Our memories are so weird, aren't they?" I asked.

"Indeed. I remember all of that so well, but I don't remember where we went next for our home. It feels so strange to me."

"It is strange. Thanks for sharing this with me," I said.

"You are most welcome. I am glad to be able to share my life with someone."

Meeting Papa

Halfway through my second slice of pizza one night, I noticed Marty seemed uneasy. "You okay?" I asked.

"Oh, fine. Yeah. I'm okay."

"You seem shifty, like you can't sit still."

"It's just… Well… my dad wants to meet you." It was the first time I'd heard him refer to his dad *as* dad and not Papa.

"Does he?"

"Yeah. I guess I've been talking about you so much he wanted to meet you."

"When?"

"Any time."

"Let's go now!" I was excited to finally meet him after all the time Marty and I had spent together.

We finished the slices we were working on, left the box on my chair, and headed toward Marty's house.

I'd never walked there from my house before. Any time I'd have gone down that far, I'd have driven. Even as a kid, I'd always been on a bike heading down to that part of the neighborhood.

"He's very excited to met you," he said.

"Meet you," I corrected him. I was often reminded that Marty's native language wasn't English, and I tried to help him learn a correct word or phrase. "Met is the past tense."

"Meet you, yes. He's excited to meet you."

As we made our way up the driveway, I could tell Marty was nervous, though I was unsure why.

"He's quite strict," he said. "He's very nice, but he is very strict with things. Please be polite."

"Of course. I'll be completely respectful."

"Vader we zijn er," he called out as we entered the front door. "I've just told him we're here, in Dutch."

"Does he not speak English?"

"Oh, no. He does. It's more out of habit than anything else."

"Okay, phew." For a moment, I panicked that I wouldn't be able to communicate with him.

"Hallo zoon," I heard a booming voice call out from another room.

"Hello, son," Marty translated almost immediately. "Dad, where are you?"

"Kitchen. Who is with you? You said we are here, not I am here."

"Matt is here. You said you wanted to meet him."

"Wonderful! Please come join me."

I followed Marty through the living room, which was sparse with decorations. Only the bare minimum furniture, all pointed at an older-looking television. No family photos anywhere. No magazines on the coffee table. No real sense of people living there. In hindsight, it made sense. They were still new to the house, so maybe they hadn't settled in.

As we entered the kitchen, I was immediately struck by his father. He was a large man, much taller than both Marty and I. Perhaps six foot five or six foot six. He towered over me. His facial features resembled Marty's so much they could have been twins. Their haircuts were the same, though Marty's was a little shaggier. Their hair was the same shades of brown, their eyes matching crystal blue.

"Hello, Matt!" He bellowed as he continued turning back and forth from his cutting board to various pots and pans simmering away on the stove. "I'm making beef stew and stoemp."

"Papa loves to cook," Marty added.

"I am Jean Luc," he said. "It is so wonderful to meet you and have you in our home. Please, make yourself comfortable." He gestured toward the table on the other side of the kitchen.

"Have you had stoemp before?" Marty asked.

"Had it? I've never even heard of it," I laughed.

"Papa, we've had some pizza already."

"You and your pizza," he laughed. "You have surely come to love American food so quickly."

"I could eat," I said. I didn't want to be rude and felt that Marty saying we'd already eaten some pizza was his way of telling his dad that we wouldn't eat with him.

"Are you sure?" Marty asked.

"I don't mind if you want to take some home with you," his father said, still bustling about, popping vegetables and spices into the various items cooking on the stovetop.

"I only had two slices," I said. "I've got room."

"Prachtig!" Marty's father exclaimed. "That means wonderful in English," he added. "Michel, please set the table." I assumed that it was Marty's Dutch name. He pronounced it very matter-of-factly, me shell.

"Yes, Papa." He sprung to his feet, poking in and out of cabinets and drawers, grabbing plates, utensils, and glasses.

"Can I help?" I asked.

"Guests need not help," Jean Luc said, still facing away from me.

Marty placed the empty plates to Jean Luc's right, filled the glasses with water, and placed the full glasses and utensils on the table.

I grabbed some napkins from the holder in the middle of the round table, placing them under each person's fork, knife, and spoon.

"It will be ready shortly," he said, turning halfway around to make eye contact with me.

"What's stoemp?" I asked Marty, trying to keep my voice down for some unknown reason.

"Just wait," he said. "It's a delicious Dutch dish. It's like mashed potatoes but with delicious vegetables mixed in. Father makes it wonderfully."

I'd never heard of it before, but it sounded right up my alley.

The clang of ladles and spoons suddenly filled the kitchen with the sounds of plates filling.

Jean Luc turned, arms full of plates, and stepped toward the table, ducking under the chandelier hanging from the ceiling over the table. "Let us eat," he said. "Zegen dit voedsel. Bless this food," he said, looking up at the ceiling.

"Thank you so much," I said. It looked wonderful. The aromas filled my nose like nothing I'd ever smelled before. The chunks of beef floated around in the bowl of the stew like tiny logs floating down a river to a mill. The vegetables popped up through the top of the mashed potatoes. Carrots, peas, Brussels sprouts, and leeks. I'm sure there were more, but those were what I could see. The potatoes themselves were a little more brown than traditional mashed potatoes.

As Jean Luc commented, I must have stared at the food too long. "You're unsure why the potatoes are brown, yes?"

"I've never seen mashed potatoes so brown before."

"Ah," Jean Luc said. "They are not mashed potatoes. That is why. This is stoemp. It is similar but prepared differently from traditional American mashed potatoes."

I grabbed my fork and scooped up a mouthful. Once I'd brought it up to my nose, I knew it would be one of my new favorite foods. I inhaled deeply and fell in love with it even more. That first mouthful changed me. It was all I ever wanted to eat again. "This is sublime," I said, food still mostly filling my mouth. The words came out jumbled and muffled. I finished chewing and swallowed. "Sublime," I said. "This is sublime."

"Prachtig!" His father exclaimed. "I am so happy!"

The stew was thicker and richer than I was used to. But the beef was cooked to perfection. It was soft and tender, juicy, and seasoned so perfectly. As much as I hate the cliche, it melted in my mouth.

"Papa loves to cook," Marty said again.

"Why have we been sitting in my driveway eating pizza so many nights?" I laughed, still shoveling food into my incredibly happy mouth.

"Michel loves American food," Jean Luc responded. "I can cook until I am dead, but Michel will prefer to eat your pizza to my cooking."

"Papa," Marty said. "That is not always true!"

"If my father cooked like this, I'd be home every night for dinner," I said.

Jean Luc smiled. He sat across from me, and although he was so much bigger than I was, I didn't feel intimidated. I saw none of the strictness Marty had warned me about, but I'd only been there for twenty minutes. Perhaps, behind closed doors, things were different.

"Marty tells me you've become good friends," he said.

"We have," I said. "One night, he just came walking down my road, and we chatted briefly."

"I understand you live near?"

"Yes, just around the corner."

"His is the gray house over at the back of the neighborhood," Marty added.

"Ah, yes. We've admired it."

"Thank you. I had nothing to do with it," I laughed. "My parents bought it when I was little; we've been here ever since."

"We've only been here one month," Jean Luc told me. "I came here for work."

"Can I ask what you do?" I asked.

"I'm afraid I'm not able to talk about it," he said. "I would love to share, but it's prohibited." He looked to his left at Marty, making sure he made eye contact. It seemed to be a reminder that Marty was not supposed to talk about it.

"I understand," I said. "Whatever it is, I'm glad it's brought you two here."

"As are we," he said. "Michel has quite enjoyed getting to know America and American life." He reached out with his right hand and grabbed Marty's left hand, squeezing it before returning to his meal.

"This food is so good," I said. I couldn't help but confirm to Marty and his dad how much I enjoyed the meal.

"I am pleased you like it," he said. "Tell me, Matt, what do you do?"

"You mean for work?"

"Yes. I assume you have a job?"

"Yes, sir. I work at an insurance agency. I'm what they call an underwriter."

"What is this? An underwriter."

"It's boring," I said. "I only got the job because my aunt works there."

"You are not happy with your job?"

"Most people here aren't," I laughed a little. "But all those pizzas we eat aren't going to pay for themselves."

"Ah, yes. American food is quite expensive. We're used to much more reasonably priced meals."

"I think most of the world is," I added. "America is a strange place if you're not from here, I'd guess."

"It is," Marty said, chuckling.

"Your family life is well? Your home?"

"Everything there is great," I said. "It's just my mom and I. Dad's been gone for years. I don't see him much. But I'm fine with it."

"Your mother, she is well?"

"Mom's great," I said. "I'm sure she'd love to meet you sometime."

"Excellent," he said. "I would like that, as well."

Before I knew it, my bowl of stew was empty, as was my plate of stoemp. He'd given me a fairly healthy portion, but I'd finished it all on top of the two slices of pizza I'd already eaten earlier that night.

"You liked it quite much," he said. His accent was much stronger than Marty's, and his English was a tiny bit more broken, though not to the point of having any trouble communicating with him.

"That could have been the best meal of my life," I said. "Please don't tell my mother."

Jean Luc made a lip-zipping motion, which caused Marty to chuckle again.

"I'll get the plates," Marty said, getting up from the table.

I followed his lead, bringing my plate, bowl, and cutlery to the sink. Marty then washed everything by hand, though a dishwasher was just off to his left.

"I'll dry," I said, grabbing a towel from the dish rack in front of me.

"Thank you, boys," Jean Luc said, still seated at the table.

Marty and I washed everything and dried it, placing it right back into the cabinets and drawers the items had come from. It was something I didn't recall ever doing in my house. Either we'd put stuff in the dishwasher and empty it when it was done, or we'd wash something by hand and put it in the dish rack to dry.

"I would like to talk with you again," Jean Luc said, finally standing.

"It was so nice to meet you, sir," I said, reaching to shake his hand.

"In Belgium, we hug," he said, grabbing my hand and pulling me into his chest. His giant arms felt like they could wrap around me twice. I did my best to squeeze him back, but honestly, I was trying to survive the biggest bear hug I'd ever gotten.

"Papa, we'll be going now. Is that acceptable?"

"Yes, yes. Go, go. I'll see you when you're home later."

"Thank you again," I said.

"Matt, you are welcome here any time," he said. "I cook every night I am home. Michel will tell you when there is food for you to eat."

It was the first of many meals I'd have at their house. Jean Luc wasn't just a master cook in Dutch cuisine, though. Have you ever had homemade Chinese food? I have many times. It's leaps and bounds better than what you can buy. He seemed to know how to cook every type of food there was. None of it was ever bad, as if he'd mastered every single thing he'd ever tried to make.

We walked back to my house, laughing. I'd been so nervous for nothing. Jean Luc was wonderful, warm, and welcoming. Perhaps there was more to the story I didn't know, but that first night was memorable and great.

The night was capped off with us approaching my driveway and seeing a family of raccoons just having begun grabbing the box of our leftover pizza and hurrying off, each of the four with a slice in their hands.

Everyone's bellies were happy that night, Mother Nature's included.

Marty Meets Brooke

The very next night, I was scheduled to meet up with Brooke in the city. As I was heading out to my car to leave, Marty approached on foot at a more rapid pace than I'd seen him move before.

"Matt, hi," he said, waving while still far from me.

"Marty?" I questioned, making sure it was him under the street light.

"Hi. It's me," he said.

"What's up? I'm just about to go meet Brooke," I said.

"I know. I remember. You told me that last night," he said. "I had this terrible feeling that something was wrong, so I came right over."

"You could have called me," I said. "I have my phone on me." My giant Nokia phone, the size and weight of a brick, was never far from my person.

"I wasn't sure you'd answer," he said. "So I rushed here to catch you."

"You okay?" I asked as he got closer. His face was as white as a sheet.

"I had this feeling," he said. "That something was going to happen to you."

"That's odd," I said. "I'm fine."

He took the last few strides toward me quickly and hugged me before I knew it. It sticks out in my mind so vividly because it was the first time he'd hugged me. He wrapped his arms around me so tightly that I felt like I was suffocating. "Easy, easy," I said. "I'm fine. Everything's fine." I hugged him back, giving him a gentle pat on the shoulder to let him know everything was okay.

"I am so glad," he said. "I was so worried, though I don't know why."

"Everything's fine, buddy, I promise."

He eventually let go of his hug and took a step backward. "I am so relieved."

The color began returning to his face, albeit slowly.

"Are you okay?" I asked him.

"I feel better now, yes, thank you."

"What are you doing right now?"

"Nothing," he said. "I'm just going to go back to my home."

"Come with me," I said. "Brooke's great, and I think you should meet her and her roommates."

"I couldn't," he said. "I don't want to force myself into your date."

"You wouldn't be," I said. "We're just going to hang out and watch a movie with whichever of her roommates are there tonight."

"Will you be getting the New York Pizza you talked about before?"

"Probably," I said. "It's a big hit amongst the girls."

"I will join you, then."

"Great, I'll text her and let her know."

Texting back then took a lot longer than it does now.

666 66 6 999 6 2 999. 6 2 777 8 999 444 7777 222 666 6 4444 66 4 9 444 8 44 6 33. 7777 33 33 999 666 88 7777 666 666 66.

Which translated to "On my way. Marty is coming with me. See you soon." Texting was *so efficient* before Blackberries and iPhones.

Ok, see you soon she replied a minute later.

"Let's go," I said, opening my door.

Marty walked around to the passenger side, opened his door, and hopped in.

As it became accustomed to us doing, I started the car, and Marty jumped from radio station to radio station to find a song he liked. We always waited until we were sufficiently satisfied with the choice before we drove off.

He settled on "The Remedy" by Jason Mraz.

"I really like how fast he sings," Marty said, buckling himself in.

"Works for me," I said over the sound of my seatbelt clicking.

Based on what I'd seen of Marty visiting a new place for the first time, I knew the city of Boston would astonish and amaze him. As soon as we pulled off the highway, I knew he'd start darting his head around, looking at the buildings, all the traffic, and all the people on foot.

I weaved through the city streets, making my way to the same parking garage I'd been using—though, in hindsight, not the cheapest parking solution—the underground lot beneath Boston Common.

As we approached Park Street, the buildings to our right disappeared, revealing Marty's first glimmer of the Commons. A wide-open park in the middle of the city, flush with people walking, hanging out, vendor carts selling pretzels and fried dough, their proprietors bundled up against the frigid October evening. Dusk just settled over the horizon, the rising moon tucking itself neatly behind the Prudential building, a tiny sliver sticking out from one side as if placed there by a skilled painter.

"Matt," Marty started. "Wow."

"It's pretty beautiful, isn't it?"

"Beautiful isn't the right word," he said. "This is incredible."

I'd been there plenty of times in my life, more frequently in recent weeks since I'd met Brooke, but something about the Common always felt special—it still does, to this day—it felt like a fairy tale—beautiful greenery in the middle of an iron jungle of buildings.

"Is this where Brooke lives?" he asked.

"There," I said, pointing to the far end of the block, to the building her dorm was in.

"Where do we store the car?" he asked.

"You'll see."

We drove to the end of the block and made the right at the Dunkin' Donuts with the Baskin Robbins in it that I'd been to a dozen times, heading to the opposite end of the Common that we'd first arrived at just a few short minutes ago. Marty's eyes never left the park.

"Look at him!" He yelled, pointing. I did my best to look at what he pointed to but could not see, as we'd already passed the person.

I made the right into the garage and progressed down the ramp, stopping at the automated machine to grab a parking ticket.

"How did this happen?" he asked.

"What?"

"We're under the park."

"Yes. We are. And I have no idea how they did this, but it's pretty astonishing."

We had to drive down to the third level before we found a place to park.

"I'm a little nervous," he said. "My stomach feels like it's in knots."

"Why are you nervous? You're not going on a date!"

"I do not know," he said as I pressed the button to call the elevator.

"You've been on an elevator before, right?" I said, half joking.

"I have," he smiled.

The ding startled me a bit, as it usually took longer for the elevator to come down. "Okay, let's head up."

Together, we walked from the garage exit across the park. I intentionally walked slower than usual for two reasons: I knew Marty wanted to take his time and see everything Common had to offer. Two, I was early. It's a character flaw I see in myself where I always get someplace early and then kill time until I'm on time. I hated—still do—being late to anything.

He was speechless, following just a step behind me, staring at every inane object, listening to every person who spoke to him, sometimes striking up a conversation, really enjoying himself.

"C'mon," I said, looking at the clock on my phone. "We've gotta go." I had to pull him away from a conversation with a homeless man who'd asked Marty for money.

"I'm so sorry, sir. I haven't any," he said, as politely as could be.

The pedestrian signal turned to walk, and we scurried across the street toward the building Brooke's dorm was in, pausing briefly in the middle of the road for Marty to look up toward the top of the building like a typical tourist would do in a big city.

Going inside and up to the desk to check in had become slightly second nature. I'd been to the dorm a dozen or so times in the month since I'd met Brooke and was familiar with a lot of the folks who worked the desk. They'd take your ID and put it in a little slot on a page for the floor you were going to. It was a very low-tech way of tracking who was in the building. It also prevented people from having overnight guests. Well, it was supposed to, anyway.

We hopped in the elevator and got off on the twelfth floor, hanging a right toward Brooke's suite.

She greeted us at the door. Me first, with a big hug, then a handshake for Marty.

"It's nice to meet you!" She said. "Matt's told me so much about you."

"Likewise," he said, closing the door behind him.

We stood in the common room for a moment before a couple of Brooke's roommates came out to greet us: Danielle and Amanda.

"I ordered pizza," Brooke said. That was code for "can you go down and pick it up and pay for it," which I was fine with.

"Would you mind?" I gestured toward Danielle and Amanda, reaching for my wallet.

"Of course," Amanda said. "We'll go get it."

Brooke gestured to the standard dorm-issued couches, and we all sat.

"Marty, Matt tells me you're new to his neighborhood."

"That's correct. I've only been there a short while. But Matt has been wonderful in showing me around and teaching me new things."

"He's very smart, isn't he?"

Marty smiled.

"What are we watching tonight?" I asked.

"I rented *28 Days Later*," she said. "It's supposed to be really good. It just came out." The small DVD case from Redbox sat on the table in front of us.

"I've not heard of it," Marty said.

"I have," I said. "It sounds pretty good. Scary, but good."

A few minutes later, Amanda and Danielle returned with the pizza. Brooke excused herself to grab plates, napkins, cups, and a 2-liter bottle of soda.

I dished out the pizza for Marty, Brooke, and me before getting up to put the DVD into the DVD player I'd bought for the suite a week or so before. It may seem weird having bought them a gift like that so soon after meeting Brooke. But, in my defense, it was sort of a selfish thing. We'd previously been watching DVDs on her tiny laptop screen, and it wasn't a super fun experience. So I bought the DVD player to watch movies on the still-small-compared-to-today's-sizes-but-bigger television.

The movie was great. Everyone seemed to really enjoy it, though occasionally letting out a small gasp or, sometimes, even a bit of a scream.

We stuck around for a little conversation after the movie, but I knew Brooke had an early class the next morning.

"We should head out," I said in Marty's general direction, breaking up his conversation with Danielle.

"Is it late?" he asked. "Yes, we should go."

I hugged Brooke and high-fived Danielle and Amanda on the way out, something that'd become the norm for quite some years.

"It was so nice meeting you," Marty said. "Thank you for your hospitality."

"You're so welcome," Brooke said. "It was great meeting you, as well."

I hugged Brooke again before closing their suite door and heading down the hall to the elevator.

Marty was silent the whole way down while we grabbed our IDs from the desk and got outside.

"You okay?" I asked as we waited for the walk signal.

"I..." he started. "I... I'm not sure."

"Was it the pizza?"

"Oh," he said. "No, not like that. The pizza was good, though you were right in saying that Papa Gino's is better."

"So what is it?" I asked, motioning for him to head across the street as the signal had turned to walk.

"I didn't get a good feeling."

"From what? The movie? You said it wasn't the pizza."

"From Brooke."

"What do you mean?" I asked.

"I'm not sure. I know we didn't spend much time with her, but I didn't get a good feeling from it."

"Oh," I said. "You didn't like her?"

"It's not that. I'm not sure how to describe it. It's an odd thing to try to put into words."

We were halfway through the Commons, back to the garage, when he spoke again. "Let's not worry about it for now. Perhaps it was nothing. Maybe we can try again some other time?"

"Okay." I felt a weird flash of panic and guilt flush over me. "You're sure it wasn't that you didn't like her?"

"I'm sure. It was just an off feeling. Maybe you're right; maybe it's the pizza, after all."

I laughed. "Maybe."

We paid the $24 for parking and returned to the elevator to get to the car on level 3.

"This was an enjoyable evening," Marty said. "I quite love the Commons here."

"Me, too," I said. "I'll have to bring you back sometime in the Spring to show you the Public Gardens. It's just across the street."

"Is it what it sounds like from its name?"

"It's a big garden. When the flowers are in season, it's breathtaking. Flowers as far as the eye can see. All sorts of colors, shapes, sizes, varieties. It's incredible."

"I hope we get to do that," he said. "It sounds so wonderful!"

We got back to the car and drove up and out of the garage, circling through the city's one-way streets before getting back on the highway to head back to our neighborhood.

Although I wanted to dig into Marty's feeling more, I let it go for the evening.

2005

The First Block Party

After a blistering winter, Spring was more welcomed than it'd been in a while. While enjoyable, All those nights sitting out in the garage were sometimes brutal. Keeping with the tradition that we absolutely made up ourselves, we kept the door open every night. Even when it was snowing, it just felt like it was our thing, as odd as that seems.

So when the weather warmed up, it made sense to take advantage of it.

"We should throw a block party," I told my mom.

"That's a great idea," she said. "We haven't done one since a couple of years after we moved in. You were just a kid."

I invited everyone I knew. Eric, at the end of the street, who I used to be close with but hadn't been since we went to different high schools. Sarah, who I'd always had a crush on as a kids, and her brother, Josh. Kevin, Derek, Charles, Michelle, Megan, Mike, Allyson. Everyone I could think of, I told.

Marty and I walked around the neighborhood, knocking on doors together. Even doors of people we didn't know, we'd knock, introduce ourselves, and give them the details of the party.

Since my road was at the back of the U, we figured we'd block off both ends from traffic and just set up everything on the street. We'd have people wheel their barbecues out and cook whatever food they wanted to contribute. It felt like the world's best idea. And, for once, it was a practical use of our time together. When we'd normally sit and eat pizza, we walked around knocking on doors.

Marty, ever more organized than I was, kept a notebook of all the addresses we'd gone to and which ones no one was home at so we could try again later.

We even drew up a simple flyer on my computer advertising the event. I xeroxed a bunch of copies at work, and we'd leave them in the mailbox or by the door of the houses we couldn't contact after a couple of attempts.

"This is going to be so much fun," I said. "Do you think your dad would make some food?"

"I have a feeling he's already at the market buying tens of pounds of meat," Marty laughed. "He was so excited when I told him what we were doing."

For some reason, the image of Jean Luc carrying a cow on his giant shoulders popped into my head. Almost cartoon-like, just a whole cow propped up there, mooing as if it was to say, "Hey, humans shouldn't be carrying me. Can someone help me?" as Jean Luc trudged on, bringing the cow home to make his world-famous beef stew for hundreds of people.

• • • • • • • • • •

When the day of the block party arrived, it was chaos. People showed up in droves with tables and chairs, meals they'd prepared. One of the neighborhood families owned a mobile barbecue truck. They pulled up with a tow-behind smoker that looked big enough to cook the entire imaginary cow I'd pictured on Jean Luc's shoulders.

From side dishes to full meals, people showed up in spades.

I overheard the casual conversations of so many people. Families that were new to the neighborhood meeting new people. Couples who'd lived here for years but didn't know some other family that had been around just as long. Friends who had known each other since they moved in, reconnecting after not seeing each other over the winter. Casual acquaintances waving to one another, as they'd done each time they passed on the street, coming or going to or from the neighborhood on one of the streets leading in or out.

It made me so happy that so many people had shown up. "This is awesome," I told Marty, digging into Mrs. Peterson's pasta salad.

"I didn't know this many people would show up," he said.

"Me either." I flashed back to the only other party I could remember hosting: my high school graduation. The party where I'd invited almost everyone I was friendly with before graduation. The same party where the only people to have shown up were my family. I think I abandoned my party that night and went out in search of someone else having a better party.

Marty high-fived me. "We did a good job," he said.

"Hell yeah, we did," I said.

His phone buzzed from his pocket. "It's Papa," he said, looking down at the screen. "He needs help."

I'll never forget the sight I saw when we walked through the living room into the kitchen at Marty's house that day.

"I may have gone a bit overboard," Jean Luc said.

There were plastic Tupperware containers stacked everywhere. The countertop, the table, the chairs, the small table by the back door where they kept their mail.

"Oh, Papa," Marty said.

"Oh my," I added.

"There's more," he said. "I made many speculoos, too."

I looked at Marty.

"They're like a little cookie. Kids would get them as a reward for doing well in school back in Belgium."

Jean Luc opened the fridge. "I may have made some fresh whipped cream for waffles," he said.

Top to bottom, front to back, the fridge was full of more Tupperware containers everywhere I could see.

"I see why you need our help," Marty said. "Shall we load up the car?"

"I think that's a good idea," I said. "I don't think we can carry this all around the block ourselves."

And off we went. We loaded up every Tupperware container and every serving utensil they had. He'd also bought enough Sterno to heat all the food everyone else had brought. Countless sleeves of plastic bowls.

Boxes of plastic utensils. It felt like we were heading to a homeless shelter to feed the population of Vermont, but we were bringing all the food with us.

"Papa," Marty said from the front of the car, just about out of earshot. "This is incredible. Thank you."

The two of them embraced. It was the first time I'd seen them physically touch each other. It was such a brief but sincere moment. It made me happier than I'd already been.

· · · · • · • • · ·

Jean Luc honked when we pulled up to the barricade we'd made at the end of my street. One of the neighbors ran over, saw who was in the car, and quickly moved the garbage cans we were using as a barricade out of the way, allowing us to drive down the street.

He was careful to avoid hitting any people, tables, or chairs. We got almost up to where my house was, about mid-way up the street, before we had to park.

"Anyone have an empty table?" I asked, getting out of the back seat.

"Here," Mrs. Franco called out. "I do."

"Thank you," I said, popping the trunk.

The three of us unloaded and set up Jean Luc's food on the table, eventually having to borrow a table from another neighbor. It sprawled out wide in such a vast assortment. People started noticing.

Though we hadn't finished unpacking everything yet, Jean Luc said, "*Eet, eet*! Eat, eat!"

The crowd around us queued up, grabbing a little of everything as they scooted their way down the table from right to left. It was the most organized I'd seen a group of people that large be around food.

"Oh my God," I heard Mr. Wilkinson call out from the far end of the table. I was still grabbing things from the back of the car but was happy to listen to people already enjoying the food.

"Hi, I'm Kelly," I heard someone say, but I couldn't see who it was.

"Marty. Very nice to meet you," Marty said. I looked up and noticed him talking to a girl I didn't recognize but looked to be about our age, maybe a year or two younger.

"Hello," an older woman said. I didn't recognize her, either. "I'm back for seconds. This is wonderful. I'm Melissa." She reached out to shake Jean Luc's hand.

As he did when I met him, he grabbed her hand and pulled her in for a hug. "In Belgium, we hug!"

"Oh, oh my!" she exclaimed as he engulfed her. "It's nice to meet you, too." I heard her say.

• • • • • • • • • •

I lost count of how many people he hugged that day. It seemed like everyone flocked to him. They surrounded him, introducing themselves and becoming his new best friend until he met the next person. He seemed like he was the happiest a person could be. Sharing his cooking with all of these people who were strangers until that day made him flush with love and happiness. Marty and I watched from a distance in awe.

"He's truly remarkable," I said.

"Papa is wonderful," Marty said.

"Do you have more waffles?" I heard someone almost cry out from thirty feet away.

And he did. He had more waffles than a Waffle House that day. More whipped cream than the Hood factory. And more smiles on the faces of more people than I'd ever seen before. Jean Luc was the neighborhood's new favorite person.

Foo Fighters & Dinner

The next morning, my phone buzzing from the coffee table in front of me woke me up. I thought I was imagining the sound. I was so exhausted from cleaning up the block party until well into the early morning hours.

I got four tickets to Foo Fighters.

It was a text from Brooke.

9 44 33 66? Which worked out to "when?"

Tonight. I won them!

Cool. I replied.

Meet me at the Garden at 7? Bring Marty.

Yeah?

Yes.

It was still early, just after seven. I knew I had to work that morning, but I had plenty of time before I had to start thinking about getting up and getting ready.

My body ached as I sat upright, reaching for the armrest to help balance myself. Muscles stretched, and joints cracked. I was sore. Perhaps sleeping on the couch wasn't the best idea after such a long day of doing so much *stuff*.

Marty answered on the fifth ring.

"You okay?" he asked immediately.

"I'm good," I said. "Sorry to call so early. I've got to get ready for work, but I wanted to see if you wanted to go to a concert tonight. Brooke got tickets."

"For who?"

"I know you're going to love this," I said. "Foo Fighters."

"Shut up!" He went from just waking up to wide awake in a flash. "I love them!."

"I'll pick you up at six," I said. "Be ready."

• • • • • • • • • •

We got to the parking garage under the Garden right on schedule. I knew from having texted Brooke throughout the day that we'd meet by the parking garage elevators at seven.

Level after level, we went down, over and over again. The garage seemed to go on forever, though every level was full. We finally found a spot after what felt like an hour of driving.

"It's going to take forever to get out of here," Marty said.

"Ugh," I groaned. "You're right."

Much like any other event, parking in Boston was atrocious. It was great to park so close to the event, but then everyone at the event was leaving all at the same time. Thousands of cars waiting to reverse out of their spots, holding up traffic as they did. It was always a nightmare, though welcomed, most of the time.

After putting the paid receipt on the dashboard, so we wouldn't be towed, I locked the car.

"I'm so excited!" Marty yelled.

"Me too!" Truth be told, I wasn't that big of a Foo Fighters fan at the time. After that show? Yes, absolutely. But before I saw them live, I'd just occasionally heard them on the radio, never having sought out their music. I'd never pass up a concert, though. Live music was just so enjoyable for me. The way the band feeds off the crowd, and vice versa, is something you can't explain to someone who hasn't experienced it. It's life-changing in some cases.

We found Brooke and Danielle, who looked to be our fourth ticket holder, pressed up against the back wall when we came out of the elevator, along with a dozen other people.

"Hey," Brooke said, hugging me.

"Hey, this is so exciting," I said.

"Hi," Marty said, waving from a short distance.

"Hey, Danielle," I said, quickly hugging her.

"Let's go find our seats," Brooke said.

Marty and I followed behind the girls, making sure not to lose them from our sight.

Like everyone else who wasn't there to catch a train out of the city or grab a quick bite from the McDonald's by the train station, we headed up the long escalators to the first floor of the Garden.

People were everywhere, shoulder to shoulder, increasing my anxiety. As I often did, I brushed my hand against my back pocket to ensure my wallet was still there. Although it'd never happened to me, I had a chronic fear of being pickpocketed in close quarters with a lot of strangers.

"Women this way. Men that way. Empty your pockets. No backpacks. Purses open," a security guard said, pausing for a few seconds, then repeating it all.

"Meet you right there," Brooke said, pointing to a framed Bruins jersey hanging on the wall, just past a group on the other side of the security checkpoint.

I nodded.

"Have you been to a concert like this before?" I asked Marty over my shoulder as I was patted down by a security guard who could have definitely not cared any less.

"No! I have never been to one but am familiar."

"This is going to be so great," I said as he finished his pat down and caught up to me.

The girls took a little longer, as security had to go through their purses. The female security guard also cared a bit more than the male one. They were patted down a lot more thoroughly than we were.

As we waited for the girls to catch up, we stood by the Bruins jersey on the wall. The plaque said it was Bobby Orr's game-worn jersey from the infamous photo of him flying through the air that virtually every Bruins fan owned a copy of. I smiled at its historical significance.

"We're in section 329," Brooke said as she got within earshot.

"Nosebleeds," I said.

"Free nosebleeds," she said, poking my ribs.

"Free nosebleeds are better than no nosebleeds," I said.

In hindsight, we could have easily bought those tickets for less than a few hundred dollars. But it wasn't something we'd have spent that money on, so we weren't planning on going before she won the tickets. They weren't very expensive, but it wasn't about the money. The excitement was just in being there, in having won the tickets.

"How'd you win?" I asked her.

"I called in at the right time," she said.

"We were just goofing off," Danielle said. "We all got new cell phones today, so we tried to see if we could win if all the suite mates tried calling simultaneously. Brooke won!"

"That's cool," Marty said.

We took another escalator from the first floor to the second and then to the third. We walked around the venue's perimeter, periodically peaking through the curtains that blocked the light from seeping in during the show.

The stage was at the far end of the arena from where we were. From the quick peeks I snuck, I could see the setup for the opening act. If memory serves, it was Weezer. But I could be misremembering that.

"Here we are," Brooke said, pointing at the painted numbers above the entryway. 328 - 329.

"After you," I said, holding the curtain open for her and Danielle.

An usher inside the curtain looked at the tickets and walked us down to our row, pointing to the four open seats in the middle of the otherwise filled row.

We were straight back from the stage. Literally as far away as you could be from where the bands would be playing. But we had a good view, straight on. They would seem like ants from the distance we were, but I don't think any of us cared.

The crowd filled in around us and below us. Almost every seat was full, and the standing-room-only floor filled with people pressing up against the barricade, hoping to get that one inch closer to the band by pushing the person in front of them a little harder than necessary. The area around the sound booth was empty, as all the people with the floor tickets were pressed against one another.

The lights began to dim, and I couldn't help but smile.

I looked over at Marty; he also had a huge grin on his face.

"Thanks for inviting us," I yelled over the house music to Brooke.

"You're welcome," she said. "Glad you guys could come. I hope this helps win Marty over a little."

"I'm sure it will," I said. I looked past Brooke to Danielle and saw her smiling. All four of us were very excited about the show.

• • • • ● • ● • • •

I couldn't tell you much about the opening act, but I *think* it was Weezer. They were fine, but I never paid much attention to them. I was watching Marty a lot throughout. Seeing someone experiencing a concert for the first time is something I'd never done before. It was incredible watching his eyes dart around the arena, following spotlights, watching the singers moving around on stage. The pyrotechnics surprised him the first time they went off. I don't think he was prepared for the spectacle a big rock show can sometimes be.

Between acts, the black banner behind the opening act was pulled down, revealing the Foo Fighters logo. The crew ushered the opening act's gear off stage, making way for the Foo Fighters' stuff to get brought out. The crowd cheered at the various techs as they sound-checked everything on stage, making sure it all worked before the band came out.

The lights went out, and the crowd went berserk.

I'll never forget that moment I first heard Dave Grohl speak live for the first time.

"Hey Boston, how we doin'?" he said as he approached the microphone.

The crowd got even louder, almost deafeningly loud.

I could feel—and see out of the corner of my eye—Marty jump up and down like an excited kid on Christmas morning. I thought, for a brief second, I heard him squeal. But it could have been anyone. I like to tell myself it was Marty because it helps me remember the event more positively.

"You ready for a rock show?" Grohl asked. The crowd roared. Of course, they were ready for a show.

They blasted right into "In Your Honor." Marty must have been a bigger fan than I was because he continually leaned over mid-song and told me the name of it.

Some of them I recognized as they came on. I suppose, in hindsight, the more popular ones were the ones I recognized. Thinking back, there were many songs: "All My Life," "My Hero," "Best of You" (which had been on the radio non-stop at the time), "Learn to Fly," "Times Like These," "Everlong," "Monkey Wrench."

They played all of their hits over the next hour and a half.

Marty sang along to almost every song, his voice getting fainter and increasingly hoarse as the night went on. It didn't slow him down any, though. He was having the time of his life.

I periodically looked over at Brooke and Danielle, who were also enjoying themselves.

At one point, Brooke wrapped her arm around my waist and pulled me in close to her, giving me a little hip check. She'd do that quite a lot throughout our relationship. She would eventually call it a "butt bop," though I'm not sure I ever knew why, and I never questioned it.

The crowd continued to roar for quite a while after the band had finished playing and left the stage. We stayed put, hoping for an encore, but there wasn't one. After a few minutes, the house lights came on, signaling it was time to leave.

"Do you guys want to get something to eat?" Danielle asked once we were back out into the walkway, heading toward the escalators.

"All the vendors are closed," I said, pointing to one with the lights turned off.

"There's a bunch of places outside that I'm sure are open," she said.

"What do you think?" I asked Marty.

"It's just before midnight," he said, looking at his phone's clock. "It would solve our garage problem."

"Garage problem?" Brooke asked.

"There are thousands of cars trying to leave right now," I said. "We're on the bottom floor of the garage."

"Oh, geez," Danielle said. "Let's go eat then. There'll still be people leaving when you guys get back."

"Sounds good," Marty said.

"Let's go," I said, following the girls' lead down the escalators and outside. The crowd, some likely fairly intoxicated, was still rowdy as they poured out onto the streets of Boston.

We didn't spend much time deliberating where to go. I pointed to the first bar I saw, and we got lucky that they had a decent-looking menu posted out front.

• • • • • • • • • •

We sat in a booth away from the bar, which was incredibly packed for a Wednesday night. I expected it to be busy after such a big event just across the street.

"Menus?" someone asked, barely stopping to hear an answer.

She flew back by a moment later, dropping a stack of menus on the table and tossing some coasters down.

"I'm starving," Marty said.

"Same," I replied.

"Me too," Brooke and Danielle both said.

I fumbled through the menu for a bit before settling on just getting a burger. I told myself that it would be hard to screw up a burger, not knowing how good the rest of the food would be in a place like that.

We all did the usual small talk while waiting for the server to return. That casual "what are you getting?" "Oh, that sounds good," small talk that everyone does at a restaurant.

Did it actually sound good? No, not really. It was bar food. We were hungry, and it served its purpose. We weren't expecting Wolfgang Puck to be in the back preparing it.

"How did you like it?" I asked Marty, who was sitting across from me.

"Brooke," he said. "Thank you so much for this. This was amazing."

"So lucky I just happened to win tickets," she said. "I'm so glad you liked it!"

"I love music," he said. "I didn't realize seeing it live would be like that."

"I saw you singing," Danielle said, smiling.

"My throat hurts a little," he said. "But it was worth it."

"I wish I knew more of the songs," I said. "I had fun, but I didn't know very many of the songs."

"It doesn't matter," Marty said. "I think we all had fun. That's all that matters."

The server circled back, took our order, and was gone in the blink of an eye. She dropped off four glasses of water a second later. Marty gulped his completely and turned around, signaling her for a refill.

"That helped," he said. "My throat has never been so dry before."

"That'll happen when you yell and sing for so long," Danielle said.

"I barely sang, and my throat is killing me, too," I added.

"Marty, where are you from?" Danielle asked before getting a glare from Brooke. "What?" she said in Brooke's direction.

"It's okay," Marty said in Brooke's direction. "I don't mind. I'm from a small place in Belgium."

"Your English is excellent," Brooke said.

"It is, isn't it?" I added.

"Growing up, I didn't have a lot to do. We were lucky enough to get American television, so I watched a lot of that. It really helped with learning the language."

"I've heard that before," Brooke said.

"Me too," Danielle added.

"It seems to be a very easy way to pick up the language. And not just the language, the slang, American mannerisms, inflection. You learn more from watching someone natively speak the language than you can from learning it in a book or classroom."

"What brought you to America, then?" Danielle asked.

"Danielle quit it with the twenty questions," Brooke snapped.

"It's all right," he said. "I don't mind."

"His dad got a job here," I said.

"Well, no. Not got a job. He had this same job in the last place we lived, but it transferred him here."

"Oh, I thought it was a new job," I said.

"Apologies. No. Same job, new place. He has had this same job since I was a child."

"What does he do?" Brooke asked. It seemed like she wanted to ask a lot of questions of Marty, but let Danielle do some of the heavy lifting so as not to be perceived as the bad guy.

"I'm afraid I can't say," he said.

"If it makes you feel any better, I don't even know," I added. "It's some secret or something."

"Something like that," Marty chuckled.

"Do you like it here?" Danielle asked.

"I do, I quite like it. Matt has made it a lot more enjoyable since I met him."

"Aww," Brooke said, sliding a little closer to my left side.

"It's easy," I said. "Marty is so chill. It's really easy to be his friend."

He looked across at me and half winked. "You too, buddy."

"So, this was your first concert?" Brooke asked.

"It was. I'd seen them on television before, but being there in person is so different. It's just incredible. I want to go to more of them," he said.

"I remember my first concert," I said. "You never forget that."

"Who was it?" Brooke asked.

"Van Halen. I saw them about ten years ago. With Collective Soul."

"Shut up!" Danielle said. "In Worcester?"

"Yeah, were you there?"

"My older brother took me," she said. "It was my first concert, too!"

"Small world," Brooke said. Looking back, I could tell she was always a little uneasy about the bond Danielle and I had. It was never—not even for a minute—flirtatious or romantic. We were just friends right from the get-go. She and I were so similar, which made sense why Brooke liked us both.

"Do you go back to Belgium sometimes?" Brooke asked, turning the conversation back to Marty.

"No. We've moved a lot since I lived there. I was young when we left, so I am not obligated to go back and visit."

"Do you have family there?" she asked.

"No. Not anymore."

"Where did you live after that?" Danielle asked.

"Let me think," he said. It was a question I'd never thought to ask him myself. I had always assumed he went from living in Belgium to living down the street from me. "Beijing, Tokyo, Sydney, London, São Paulo, back to Sydney, and then here."

"That's a lot of places!" Brooke said.

"We go where father's job tells us to go."

"That's gotta be tough," Danielle said.

"I wouldn't want to do that," I added.

"It can be hard, especially if you don't get to stay someplace for more than a year. But you do what you have to do. I've never questioned it."

"Never? Not even once?" I asked.

"No. Father's job is how we live, so I do what I'm told. I go where he's told to go."

"That seems like a complicated life," Brooke said, her thoughts interrupted by the server delivering our food.

I took a big bite of my burger. My thought of a cook not being able to screw up a burger was right. It was delicious.

"Good?" I motioned, in general, to the table. They collectively nodded, Marty raised his hand in the direction of the waitress to get even more water.

"I'm glad you like it here," Brooke said.

"Me too. I hope I get to stay for good," Marty replied.

"Me too. I can't imagine life without you after this long," I said.

"How long have you been here?" Danielle asked between bites of her pasta.

"I think it's been just over two years now," he said, looking to me for agreement.

"I think that's right." I tried to remember when I'd met him. I knew it'd been a couple of years, but I was unsure of the exact date.

"How long were you in your last place?" Danielle asked.

"Our second time living in Sydney was four years," he said. "The first time was just six months, but they needed him to go to London urgently. So we went."

"At the drop of a hat? Just like that?" I asked.

"Just like that."

· · · · • · • · · ·

After some careful math, we wrapped up our meal and split the check out so we all only paid for what we had. Although I had offered to pay for the whole meal, everyone wanted to chip in.

It was just after one in the morning by the time we put Brooke and Danielle in a cab back to their dorm and headed toward the Garden to retrieve my car from the garage.

As we suspected, a steady stream of cars was still pulling out of the garage. Not bumper to bumper or standstill, like it'd have been if we tried to leave right after the show. But a steady enough flow that it was obvious people were still leaving the show.

"I'm so tired," Marty said as we got into the elevator.

"Same," I said. "Exhausted."

We got in the car and sat briefly, relishing the evening.

"We have to do this again," he said. "But maybe not with the interrogation at the end of the evening." He looked out the window at the mostly empty lower level.

"I'm sorry about that," I said. "You could have said something if you didn't want them grilling you."

"It's fine. I'm just joking," he said. "Mostly joking."

"I think they just wanted to get to know you better," I said. "It's their way of learning about you. And they asked some stuff I didn't know."

"So you got to know me better, too," he said.

"Yes. So it was worth it."

"Seeing the concert made it all worth it," he said. "I think we should definitely do it again sometime."

We left the garage and headed north. I knew the general direction of how to get us home, so I followed my gut instinct and got on 93 North. Once I got my bearings, I was confident I'd be able to get us back home.

Somewhere along the way, Marty stopped responding to our conversation. I looked over, and he'd fallen asleep.

I drove the rest of the way home in silence. I turned the radio down to the bare minimum to not wake him.

"Hey," I said, gently shaking his arm as I pulled into his driveway. "We're at your house."

"Did I fall asleep?" he asked.

"You did. It's just before two."

"I better get inside," he said. "I don't want to wake Papa."

"Night bud. See you tomorrow?"

"I'll be there."

A Bad Feeling

"Was she trying to win me over?" Marty asked as I answered my phone the next morning.

"Huh? What?" I was still mostly asleep and disoriented by the sudden sound of the phone vibrating on my nightstand.

"The concert. Dinner. Was that her attempt to win me over? Is that what you say in English?"

"Ah," I was catching on. "You think Brooke knows you're not a big fan of her?"

"I think it's pretty obvious, don't you?"

"I think the opposite. You do a good job of hiding it. Especially when she's around."

"It's not that I don't like her; I hope you know that. I just got a bad first impression, a bad feeling. And, since then, I feel that my gut reaction was right."

"I don't fault you for being critical. I'd do the same if the situation were reversed."

"I know you would," he said.

"But, yes, I think the concert was her way of trying to win you over, to get you to see that she's not all bad and actually a good person."

"I'm sure she's a good person," he said. "I just think there are things about her that should concern you more than they do."

"I'm concerned," I said. "But, at this point, I'm willing to overlook those concerns to see where this goes."

"I understand that."

"Sometimes you don't know until you know, right?"

"And sometimes you need a close friend to help you know. Which is all I'm trying to do."

"Well, I have some news to tell you that you may not be super jazzed about."

"Oh?"

"We're going to move in together."

"Yeah?" he seemed less than thrilled.

"It just makes sense. We've been together for two years, and we'd save money between rent, driving back and forth between my house and her apartment."

"Well, if it makes sense..." he said sarcastically.

"It's more than that, but you know what I mean."

"If you're happy, I'm happy for you. You know that's what I've always said."

"I know," I said. "And I appreciate that."

Moving In With Brooke

Moving day had finally come around. It'd been a few weeks since I told Marty I was moving in with Brooke, and he'd started to warm up to the idea. She worked a lot of late hours, so when I pitched it to him as us having more time to hang out, he got on board with it a little more than he originally did.

It felt weird looking at my childhood bedroom, empty of everything except the twin bed I'd slept in since I was a toddler. Everything I owned was packed into boxes, as haphazardly as a twenty-something would pack.

I wouldn't go as far as saying my mother was sobbing, but she was upset. I was her only child, and it'd just been the two of us since my father left all those years before. It was hard not to see it from her point of view. While she had nothing against Brooke and certainly didn't have the same concerns that Marty did—because I never told her any of the stuff I'd told him—she was still upset that I was moving out.

"You don't need me anymore," she said on one of my trips downstairs, arms full of boxes.

"Mom, that's not true," I said. "I've never lived on my own before. I'm going to call you every night and ask you how to do stuff."

She laughed, shooting a tiny bit of snot into the tissue she'd been holding onto for the last hour, clearly soaked through with tears. "Just remember to turn the stove off. You'll be fine."

"I'm going to miss you," I said. She'd always been such an important part of my life. I didn't know what life would be like without her.

"Me too, bug." She'd called me Bug since I was a kid—a nickname I never understood but also never questioned.

I put the last box in the moving truck, just as Marty had finished organizing the previous box I'd brought downstairs, playing a game of quasi-Tetris, making sure everything lined up, was secure, and that we'd have enough room to get Brooke's things, which was our next stop after leaving my house.

"That's the last one," I said, handing him the last box. I knew contained therein were things I'd need that first night in the new apartment. My alarm clock, toothbrush, toothpaste, favorite pillow, and plastic tumbler so I could have a drink and laptop.

"Got it," Marty said, placing the box in a perfectly thought-out spot he'd prepared as if he knew how big the last box would be.

"Drive safe," my mom said, waving as we got into the truck.

Marty had offered to drive, but I decided to do it myself. Not that I doubted his ability to drive the U-Haul, but I wanted to do it. Something about driving a truck that big made me feel powerful, as dumb as that sounds to share with you.

"You ready for this?" Marty asked as I pulled out of the driveway, nearly running over my mom's mailbox.

"I'm ready," I said. "Ready as I'll ever be, anyway."

We drove from my house—well, I guess my mom's house—to Brooke's apartment, where I'd basically been living for the last year, anyway. I'd previously arranged it so the other tenants would park on the street the night before so I could back the truck into the driveway, making it easier to load up out the back of the building. Thankfully, her apartment was on the first floor, so there were very few stairs to go up and down.

Marty and I fumbled with the ramp for a few minutes before we rang the bell. I was hoping we could find some way to line the ramp up with the porch to eliminate the stairs, but we couldn't make the geometry of it all work.

I finally pressed the buzzer once we were ready to get going.

"Hey guys!" Danielle answered the door, swinging it open to let us in.

"Good morning," I said, high-fiving her, as I always did.

"Hi, Danielle," Marty added, looking around for something to prop the door open with. Although Brooke's apartment wasn't in the best part of town, we weren't worried about keeping the door open, knowing how frequently we'd be going in and out.

"Morning," Brooke said as we entered her apartment. The boxes were everywhere, some filled, some not. Rolls of packing tape sat atop the small kitchen table, ready to be used.

"Are you not ready to go?" Marty asked, obviously annoyed.

"I thought the plan was that we'd get here and just load the truck and go," I added. I tried not to let my annoyance show as much as Marty's clearly did.

"Almost ready," she said, feverishly tossing things from the kitchen cabinets into the boxes by her feet, paying no mind to what things were going in which box. Just haphazardly tossing item after item into the empty boxes.

"I'm helping," Danielle offered from the living room, where she, too, was tossing things into boxes. I don't know why, but it drove me a little mad. Not just that they weren't ready when they were supposed to, but that they were so disorganized with their packing. My stuff was meticulously packed. Granted, I only had a single bedroom to pack up. But I knew exactly where everything was. Each box was labeled with what was in it and what room it was supposed to go to.

"Why don't we start bringing the furniture out?" Marty asked, looking at the living room, seeing that the loveseat and couch were still covered with unpacked items, flattened boxes, and the remnants of the Chinese food they'd clearly eaten the night before.

"Good idea," I said, moving toward the table in the kitchen, knowing it would be the most awkward shape to get into the truck.

I nodded to Marty, indicating I wanted him to grab the other side.

Marty spoke when we got outside the apartment door and into the hallway. "I'm not the only one annoyed with this, right?"

I groaned. "No."

"Moving sucks enough when all parties are prepared."

"And they're clearly not prepared," I said. "I told her days ago to make sure she didn't wait until the last minute."

"She usually does, doesn't she?"

"Her concept of time does not align exactly with mine."

"Concept of time?" Marty laughed. "You have a panic attack if you're more than thirty seconds late to being somewhere."

He wasn't wrong. And while we weren't late for moving, per se, it still felt like we were getting off to a rough start.

"You're right," I said. "I'm annoyed."

"Was you guys moving a surprise?" he asked snidely.

"Yes!" I laughed as we made our way up the ramp, struggling slightly to balance the top-heavy table. "I just thought, all of a sudden, 'Hey, let's move in together!' and then sprung it on her first thing this morning."

We were clearly poking fun at how unprepared she was. As if we hadn't been planning this move for months. As if, all of a sudden, the date that'd been marked on her calendar for months was here, and she didn't realize it.

"She had the forethought to invite Danielle over last night," Marty said.

"Mhmm," I nodded, dropping my end of the table into the far right corner of the truck, making sure it'd fit where I thought it needed to go.

"More that way," Marty said, pointing to my right. "Hopefully, there's not much left to pack."

"I'm sure there is," I said, letting my annoyance show more than I'd have liked.

"Let's see what's next."

"Okay," I said, following him back inside.

The two of us stood in the doorway, surveying the apartment. Personally, I was comparing the state of my bedroom when Marty showed up that morning to what Brooke's apartment was. Every box from my room was neatly packed, label facing out. The floor was vacuumed, the lights on, and the curtains pulled back. It was ready for a team—well, Marty and I—to come in, scoop everything up and move it into the truck. Brooke's apartment looked like a hurricane had just swept through, hitting every single thing she owned.

"Couches?" I asked, making my way to the far end of the bigger couch without waiting for Marty's response.

He nodded, grabbing the end closest to him and walking backward toward the door, trying not to trip over any items left on the floor between our origin and destination.

"Good thing it's not a recliner," I said.

"Why?"

"They're heavier," I joked. "This one's relatively light." I flashed back to having helped my mom move a new couch into our living room a few years back. It was a sectional with two recliners and weighed a ton.

"Ha," Marty said, not actually laughing. I couldn't tell if he was mocking me or not.

We placed the couch into the empty spot in front of the table we'd previously put in. "This is going to take forever," I said.

"Yep. Let's go get the loveseat," he replied.

"Okay." I followed him back into the living room, grabbing the smaller, lighter couch.

We were able to almost toss it on top of the bigger couch, given how light it was. "At least we're getting the heavy stuff out of the way," Marty said.

"Good way to look at it."

"The bed is staying here," Brooke said as we entered the apartment. "We have a new one being delivered later today."

"Good timing," I said, knowing it'd probably get delayed somehow, and we'd sleep on the couches on our first night in the new apartment.

I grabbed the coffee table, brushing off the items on it onto the floor. Marty grabbed the television under one arm and the DVD player under the other.

"We're going to end up sitting here waiting," Marty said, walking up the ramp to drop the latest items into the back of the truck.

"Probably," I said. "I'm sorry."

"It's not *your* fault," he said. "Well, it kind of is. You picked her."

I laughed. "You're right. This is all my fault."

As we re-entered the apartment, I surveyed its contents again. All the heavy or bulky items had already been loaded into the truck, and it didn't seem like any boxes were ready to go. Those that seemed filled weren't taped shut, nor were they labeled.

"Let us know when you're done in here," Marty said, clearly not caring about repercussions. "We'll be out by the truck."

I smiled and nodded slightly as I followed him out of the apartment, sitting on the back of the truck, one of us on each side of the ramp.

"Hopefully, it's not long," I said.

It was. It took them three hours to finish packing up the contents of Brooke's apartment.

· · · ● · ● · ● · ·

Once we had finished loading the truck, which thankfully went quickly due to the dolly we'd rented with the truck, Marty and I headed out to the new apartment. Brooke and Danielle followed us somewhere behind us in Brooke's car.

Our apartment was on the first floor, making it incredibly easy to move in.

"It's the middle of the day," Marty said as we pulled into the apartment complex's parking lot. "Just back into the spot right by the door."

"It's handicapped," I said.

"We'll move if someone needs us to, but I'm sure they're used to this. People move in and out of these big complexes all the time."

I took his direction and started backing in. He jumped out to guide me, helping space out the distance between where the end of the ramp would fall and the door into the complex.

We were moving to Somerville. Not the most glorious location, but it was close enough that she could get to school and her part-time job at Macy's, and I could get to my job. The rent was low enough to afford a two-bedroom, allowing us to share the second bedroom as a joint home office, primarily for our computers and the start of our burgeoning DVD collection.

"Perfect," I heard him call out as he raised both hands in the air like an air traffic controller telling a 747 to stop.

The air brakes on the truck made a whooshing sound as I jumped down out of the cab.

"Do you have the keys?" Marty asked.

"Yep," I said, pulling the key to the complex door out of my pocket. We propped it open with a rock that had been conveniently left in the mulch bed behind the door. Someone had the same idea we did when they moved in or out and left the perfect-sized rock that held the door open to its widest point.

"Let's go inside and make sure the key works to the apartment before we lug anything inside," I said.

Marty followed me down the short hallway, past the mailboxes, to my new home. The apartment was an end unit, directly to the left, when we got to the end of the hallway. I first looked to my right to see the massive expanse of the rest of the hallway. Door after door, lining down it, as far as the eye could see.

My key worked, and Marty and I went inside, closing the door behind us.

I gave him a quick tour, explained which bedroom would be which, pointed out roughly where I wanted to put the furniture, and then double-checked to see if the bottled water the leasing agent promised to stock the fridge with was there.

"Delicious," Marty said, gulping half of what would become his first bottle of Poland Springs. "This is a nice apartment."

"It's not bad for a first apartment, right?"

"It's not bad for any apartment," Marty said reassuringly.

"Hi," Danielle said as she and Brooke came in, surprising us.

"We're just getting a lay of the land," I said. "We'll start unloading momentarily."

"Take your time," Brooke said, kissing me on the cheek.

Inside, my anxiety was in high gear. Although we had the whole day, in my head, we were already three hours behind schedule due to Brooke being unprepared for the move. "Okay, we'll go out now."

"Let's go, boss," Marty said.

He followed me outside and grabbed the dolly from the back of the truck.

"Should be easy to load out," he said, tossing a handful of boxes onto the dolly.

"I think so, too. Want me to be the runner?"

In hindsight, we should have rented two dollies. Since there was only one, one of us would have to stay behind with the truck, moving boxes toward the top of the ramp so the other person could just come out, scoop them up, and run them inside.

"Think they'll come help?" he asked.

"Carry boxes?" I scoffed. "How many did they help carry out when we loaded the truck?"

"Did they?" he asked, knowing full well that neither of them carried a single box when we loaded Brooke's apartment.

"Probably faster if they're out of our way, anyway," he said. "We can plow through everything quicker."

I grabbed the dolly and ushered the four boxes down the ramp and inside the apartment, dropping them in the various rooms they needed to be left in.

"Thanks, honey," Brooke said as I whipped by her with the empty dolly, trying to get the unloading done as quickly as possible.

Marty had the next batch of boxes ready by the time I got back out there.

We continued that routine until every box was inside, conveniently placed out of the way of where we'd need to maneuver the furniture.

Through a stroke of good luck, the bed delivery happened just as we got the last of the furniture off the truck. Brooke escorted them into the bedroom and told them where she wanted the bed assembled.

"Glad we paid extra," I said.

"For assembly?" Brooke asked.

"Yeah. I'm too tired to put a single thing together," I replied. "You too, Marty?"

"Exhausted beyond words. Be right back." He excused himself to the bathroom.

I used the kitchen sink to flood my face and head with cold water. While it was only May, it was unusually warm for that time of year. I was thankful we hadn't moved in July or August, but I still felt the sweat sticking my clothes to parts of my body that clothes weren't supposed to stick to.

Brooke and Danielle were seated in the living room, one on each couch, as I fumbled with some boxes in the kitchen, hoping I'd find some plates and cutlery to order some dinner. It wasn't late enough for dinner, but it was too late for lunch, and by that time, I was famished.

"Moving really takes it out of you," I called out in their general direction. Neither responded, presumably because they either didn't hear me or didn't care.

The two men who had delivered the bed finished constructing the frame and were carrying the trash out. "Thank you," I said. "Brooke, do you have any cash?" I asked after checking my empty wallet.

"I've got it," Marty called out, rounding the corner from the hallway leading to the bathroom. He handed them each a ten-dollar bill. "Thanks again, guys."

"Thank you," Brooke called out from the living room.

"Thank you," one of the two who spoke better English said as the door closed.

"What should we eat?" I asked. We had no internet in the apartment yet, and the concept of smartphones hadn't quite made it to me or the other people in the room.

"Should we go out and see what we can find in the area?" Brooke asked.

"Good idea," Marty said. His annoyance with her seemed to have dissipated since the truck was fully unloaded.

"When do we need to bring the U-Haul back?" I asked in Brooke's general direction.

"I think they said by seven."

"Perfect. Why don't you follow me there, and I'll jump in the car once I drop it off."

A New Place To Live

I woke up the next morning, slightly confused. My brain not yet having recognized the walls of the new room I'd never slept in before. The slight sliver of sun shining through the slit in the blinds seemed to be making my eyes a target, hitting me directly in the face.

My brain also assumed my phone would be on the nightstand next to the bed, but we didn't have nightstands yet. I leaned over, fumbling for the phone on the floor, to find out it was just after seven in the morning. I rubbed my eyes, adjusting my position so the sun didn't hit me in the face anymore, and looked over at Brooke. She was still asleep. "Must be exhausted from all the moving," I said, mostly to myself, sarcastically.

The joints and muscles in my body ached, and although we'd finished moving mid-afternoon and I'd gotten a good night's sleep, I still felt incredibly sore. Every part of me seemed to revolt as I tried to sit upright. The cracking and popping of joints felt so loud that I was convinced it would wake her up.

Sliding out of bed, I walked over to the closet and found a box that had some of my clothes in it before sneaking out of the room to the bathroom across the hall.

I peeked down the hallway, seeing Marty's feet on the end of the couch that was visible from my line of sight. He and Danielle had slept in the living room, Marty on the couch and Danielle on the loveseat. By the time we'd gotten back from dinner, we were all too exhausted to get them back to their respective homes. My plan had always been to have Brooke drive Danielle home, then drop Marty at his house and pick up my car from my mom's driveway. But we were so beat that we all fell asleep around nine that night.

My plans for starting to unpack were all foiled by my exhaustion. My thoughts that I'd get the kitchen all set up and then go for our first grocery shopping the next morning did not come to fruition, not even close. I had wanted to go for a walk around the apartment complex to see what things were within walking distance. I'd seen a Whole Foods not that far away when we drove there to see the complex for the first time, but I wasn't sure if it was walkable or not. I had wanted to explore a lot of things, but knew my day would end up dropping people at home and getting my car. Sure, there'd be more time to do the stuff I wanted to do, but I knew unpacking was an uphill battle. Especially seeing how disheveled Brooke's packing was.

That first shower felt better than any other I can remember in that apartment. The hot water was endless. I'd turn it up so hot that I felt uncomfortable, in hopes the heat would help my sore joints. That it'd help relieve some of the tension in my muscles.

A gentle knocking on the door startled me. "Can I come in?" It was Brooke.

"I'm in the shower," I called back, not really answering her question.

I heard the door open and close quietly. "I don't remember saying yes," I mumbled under the sound of the rushing water. It was the first—and only—time Brooke ever used the bathroom at the same time I was in there. It felt so weird, so foreign to me. It was surprising that it'd never happened before in the two years we'd been together. I'd hoped it was a fluke, secretly, and that it was just adjusting to the new environment that led her into the bathroom while I was showering.

"I'm going back to sleep," she whispered. The sound of the door closing was barely audible over the shower.

Another ten or fifteen minutes went by before I felt fully relaxed and clean. My preparedness to have a box of shower items had paid off. I probably should have showered the night before, but, as I previously mentioned, we were all exhausted.

We'd found a great little Chinese restaurant that had a few tables outside, just down the street. I brought a menu home and put it on the fridge with the only magnet we had. It was from the leasing office and said "Welcome Home" on it.

Once I was dry and dressed, I headed out to the living room to see if Danielle or Marty had woken up. The clock on the microwave in the kitchen read five past eight. It was still early, and the two of them were still sound asleep.

I maneuvered around the piles of boxes, the coffee table oddly placed in the middle of the room, and made my way over to the big picture window. It was one of the things that sold us on that particular apartment. The picture windows were only in the end units, and we had almost decided against the complex when the leasing agent said that we might like an end unit better than the middle unit she'd first showed us.

Without opening the blinds too much, not wanting to let too much sunlight in, I peeked through, looking at the buildings around us. I could see the Whole Foods sign off in the not-too-far-off distance. A McDonald's was just up the block. Some other businesses here and there, a small market that looked to be setting up fresh produce out front. The Best Buy sign was high in the sky, to be sure it could be seen from the highway.

It'd have been picturesque if I had a cup of coffee in my hand. I could have been in the opening credits of some sitcom where the boss looks out his window, surveying his surroundings, before turning and telling the main character to get back to those TPS reports.

"Morning," I heard Marty say.

I turned around and saw him sitting up. "Hey, buddy."

"My back is killing me," he said. "This couch sucks."

I chuckled.

"He's not wrong," Danielle added, stretching her limbs and eventually sitting upright.

"Brooke's still sleeping," I said, trying to lower my voice.

"No, she's not," Brooke called from the other room. "I'm up."

The three of them took their time getting ready for the day. I did my best not to be anxious about it, allowing them all the time they needed, despite how much I knew I needed to get done that day. The still-packed boxes seemed to surround me everywhere I looked. I knew that I'd be the one who had to unpack most of them and find homes for all of their contents. I'd be the one who decided which drawer the silverware went in, or which cabinet the plates would get put in. I'd be the one who decided which side of the fridge the 12-pack of Coke would go on, or where we'd keep the pizza cutter I knew we'd need because no pizza place ever *really* cut all the way through the crust.

I knew I'd be the one saddled with all the responsibility of doing all that work. It's not that I minded, but I knew how Brooke was. She'd take one box and then obsess over every single thing in it, deciding if she should keep it and, if she did, where it should go. Should the photo of her grandparents go on the window sill in the bedroom, or on the little shelf between the kitchen and the dining room? Should she leave a brush by her side of the bed, so she could brush her hair before going to sleep? All of those things—all stemming from a single box being unpacked—would take her just as long as it'd take me to unpack just about everything else. Again, not that I minded. It was more that I knew what to expect at that point in our relationship. She was the dilly-dallier, and I was the get-it-done person. I'd say we complimented each other well, but we didn't, really. Not in that regard, anyway.

I stood in the doorway to the shared office we'd set up over the coming days, imagining myself in there, someday, working away on some big project, or working remotely for some company who would trust their employees to do so. I imagined the two of us in there, with the small television I'd had in my bedroom back home, playing old reruns of shows that we both loved and bonded over. I pictured my future in that room that day. I pictured my future, not just with Brooke, but with myself. Imagining all the things I could be. All the things I'd hoped I could become. So many visions and dreams all flooding me at the same time. Things I didn't even know interested me until they flashed before my eyes.

"You ready?" Brooke called out from the opposite end of the hallway, directly behind me.

"You guys ready now?" I asked, trying not to show any impatience.

"We're ready," she said. "You okay?"

"I'm okay," I said, smiling. "I'm good."

2008

Trust Issues & A Planned Proposal

Over the years, Marty and I had become closer than ever. We spent more time together than Brooke and I did. We referred to one another as brothers. That's how close our bond was.

So when I knew, after almost five years of dating, that I was going to ask Brooke to marry me, Marty was the first person I told. Before I'd planned anything. Before I'd bought a ring. Before I'd asked her parents. Before I told my mom. I called Marty and told him.

Truth be told, the two of them never got along that well, even after all the time they'd spent together over the years. For a brief moment, he even went on a few dates with her best friend, Tracy.

"Hey hey hey," he said, answering the phone. He'd gotten a lot less formal over the years, his accent barely audible anymore.

"Hey bud," I said. "I've got some big news to tell you."

"You're pregnant," he laughed. His sense of humor had picked up, as well. I think part of it was that I'd rubbed off on him so much. He was a lot like me by that time.

"No, dipshit," I said. "But that's hilarious."

"So what is it?"

"I'm going to ask Brooke to marry me."

He paused a moment. I wasn't sure if he was thinking of how to respond or just that he was shocked. "Oh, that's great. Congratulations!" I could tell he was forcing out the excitement.

"Thanks. It's a big step, but I think we're ready." We'd already been living together for about three years at that point. It only seemed natural to want to get married.

"It is a big step," he said, pausing again. "But if you're ready, you're ready."

"I think I am," I said, wavering a little.

"I support you, you know that. You're my best friend, and I'm there for you, no matter what."

"I appreciate that, you know that. And, look, I know you and she aren't best friends. That's fine. I'm fine with it. I get it. So I appreciate your support even more than I can tell you."

"That's what friends do, right?" he often parroted back things I'd said to him years ago as if he coined the phrase himself.

"That's what friends do."

"When are you doing it? What's the plan?"

"I don't know yet," I said. "I have to get a ring and talk to her parents first."

"Ring shopping sounds expensive."

"Tell me about it," I laughed. I had been preparing, putting away a little money here and there over the last year, trying to save enough to buy something nice, but not the traditional "three-month salary" I'd always heard about.

"Let me know how I can help," he said.

I had already known I was going to ask him to be my best man. There really was no question about it. He was the right person for that responsibility. He was the right guy that I knew would have my back, no matter what. So I didn't ask him then. Knowing he had already asked how he could help was answer enough that I knew he'd do it when I officially asked.

"Thanks bud. Pizza tonight?"

"You bet." Marty still lived in the neighborhood where I used to, but I'd moved in with Brooke about half an hour south of there. Although Marty was good at driving, thanks to my teaching, he still didn't own a car or drive anywhere. He worked what seemed like full-time hours but didn't spend any money on a car. So, needless to say, I'd always make the drive from our place to his, grabbing the pizza on the way.

Instead of sitting in the driveway at the house I used to live at—although my mom still lived there—we sat at the end of the cul-de-sac near Marty's house. We sat in the same chairs, in the same configuration we always had—me on the left, Marty on the right—facing down the street toward oncoming traffic. We were only a handful of feet from the end of Marty's driveway.

· · · · • · • · · ·

You'd think Papa Gino's would have gotten sick of us after all those pizzas over all those years, but they didn't. The staff would turn over pretty frequently, but I'd always get to know the new people after a few visits. They probably loved me because the order was always consistent and easy. Large cheese pizza and two Cokes.

As usual, I grabbed the food and drinks and drove to Marty's house.

He was already waiting in his chair, mine set up next to him.

It was a beautiful June evening. The sun was still high overhead, not a cloud in the sky. It had rained earlier, but the sun came out so that everything had already dried up.

I pulled up next to my chair, parked the car under the same giant oak tree I had always parked under since moving, and hopped out.

"Hey bud," I said, handing him the pizza box and taking a plate he handed me.

"Hey, hey," he replied.

He took a slice from the box, plopped it on my plate, and then did the same for him. I placed my Coke down by my right side and handed his to him.

"Engaged." He said between bites.

"You think I'm crazy, don't you?" I asked.

"Look, Matt. You're my brother. I love you like my own family. There's nothing in this universe I wouldn't do for you."

"I sense a but coming on," I said.

"But..."

"There it is."

"But, are you sure?"

"I guess I'm as sure as I can be," I said. "Brooke's been everything to me over the last years."

"I know you love her," he said. "And I know she loves you."

"Isn't that all you need? Love?" Then I cheesily did the bum bum bum from the song that's probably going to be stuck in your head now. I'm sorry.

"Not always," he said. "Sometimes love isn't enough," he quasi-sang, mocking my stupidity.

I knew, on some level, he was right. Love wasn't always enough, but it felt enough. It felt right with Brooke. "I know. But it feels like it's time."

"It's time?" he asked. "You don't get married just because a certain amount of time has passed."

"You're right," I said. "But it's not just that."

"She doesn't trust you," Marty said, kind of matter-of-factly. "She never has."

"How did you..." I started. "How did you know that?" I'd never told anyone how Brooke didn't trust me. She always seemed to suspect I had a fling early on in our relationship—though that wasn't true—and had very little trust in me because of it. I think part of it was due to low self-esteem. Her's, not mine.

"I know she's looked through your phone before. Read your emails and texts."

"How do you know?"

"One time when we were at your place, after dinner, you and Danielle went into the other room to look at your new computer or something. So she and I were alone, talking. It doesn't happen often, but it was just us. And she said some things about a conversation you and I had over text. One that I'm absolutely positive you'd never told her about. It wasn't anything big or scandalous, but it was a private conversation between you and me. And she knew about it. When I alluded to the fact that I didn't think you'd told her about that, she changed the subject."

"Why didn't you mention it to me before?"

"You don't want to be the one to pop your best buddy's bubble, right? I didn't want to upset you."

"I appreciate that. And I know she's been nosey over the years. She snoops a lot, but, like, I can't just change my passwords to something she doesn't know."

"Then she'll have even more reason not to trust you. She'll think you're hiding something."

"Bingo."

I grabbed another slice of pizza from the box, holding it open toward him to offer a second slice to him. He grabbed it and took the box from me, placing it on the small table between us.

"You're okay with living the rest of your life like that?"

"Like what?"

"Walking on eggshells. Hiding things without hiding them. Having everything you think is private, not be private."

"Well. Married couples don't hide anything from each other, do they?"

"I suppose they shouldn't. But should they share every single tiny detail? I know I'm not married and have never had a serious relationship, but should you know everything she talks to every one of her friends about? And vice versa?"

"I hadn't thought of that before. I guess not. I suppose that there should be some secrets somewhere."

"Not even secrets," he said. "Everyone has secrets. I even have secrets I don't tell you. It's not a matter of secrets. It's about privacy. You should be able to have a private conversation with anyone, not just me, and not have her read the whole thing. Why would she do that?"

"Trust. Or lack thereof, I suppose."

"Exactly."

I paused, finishing the crust of my second piece of pizza. "Maybe it's something we can work on together."

"Bro," he said. I always found it funny when he called me bro because his accent would slip out just a tiny bit, and it sounded so funny to me. "It's been five years, right? Why would she change now? She's gotten away with it for so long."

"I hadn't thought of that." I said, thinking about how he said 'gotten away with it' like she was a criminal and I was a schmuck for not correcting the behavior the first time it happened. "I confronted her about it once or twice."

"When?"

"A while ago. She confessed to reading my email while I was over here. As soon as I got back, she said she felt guilty and would never do it again. I asked her why she did it, and she said she was curious about what I was talking about."

"In email?"

"Yeah. Here's a bunch of boring emails about work stuff. Good luck reading through my horrible PowerPoints. Have fun wasting your time."

"Would she have found anything she would be mad about?"

"Not a thing. Which is why I don't get why she doesn't trust me. It's not like I'm out sleeping around. Even if I wanted to, when would I? I'm either with her, at work, or with you."

"Not like you've got an abundance of free time."

I took my third—and probably last—slice of pizza, Marty following suit.

"I'm just saying," he said. "Be careful. Do what's right for you, but be careful."

I knew he was looking out for my best intentions. "I will," I said.

We stayed another couple of hours before I headed back to the apartment. We talked about our days at work, mostly. Marty told me about a new project he'd just been assigned to that he was having trouble with. He, much like what he told me about his dad's job, couldn't talk about what he was doing for work. So he'd often talk in vague ambiguities, which was fine. I knew if he could tell me the specifics, he eventually would.

Two's Company, Three's a Crowd

Although Marty wasn't fully on board with my proposal (or the marriage), he helped me plan the whole thing out. From ring shopping to planning how I'd do it to planning what I'd say, Marty helped with everything.

"You know I'm happy for you," he said one day while driving from his house to my apartment. We planned to hang out with Brooke, watch *Sky Captain and the World of Tomorrow*—which was terrible if memory serves—and get some dinner.

"I know," I said. "I appreciate that you are, despite your doubts."

"Listen, if everything were perfect, I'd still have doubts. I feel like I'm your guardian. Like no matter who it is, they wouldn't be good enough."

"A little overprotective, eh?"

"A little bit, I suppose."

We pulled into a parking spot just around the corner from my building, further than I usually had to park.

"What are we getting for dinner?" Marty asked.

"I bet you want pizza, don't you?" Much to my chagrin, there was no Papa Gino's near my apartment, but there were plenty of other good options.

"I'm not sure. Let's go in and see what Brooke wants to do."

The two of us walked around the corner of the building and went inside. My apartment was just right across the hall from that entrance to the building, the door already unlocked, Brooke whipping around in the kitchen.

"Hey!" she said as we entered, taking our shoes off by the door.

"Hi," I said, kissing her on the cheek.

"Hi, Brooke," Marty said, making his way to the living room through the kitchen. "It smells wonderful."

"I was hoping you'd hit a little traffic," she said. "Dinner would have been ready. I thought I'd cook."

I was a bit skeptical. Although a great baker, Brooke wasn't the best chef. "What are you making?" I asked.

"Pasta."

A short sigh of relief escaped. "Great," I called back from the living room. "Pasta means boxed pasta and jarred sauce," I whispered to Marty. "Hard to screw that up."

He chuckled, seating himself on the far end of the couch.

"Thanks for cooking," I said, sitting beside Marty.

We had no plans for what to do before the movie, so we just sat and waited for dinner to be ready, making small talk.

"Two more minutes," Brooke called from the kitchen. "Just about done."

Marty stood and headed toward the bathroom. I headed to the kitchen to get plates, silverware, and drinks ready for the table.

"He doesn't like me," she said once Marty had closed the door.

"Stop," I said. "He does. He's just different. His personality is a little off sometimes." I fumbled for what to say to her to stop the conversation or change direction.

"Did I do something?"

"No, no," I assured her. "He likes you just fine."

The toilet flushed, so I scurried over to the cabinet where the plates were, grabbing three pasta bowls and three glasses.

"Coke?" I called out in the general direction of the hallway.

"Please," Marty called back from behind the closed bathroom door.

"Coke for you, too?" I asked Brooke.

"Thank you."

Once the plates were full of pasta and Marty returned from the bathroom, I set everything on the table.

"Thank you, Brooke, for cooking. This smells wonderful," Marty said.

As I suspected, it was boxed pasta and jarred sauce. The same stuff we ate at least once a week. Not that there's anything wrong with boxed pasta and jarred sauce. Not by any means.

Like always, I poured too much parmesan cheese on my penne before swirling it all together. As much as I love pasta, it's really just an excuse to shovel cheese into my mouth. Everyone knew that about me.

"Very good," I said, being supportive of Brooke's effort to do something nice for Marty and me.

"Thanks. I wanted to make rolls too, but I forgot to heat the oven."

"It's fine," Marty said. "This is great as it is."

I knew, in his heart, he'd have preferred pizza. He loved pizza more than any other food.

"The movie is supposed to be pretty good," I said, trying to move the conversation along as we all continued to eat.

"Yes, I've heard the same," Marty said.

Something about the conversations was always off when it was just the three of us. It always felt forced, like the three of us had no chemistry. Marty and I alone? Great conversations, almost nightly, for five years. Brooke and I? We could talk about anything and everything under the sun. Never a quiet moment—though when we had those quiet moments, they were great—we always had something to talk about. But when we were all together, it was this odd awkwardness. It just felt like we were strangers and could *only* make small talk.

I was the first to finish my pasta, so I got up to place my dish in the sink to be rinsed later and put into the dishwasher.

Before I was able to get back to the table, Marty was on his way to drop his plate in the sink, following my lead. Brooke followed a moment after. All of us still silent. The tension was palpable.

For years, I'd hoped that the two of them would have some magic moment where they'd find a topic they both loved and talk about it. Or they'd bond over some quirk I had that they both hated. I'd hoped for something, some minor thing, that would allow them to become friends. Maybe not the best of friends, not the type of friends who would hang out without me. But friends of some kind. Buddies. People who could be in the same room as one another, without me, without awkwardness.

But that moment never came.

I would say they tolerated one another, but it was more than that. They were pleasant to one another, having plenty of casual conversations over the years. But there was always this level of Marty's disapproval and Brooke doing her best to win him over.

Though he never confided in me about his disapproval more than the day we talked about her trust issues; I knew there had to be more to it than that. I knew, somewhere, Marty had something else he was holding back about why he didn't fully trust Brooke.

The three of us sat down on the couch almost in unison. I sat between the two of them. The couch was long enough that all three of us could sit comfortably without touching one another. And while I'd usually have sat closer to Brooke, I remained neutral, sitting right in the middle of both of them, on my cushion, right in front of the glass coffee table.

"One of us should put the movie in," Marty said, chuckling.

"Oh, is that not automatic?" I joked.

"I'll get it," Brooke said, hopping up and grabbing the Netflix envelope from the coffee table. She slipped it into the DVD player and turned the television on.

Normally, I'm a talker during movies. I like to discuss what's happening as it happens. I always ask, "What did he say?" because my hearing is terrible. I miss important plot points because I go to the bathroom and insist no one needs to pause the movie, and then I am lost when I come back.

But that night, that movie, I said nothing. I kept my mouth shut. I don't know if it was because of the awkwardness between Brooke and Marty or if it was something else. But I was compelled not to speak a single word. It also probably reflected how bad the movie was, too.

• • • • • • • • • •

Marty was the first to speak when the movie ended, and it was time for the night to conclude. "I suppose I should go," he said.

"Oh, right," I said, looking at the clock on the cabinet next to the television. "It's getting late."

"Thanks for coming," Brooke said. "It was nice to see you."

"You as well," Marty said, extending his hand.

She shook his hand but pulled away almost instantly. It felt odd to me, so it's stuck out in my mind for all these years.

"I'll be back in a bit," I said, kissing her on the cheek.

As the door to the building closed behind us, Marty grabbed my arm. "It's more than that," he said. "More than the trust issues."

"What do you mean?" I asked.

"I got a bad feeling when she shook my hand. I felt a negative energy."

"You're being a goof," I said. "That's silly."

"No. Matt. I felt something bad."

"Okay. Can you elaborate a bit on what you felt?"

"I don't know how to put it into words. But something didn't feel right."

Marty didn't say much on the drive back to his house. Occasionally, he'd point out the window at something he hadn't seen before, calling it to my attention. He'd often see a car in a color he didn't know you could get a car in and point it out to me. But we didn't have any more deep conversations on the way back. I didn't bring up his feeling again until a few days later.

That Bad Feeling

It'd been eating me alive, the few days between when Marty told me he had a bad feeling about Brooke and the next time I saw him. I'd written countless text messages asking him to talk more about it. Only to delete them all before sending them, one after another. The words just never felt right enough to send. The fear of, perhaps, he was right, and something was off. Maybe he saw, or felt, something that I didn't. Something I didn't pick up on.

But why did it seem to happen only when he touched her hand? What was that all about?

"Papa Gino's tonight?" I finally texted.

"7?" was all he replied.

"See you then."

It was the shortest text conversation we'd had in a long while. Short, to the point, and of very few words. Just enough to get the point across.

• • • ● • ● • • •

I toyed with how to bring it up the entire ride to his house. What to say? How do you say it? When to say it. My anxiety was through the roof, higher than I can remember until that point in my life. But he had to say more. He had to tell me what he felt, what this bad feeling was that he was holding on to.

For the first time, he wasn't waiting outside. He wasn't in the driveway or waiting in his lawn chair—though they were both permanently set up in the cul-de-sac—he wasn't anywhere.

I parked in the same spot I always did, turning the radio off and shutting the engine down. "I'm here," I texted.

"Be right there," he replied. "One sec."

Before I knew it, he came bounding out of the woods directly in front of me. A big smile on his face, a bigger appetite surely in his stomach.

"I ordered the pizza," he said, pulling the passenger door open and climbing in. "Let's go, it should be ready."

I nodded silently, started the car, shifted the car into reverse, turned around, and headed out of the neighborhood. I'd been into that Papa Gino's countless times in my life, well into the hundreds, but something about that night felt different. It felt off. Perhaps it was the dark clouds looming overhead. Perhaps it was the ball sitting in the pit of my stomach, knowing I had to talk to him about something I really didn't want to discuss. Perhaps it was just my anxiety about everything. I'm not sure.

"Hey guys," Kevin, the cashier, greeted us. We were both familiar faces at that point.

"Hey Kevin," Marty said, handing over a twenty-dollar bill and taking the pizza and a small plastic bag with our two sodas.

"So, listen," I said as we got back in the car. "This has been bugging me."

"The other night?" he asked. "Me too."

"What was that?"

"I don't know," he said. "Sometimes I just get these feelings when I touch someone."

"And you got a bad feeling from Brooke?"

"I don't know if bad is the right word," he said as I backed out of the parking spot.

"So, what is the right word?"

"I'm not sure. I felt this flash of heat when her hand touched mine."

"From her hand? Like, physically hot?"

"No, not physically. Like an emotional wave of heat hit me. I'm sure it's nothing."

"It can't be nothing. If it were nothing, you wouldn't have brought it up."

"I'm sure it's nothing. I really am."

"But you felt something?" I asked.

"I did. I felt something unusual, but it happens all the time."

"All the time?"

"The first time I hugged you, that was the first time I made physical contact with you. I felt something then, too. Not like what I felt with Brooke, but I felt something that I couldn't shake for a while."

"Was it a bad feeling?"

"Quite the opposite," he said. I saw him smile out of the corner of my eye.

"How so?"

"With you, it felt powerful. It felt like we connected instantly. I felt a warmth but in a good way. I saw a small flash of light, which made me know you were good. That our friendship would be good for many years."

"That seems like a lifetime ago," I said.

"It does. I can't believe how long it's been already."

"You're sure it's nothing?"

"I've expressed my concerns over Brooke's behavior already. We both know she doesn't do well with trust, but other than that, I've not seen any concerning behavior from her."

"She's sometimes a little bossy," I blurted out, not realizing that was something I'd, until that point, kept to myself.

"What now?" he said as I felt him grab my right forearm.

"I... well. Sometimes, she can be a little bossy."

"How so?"

"I'd eat pizza with you more than twice a week if I had my way. Let's just say that."

"She doesn't let you spend as much time with me as you'd like?"

"No. I get it. She's my fiancé, my future wife. I should give her most of my free time."

"Right, but not all of your free time."

As we got closer, the headlights illuminated our chairs at the end of the street. Those chairs felt, on some level, like our sanctuary. No one ever bothered us when we sat there, talking, eating pizza, hanging out. Whatever we did, it was a quiet space where the only people we'd ever encountered were Marty's neighbors pulling into their driveways and immediately entering their houses. Sometimes, they'd wave. Periodically,

Mrs. Harriman would say hello when she got home from work, but never more than that. No one ever approached us to ask us what we were doing or why we were sitting in the middle of the cul-de-sac, eating a supply of pizza that, to the casual eye, seemed never to end.

"It's one of the few things that really bothers me," I said, shifting to park.

"Have you brought it up?"

"C'mon," I said. "You know I'm as confrontational as a monk. I don't like conflict at all."

"Matt, this is your life. You can't just be complacent forever. Make things happen. Speak your mind. You can move mountains if you want to."

"It's not that simple. You wouldn't get it," I said, looking away as I stepped out of the car.

"Why wouldn't I get it?"

"You just wouldn't." I sat, took my first slice of pizza, and placed it on the paper plate already waiting on my chair.

"You think I don't understand love because I've never been in love?"

"How the fuck did you know that's what I was thinking?"

"It's obvious," he said. "I can tell. And you're right. I don't understand love. Not the way you do. I've never experienced it the way you have. I've felt the love of others, but not a romantic love. Not like you and she have. Until now, I've never stayed in the same place long enough to find someone."

"I didn't mean it that way."

"What other way did you mean it?"

"I don't know. I just... I'm sorry."

"It's fine, really. Don't even worry about it."

We ate the whole pizza that night. We laughed so much once we'd moved on from the serious conversation. We laughed until the rain started suddenly pouring down, drenching the two of us.

"Run, I'll go," I said, pointing to his house.

"Bye," he said before breaking out into a full sprint to get into the house.

I sat for a minute in the car, trying to warm up. Although it was a warm July evening, the rain was cold. The air conditioning in the car blasted as soon as I turned the engine on, making the cold water covering me even colder. I shivered for a minute before warming up.

The Best Man

Unbeknownst to me, you have an engagement party when you get engaged. I'd love to bore you with the proposal's details, but it wasn't anything spectacular. I had a big, elaborate plan that I'd worked out with Marty's help. But it all fell to shit. Brooke and I had a big fight the night before I proposed, and I felt guilty. One of the ways I try to make amends when I've done something bad is with gifts. And what better gift than an engagement ring, right?

So I proposed, in our apartment, on a commercial break from "How I Met Your Mother." The episode where Britney Spears guest starred. It'd been on our TiVo for a few months, and we were finally catching up.

In the most unromantic way possible, I excused myself from the room, got the ring, and threw her a super loving "Do you want to get married?"

Cut to the engagement party. Marty and some of Brooke's friends had put it together. They'd rented out the function room at our apartment complex for the evening and had a catered meal brought in from our favorite Italian place in town.

It was a nice surprise for us. We had no idea they'd planned it and thought we were meeting Danielle and Amanda up there for a game of pool, as we'd done so many other times.

But when the doors opened, and virtually everyone we knew was there, yelling, "Surprise!" it was one of the highlights of my adult life. It made me feel so loved.

Having never been to one before, I didn't know what to do or how to act. The women had it easy; it was all "show me the ring, " "How'd he propose," and the like. On the other hand, I went around hugging people and shaking hands. Giving the usual "nice to see you"s and "how've you been"s. Had there not been so many people I knew there, it could have been any other evening. Besides a wonderful meal being brought in and served, it didn't feel like a party. It didn't feel special.

"Thank you," I said as I approached Marty in the back corner of the room. "I know you had a hand in this."

"A small hand," he said. "It was mostly her friends. I think they just let me participate so I wouldn't feel left out."

"Well, I appreciate whatever part of it you put in."

"Any time."

"Speaking of time," I said. "Now that it's official, I suppose I should make it official with you, too."

"Make what official?" he looked over at me.

"You being my best man."

"Wow! Really?"

"Really."

"What about her brothers? What about... I don't know, anyone else?"

"Marty, you are *my* brother. That trumps her brothers by a landslide."

"Yes. I'll do it. It'd be my honor to stand up there with you."

I didn't feel any sense of negativity or sarcasm. No judgment. No moment where I felt like he was being insincere. I knew he wasn't Brooke's biggest fan, but he had no problem supporting me and my decision. He spent more time with me over those five years than almost any other person did and, as a result, knew me better than anyone. He knew that if this was my decision, it was the right one for me.

A Wild Bachelor Party

To say I had butterflies in my stomach would be an understatement. I felt more nervous about the wedding than I had any other time in my life. Which, in hindsight, feels weird. There was so much time to prepare for it once I decided to propose, but I still felt nervous.

No matter how many times I'd talked about it with Marty, I still felt like I could throw up at any minute.

The night before the wedding, he came over to the apartment. Brooke had stayed at a hotel near the wedding venue with her maid of honor and bridesmaids so they could get ready more easily on the day of.

Marty and I had a wild night planned for my bachelor party. We ordered dinner—yep, you guessed it, pizza—and did what any bachelor in his late twenties would do: We played Guitar Hero 3.

I wasn't into gaming much in my twenties. As a kid? Sure. Sign me right up for Super Mario Brothers, The Legend of Zelda, and countless other Nintendo and SNES games. But I phased out of it at some point.

When Guitar Hero 3 came out in 2007, I had gotten into it in a big way. I'd always fantasized about becoming a rockstar. Playing a tiny plastic guitar and a video game was as close as I'd get, but it made me fall back in love with playing games.

That night was no different.

Marty was a fan of the game, as well. But he wasn't as into it as I was and was nowhere near as good at it. But he still enjoyed it and had fun playing.

"Try it again," he told me after failing miserably to finish The Number of the Beast by Iron Maiden on Expert. Again, memories are weird. Why do I remember that was the song I failed that night? I'd made it through it other times before and since, but it sticks out as the memory of an otherwise normal night of playing games with my friend, as the song I'd failed at.

"Okay," I said, queueing the song back up to try, shaking my wrists as if the increased blood flow would help my dexterity.

And off I went, flying through the opening riffs, powering into the first chorus, when my phone rang.

I tried to look down at it on the couch behind me without losing my place in the game, but I couldn't see it.

"It's Brooke," Marty said. "Do you want to answer it?"

I paused the game and grabbed the phone. "Hey."

"What are you doing?"

"We're just playing Guitar Hero at the apartment."

"Are you ready for tomorrow? Did you finish your vows?"

"I did." I lied.

"Good. Don't let Marty keep you up too late. You have to pick up the flowers in the morning."

I used my hand as a mouth and mimed her talking, rolling my eyes. "Yes, I know." I knew because she'd already told me three times. And left a note on the back of the apartment door. And texted it to me twice. My memory sucked, but not as much as you'd think, knowing how many times she reminded me about those stupid flowers.

"See you tomorrow. Good night, I love you."

"Love you." I hung up.

"Hey, don't forget about the flowers," Marty sneered.

I laughed. "I know, I know, I know."

"How many times does she need to remind you?"

"All of the times, apparently."

"I'm surprised she hasn't texted me to tell me to remind you."

"It's still early," I laughed, unpausing the game. "She still might."

Panic Before The Wedding

The next morning, I woke up on the floor next to the couch. Marty was lying on the chaise lounge portion of the couch, still snoring.

I creeped out of the room into the bathroom and jumped in the shower, trying not to wake him.

As I cleaned myself for arguably, the most important day of my life, my anxiety spiked. I don't think I had a full-blown panic attack in the shower that morning, but it felt pretty close to one. My chest tightened. My vision blurred. My heart raced. My head felt like it was spinning. Everything felt so far away, out of reach. It felt horrible. There's no other word for it. Horrible was how it felt.

"Hey, you almost done?" Marty called out a few minutes later.

"Yeah," I said, bracing myself against the back wall of the shower, hoping I didn't fall out and yank the curtain down on top of me. "Be there in a few."

"Ok," he said. "I'll wait."

The anxiety hadn't subsided when I got out of the shower. Although the panic attack symptoms seemed to have faded, I still felt like I was going to pass out at any moment.

Thankfully, I didn't.

Marty and I got dressed for the wedding, without issue, without forgetting anything. We drove straight to the florist from the apartment, picked up the flowers that were too incredibly important to have forgotten, and made it to the venue hours before we needed to be there.

It was eerie. Walking into the venue without any of it having been set up yet. No lights. No tables. No chairs. Nothing was ready to go. I didn't panic, though; there were still hours before any guests would show up.

"Oh, hi, Matt," the event coordinator said, entering the room from the back. "Brooke said you'd have the flowers."

"Yes, they're out in my car, out front."

She said something into a walkie-talkie she was holding, and a man came running from behind me and took my car keys to fetch the flowers.

"You're very early," she said. "Head through that door to the back room. That's where we'll do the pictures after. For now, I've set up some refreshments and snacks. You can wait in there."

"Thanks," I said, following Marty across the parquet dance floor, past the spot where the DJ had just started setting up, and through the doorway.

The room back there was fairly large, to my surprise. It could have easily held twenty or more people comfortably.

On the right was a long table covered in an off-white tablecloth. It had all sorts of hors d'oeuvres, some prepared meats, like pepperoni, salami, and ham, an assortment of cheeses, and some crackers. While certainly not a replacement for a whole meal, it was enough to tide us over until we could eat later that day.

It was just the two of us back there. We could hardly hear the staff bustling around just outside the door, getting everything ready for the big event.

"I don't know," I said, breaking the silence. A piece of pepperoni still stuck to my upper lip.

"You don't know what?" Marty replied.

"I don't know. I don't know if I can do this." My nerves had kicked into high gear. The anxiety felt stronger than it ever had before. It was, suddenly, very terrifying to me. The idea of walking out in front of all of those people, all of those loved ones, and friends, and extended family, and being the center of their attention. For an hour. Or more.

"You can do it," he said, approaching me from the far end of the snack table. "It'll be fine."

"I need to sit," I said. "Is there a chair?"

Marty ran out of the room to see if he could find a chair I could sit on. I didn't wait for him to return and almost threw myself onto the ground, doing my best to tuck my head between my knees, almost hyperventilating. The walls started closing in, my breathing sped up, and my head spun.

"I'm back," I heard him say but didn't look up to see whether he had a chair or not.

"C'mon, get up," he said. I felt him grab my arm and pull, but my body didn't move. "If you wrinkle that tux, I will be the one that's at fault. Let's go." He pulled again. This time, my body cooperated, and I was sitting in the chair, upright before I knew it. The world around me still rebelling against me, circling in on me, trying to crush me.

"I think... I think I'm having a panic attack." I said. I'd never had one before. I thought I may have once or twice, but, in hindsight, it was nowhere as bad as I felt that day, in that room, before my wedding to Brooke. It was worse. So much worse. A factor of ten, twenty even. I didn't know what to do.

"You're going to be okay," Marty said, still holding my arm, though I'd been seated for a minute. "Just breathe. Everything will be fine. You're a rockstar. You're amazing. You can move mountains. You can swim oceans."

"You sound like Tony Robbins." I tried to force myself to laugh as if it were a magic spell that would help me calm down. Laughter's the best medicine. Isn't that what they say?

"Trust me, Matt. Just trust me."

I felt him loosening my bow tie and unbuttoning the top button on my shirt.

The cool air felt nice, flowing down my shirt to my chest. It felt relieving.

"This is going to be weird for just a minute," he said. "But trust me."

He put his hand on the back of my neck, by the base of my skull. "Hold on," he said as he pressed in.

Everything turned stark white. Like a giant flash of lightning had just struck the room. Like how they portray death in the movies. Like I was walking toward that proverbial white light that indicated my life was over.

And then it was gone. I was left with a warm feeling. A safe feeling. My breathing had slowed to normal. My heart didn't feel like it was beating out of my chest anymore. The walls were back where they should be, no longer closing in on me. Everything felt, for lack of a better word, normal.

"What was that?" I asked.

"Old Tibetan relaxation trick," he said. "I read about it on your computer once. I always wondered if it worked." He quickly stood up and grabbed a Ritz cracker at the snack table.

"It did," I said. "It worked. It worked a lot, like really fast."

"I'm glad. I'm happy that it calmed you down."

"You've been hiding that from me for our whole friendship? I could have used that a time or two," I laughed.

"Sometimes you just need a reset," he said. "Sometimes you can't do it on your own."

We sat, together, in that room, for the next couple of hours while the rest of the wedding got set up. We had them refill the pepperoni and crackers four times while we waited. I don't remember how much the whole wedding cost, but I am pretty sure we got our money's worth in pepperoni alone.

It was one of the lowest points in my life, that day. The anxiety leading up to that wedding was unbearable. I know, for certain, I would not have made it through if it weren't for Marty. Whatever voodoo black magic crazy nonsense thing he did to me that day—and he can call it whatever he'd like—worked. If I could bottle that, somehow, and sell it, I'd be rich and retired by now.

Red Sox

"Hey," I said as Marty answered the phone. It'd been a few weeks since I got back from my honeymoon, and I had only seen him once since. It felt so odd and foreign to have spent so much time apart from him, given how close we were.

"Hey, buddy," he replied. "We still on for tonight?"

"Actually, change of plans."

"Everything okay?" he asked.

"Everything's great. I scored us some tickets to the baseball game tonight."

"Baseball? I've never been," he said, sounding excited.

"I know; I thought it would be a fun change of pace. But there's some small bad news."

"Oh?"

"There's no pizza there," I said, laughing.

"But I hear there's world-famous hot dogs, right?"

"Right," I said. "You'll love it. The game starts at seven, so I'll pick you up at six."

"See you then!"

A guy from work had extra tickets and asked if anyone wanted them, and I was never the kind of person to turn down free tickets to a sports event. Things were wild in Boston after the Red Sox broke their decades-long curse in 2004 when they won the World Series. I had always enjoyed baseball and knew Marty would have a good time at the game with me.

· · · · • · • · · ·

He was waiting at the end of the driveway when I got there. I laughed as soon as I got close enough to see him. He was dressed head to toe in Red Sox merchandise. I'd never seen him wear a Red Sox hat before, and I could tell it was brand new—he hadn't even bent the rim yet—along with a t-shirt that still had creases, and I thought I spied a label still on the sleeve.

"You look like a walking billboard," I said as he got into the car.

"It's great, isn't it?" he laughed at himself.

"You look like a pro. You've been at this a long time, haven't you?"

"Shut up," he joked. "I've never been before. The only time I ever watched a baseball game was four years ago. You remember?"

"Oh man, I remember. I couldn't stop talking about the World Series."

"What you meant to say is that you couldn't shut up about it."

"Well, yeah. How often does that happen? Especially to our teams?"

"I think the thing they call me is a fair-weather fan, right?"

"No, not exactly. But who cares what they call you? We're going to have a blast."

Marty's zest for life had never changed in the five years I'd known him. He was still just as fascinated with new things as when I first met him. I'll never forget that first night in Lil' Peach, where he looked at every single thing as if he'd never seen it before. The same marvel of his astonishment happened the whole ride down the highway into the city. Every building, every sign, every off-ramp. He loved it all.

"In Belgium, we didn't have roads like this," he said.

"Freeways? Highways?"

"No," he said. "In our little town, one road led to the city. We hardly ever went there because it was so far away."

"It's how we get around here," I said.

"It's so amazing. You drive so fast and get places so quickly."

"It really is pretty cool. I think we take it for granted because we grow up with it. We're so used to it that it doesn't feel as impressive."

"I'm impressed," he said.

We got off the highway on the Storrow Drive exit, as I'd done so many other times in my life, heading toward Fenway Park. "It's such a marvel to see," I said. "There's only one other ballpark that's as old as Fenway. There's so much history there; you'll love it."

The one thing Fenway didn't have—and still doesn't—is parking. Many businesses around the field close during games and just rent out their parking lots for $40, $50, $60, and sometimes even more. And since there's no official parking lot, people pay it to be close to the field and not have to walk. A fair bit of people do tend to take public transportation, too. They park in other parts of the city and take the Green Line to the Fenway or Kenmore stop. It's only a short walk from there.

There was a Mobile station up the block from the park where I usually parked when I'd go to games, albeit infrequently. I knew it'd be closed for business, and I could get a spot for $30.

The guy handling the lot pointed to an empty spot and took my cash. No receipt, no ticket on the dash, and no indication that I'd paid. Just the fact that my car was there seemed to be proof enough. The wad of cash he had was enormous. Probably tax-free money, too. Smart.

We were completely boxed in before we even got out of the car. Which, on its face, feels like a bad thing but is quite normal. It's not like you need to get out any time soon, and everyone parked around you will be leaving at the same time you are. It made sense.

"That filled in quick," Marty said.

"It usually does. I'm glad we got a spot."

I exited the car first, grabbing my Red Sox hat from the backseat, where I'd often toss it once I took it off. Marty got out a minute later, adjusting his brand-new hat and tugging his shirt down to ensure the giant red B was visible to anyone and everyone.

"I'm so excited," he said. "Go, Red Sox."

The crowd around us, all heading to the same place, cheered. It was evident a few folks had started pre-gaming and were a little tipsy already.

As part of that crowd, we walked down the street, passing all the restaurants with their windows and doors open, many with outdoor seating. The pre-game show was on most of the televisions in almost every place. The sound of excitement filling every piece of empty space around us. The fandom was something else. There are, arguably, no fans with more passion than the Red Sox fans on game night in the city.

As we approached the park, the bootleg t-shirt and hat guys started showing up on the street corners. "Shirts heah! Ten dollahs! Hats heah! Five bucks!" One of them shouted. Had Marty not already been adorned with his Sox gear, I'm sure he would have wanted to stop and buy a shirt and or hat. I knew it was fake merchandise. The guys selling it knew it was fake. Most everyone walking by the guys selling it knew it was fake. I'm sure the police knew it was fake, too. But no one seemed to care. Those guys still sold tons of merchandise, made a ton of money, and were gone before the game even started.

We walked past all the historic memorabilia that adorned Landsdowne Street before turning onto Jersey Street. The park was so close to us that it was hard to tell how big it was.

"This is it?" Marty asked. It was the first time I could remember him not being amazed by something new.

"It's more impressive when you get inside," I said. "I promise."

He followed me through the crowds of people picking up their tickets, buying official merchandise, or getting food from outside vendors. We got to the appropriate gate and scanned our tickets to go inside.

There's something that—still to this day—amazes me about Fenway. It just has this smell to it once you get inside. When you're under the stands, making your way past the food vendors, all the bathrooms, and all the stores selling hats, t-shirts, gloves, pictures, etc. It just hits you. It's not a bad smell, don't get me wrong. It's this incredibly unique smell. A combination of beer, hot dogs, pretzels, old steel, people, and happiness. This overwhelming smell of joy. A perfect blend of everything you'd want to smell at a baseball game. It never failed, either. Every single time in my entire life that I'd been to Fenway, the smell was there.

"Oh, me," Marty said. "You were right. It's much bigger inside."

"We're not even outside yet," I said. "Wait until we go up to where the field is, where we sit."

We stopped along the way, grabbing some Cokes, a pretzel, a hot dog for me, and two hot dogs for Marty.

The walk from the gate to our seats was fairly long, just due to the layout of the underneath part of the field. By the time we got to the hallway leading out to the field, we'd eaten most of our food. Perhaps it was excitement. Perhaps it was because it was after the time we'd normally have eaten dinner. Whatever it was, it just meant we needed to get more food once we got settled.

I let Marty walk down the hallway first, weaving and dodging other people coming and going. I had wanted to walk next to him so I could hear his excitement when we got out from underneath to see the field, but there were too many people. I was just a couple of steps behind him.

When he finally got outside, I heard him say something I'd never, in the whole time I knew him, say.

"Holy shit." He swore. He'd never cussed before, at least not in front of me. I'd joked with him about it, even giving him a little bit of a hard time once or twice. But he'd never done it before.

"It's pretty breathtaking, isn't it?" I said as I caught up to him. He was standing in the doorway, the stands in front of him, the wide open view of the Green Monster off in the distance, in all its glory.

"If I had known it was like this, I would have come sooner."

I couldn't help but laugh. Marty always had this way of saying just the right thing.

The usher walked us down to our seats. Third row, right by first base. The seats were better than anything I'd ever had, especially since the prices skyrocketed after 2004.

"These seats are great," Marty said, sitting on my right.

"Let's go, Red Sox," the guy behind me yelled repeatedly. It was too early for a chant to start, but that didn't stop him from trying.

The players were already out on the field, tossing balls around, warming up. We were so close that I could read Kevin Youkillis' name on the back of his jersey. He and Dustin Pedroia tossed a ball back and forth. Occasionally, Pedroia would throw it over to Mike Lowell at third base or Julio Lugo at shortstop. I wasn't the biggest Sox fan in the world, but I knew the team well enough to know who was who, even if I couldn't read all the names of those too far away from me.

It was late in the season at that time. Sometime in early September, if my memory serves. They played the Rangers the whole weekend, three games. I think it was a shutout, but I could be misremembering.

"Ladies and Gentlemen, please rise for the national anthem."

We stood and removed our hats, placing them over our hearts. Although Marty wasn't American, he still showed tremendous respect for the country. He was always polite, and this time was no different.

The teams lined up along the first and third base lines, placing their hats on their hearts like the crowd.

Once the announcer said, "Play ball," the crowd went wild. The screaming and cheering were so loud that I had to cover my ears temporarily.

"This is great," Marty said. I read his lips. It was so loud that I couldn't hear him sitting, not even a foot away from me.

We took turns getting more drinks and more food. I lost count of how many hot dogs I ate that night. I don't recommend eating however many I had, though. I felt like I was going to burst by the time we left. I made more trips than Marty did, mainly so he could stay and enjoy more of the game than I would. We made friends with the guys behind us—who eventually got that "Let's go Red Sox" chant going successfully—, and we'd pick up a round of beers for them sometimes, and vice versa. A you scratch my back, I'll scratch your's type of game-going relationship.

Marty leaned over as the game wound down and asked, "Is this too expensive to do every time there's a game?"

I laughed. "You want to get season tickets?"

"How much would that cost?"

"I think like ten grand a seat or something."

"Oh. Okay. So maybe we come to a game or two a season?"

"That sounds like a great plan." I was still laughing. As much as I'd have loved season tickets to the Red Sox, especially during those years when they dominated the league, I made nowhere near enough money to spend on season tickets.

The Red Sox won the game; I remember that for sure. They had a pretty rough year, but I remember they won the game we were at. They won at Marty's first game.

Annual Block Party

The buzz in the neighborhood was starting to ramp up. I'd seen several people posting on their newly found obsession, Facebook, about it, as well. Although I hadn't lived with my mom for over three years, I was excited to go back and help with the annual block party.

"Matt, hello!" Jean Luc called out as I walked into their house, through the living room, into the heavenly-smelling kitchen.

As usual, he'd been prepping for the block party for days. The Tupperware was everywhere like it always was. The stove was covered in simmering pots and pans. The smells were divine. "Looks like you're ready," I said.

"Not even close," he scoffed.

"Tick-tock," Marty said, entering the kitchen behind me.

"Kalmeren," Jean Luc said. "Quiet down, you." He shook his fist but in a very playful way.

"Shall we start bringing food down?" Marty asked.

"Ja graag. Yes, please. I'll be there soon."

"Okay, Papa," Marty said, grabbing a stack of Tupperware containers stacked so high I couldn't see his face. "Your car out front?"

"In the driveway, yeah." I followed suit, grabbing as many containers as possible and struggling to find my way through the front door.

"Your father must love this," I said.

"You have no idea. He calls it his 'doel voor het leven'. It means the purpose of one's life. It gives him something to do that isn't work."

"That's great," I said. "I'm so glad we decided to do this."

"Can you believe this is the fourth year?"

"Time flies," I said, following him back into the house to gather more Tupperware.

"Okay, Papa, I think this is it," Marty said. He tried to lean in and receive the hug Jean Luc offered, but he stepped back when the stacked-high Tupperware started to topple. "See you in a bit."

"Bye, sir," I said, grabbing the last of the filled containers. "We'll see you down there."

Jean Luc wasn't the only one excited by the annual block party. It seemed like everyone in the neighborhood was. From the first year to the second, attendees seemed to grow exponentially. I'd guess that in the second year, it had doubled. I wasn't ready to see how many more people there would be this time.

Someone must have seen us coming because as we rounded the corner onto my mom's street, they'd already moved the barricade, and the people closest to that end were applauding. I couldn't help but laugh.

"Is this for us?" Marty asked.

"Kind of."

"Kind of?"

"I think it's more for what we're bringing," I said. "Your dad's cooking."

"Look at all the people," Marty said. "Word's gotten out!"

There were people everywhere. Hundreds of them, maybe even in the thousands. As if by some biblical means, they all parted, making way for me to drive down the street to the already set up tables in front of my mom's house. She was standing there, waiting for us. Hands on her hips as if we were late.

"Good," she said as we got out of the car. "You're here!"

"Help us unload?" I asked.

"Yes, of course. It's almost time that people will be hungry."

"There's plenty of other food," Marty said, gesturing to the other tables.

"But there's not this food," my mom said.

Marty and I laughed momentarily before placing the food on the waiting table, ensuring the hot food went into the heated trays, already steaming from the sternos below.

People had flocked to the table before we could even finish unloading the car. It was as if people had never eaten before. Their mouths agape, their arms outstretched with empty plates and bowls. Their excitement palpable and infectious.

It was, on some level, like Marty and I were at a soup kitchen, feeding the homeless. Person after person flowed through the line, taking a scoop of everything, not caring if the food all mixed on their plate or in their bowl. One person brought their own Tupperware, asking if we minded if she filled up. There seemed to be enough food for everyone, so we let her.

"They love this stuff," I said. "Your dad should open a restaurant."

"Maybe someday," Marty said. "When he retires from work."

"He'll make a fortune," someone in the crowd said, asking for a refill on her already emptied bowl.

I couldn't help but smile. The thought that everything that happened was all because of something Marty and I put into motion all those years ago. Had we not had the idea, none of those people would be together, in the middle of the road, eating food, making friends, being social. None of it would have happened had the two of us not gone and knocked on every door in the neighborhood, some more than once.

"Good work, boys," my mom said before scurrying off to pick up some dessert from Mrs. Wilkinson's table. She owned the best bakery in town, so her table was the only one that was as flooded as Marty's dad's. The two seemed to work well in conjunction with one another. We fed them their primary meal, and she fed them cakes and pastries for dessert. Although Jean Luc made some great Dutch desserts, sometimes people wanted an old-fashioned apple pie or a giant chocolate cupcake.

"Hey, where's your dad?" I asked after noticing that a few hours had passed and the food supplies were running low.

"He should have been here by now, shouldn't he have?"

"Hey, Mom!" I called her over, waving. "Can you keep this under control? We're going to go back and get more food and see where Jean Luc is."

"Of course, be careful." She usually said that anytime I was driving anywhere—she still does, to this day—even if I wasn't going far.

Again, the seas of people parted. This time, many people stood from their seated positions, moving their chairs out of the way to let us through.

"I'm telling you," I said. "Your dad will make a killing selling this stuff."

"I'll be sure to tell him," Marty said.

A Great Loss

"Papa?" Marty called out as we entered the house. The smells of heaven still lingered in the air, but the sounds of the clanking pots and pans we'd come accustomed to weren't present.

"Be right there," I said, stopping to tie my shoe by the couch in the living room.

Suddenly, I heard a loud thump, and then Marty called out to me in a tone I'd never heard before. I felt the fear in his voice. "Come quick, Matt!"

There'd never been a time I ran through his house faster than I had that afternoon.

"Call 911!"

Jean Luc was laid out on the floor in front of us. Marty by his side, kneeling, starting to pound on his father's chest.

I fumbled for my cell phone in my pocket, only to find it was dead. I nearly jumped across the entire kitchen to the phone on the wall, grabbing it and dialing 911 without even pausing to ask what was happening.

"911. What's your emergency?"

"My friend's father. He needs help. Please send help."

"What seems to be the problem?"

Marty continued to pound on his chest in some form of CPR that he'd learned but forgotten. "Papa, no," he cried out.

"We just found him on the floor."

"What's your address?"

"3 McClure-Keller Road."

"Help is on the way. Please stay on the line. Is he breathing?"

"Is he breathing, Marty?"

Marty paused the pounding and checked. "No, he's not."

"He's not," I told the operator.

"Do you know CPR?" she asked.

"No."

"Okay, I'm going to tell you what to do."

I don't remember anything else of what she said. I know that, between Marty and I, we tried to give him CPR for what felt like an hour. We continued compressions and breathing for him, eventually hearing the sirens getting louder.

We didn't speak to each other other than to signal we needed to switch because the person doing compressions was getting tired.

"Hello?" someone called out from the front door.

"Back here!" I yelled as loud as I could. "We're back here!"

"How long has he been like this?" the EMT asked as he and his partner dropped their bags. The EMT on the far side of Jean Luc from me pulled out an oxygen mask, strapping it around his head and neck, forcing air into his lungs.

"I don't know," Marty said. "We saw him a couple of hours ago and returned to get more food for the party."

"Party? What party?" the other EMT asked.

"We're having a block party around the corner," I said.

"We came back to get more food, and I found him like this," Marty said.

"Did he fall?" the EMT asked.

"I don't know. He was like this when we got here," Marty said.

"I heard a thump," I said.

"Was that him?" The EMT looked back and forth between Marty and me.

"No," Marty eventually spoke. The EMT continued compressions. "It was me. I fell to my knees when I found him."

"OK, step back, guys. Let us work on him."

The EMTs would stop and check his pulse every few minutes before resuming CPR. One would signal to the other; he'd stop, check his pulse, and shake his head before resuming.

At one point, they tried the defibrillator. The sound of the shock reverberated through the otherwise silent house. Jean Luc's body jumped off the floor for a fraction of a second before slamming back down with the loudest thud I've ever heard.

"Papa, no," Marty cried out again.

I did the only thing I could think of; I walked over, stood next to my friend, and put my arm around him. Thirty-seven minutes had passed between when I called 911 and when the EMTs stopped compressions entirely.

"I'm sorry," one of them said. "There's nothing else we can do."

"I'm so sorry," the other EMT said. "He's gone."

Marty turned to me and buried his head in my shoulder and neck. I felt him weep, his tears pouring down the back of my shirt. "How?" he kept asking the same question over and over again. "How?"

"It seems like he had a heart attack," one of the EMTs said. "But we won't know for sure until they can examine him. Do you know which hospital you want us to take him to?"

"It doesn't matter," I said. Marty still buried in my neck, not showing any signs of wanting to move.

"Can I say goodbye?" he asked, still not moving from the comfort of my shoulder. "Do I need to say goodbye?"

"You don't need to right now," I said, looking to the EMTs for reassurance. "We'll see him at the hospital."

That day, one of the worst of Marty's life, was the only time I'd ever seen him cry. Not when I got married. Not when he got married. Not at the birth of my daughter—his goddaughter—not at the birth of his son. No other moment in his life, that I saw, ever led to him shedding a tear.

I didn't judge him. I didn't scold him for being emotional. I didn't try to rush him. I stood in the heavenly-smelling kitchen, holding onto my friend as if our lives depended on it. I clutched him in my arms and let him cry on me. In those moments, I let him do whatever he needed that afternoon. I didn't know what else to do. I didn't know what to say other than the "I'm sorry" I'd said over and over again. I didn't even know how to process my own grief at that time. All I knew was that Marty needed me. He needed me to stand there, silent, and let him cry.

The EMTs eventually moved Jean Luc to a stretcher, handed me a card with the hospital's address, and wheeled him out of the house.

Marty fell to the floor, pulling me down with him. His face was red from emotion, his eyes swollen from the tears, and his voice raspy.

"How could this have happened?" he asked me.

I grabbed his hand, squeezing it tightly. "I don't know, Marty. I'm so sorry."

"How can I live when my Papa does not?"

"I don't know," I said, reiterating my sorrow for him.

The two of us sat on that kitchen floor for half an hour. I held Marty while he continued crying. I held his hand. I rubbed his back. I did everything I knew I'd want someone to do for me to comfort me should it ever happen to me.

I sat, as silent as I could, until I couldn't be silent anymore. Suddenly, the two of us sat on the kitchen floor, crying. I cried quietly at first, but I was balling once I couldn't hold it back anymore. I was sad for the loss of such a great man who'd meant so much to me and the great loss my best friend had just suffered. I cried because there was nothing I could do. I cried because I felt hollow.

"We should go," Marty said.

"To the hospital?"

"Yes. Will you drive?"

"Of course," I said. "Anything you need."

• • • • • • • • •

I have no idea how I found our way to the hospital. In a world before phones with GPS or in-dash navigation systems, it was a feat that I got us there at all.

We parked in the emergency lot, not knowing where else to go, assuming Jean Luc would still be in the emergency department.

"Wait," Marty said as I reached for my seatbelt. "I don't know if I can go in yet."

"Take all the time you need," I said, clutching his hands in mine. "At your pace."

"How?" he asked again, almost pleading.

"I don't know." I felt so useless.

Minutes passed. The lights of other ambulances flashed as they drove by us toward the bay where they'd unload. The faint whooshing of the emergency room doors sliding open was audible through the crack in the window I'd left open.

"I'm ready," Marty said, pulling his hands free of mine and opening the door in one motion.

"I'm right behind you," I said, jumping out and hurrying to catch up with him.

"Janssen," I heard him tell the woman behind the desk. "Jean Luc Janssen."

"Go through those doors and follow the hallway to the end. Go through the red door, and someone will take you the rest of the way," she said. "I'm sorry for your loss."

Marty was brave. Although I started crying again at the sound of the word "loss," he did not. He stood straight, nodded, and turned back to make sure I was behind him.

We stood briefly at the doors the nurse pointed us to, waiting for them to be unlocked so we could go through.

It felt like eons.

They eventually swung open, and we stepped inside. The moment they closed behind us, the sounds from the emergency room disappeared. I wondered if they intentionally made them soundproof or if that was just a coincidence.

Marty and I walked, side by side, down the long hallway. The red door at the end grew larger and larger as we approached. It seemed right in front of us but miles away at the same time.

We knew that Jean Luc was on the other side of that door. Somewhere. Waiting for us to come in and say our goodbyes. For us to identify that it was, in fact, him and that they could begin to do with him whatever they did with people once they'd died.

He grabbed my hand and squeezed it without a word.

He pushed the red door open with his free hand and stepped inside, pulling me in behind him.

It was quiet in the room, cold but not freezing. We must have gotten there fairly quickly after the ambulance. They hadn't had a chance to move him into one of those fridges with the slide-out drawers you see in the movies and on television. Though covered with a sheet, he was laid on the table directly across the room.

I, again, cried. Marty was stoic. His emotions kept on the inside; his ducts out of tears, possibly.

"Hello," a man in a white coat said as he approached.

"Hello. I believe that's my father," Marty said, extending his arm in a completely unintentionally dramatic way, pointing to the table with his father's body on it.

"I'm so sorry for your loss," the man said, leading us back toward Jean Luc's body.

The man in the coat pulled back the sheet, revealing Jean Luc's face. I'd seen it a thousand times before but couldn't remember looking at it that day. I couldn't remember looking up at him when we tried to save him just an hour ago.

Marty said his farewells in Dutch. He didn't offer any translations, and I didn't ask. What he said was private, between himself and his father.

I offered the only thing I could think to say, firmly believing that Jean Luc could hear and see us in his afterlife. "I'll take care of your son," I said. "I will make sure Marty is okay."

We stayed with him for a short while. Marty periodically touched Jean Luc's hand or his face. After getting permission from the man in the white coat, who I assume all these years later was the coroner, Marty removed Jean Luc's chain with the cross on it. Jean Luc had always had it on whenever I'd seen him.

"Can you put it on me?" Marty asked, turning his back to me.

"Of course," I said, fastening the clasp.

To my knowledge, Marty never took it off. Not to shower. Not to swim. Not to give to his son. Never. It stayed on him every moment of every day that I saw him.

2009

The Beginning & The End

The six months after the funeral were really difficult for Marty. He'd spent the majority of his life just having his dad by his side. All the countries they'd been to, all the places they'd seen and lived. Through everything, his dad had been there.

   I learned a lot about life during those times. Did you know you could get an emergency passport? In most cases, they're only good for seven days, and they grant them immediately. I learned that. I also learned how expensive it is to transport a body internationally for said funeral. I learned Dutch is much harder to learn than I thought, even with being immersed in people speaking it all around you for a whole week. Marty did his best to translate but was busy with other things.

   By the time we got back from Belgium, Marty was exhausted. He'd seen so many people he'd never met. He'd heard stories about his father that he'd never heard before. I heard some rumblings that people from eleven different countries attended.

   "Thank you," Marty said one day out of the blue. We were sitting at the end of the cul-de-sac, eating pizza. It seemed to be the only thing that gave him any comfort. That silly pizza from Papa Gino's was like his fuel. Any time he'd start to show signs of being down or needing a break from reality, I'd show up with a pizza, and it'd seem to recharge him for another couple of days, maybe a week. Or maybe it was the company. I did my best to talk about happy things, about positive things. I tried to keep his mind occupied with other things and not focus on the death of his father.

All the grieving I did, I did in private. I tried not to even grieve in front of Brooke because I knew she wouldn't understand. She never really supported my friendship with Marty. She never discouraged or tried to end it, but she didn't get it. She had her own group of friends, but none of them were as close to one another as Marty and I were. It was more than just a friendship. It was a bond. A bond made even stronger with us having both gone through his father's death together. When Jean Luc was found, both of us being there was a big experience for us. It brought us closer together.

The months after that just bonded us more. I was there for him any time he needed it. It was frequent, but I didn't mind. I always would tell him, "That's what friends are for." I knew he'd do the same for me.

"Truth be told," he said. "I'm struggling."

"I know, man. I see it. I'm here for you."

"Not just that," he said. "Sure, the emotional part of it is hard. But it's more."

"More how?"

"Papa made a lot more money than I do."

"Oh."

"I'm struggling to pay the bills."

"Did he have insurance? Any savings?"

"He didn't have insurance. In Belgium, the government helps your family if you pass. We didn't know America didn't."

"Can't they help you now? You're still a citizen, aren't you?"

"I am. But I haven't lived there in too many years, so I'm not eligible."

"Savings?"

"I've spent most of it already. All the money he worked hard to save is almost gone, and I feel terrible because of it."

"I'm so sorry, Marty."

"I know. I don't mean to complain. I'm sorry."

"You're not complaining. You're talking to a friend."

"I know."

"If I had any money, I'd give it to you. You know that."

"I know you would. I'm not asking for money."

"I get it. Just venting."

"Just venting."

"How bad is it?" I asked.

"I've been using his savings to cover the difference in the money I make and the bills for the house."

"Didn't his company pay for the house?"

"Only for the first year, since they had us move here."

"Jeez," I said. "So you're on your own. How much difference is there?"

"After taxes, I need to use around two thousand from savings to cover all the bills. Thanks, America, for your tax system!" He shook his hand at the air, careful not to drop his plate.

"That's worse than I thought," I said.

"Everything in America is so expensive. It costs money just to be alive, to be human."

"I know. I feel that, too."

"Should I work more? Do people have more than one job?"

"They do. But you shouldn't need to, to survive. Why don't you move in with Brooke and me?"

"Oh no," he said immediately. "I couldn't possibly."

"You can. You should. We can give you that second bedroom. It's just an office for us now. We don't need an office. Neither of us works at home."

"Brooke would not like it," he said.

"You're probably right," I agreed. "But you need a friend, and I'm your friend." The thought of asking Brooke if it was okay never even entered my mind.

"She's going to hate it," Marty said.

He was right. I knew it. He knew it. Brooke would soon show it. But I didn't care. "We'll figure it out," I said.

• • • • ● • ● • • •

The first few nights, before I was able to clean out the second bedroom and put most of it in storage, Marty slept on the couch. That same couch he'd slept on the first night we'd moved into that apartment. It was still just as uncomfortable as the first night. He didn't let me forget it, either.

Brooke was, in fact, furious. Not that I brought Marty to live with us, but because I hadn't talked to her about it before making the decision. The reality is that I didn't talk to her about it first because I knew she'd say no. I knew she'd push back and find some excuse not to let him move in. She'd rather get her way than help my friend out.

We spent the first week pretending everything was okay and arguing in our bedroom after we'd "go to bed." Silently screaming at one another about how I was ruining their lives, about how she was selfish and only cared about herself or *her* friends. We'd argue, as quietly as we could, about how she gave more to her job than to our relationship.

Truth be told, things were rocky with Brooke before Marty moved in. We'd had our fights, but I'd always held back. Like I mentioned before, I'm as confrontational as a monk. I don't like arguing, I don't like getting into fights, and I surely don't like saying things out loud that I'd keep to myself and let rattle around in my brain until they drove me up the wall.

On the seventh night, things got so heated that Marty came and knocked on our closed bedroom door to check if we were okay. He'd heard the arguing and wanted to make sure things weren't being said that couldn't be unsaid.

I opened the door just a crack. "We're okay, bud," I said. "Just having a heated debate."

"I can go," he said.

The door jerked open so hard in my hand that I almost put the doorknob through the wall behind it. "You'll do no such thing," I said, loud enough for Brooke to hear me in the far corner of the bedroom.

"This is my fault," he said. "I shouldn't be here."

"You're my best friend and are not going anywhere." I reiterated.

"Should I go, then?" Brooke asked, half serious.

"Has it come to that?" I asked. "Do you want to go?"

"I want to be respected," she said, crossing her arms.

"Ditto," I called back. "You need to give it to get it."

"I'll let you continue," Marty said, pulling the door out of my hand and closing it.

Something about that night caused me to let loose, to break out of my shell. I don't know if it was out of concern for my friend or if I was still feeling the raw emotions of Jean Luc's death. I'm not sure what it was. But, on that night, in that room, with my best friend just twenty feet away, outside the door, I let it all out.

"You don't trust me," I said. "You've never trusted me."

"That's not true!" she said.

"You read my email. You read my text messages. You look at my phone all the time."

"No, I don't!." I knew she was lying.

"I set a trap once, and you fell into it."

"What?" she screamed. "You did what?!"

"I sent myself an email from a fake email address I made up. It talked about plans I was going to make with my high school girlfriend, Jill. And you read it and then tried casually bringing Jill up in conversation a couple of days later. Out of the blue."

"That's not true. I saw her come up on Facebook as someone I might know."

"Quit the bullshit, Brooke. You're lying. You've always lied about this, and I caught you."

"I've never been so insulted in my life," she said, reaching for her purse on the nightstand.

"You're only insulted because you got caught. You're mad because I've known."

"I'm mad because you're making things up. You let him," she pointed to the living room, through the wall, "come between us!"

"This isn't Marty's doing," I said. "He only helped me see the truth about what you've been doing. You treat me like your property, not your partner."

I shocked myself. I couldn't believe the words that I'd just let come out of my mouth. I don't think I'd ever spoken to another person that way, certainly not someone I loved. But, the reality was, sometimes love isn't enough. That's what they say, right?

She didn't respond. She grabbed her purse and phone and stormed over to the door, yanking it open and walking out into the hallway.

"Fuck you," she said in Marty's direction. Before grabbing her keys and walking out the apartment door, she flung her coffee cup in his general direction, only narrowly missing his head, but only because he ducked. She stormed off through the kitchen, slamming the door behind her.

"Guess that didn't go so well," Marty said, shrugging.

"I said a lot of things I'd been holding back," I said. "I'm sure you heard most of it."

"These walls aren't as thick as you might think," he laughed.

The Vanishing Act

It felt weird sleeping in "our bed" without Brooke. I won't go as far as saying it felt lonely, but it felt different and strange. I'd roll over and expect to see her there, curled up in the ball she often slept in, or to be woken up by her getting up to go to the bathroom in the middle of the night. But she was gone. She never came back that night.

When I woke up the next morning, her side of the bed was cold. There was no indentation to show she'd been there, but maybe she got up a little bit ago. Her pillow was still cold. Her alarm clock was flashing as if we'd lost power. I didn't remember her touching it before she left, but it had all happened in the blink of an eye. Maybe she turned it off or messed with it in some manner.

"Hey," Marty said as I exited the bedroom.

"What time is it?" I asked.

"Ten. A little after."

"Oh shit, I have to get to work!"

"It's okay. I sent an email to your boss saying you were sick. I pretended to be you."

"You what? After I just fought with Brooke about snooping on my phone!"

"I, uh..."

"I'm kidding," I said. "If I can't make light of it, it'll never feel better."

"You jerk! You scared me!"

"No sign of Brooke, huh?"

"She didn't come back last night. Or she's a ninja, and I didn't hear her."

It wasn't like her to leave and not come back. The only other time we'd had a big fight, she left for a couple of hours, but she came back. We'd made up then. She forgave me. I forgave her. I don't even remember what that other fight was about, honestly. I just know it was unlike her to leave and not come back.

"Why don't we go grab some breakfast?" Marty asked. "That diner up the road, over by the Whole Foods?"

"You know I can't say no to that place," I said. "Their bacon is to die for."

"Die for? You know my dad just died," Marty said.

"I, uh..."

"I'm kidding. My turn!"

I damn near had a heart attack. Which is what we came to learn took Jean Luc from us. While cooking his favorite foods to share with his favorite people, his heart had just given out. The coroner said he probably didn't suffer and was likely dead by the time he hit the floor.

"You son of a bitch!"

Marty then did something I hadn't seen him do in a long time. He smiled. A big one. So big that he got smile marks on his face.

"Let's go," he said. "Go get dressed."

"Okay."

• • • • •●• ●• •

After breakfast, we decided to walk to the park near my apartment. It was a nice day, and I figured it'd do me some good to get some fresh air and think through what I'd say to Brooke when she came back.

Kids were playing on the swing sets, their mothers nearby, keeping a close watch to make sure no limbs were broken. A group of men were playing with their dogs on the far side of the park, occasionally letting them off their leashes to run free, only to quickly grab them and re-leash them when they got close to a person who seemed uncomfortable.

It felt peaceful there like there were no troubles anywhere in the world.

"I'm sure everything will be fine," Marty finally spoke.

"I know it will," I said, agreeing. "Things just got a little heated. Maybe I said some things that I'd like to take back."

"Do you?" he asked.

"What do you mean?"

"You've been bottling that stuff up for months, haven't you?"

"Months? No. More like years."

"And you finally let it out. That's healthy."

"Is it? Why do I feel like shit then?"

"Sometimes speaking up for yourself hurts," Marty said.

"I guess you're right."

"Sometimes you have to go through the hard part to get to the good part. I'm sure you guys will work it out."

"I'm sure we will," I said.

We sat in the park for an hour, maybe a little more. We sat, enjoying everything around us. I watched the tops of the trees as they swayed in the breeze. It felt soothing to me for some reason. I'd never taken comfort in nature before that day, but it felt so, I don't know, natural. It felt welcoming, like I was at home and everything was perfect.

At one point, Marty played on the swings with some kids. They looked to be around eight, maybe ten years old. They really loved him coming over and showing them how to swing higher than they thought was possible.

"Marty," I called out. "We should get going." It was getting to be almost one in the afternoon, and I decided to get back and try to get in touch with Brooke.

"Okay, let's go," he called out, doing one final jump from the swing at the height of its arc.

The children cheered as he landed and bounced up immediately.

• • • • • • • • • •

We walked back to the apartment together. I spent the time looking at all the things that I found comfort in, mostly feeling sorry for myself.

"It'll be okay," he reassured me. "You'll call her when we get back, and you guys will work it out."

"I hope so," I said. I felt bad about what had happened. I think most people tend to feel bad after a fight with their partner once the adrenaline wears off. And I did. I felt terrible.

I unlocked the door, stepped aside to let Marty walk in, made a grand "after you" gesture, and followed him inside.

All of the lights were on. The dimmable lights were at full brightness. There were so many lights on that it hurt my eyes temporarily.

That's when I noticed that everything was a mess. There were clothes thrown all over the living room. Blankets were tossed from the couch onto the floor.

"Hello?" I instinctively called out. "Is someone here?"

There was no response.

I peered down the hallway to see the lights in the bathroom, the hallway, and both bedrooms were all at full brightness.

"Brooke?"

No response.

"Hey, Matt," Marty called from the kitchen.

"Yeah?"

"Come here."

"Just a second," I said, walking to the end of the hallway. From where I stood, I could see into both bedrooms and the bathroom. They, too, were all seemingly trashed. Picture frames were knocked over, my pillow was thrown on the floor, and my desk was in shambles. It seemed like, maybe, we'd been robbed.

"You coming?" Marty asked.

"Did we lock the door when we left?"

"You weren't robbed," Marty said. "Come here."

I found him standing at the stove in the kitchen, with his back to me. "What is it?"

He turned to face me, stepping out of the way.

On top of the stove was a pile of something I couldn't make out from where I stood. As I stepped closer, I could tell it was pictures. Well, it *was* pictures. It was all of the photos of Brooke and me together. She'd torn them all up and left them in a pile on the stove.

Our entire relationship's worth of photos was now small, one or two-inch pieces of their former selves. Torn into shreds to make a point, a statement of some kind.

"There's a note," Marty said, reaching out to hand it to me. "I picked it up before realizing what was happening."

Without a word, I took it from him and flipped the paper open.

I never thought you'd actually choose him over me. I thought we were in this together. That's what you said.
I took all of my stuff while you were at work.
I wish the best for you.
I love you.
Goodbye
B

"She did this," I said, gesturing broadly to the rest of the apartment.
"What'd it say?" Marty asked.
"She's gone. She left."
"What? No. She left?"
"She left. She said I chose you over her."
"Is that it?"
"More or less."
"But we both know it was much more than that," Marty said.
"I know. You know. She knows. That's not the picture she'll tell everyone, though. That's not how she'll paint me when she retells last night to her friends or her family."
"Who cares?"
"I mean, I do. A little, anyway."
"Time heals all wounds. Some American television person said that, I think."
"In time, yes."

I couldn't believe she'd left. She just came while she thought I was at work and took her stuff, leaving behind a disaster—one more, final mess for me to clean up.

Part of me was hurt. Part of me was relieved. Part of me felt anxious, wondering what would have happened if we skipped the park after breakfast. Would we have stumbled onto her, packing her things when we got back? Were her friends with her? Where was she going to go? Would she move back in with her parents? Would one of her close friends take her in, as I had with Marty?

My mind was racing faster than I could keep up with it.
My heart was racing as well.
"You okay?" Marty asked.
"I think I am," I said, letting out a big sigh. "I think I will be, anyway."

Keeping Up With Tradition

Over the next several weeks and months, I tried to reach out to Brooke. To talk. To reconcile. To apologize. She sent me right to voicemail every time and never returned a single call. Text messages went unanswered as well.

After all those years together, I figured she would at least want to try to fix things. I knew she loved me, and she knew the same.

The annual block party was in just a few days. And while I was excited about it, I also dreaded it quite a bit. Although Brooke had never attended—there was always some reason for her not to, but I think the primary reason was that Marty was there—so I didn't mind her not being there. My headspace wasn't the best due to the sudden end of our relationship. What weighed more heavily on my mind was that Jean Luc wouldn't be there. I knew it'd be hard on me, as well as on Marty. Most of the people who attended the year prior probably didn't know Jean Luc had passed. They would likely show up expecting to eat his wonderful food, eventually hearing him come barreling down the street, laughing his giant laugh. They didn't know he was gone, and telling them would be hard. I knew he made a lot of friends in the years prior. That annual block party was his way of getting to know everyone in town. He really loved it.

The folks who lived on the cul-du-sac with Jean Luc and Marty probably knew something was up, especially when they stopped seeing either of them around. The For Sale sign out front probably solidified that something had happened. Either they'd moved away suddenly or something worse. Unfortunately, it was the something worse that Marty and I would have to tell people.

• • • • •●• • • •

When I woke up the day of the block party, I lay in bed, scrolling through Facebook on my phone. Looking at the Event page that we'd set up the year before, once people started really using Facebook. It was full of pictures from years prior. Pictures of people smiling, eating, talking, playing games, sitting, walking. It was full of happiness.

A few minutes after I woke up, I heard a clang from the kitchen just after I got through my email.

"Marty?" I called out through the closed door.

"Sorry, did I wake you?"

I hopped out of bed, tossed on the first shirt and pants I found, and opened the door.

The aroma hit me immediately. My mind flashed back, instantly, to Jean Luc's kitchen. To that last day we saw him. Those smells transported me back to that day.

"Are you cooking?" I asked before even getting to the kitchen, still standing in the hallway, unable to believe what I was smelling.

"I wanted to surprise you," he said. "To surprise everyone."

As I walked into the kitchen, I saw it. Pots and pans boiling and simmering. Tupperware was everywhere, filled with food that looked just like Jean Luc's.

"I hope you don't mind," Marty said. "I took your car last night after you went to sleep. I went to the storage unit and got Papa's recipes and Tupperware. I've been up all night cooking."

"How did I not wake up earlier? The sounds and smells should have done it."

"I did my best to be quiet," he said. "I wanted it to be a surprise."

"Color me surprised."

"Can you grab the paper on the printer for me?"

I looked over at the kitchen table, which we'd turned into a home office for our laptops and a shared printer. On the printer was a single piece of paper. From where I stood, I could see a photo of Jean Luc on it. "Got it," I said.

"There's a frame in the bag on the couch. You mind?"

Once I'd grabbed the paper, I could read the wording. "In loving memory" was above the photo, and "1951 - 2008" was below it.

"This is wonderful," I said, popping the picture into the frame. "It's a great way to remember your dad and, at the same time, tell everyone he's gone."

"I don't know if I'm ready for this," Marty said.

"I feel the same. It'll be tough to talk about him."

"Yes. I hope I'm able to keep a positive mind about it."

"I'm going to try to focus on the good stories. The happy thoughts."

"It's so hard without him," Marty said.

"I can't imagine what you've been through," I said. "My dad hasn't been around in a decade, but I know he's out there. If I wanted to talk to him, I could."

"I know you understand," he said. "It's just so hard to believe he's gone and gone in such a flash."

I went into the kitchen and gave him a big bear hug. "We'll get through it," I said. "Together."

"Oh no!" The water had started boiling over, so he broke free from my hug.

• • • • • • • • • •

We made it back to my mom's neighborhood on time without spilling a single drop of the food, which felt like it was bouncing around in the back seat and trunk the whole way up the highway.

As usual, the tables in front of my mom's house were reserved for Jean Luc. Well, for his food, anyway.

The neighbors parted ways and allowed us to drive up the street, parking in my mom's driveway.

Before we unloaded the food, Marty got out of the car, picture frame in hand. He placed the framed picture right in the middle of the table where we'd shortly serve hundreds of people the food they'd come to love.

"Oh no." I heard someone say when they saw the picture. "Jean Luc is gone?"

"I'm afraid so," Marty said.

"What happened?" another person asked.

"He had a heart attack," I said, trying to relieve some of the pressure of Marty being the only one to talk about it. "A year ago."

"I had no idea," someone said. "I'm so sorry."

"It's okay, but thank you," Marty offered.

"Jean Luc lives on," I said. "Through Marty."

I popped the trunk of the car, and it smelled like a little slice of heaven leaked out. We began grabbing the Tupperware and popping them onto the table.

People lined up, just like years past, filling their plates and bowls to the brim, getting seconds when they finished their first serving.

"Thank you for continuing your dad's legacy," Mrs. Wilkinson told Marty. "I'm sorry for your loss."

Marty nodded. It was how he acknowledged almost everyone who offered condolences that day: a slight nod to accept that they'd said something but no words to acknowledge it. If he had kept talking about his dad, I felt he'd have broken down that day.

Life had changed for him and me, so much in the last year, that we were both having a hard time dealing with it. I know I was thankful that I had him to lean on, and I hoped he felt the same. I knew I could always talk to him about anything without judgment.

Every so often, I'd look over at the photo of Jean Luc, his smile beaming, a spatula in his hand, the steam from a boiling pot seen over his shoulder. It was as if he was there with us that day. As if I could hear his voice telling stories of all the places he'd lived, of all the places he'd traveled to. How he'd make that "shush shush" sound when someone would ask him what he did for work. How he'd play dumb and act like he couldn't speak English suddenly when someone would press him on his job. I could sense his presence standing behind me, making sure I scooped enough beef stew into someone's bowl when they asked for extra. Even though he was gone, it felt like he was there with us. That feeling would continue every year when Marty and I would continue his legacy and show up, cars full of food, to feed the neighborhood.

Boston Bruins

Occasionally, one of the sales guys at work would send an email asking if anyone wanted extra tickets to a sporting event. The company had boxes at all the local venues: Fenway, Gillette Stadium, and TD Garden. It was one of the easiest email replies I've ever sent in my entire professional career.

I would usually give Marty a heads-up about where we were going, but I decided to surprise him that night.

"It feels like we're heading into the city," he said as we were crossing the bridge.

"You're right. But for what?"

As usual, I drove, allowing Marty to take in all the scenes and sights he'd missed all the other times we'd driven into the city. His astonishment for new things never ceased to amaze me; it was something I wished I possessed.

"Is there another concert?"

"Not tonight."

"A baseball game?"

"Close," I said. "Not quite."

As we pulled into the parking garage under the Garden, he immediately knew where we were going.

"Hockey game?"

"You got it!"

"I am so excited! I've never been before," he said.

"I got tickets for free at work."

"That's a great perk," he said. "Are they good seats?"

"They're pretty decent," I said. "I've been a few times."

I loved hockey. I always had. I don't know where my love of the sport came from, but I'd been a big hockey fan, specifically of the Boston Bruins, for as long as I can remember. Going all the way back to childhood, I could remember watching games by myself while my mom watched nighttime sitcoms in the other room, the volume of my television competing with hers. We'd often yell, "I can hear yours," or "Turn it down." Usually, my mom won, and I watched at a lower volume.

Something about the sport just spoke to me. The skill and grace of the players. The coordination. But also the violence and toughness. Not many other sports have the level of skill hockey players have. At least in my opinion.

There's something special about seeing it in person. It's one thing to watch it on television. But when you're up close, and the players are flying by, they seem larger than life. On-screen, they're just regular people because you have nothing to compare them to. But, in person, you can see yourself standing close to them if you're near the ice. I'll never forget the first game I went to, where I was able to get up close to the glass during warmups, and Zdeno Chara skated by me. He was six-foot-nine without the skates, so he was probably well over seven feet tall with the skates on. More than a foot taller than me, and it felt so obvious in person.

"Who are they playing?" Marty asked.

"Montreal."

I knew he didn't follow hockey much, but I knew he knew it well enough from me talking about it to know that we had a rivalry with Montreal. I wouldn't go as far as saying they're our arch-enemy, but it was pretty close.

"It should be a good game then, right?"

"I hope so. Especially for your first time."

It seemed all too common that when I parked in the garage under the Garden, I had to drive down to the bowels of the Earth to find a spot. Thankfully, there was an elevator that brought you out to the right place.

We popped into the Pro Shop, where I bought Marty his first Bruins hat, which he donned proudly during every hockey season from that day forth. It was his favorite hat, even though he wasn't the biggest hockey fan.

"Where to now?" he asked.

"Upstairs," I said, pointing to the crowd making their way up the escalator. "Just like when we went to the concert here."

People were flooding up the escalator from the concourse to the main level of TD Garden in droves, everyone seemingly excited by the evening's event. A select few, already having had too many drinks in their pre-game ritual, were making quite the ruckus from the top of the escalator.

Marty and I made our way from the Pro Shop over to the escalator, Marty fidgeting with his new hat, trying to make it as comfortable as possible on his head.

"You like it?" I asked.

"It's my new favorite hat," he said, beaming.

We scanned our tickets, got patted down by security, and headed toward our seats. The company paid for premium Loge seats, which were a nice upgrade from the seats I'd normally have paid out of pocket for. They were extra padded, had their own bathroom area, and had in-seat food and beverage service. Not having to wait in line to get more drinks or food was excellent, even if it was at a premium price.

As we approached our row, my gut felt heavy. There were red jerseys everywhere where I could tell our seats were. As if a bus full of Canadians came down together after having bought out almost all the seats in that section. I could see six empty seats smack dab in the middle of the sea of red.

"That's us," I said, pointing from the end of the row. That universal pointing to seats further down the row was sports-speak for "I need you to stand up, so I can squeeze by".

A wave of red stood up, allowing Marty and I to scurry down the row to our seats, quickly followed by Mike, one of the sales guys I knew from work. He introduced the woman with him as his girlfriend, but I didn't catch her name.

"Montreal fans everywhere," he laughed.

"This should be good," I said in Mike's direction.

• • • • • • • • •

The Bruins took the ice with a few minutes left before the puck dropped. The crowd was thunderous, applauding the home team and welcoming them out to the ice. All the usual faces were present: Chara, Bergeron, Krejci, Boychuk, Lucic, McQuaid. So many familiar faces that I knew but knew Marty wasn't familiar with.

I stood and clapped, shouting, like the rest of the almost-twenty-thousand people. There was a staggering amount of red shirts throughout the arena, which wasn't uncommon. Similarly, when Boston played in Montreal, there was a lot of black and gold present. I never looked into it, but I was sure some tour group shuttled people back and forth to games up there when I'd see our fans on television.

The applause continued through the remainder of the warm-up, well into announcing the starting lineups for both teams.

Marty seemed like he was enjoying it. He clapped when I clapped. He booed when I booed. He took all the right cues from me, even though I was sure he didn't fully understand what was happening.

I did my best to explain the game to him, particularly when the whistle blew or there was a penalty of some kind. Hockey is much more enjoyable when you understand the game.

We ordered a round of drinks and some hot dogs from a server, including Mike and his girlfriend.

"I've got it," Mike said. "We'll make the company pay." He leaned past me and looked at Marty. "You're a potential client if anyone asks," he laughed to himself.

"Got it," Marty said. "We talked business during the game!"

We all got a good laugh out of it. It wasn't a ton of money, but it was nice to have Mike get the company to take care of the expense.

• • • • • • • • •

The place erupted when the Bruins took the lead late in the first period. Boos barely made it through the applause and cheering. Montreal fans felt the linesman missed an offside call, which would have made the goal not count. Bruins fans felt they got the call right and were happy our team was winning the game.

"The Montreal fans think our guy crossed the blue line before the puck did. That's called offsides," I explained to Marty.

"So the puck has to go past it first?"

"Right. And if a player from the team with the puck crosses that line first," I paused to grab my food from Mike, who'd had it handed down the row to him. "Then it's offsides, and the play is supposed to stop."

"But our guy didn't go over too soon, right?"

"We certainly don't think so," I laughed, pointing at the scoreboard.

"After review, the play on the ice stands. Good goal," the referee called out over the PA system.

The crowd went bonkers. Not only did we get the goal legitimately, but Montreal would now have a penalty for challenging the play and losing the challenge.

"Why is everyone so excited now?" Marty asked.

"We get a power play."

"What's that?"

"When the other team gets a penalty, we get to play with a man advantage," I explained. "See how that one guy is on that bench over there by himself?"

Marty looked down in front of us. "Yes, I see him."

"That's the penalty box. That's where a player goes when they do something wrong."

"What did he do wrong?"

"Well, nothing. His coach did. He tried to tell the referee he was wrong and lost that battle. So, the guy sitting there is serving out the penalty for the team."

"Got it. Let's go Bruins!" He shouted.

• • • • • ● • ● • • •

The Bruins won the game 6-2, having gotten four goals in the last period.

"This was a lot of fun," Marty said. "I like hockey!"

"I'm glad you had fun," I said, climbing into the driver's seat. A lot of the other cars had already left the parking garage. Many folks had the mentality of "there's no way they're going to lose now. I'll beat traffic if I leave early", which helped us get out of the garage faster than if everyone had stayed.

"It helps," he said.

"Helps what?"

"It's a distraction. Doing things helps me not miss Papa."

"It's okay to miss him," I said, not knowing what else to say.

"I know. And I do. But some days are harder than others. Sometimes it's all I can do. I think about him all the time. All that he did for me."

"I can't imagine what it's like losing your dad like that. I never really had one to lose."

"I don't expect you to understand," he said, looking out his window as we drove over the bridge, heading home.

"I'd like to," I said. "At least I can try to help you if I can."

"You do help. Just being my friend is helpful. Taking me into your home was more than anyone else would have done. Especially given what it cost you."

It'd been about six months since Brooke moved out. I knew what he meant immediately when he said: "cost you." My relationship. My marriage. "I don't look at it like that."

"Why not?"

"If she was so willing to leave, so quickly, I think she already wanted to leave. She was just looking for an excuse. She blamed you because it was easier than telling me the truth about wanting to leave."

"You think that?" he asked, turning to me. I caught his glare out of the corner of my eye.

"People don't just throw marriages away so quickly over something so small, right?"

"I suppose you are correct. I'm just sorry it happened."

"Better now than ten years from now, I guess. No kids. No house. No shared assets. It'll be an easy divorce."

"Is that the plan? Divorce?"

"I'd assume so," I said. "She hasn't spoken to me since she left. No response to my voicemails, emails, or texts. I even reached out to her parents and got no response there, either."

"That feels kind of cold, doesn't it?"

"Who knows what's going through her head. Maybe she sees me as the bad guy. Maybe I am, I don't know."

"You're not," he said. "No one is. Not in this situation."

"If I knew where she was, I'd go and try to talk to her."

"Do you feel like you could reconcile? Fix things?"

"I'm not sure. But I feel like I at least would have liked to try."

"I feel like that would have been the right thing to do," he said. "If you tried, and it didn't work, you at least did all you could do."

"Life's too short not to try."

"Life is too short," he agreed.

I thought about Brooke a lot on the rest of the drive home. She'd popped into my head periodically over the previous six months. I'd wondered where she was. I'd wondered how she was doing. I hoped she was safe and healthy and had support from her family and friends to get through our difficult time. I figured she probably hated me or at least was mad enough at me to lock me out of her life. I didn't understand the decision entirely. I didn't get how something I perceived as such a small thing—helping a friend in need—turned into an event that would destroy our marriage. But, I suppose, underneath, there was something else brewing. Something she was feeling or thinking that she hadn't shared with me. Something that I didn't know about or have any suspicions about. Something that had her looking for a way out. Something that would be an excuse to up and leave. Some reason, some thing, to let her walk away, not feeling guilty. Something that would allow her to not feel like the bad guy.

My mind wandered as I drove on quasi-autopilot the whole way home. I wondered if I'd ever get closure. I wondered if there was hope to reconcile. To fix things. I wondered if she'd ever speak to me again. But, ultimately, I wasn't sure what I wanted. I wasn't sure if I wanted to try to fix things. Truth be told, I wasn't happy with a lot of our relationship. On some level, I knew that all the things Marty helped me see—that I'd been ignoring unintentionally—were real. They weren't made up. They weren't a ruse by my friend to break us up. They were real problems. And they needed to be addressed. I had a knack for not bringing up things that bothered me until we got into a fight. We didn't fight that much, so I bottled a lot of my feelings inside. I kept them to myself, hoping that they'd resolve themselves. Hoping that I'd be able to work through whatever it was on my own or that the cause of the problem—often Brooke—would change. She didn't change, and the problems didn't fix themselves. When I eventually started therapy and recounted my life, my therapist literally scoffed at me when I told her I'd hoped everything would magically fix itself. "Hurt people hurt people," she said. Something I'll never forget. Brooke was, for whatever reason, hurt. Maybe from my relationship with Marty. Maybe from past trauma. Maybe from something she didn't tell me about. Perhaps from something she wasn't even aware of. But she was hurt, and she used that as a reason to try to hurt me.

I suppose, on the drive home that night, while lost in my thoughts, I realized that although I wasn't able to save my marriage, I'd be okay. So much of my life had revolved around Brooke over the past six years that it felt like it was *all* my life was. Like I didn't exist anymore and was only an offshoot of her.

Don't get me wrong, I loved her. With all that I was. And I don't want to diminish our relationship, but I felt, almost, perhaps a tiny bit, of relief when she left. I don't want to be dramatic and say that I felt "free," but on some level, I did. I felt a weight lifted off my shoulder. Like I no longer had to walk on eggshells. I no longer had to keep things inside and bottle them up. I felt like I was a new man.

And yes, that probably makes me a bit of a terrible person. It probably sullies your opinion of me some, and I get that. Even all these years later, I question things. I wonder if I'd done things differently, or thought differently, or acted differently if things would be different. Would it have been such a big deal if I had just talked to her about moving Marty in first? Or was that just her excuse to start a fight and leave?

So many times have I questioned myself about that night and the weeks and months after when I almost desperately tried to contact her to sort things out.

I recalled so many nights of tossing and turning, sleeping just a few hours. So many hours of laying awake, replaying the events of that evening in my head, over and over. Wondering what the trigger was. Was it really Marty? Was it me? Was it her? There had to be more to it.

But, still, that sense of relief washed over me. Every time I felt like I was going crazy trying to work out what happened or why it happened, I remembered that the last six months had been okay. Did I have bouts of sadness? Sometimes overwhelmingly so. Did I hate myself for a long while? Absolutely. But, overall, I'd been okay. I'd leaned on Marty. I'd leaned on my mom. I'd eaten more Papa Gino's at the end of the cul-de-sac, in front of the house that used to be Jean Luc's and Marty's, than I could count. Slice after slice, conversation after conversation, Marty helped me through one of the most difficult times in my life. And he did it without even thinking twice. He knew it wasn't his fault, and he only blamed himself for it one time. Just once. I corrected him and never let him blame himself for my failed marriage ever again.

Christmas Decor & A Marriage No More

"Remember the night we went to the hockey game?" I asked Marty from the living room.

"What about it?" he called back from the kitchen.

"We talked about trying to locate Brooke."

"Did you find her?" he came running back to the living room and sat down across from me on the couch.

"No, but I think I finally have some answers."

I handed him the legal-sized manila envelope that had come in the mail. "Look at it," I said as he'd already started sliding the papers out from inside.

"Oh, me," he said. Despite my correcting him several times, he'd occasionally say 'oh me' when he meant 'oh my.' "Divorce papers?"

"I guess she hired a lawyer."

"I guess she doesn't want to resolve your issues," he said, half-laughing.

The apartment was decorated for Christmas. And although we were two men in our twenties, I felt like we'd done a pretty decent job. It didn't feel half-assed or too masculine. I looked past Marty to the Christmas tree, watching the lights twinkle momentarily.

"She waited until now," I said.

"What do you mean?"

"I proposed at Christmastime."

"Oh, me."

"She waited to serve papers until now because she knew that would hurt me."

"I'm so sorry," he said.

"It's fine. I'm not hurt. I guess I feel relief. I have my closure."

"Do you need to hire a lawyer?"

"I guess I should, right?"

"Probably best."

• • • • ● • ● • • •

I looked over the paperwork, having no legal experience in my life except for seeing every episode of *Law & Order* and *Judge Judy*. I read and re-read legal words and phrases that made no sense to me. Things I had no idea what they meant, but all seemed to be fairly straightforward. She'd filed an "uncontested divorce," which, according to Google, means that both parties agree the marriage is over and that there's no dispute over who gets what. It seemed like she just wanted it all to be over.

Although I had come to terms with the pending divorce over the last few months, given how I was unable to track her down or make contact with her, the finality of receiving the paperwork really hit home. I felt, even if for just a brief minute or two, sad.

Periodically, while reading over the documents, I'd stop and look out the window. The townhouses across the road from my apartment were all decorated for the holiday. Their twinkling lights gave me a brief reprieve from my sadness. Christmas—my favorite holiday—had given me a small glimmer of hope that everything would be okay. Those lights and wreathes and lawn decorations that I could barely make out through the snow on the window were a small reminder that, no matter what was happening in my life, there was always something to look forward to.

"You okay?" Marty asked, bringing my attention back to the room.

"Huh? Oh, yeah. I'm okay."

"I'm really sorry," he said. "I feel like this is my fault."

"Don't be sorry. If anything's your fault, it's making me see that I wasn't happy in the relationship or my marriage. And, it seems, neither was she."

"She sure did seem to pull the plug pretty quickly," he said.

He was right. If my life were a movie, there would have been a scene where I yelled at her something to the effect of "At the first sign of trouble, you just run away?" she'd have been frantically packing and crying, telling me she really loved me. Still, she couldn't "do this anymore" or something equally dramatic. You know, if my life were a movie. Obviously, there'd be some sad, sappy song playing over the scene.

"Do you have to go to court?" Marty asked.

"I'm not sure. I guess I would have to, eventually. I should definitely get at least a legal consultation."

• • • • • • • • • •

That night, we watched *National Lampoon's Christmas Vacation* and *Kiss Kiss, Bang Bang*. Each of our favorite Christmas movies, respectively. Something that would become tradition the week of Christmas. Every year, we'd rewatch the same two movies at least once. There were other favorites we'd rotate in periodically, but we always watched our two absolute favorites every year.

We'd quote the lines. We'd do the voices. We'd talk about how they should have made sequels to both movies and were bummed they never did. We'd sit together and enjoy ourselves. No agenda. No pressure. No expectations. Just two buddies, their favorite Christmas movies, and their favorite Papa Gino's pizza.

A Picture For You & A Picture For Me

I had forgotten to shut my alarm off the night before, so I woke up at 6 a.m. on Christmas morning as if I had to get up for work. I was such a light sleeper that the spinning of the CD in the alarm clock woke me up, usually before the song even started playing. Since re-discovering my love for the band Boston, thanks to the Rock Band game a few years before, I'd woken up to "More Than A Feeling."

Before the song kicked in, I reached over and shut the alarm off, groaning, mostly at myself for forgetting to turn the alarm off but also because I'd slept funny and my back was throbbing.

As I lay awake in bed, alone, it hit me. It was my first Christmas without Brooke in six years. We'd met in late 2003 and had been together since. We'd either fly to visit her family in New York or spend Christmas with my family. But we'd always been together. And this year was the first one that she wasn't there. And probably the first where she felt a strong hatred toward me.

My prep for Christmas had been much easier than in years past. No wishlists to worry about. No searching out the perfect gift. No pressure or proposal. I only had to shop for two people: Marty and my mom. They were the only two important people in my life. The only two people close enough to me that I knew, for sure, I'd see on Christmas. And as such, I needed to have gifts for them.

I took a brief moment to say a prayer. Something I didn't do often but felt necessary that morning. I prayed that Brooke was okay and that she was happy. That, wherever she was, she was safe. Obviously, I still loved her, but I understood that sometimes love isn't enough. Who said that? Don Henley, I think.

A small sound from the other room gave me a clue that Marty was awake.

"You up?" I called out, hoping he was and I didn't just wake him.

"I am," he called back.

"Merry Christmas."

"Merry Christmas."

"You think Santa came?" I joked.

"I hope so. I had a big list," he joked back.

"You want to shower first?" We only had one bathroom, and I tried my best to accommodate him since he was technically a guest in my home. Although, in my mind, he was my roommate by that time.

"Go ahead," he called back.

I popped out of bed and went across the hall to the bathroom, turning the water on as I closed the door. One of the few things I now miss about apartment living is the endless supply of hot water we had. I don't know if it was a giant hot water tank or a tankless system, but that apartment would never run out of hot water. Sometimes, contrary to my personality, I would stay in the shower for an hour. Just basked in the hot water, letting it wash away anything bothering me.

That morning, however, I took a quick shower. It was only 6:30 by the time I'd gotten out, let Marty know he was free to go in, and gotten dressed.

While Marty showered, I made breakfast. Cinnamon rolls and bacon. A true twenty-something's breakfast: carbs and fat.

Knowing Marty had gotten me a handful of presents, I didn't wander into the living room to look under the tree. When I came out late last night to put his gifts out, I saw he'd already done the same for me. I imagined him sitting in his room, sneakily pulling presents from the hidden spot where they were stored away, hoping I was already asleep so he could sneak out and put his gifts under the tree. But, alas, I was doing the same, and it just happened that he decided to plop his gifts under the tree before I did.

"Smells great," he said as he came out of the shower, toweling off his hair.

"I made the usual."

"Pizza?" he laughed, grabbing a handful of bacon and two cinnamon rolls and tossing them onto one of the paper plates I'd left on the counter.

I followed him to the dining room table, a plate full of the same thing he had, orange juice in hand.

"Cheers," I said, clanking my coffee mug of OJ to his. "To your dad."

"Cheers."

• • • • •●• ●• • •

After breakfast, we made our way over to the couch, making eye contact and then eyeing the presents under the tree. Though we'd exchanged gifts before, we'd never been living together at Christmas, so I think neither of us was sure how to proceed. It wasn't like years past where I would show up to his place or vice versa, gifts in hand, and go into gift exchange immediately.

"You go first," I said.

He wasted no time jumping up, grabbing the first gift for him he could find, and also grabbing one for me. He handed me my gift and then tore into his. I'd done my best to get him things he needed, mostly for things around the apartment: an electric razor, the coffee machine he'd wanted, but I never had since neither Brooke nor I drank coffee, an alarm clock of his own. I also got him a handful of games I knew he liked, both board and video.

The first gift he opened was one that I had hoped he'd open later in the morning. It was a sentimental gift I'd put together. Nothing particularly special but meaningful to him. A small, plain picture frame. One of the few photos of Jean Luc, myself, and Marty is in it. From the first block party, right as we'd started cleaning up from a very successful sharing of all of Jean Luc's food. The three of us beaming with smiles and pride, happy beyond words.

"This is incredible, Matt."

"It's my favorite picture of us, though there aren't many."

"Look how happy he is," Marty said.

"Look how happy we all are. Your dad had just made so many new friends. You and I had successfully thrown a big party without the help of anyone or the internet. That was an amazing day."

"It really was," he said. "Wait. Don't open that one." He pulled the package off my lap and tossed it to the side of me on the couch. "I have a better one."

He scurried back over to the tree, poking and prodding, looking for something specific. He tossed a handful of gifts out of the way, clearly on a mission for one particular thing.

"Ah. Here it is," he said, coming back to the couch. "This one first."

"You're sure?" I said, shaking the small package.

"Yes. Open."

I tore into the package, realizing I was looking at the back of it. Once I tore the rest of the wrapping paper off, I realized Marty did the same thing I did. It was a picture frame.

When I flipped it over, I realized he'd done the same thing I did.

I looked up at him.

"It's my favorite photograph of us, too," he said.

It was the same picture I'd given him.

"Son of a ..." I said.

"Great minds," he said. "It really is a great picture."

"It reminds me of that day. I still remember all of it so vividly. Everything about it."

"Me, as well."

"Hey, listen," I said. "The last few months have been a lot. And you've really helped me through a lot of the emotions I've been going through. The ups and downs I had when Brooke first left."

"That's what friends do," he said.

"It's more than that, though. You're a special person."

"You'd do the same for me," he said.

"I would. You know that."

"You helped me through rough times the last few months, too. With dad. With my home. You've helped just as much."

"I guess what I'm trying to say," I said, putting the picture frame down and looking up at him. "I'm trying to say that I love you, Marty. You're my best friend, and I want you to know I love you."

"Matt," he said, making sure I was looking at him. "I love you too, buddy."

"I don't think I could do this without you," I said. "Life. Living. Whatever. I can't imagine it without you."

"Likewise. I wish everyone had a friend as good as you."

It was obvious over the years we'd known each other that we had a brotherly love, but that Christmas morning was the first time either of us had said it out loud to the other person.

2010

Marty's Seeing Somone

One night shortly after New Year's, Marty and I were hanging out, playing Xbox, Halo 3, if memory serves, when he paused the game.

"Matt," he said. "I have something to confess."

I put my controller down, turning to face him. "What is it?"

"I've been seeing someone."

"What?! That's great!" I said.

"Let me clarify," he said. "I've been seeing a therapist."

"Well, that took a turn," I said, trying to lighten the mood that'd immediately gotten heavy.

"After Papa's passing, the rift I caused with your relationship, and the sudden changes to a lot of my life, I needed someone to talk to."

"You can talk to me," I said instinctively.

"I know. But I needed a professional. I needed someone unbiased. Someone who isn't my best friend."

I'd never been in therapy before—I am now and highly recommend it to anyone who's struggling with any life-related *thing*—so I wasn't sure how to be supportive in this situation.

"Don't get me wrong, you're my best friend, and I know you're here for me," he said. "But a professional can be so much more helpful."

"What do you talk about?" I asked.

"Anything. Everything. We spent the first few weeks talking about my life. Talking about everything up to where we are today."

"That's a lot of backstory," I said. "It must have been hard to talk about some of it."

"It is," he said. "But that's the beauty of therapy. It sucks to talk about some of the hard stuff, but once you do, you feel better. You feel lighter having someone else listen to your troubles and offer help and suggestions on dealing with it."

"Do you think it's helping?"

"I'm not sure if it is yet. I know I feel better immediately after a session, but that feeling goes away after a short while. I go once every week and feel like it could eventually help me feel better. But," his voice trailed off.

"What is it?"

"But, for right now, I'm depressed."

"Oh man," I said, not knowing what else to say. "That sucks."

"It's nothing you did, don't worry. Sometimes, as my therapist says, depression can sneak up on you. A bunch of heavy things happen quickly, and suddenly, you can't dig your way out of it."

"Is there anything I can do?"

"You're doing it," he said. "She says to do my best to do normal things. So, pizza and video games on a Tuesday night are perfect. It's exactly what I should be doing."

"Does it feel like just a distraction?"

"It does," he said. "But that's what I need, sometimes. Sometimes, I need to sit in my room and deal with my feelings. Sometimes, I need to do something crazy, like skydiving. Sometimes, I just need a quiet night at home with my best friend, shooting aliens."

"I do love shooting aliens." I laughed.

"Maybe someday I'll feel better. Maybe the depression will go away. But, for now, I ask that you give me space if I need it."

"Of course."

"And if I need you to take me bungee jumping or rock climbing or something, go with me."

"The best adventures are ones we take together," I said. "Jesus, that sounded corny. But you know what I mean."

He unpaused the game, signaling he'd said everything he needed to get off his chest.

I felt heavier. A weight I'd not felt before sitting on my shoulders. A need to make sure Marty was okay. To do whatever I could to support him, to be there for him. I knew he was hurting over the loss of his father, something I could only imagine having to deal with. And, obviously, his life had changed quite a bit since moving in with me. But I didn't know it was as bad as Marty made it seem. I didn't know he was suffering and certainly didn't know there were times when he was isolated in his room, potentially in a deep depression, trying to fight his way back out of it by himself.

Nothing before or since has made me feel more helpless. Like I had all the power to help him get past what he was struggling with, but I hadn't. That my best friend in the world was hurting, and I hadn't done anything about it. I hadn't even noticed that he'd been struggling. I'd eventually learn that depression does that, especially as I went through it later in life. It just hits you one day, and you don't know what it is; you know you don't feel right. Just all of a sudden, everything seems impossible. Everything seems like the weight of the world is on your shoulders, and no matter what you do, you can't get out from under it. It's debilitating.

Part of me was glad Marty trusted me to tell me what he was going through. Part of me felt responsible. And a much smaller part of me felt guilty for not knowing. I felt, on the whole, like I needed to do better. I needed to be there for him more, to make more time for him. I needed to check in on him more often if he was in his room. I needed to make sure that he knew I was there for him.

He paused the game again.

"You're in your head," he said. "I can tell."

"I am, I know."

"It's nothing you did or could have done," he said. "This just happens."

"That doesn't mean I can't try harder to help you."

"You can. Everyone can," he said. "But I don't expect you to. This is why I got a therapist."

"Maybe I should get one," I half-laughed.

"It's my opinion that everyone should have one," he said. "Everyone can benefit from it."

He unpaused the game.

We went back to shooting aliens and liberating captured Marines. Something we'd been through dozens of times. We eventually switched to online play, promptly getting our asses kicked by other people around the world. People much better at the game than we were. People we didn't even know but had tons of fun with, anyway.

Playing Halo games was a staple of our friendship once we'd started living together. It was something we both loved. Something we could do together, but not need to sit and talk. We'd just get engulfed in the game, playing, shooting, enjoying ourselves. It was a sign of our true friendship that we could sit side-by-side for four, five, six, eight, or more hours, just playing and not needing to talk to one another. Sitting together silently was a sign of how comfortable we were. We didn't need to make small talk. We didn't need to encourage one another. We could sit and play. That's not something I've ever had with a friend before—that feeling of not needing to fill the silence between us, that emptiness. With Marty, it was okay to have the emptiness.

Just Like That

Having Marty live with me was helpful. Not just mentally and emotionally, but financially. He'd insisted on paying for his half of the bills, which lightened the load on me considerably. It allowed us to save a bunch of money over the year and a half we'd lived together.

After numerous discussions, we'd determined that renting didn't make sense anymore. The cost of rent was going up every time the lease was renewed, to the point where it made more financial sense to buy a house.

"I don't want to go," I said one night out of the blue.

"Go where?"

"Leave here, I mean."

"I know what you mean," he said. "I feel like we've got it pretty good here."

"I have a thought. Hear me out."

"I'm listening."

"We both have enough money for a down payment on a house, right?"

"I know I do," he said. "You do, too?"

"I do. But what if we didn't each buy a house?"

"I am confused."

"What if we bought one house? Together."

"Is that a thing grown men do?"

"I don't know," I said. "I don't see why not, right? We like living together. We're best friends. It makes financial sense."

"But what about, I don't know. What happens if one of us gets married and wants to leave?"

"We can figure that out if and when it happens."

"I like the idea," he said. "I like to live with you."

• • • • • • • • • •

We house-hunted for quite a while. Everything we looked at either felt outdated or overpriced. Kitchens from the '80s. Bathrooms with carpeting. It felt like a never-ending nightmare. Sometimes, a house would have something I'd love, but Marty wouldn't. And vice versa. Sometimes, we'd both love one or two things about it, but overall hate it.

It was such a frustrating experience. Thankfully, our realtor, Heather, was incredible. She was smart and witty. She knew about houses coming to the market before anyone else and easily got us in for showings, sometimes before the seller was even ready to get listed.

She insisted that when we found the right one, we'd know. That, as soon as we pulled into the driveway, we'd know it was the right house for us.

And she was right.

The first time we pulled into 16 Maple Wood Drive, we knew it was the house we needed to have.

From the driveway, you could see back to the fenced-in pool, complete with a small pool house with a built-in bar and two televisions mounted on the back wall. The house had three bedrooms and three bathrooms. Heather said it was a "dual master" house, which was rare for New England. We wouldn't have to compete over who got the bigger bedroom because we would both get a primary suite.

When we walked in, we were overwhelmed by how immaculate it was. A giant open kitchen with a big island and Viking range led to a small eat-in area. To the back was a spacious living room.

"The bedrooms are all upstairs," she said. "Go look around. I'll wait on the porch."

Marty and I ran around like children left alone in a toy store. He went one way, I went the other, and we'd call out to each other all the things we found that we loved.

"There's a big tub in my bathroom!" Marty yelled. "You know I love to take a bath!"

"Mine just has a shower. I love it!"

I spent a minute standing where I assumed I'd put my bed. The empty room was easy to visualize with my stuff in it. I closed my eyes and listened. I heard nothing other than Marty's footsteps. No cars. No traffic. No loud neighbors. Just silence. I'd yearned for it after living in an apartment for so long. I looked forward to not having noisy neighbors upstairs or next door. No sounds of communal doors slamming shut at all hours of the night. No voices walking down the hallway. The silence was incredible.

"I think this is it," Marty said, entering *my* room.

"I know it is," I replied.

• • • • •●• • • • •

We went back downstairs and met Heather outside. She was sitting in one of the two rocking chairs on the front porch, looking at her phone.

"This is it," I said.

"Can we afford this place?" Marty asked.

"Normally? No. But the owners both passed away, and their kids want to sell it. So, it's going to be listed under market value. By a good amount."

"Won't we get into a bidding war?" I asked.

"I don't think so. I know the seller's agent. She used to work with me. I can probably get her to stall listing it, so there won't be many offers, if any."

"I knew we picked the right person," Marty said.

"Let me make some calls," she said. "They're trying to get four-oh-seven for it. I think you are pre-approved for more than that, so you should be all set."

She excused herself back into the house, and Marty and I stared at each other for a few long minutes.

"This is really happening?" I asked.

"It seems like it is," he said.

It felt like ages before Heather came back out of the house. She was still on the phone and held up the "be right there" finger that everyone uses.

"Yep. Okay. Got it. By tonight. No problem. Thanks."

She hung up.

"If you offer the full asking price, it's yours."

"What? Just like that?" I asked.

"Just like that."

"Yay!" Marty yelled, like an excited schoolboy whose crush liked him back. "I am so excited!"

"I'll write up the offer paperwork and get it over to you to sign. Once they have it, they need a deposit while you get your loan approved."

"You make it seem so easy," I said.

"It is when you work with the best," she replied, brushing an invisible chip off her shoulder.

The Block Party In A New Neighborhood

We'd been in the new house for a few weeks by the time we got settled. We had so much furniture that we didn't need to buy much to fill the house. When Marty moved in with Brooke and me, we put all the furniture from his dad's house into storage, knowing he'd eventually need it again someday.

Neither of us had talked about it, but we knew we would have some sort of housewarming party. Likely a barbecue, and likely invite the whole neighborhood. As best we could, we'd try to continue the neighborhood block party tradition we'd started back in my mom's neighborhood all those years ago.

"Hey, I have an idea," Marty said from the kitchen.

"What is it?" I called back from the living room, just down a small hallway.

"We should have a party. What do you call it when you move into a new house?"

"A housewarming party," I said. "I was thinking the same thing. Literally just thinking about it now."

"We can invite everyone from the neighborhood. Like before..." his voice trailed off.

"Your dad would be proud if we continued the tradition of sharing his food with people who've never had it before."

"He would," Marty agreed.

• • • • ● • ● • • •

We had many neighbors on our street and the adjoining streets of our neighborhood. And, although we could have done it digitally, Marty and I walked around the whole neighborhood, knocking on doors, just like we'd done that very first time.

We introduced ourselves, explained why we were knocking on their door, and welcomed them to the barbecue we'd be throwing in a few weeks. We were near the beginning of the road, so we couldn't block the street like we did at my mom's house, but we planned to have the bulk of the party in our yard, letting people use the pool and welcomed their children to play in the yard, as well.

Many of the neighbors were very welcoming, often inviting us into their homes and introducing us to their partners and children.

Overall, they were all very nice and seemed excited about our party.

Except for Dimitrius, as we'd eventually learn, was his name. He lived at the far end of one of the adjoining streets and started screaming at us as soon as he opened the door.

"What the fuck are you knocking on my door for?"

"Oh, me," Marty said.

"Sorry to bother you," I added. "We're new to the neighborhood and are throwing a housewarming party."

"The fuck do I care?" he said, slamming the door in our faces.

"That went well," I laughed.

"Let us go before he comes back," Marty said, scurrying down the stairs.

"Good idea." I tried catching up, but he quickly got off Dimitrius' property.

• • • • ● • ● • • •

When the time came for the party, we were ready. It felt like we'd bought out every pound of ground hamburger Whole Foods had, along with dozens of various types of kebabs, hot dogs, pounds of cheese for cheeseburgers, tons of bacon—because what cheeseburger is complete without bacon—and lots of vegetarian options, as well. All in all, we'd spent around six hundred dollars on food for the party. Marty also got everything he needed to continue Jean Luc's traditions.

We also stopped at the liquor store and picked up more alcohol than I'm sure any two men had ever bought at one time in the history of humankind—Margarita mix, vodka, gin, rum, whiskey, tons of different beers. We wanted to be as prepared as possible for whoever might show up.

At some point, I had the brilliant idea to buy a blow-up kid's pool. Not to let kids swim in—we had an in-ground pool at the house—but to fill it with ice and use it as a big cooler.

"And ten bags of ice," I told the cashier as he was tallying up the alcohol.

"Thirteen hundred and eighty-five fifty," he said.

I looked over at Marty with a face that said, "Sheesh," but didn't actually say anything.

We paid, stopping to grab the ice on the way out and loading it all into the back of my car. On some occasions, I could still smell some of Jean Luc's cooking when I opened the back. I'm sure it was psychosomatic, but it made me feel a little connected to him. It helped me miss him a little less when I could smell his aromas. I knew Marty was planning to make much of the food his dad had also loved cooking. To share it with the people in our new neighborhood and to continue his dad's traditions and legacy.

As we pulled back into the driveway, making sure to park off to the side, a couple of people were already milling about in the yard.

"Oh, hi," I said, calling out to them as I got out of the car. "We're not quite ready yet."

"Hi, neighbor. I'm Rick. This is my wife, Michelle."

"Hi, Rick. Hi, Michelle," Marty said.

"We're right next door in number 18. Thought you could use a hand setting up."

"That's amazing, thank you," I said as I approached, extending my hand. "I'm Matt. This is my best friend, Marty."

"Nice to meet you both," Michelle said. "How can we help?"

"Pop into the basement through the door there," Marty said, pointing. "Grab the folding tables and chairs and set them up somewhere where it'll be shady."

Although we'd come to hate it in the Fall, our property was lined with tall trees. They allowed the entirety of the backyard, including the pool, to be in the shade most of the time.

"Can do," Rick said.

"They seem nice," Marty said as Rick and Michelle walked away.

"They do. Very nice of them to come help set up."

Marty and I went back to the car, unloading the ice right into the kid's pool I'd inflated earlier that morning. As we unloaded, the ten bags we'd bought seemed like it wouldn't be enough.

"Let's get the beer and soda in first," Marty suggested. "Then we'll see if there's enough ice or not. I can always go get some more."

"Great idea," I said. Rick and Michelle had just come out with the last folding chairs and set them up around the tables they'd brought up.

"Everyone's really excited about the party," Rick shouted.

I smiled. Marty smiled as well.

Marty and I chuckled when we finished putting everything into the kid's pool. It turned out that with everything in the pool, we had too much ice. Some had spilled over the top as we jammed all the beverages in.

"What else can we do?" Michelle asked.

"There's about twenty pounds of ground beef in the trunk if you want to start making hamburger patties in the kitchen?" Marty asked. He was a natural leader, and it showed. He took control of all the planning without me needing to ask. It further expanded here with him taking charge of what to have our neighbors do.

Rick nodded, and off they went to grab the meat from the trunk and headed into the house to find our kitchen. In hindsight, one of us should have gone in and shown them, but we were preoccupied.

I followed them over to the trunk just moments later as Marty continued to fuss with the arrangement of the beverages.

Bag after bag, armful after armful, I unloaded our haul from Whole Foods. Foods that would get cooked as is went into the cooler by the grill. Buns and condiments went onto the table next to where I'd be grilling.

"The pool is ready," Marty said as he approached.

"Which one?"

"Both. The drink pool and the pool pool." He seemed to amuse himself and chuckled.

"People will start coming soon," I said. "It's eleven, and we said noon."

"What can I do to help?"

"Go check on Rick and Michelle. See if they need any help?"

"Yes," he said, heading into the house to find our neighbors.

"While you're in there, get anything going on the stove that you need to make or heat up or finish."

"Dad's food," he called back without turning back toward me.

I smiled. "Dad's food is right."

· · · · ● · ● · · ·

The neighbors started showing up just a little before noon. Slowly at first, and then in droves. I didn't count how many doors we'd knocked on, but it took us that whole day. And it was evident once people started showing up.

Destiny and her husband Greg, Mr. and Mrs. White. Dr. Joe, his wife Rebecca, and their daughters, whose names I forgot minutes after learning them.

Allyson and her two kids, Brendan and Leah, were there. Eric and his husband, Thomas. Beverly and her girlfriend Melissa, and *their* girlfriend Morgan—don't ask, it's a complicated story.

Neighbor after neighbor piled in.

"Who's hungry?" I asked rhetorically as I began cooking the copious amounts of food.

Marty had laid out the same setup Jean Luc had used every year. The same Sternos that still, somehow, had fuel left in them. The same warming trays. The same utensils. It was almost like Jean Luc was there, prepping his usuals. It was almost like a small part of Marty was channeling his dad, trying to do everything exactly as Jean Luc would have done it.

He looked over, and I nodded. A silent assurance that I saw what he was doing and appreciated it.

I could hear him telling anyone who'd listen about the food, what it was, how it was made, what it tasted like. He went on and on about

Belgium and how lovely the country was. How amazing he hoped they'd think the food was.

As I expected, lots of people loved it and called over the other neighbors they knew. There were a lot of "you have to try this" and "Marty made this. Have you met Marty yet?" coming from that general direction. Marty and his food were a big hit.

Not to sell myself short, because I make a hell of a bacon cheeseburger, but Marty was the star of the show.

From the grill, I saw the lay of the land. Tons of people gathered around Marty's table, consuming everything they could. Kids were playing in the pool while a few parents sat at the bar of the pool house, thankfully keeping an eye on the swimming children. The residents of the whole neighborhood seemed to be hanging out in our backyard. And while it seemed like a lot of them knew each other, it also seemed like a lot of them didn't.

I could hear Destiny introducing her husband to Allyson. I heard Morgan introducing Beverly and Melissa to Colin and Jessica. I saw Derek and Josh shaking hands. I saw Sarah hug Mark.

It felt heartwarming. Although we had intended for people to come and meet us and welcome us to their neighborhood, it felt like it was a housewarming for the neighborhood. It felt like many of these people had never met before and were getting to meet—or reconnect—for the first time. They were either getting to know one another or catching up because they hadn't seen each other in a while.

Marty ran by the grill, running for the house. "I have to pee," he declared. "No time."

I couldn't help but laugh out loud. He'd been so focused on feeding everyone and getting to know them that he didn't make time to run inside and go to the bathroom.

Typical Marty. Always wanting to be there for other people and putting himself last.

WHAT IF I FAIL?

"I've been keeping a secret from you," Marty blurted out, mid-commercial break. We were watching the hockey game, and I could tell something was on his mind all night. He was fidgeting and often couldn't sit still. I caught him looking at me half a dozen times before speaking up.

"Oh?" I dug through every inch of my brain, trying to figure out what he could possibly tell me. Had he met a girl? Did he get a new job? What would be something that he'd feel the need to keep a secret from me? We told each other almost everything and had for years.

"I wanted to tell you but didn't want to jinx it."

"Out with it," I said, no longer able to wait to find out.

"I've been going to a class on Monday nights."

"A class? For what?"

"Well, as silly as it sounds, America."

"You lost me," I paused the game that had just come back from a commercial and turned to face him on the opposite end of the couch. "America?"

"Yes. To learn more about America."

"For what? I'm still confused."

"Let me finish," he said. "I took classes to learn about America's policies, laws, and history. I went every Monday night and told you I was working late. I'm kind of glad you never caught on. Anyway, I've been taking classes with the hopes that I could become a citizen. I've been here long enough now."

"I hadn't even thought of that."

"As much as I love and adore Belgium, my home is here now. I thought I would try to make it official."

"That's lovely," I said. "Did you take the test yet?"

"Not yet. That's why I wanted to bring it up."

"When is it?"

"Tomorrow. Will you go with me? I'm nervous."

"Of course I will! I'm so proud of you. What a big milestone in your life, right?"

"Oh, me," he said. "You just sounded like my dad there."

He smiled at me.

• • • • • • • • • •

We were the first in line the next morning, well before the testing facility opened. That character flaw of always being early—or quirk, depending on how you look at it—was the reason we were first in line.

"I'm so nervous," Marty said. "What if I fail?"

"You know the material, right? Why would you fail?"

"I'm a bad test taker. I've never been good at them."

"Don't think of it as a test, then. Just think of it as something you're good at. Pretend it's cooking delicious food or freeing Marines in Halo."

"If it were only that easy," he said, hanging his head briefly.

"It's too bad you didn't tell me about this sooner, you know."

"Why not?"

"I could have helped you study. Quizzed you. Asked you sporadic questions and caught you off guard."

"You're right. I don't know why I kept it a secret. I guess I didn't want to tell you until I passed the test. I wanted to surprise you when I became a citizen."

"That would have been one hell of a surprise."

"But I got nervous and wanted you to come with me. I knew you'd give me confidence."

"That's what friends do, right?"

"Right."

The line behind us started to queue up with other people probably looking to take the same test. I wasn't sure if the facility only did citizenship tests or if there were other kinds of tests they did.

After about half an hour of waiting, a woman opened the door, looking past us and down the line. She shouted, "Have your identification papers ready when you enter. If you're here with someone, they can come in with you, but not into the testing room. No phones, pagers, or weapons of any kind allowed." She repeated it a second time with the exact same emphasis and enthusiasm, which wasn't a whole lot.

"You ready?" I asked Marty as he shuffled through his pile of paperwork.

"As ready as I will be."

The woman went back into the building, propping the door open behind her. A very large, very intimidating-looking security guard stepped outside and parked himself at the open door. He began signaling people to go inside, one at a time.

"That's us," Marty said. "Let's go."

I followed him into the massive entryway to the building. A round room with an upper-floor balcony spanning the entire circular structure. Doors and lights as far as the eye could see.

A second security guard had us empty our pockets and walk through a metal detector. I must have had a weird look because the security guard on the other side of the metal detector made eye contact, said, "Government building," and shrugged.

Marty beeped as he walked through. Unenthusiastically, the security guard on the far side waved a metal detector wand over him. It beeped on his belt but nowhere else, so the guard waved him on.

We collected our belongings, returned them to our pockets, and followed the signs to the testing room.

The same woman who'd come outside to tell everyone the rules was posted at the testing room door.

"Which of you is here for the citizenship test?" she asked.

"I am," Marty said, raising his that was free of the stack of paperwork he'd held.

"I need to see your identification and the completed registration form for the test."

He fumbled with the papers in his other hand, handing me some of the less important ones to hold. "Here you are," he said, handing over the proper papers to her.

She looked them over in great detail, checking the laptop on the mobile computer station next to her. "Ah, here you are," she said. "You're all set. Go on inside. You can wait in the waiting area over there," she told me, pointing to a door directly across the atrium.

"Good luck," I said, placing my hand on his shoulder. "You'll do great."

"Thank you," he said and rushed inside.

• • • • ● • ● • • •

Walking to the waiting room, I wondered what other government things happened in the building. It was much too large to be only for citizenship tests. It seemed like every few feet, there was another door, all of them closed, most of them labeled. From my vantage point, they were all too far away to make out what any of them said. But my imagination ran wild. There was an office for people who investigated UFOs. There was one for motor vehicle accident investigation. There was one for airline disaster recovery. I'm sure it was all less innocuous than that, but my mind ran wild.

Unintentionally, I moseyed across the atrium, taking it all in. The giant crest embedded into the floor. The people milling about. The sound of the metal detector occasionally beeping. I suppose, on some level, my brain was trying to occupy itself. I was trying to stay busy so I wouldn't focus on how nervous I was for Marty. I know he'd only sprung the test on me just the night before, but the anxiety and stress of this big test for him hit me. It was a common thing between us, having been so close for so many years. We just had a connection that made us both feel this way when it came time for any big event.

Once I made my way into the waiting room, I was disappointed. Unlike the rest of the building I'd been able to see, the waiting room felt lackluster. It felt like an old basement room that had been forgotten about. The tables and chairs had all seen better days, long since worn out. The single vending machine was scarce, save for some Cherry Pop-Tarts, a bag of chips that looked to have been run over by a truck, and a pack of Juicy Fruit gum. The water fountain had so much rust on it that I'd have to consider when my last tetanus shot was, should I get thirsty.

Other accompanying people came into the room. The looks of disappointment immediately hit their faces, as it had mine. I was sure no one was expecting the Ritz Carlton inside, but I think we were all expecting a little more than what we got. The room reminded me of the waiting area from *Beetlejuice*. The only thing missing was the cloud of smoke overhead and the sound of the constant phone ringing. The wood-paneled walls felt like a flashback to our childhood station wagon.

As I sat in the chair closest to the back of the room, I felt it sag immediately. I, for a brief moment, worried it might collapse. I thought I'd end up on the floor and everyone else in the room would have a good laugh.

Others taking seats were greeted with the same squeak as I was. The look of panic washed across their faces, much like mine. I scooted myself to the nearest table, hoping moving the chair wouldn't cause it to collapse.

The table was clearly old. Its finish was so worn out from people leaning on it over the years that the bare wood poked through in almost all the spots where chairs were. The middle of the table was shiny, untouched by many human hands.

"Hi, I'm Victor," the gentleman beside me said, extending his hand.
"Matt."
"Nice to meet you, Matt. Who are you here with?"
"My best friend. You?"
"My girlfriend. She's from China. Where is your friend from?"
"Belgium."
"Interesting! Well, good luck to him," he said, turning to the other side to greet the woman sitting next to him.

The room filled with people. Boyfriends and girlfriends. Friends. Family members. We had representation from tons of different relationships. All of us nervous for our loved ones. All of us, probably, wondering how long the testing would take.

It'd been a while since anyone else had come in when seemingly the only person running this test—the woman from earlier—came in to greet us.

"They've begun the test. It takes most people three hours to complete." And, with one swift motion, she was back out the door and closed it behind her.

"Sheesh," someone from another table called out. "Three hours?"

"I should have brought a book," I joked.

I did my best to kill the time. I made small talk with anyone who'd talk to me. I got up and paced around the room. I looked—twice—at the contents of the vending machine before realizing I didn't hate myself to take my chances on any of it. I considered seeing how rusty the water coming out of the fountain was but decided against it.

"Anyone have any cards?" Victor asked. Crickets. It seemed like we were all unprepared for the amount of time we'd have to wait in that room.

Whenever I felt anxious, I got up and paced around the room. You'd have thought I was a soon-to-be father in the '50s, pacing around the waiting room while his wife was giving birth. I paced and paced, anxious and nervous.

• • • • ● • ● • • •

The door opened for the first time around two-and-a-half hours after the woman had come in. It was Victor's girlfriend, who ran over to him immediately and hugged him. "I passed." I heard her whisper to him. "I did it."

Victor picked her up and spun her around twice. I couldn't help but smile. She was the first person to complete the test and passed. It took the glum feeling out of the room, a bit. The lights felt brighter. The sadness and disappointment that hung in the air seemed to thin.

More people came in, handfuls at a time. All greeting their loved ones, all of them having passed the test. Hugs and kisses and high-fives everywhere.

The tension in the room was lifting as time went on.

Couples and pairs left, one after another. The crowd was thinning, and I began worrying about Marty. The woman hadn't said there was a time limit, but it felt like he was there much longer than most people who'd come out already.

Another couple reunited. Another successful test. Another new American.

By the time Marty came in, only three other people were in the room with me. All four of us were clearly anxious, myself still choosing to pace around the back of the room.

"I'm done," Marty said, barely audibly.

Oh no, I thought to myself. He didn't look like someone who'd just passed the test.

"Well?" I said, stopping in my tracks and turning to make eye contact with him.

"God Bless America," he said, saluting a flag that didn't exist in the room.

"You did it?"

"I did it!"

I ran across the room and gave him a bear hug. "I'm so proud of you!"

"I'm so proud of me, too!"

"So that's it? You're an American now?"

"That's it. It's that simple. I get my papers in the mail in a week or so. We can come to a ceremony where they'll give me a little American flag and take my picture."

"Marty, that's so amazing. I'm so happy for you!"

"Like I said. America is my home now. And now I have the legal proof that I belong here, too."

2011

Get My Ducks In A Row

Marty and I were sitting around one afternoon when, out of the blue, he blurted out, "I think I want to go to college."

"I'm sorry, what?"

"Well, now that I am an American, I thought I should get an American education. No?"

"I mean, that's great and all. But why?"

"There's a lot of things left in life I'd like to learn."

"You've sure come a long way since I first showed you the internet."

"You opened my eyes to things back then that I could have never imagined."

"You seemed to love learning new things."

"I had a big appetite for information. I didn't have the same access to the internet in any of the places we lived before coming to America."

It'd never really crossed my mind, honestly. The fact that Marty was so many other places before I met him walking down my street in the middle of the night all those years ago. I'd never given any of it much thought. I'd never questioned where he was or how they learned new things there. I'd done that thing I always do; I learned the new information but did not question any of it.

"So you're hoping to get that same experience by going to college?"

"I would hope so. Did you go? What do you think?"

I reached out and grabbed the remote, pausing the television. "I didn't go to college. I got a job straight out of high school and started working hard to make my own path."

"Do you think it's a good idea?"

"I think," I thought for a second, "if you want to do it, you should do it."

"Will it benefit me?"

"Well, let's look at it objectively. It costs a fortune."

"It does? Why? Schools in other countries cost very little."

"Other than calling it American greed, I honestly don't know why it's so expensive here."

"What else?"

"It'll be hard work."

"I don't mind working hard."

"What about your job?"

"I talked it over with my boss, and he said he is willing to be accommodating."

"You never really talk about work." I'd thought about saying that out loud for a long time but never actually brought it up. Marty had started working with his dad shortly before Jean Luc died, and neither talked about what they did for work.

"Much like Papa, I can't say much about what I do."

"What if I promise not to tell anyone?"

"Okay."

"What? Really?"

"No, not really. All I can tell you is that I work for the government."

"The American government?"

"No. Belgium. Our home country."

"You're not a spy, are you?"

"No!" He chortled. "I'm not a spy."

"Do you work with the American government at all?"

"There's some overlap," he said. "But that's all that I can say."

"Okay. So work is okay with you going to school?"

"Yes. As long as my work doesn't suffer, which I don't think it will."

"Will having a college education and degree help advance your career?"

"I'm not sure. I think it probably would."

"And what about money?"

"What do you mean?"

"Well," I said. "We talked about how expensive college will be. Will having a degree increase your salary enough to justify spending money on college?"

"Oh, yes, I understand. I believe it will, in the long term. It might take some time to offset the initial cost, but I believe it will."

"It seems like you've done your research on this."

"You know how I am. I like to have my geese in a row before talking to you."

"Ducks," I said. "Ducks."

"Ducks?" he looked at me, puzzled.

"It's ducks in a row, not geese in a row."

He laughed at himself. "Sometimes you wouldn't know I'm a foreigner. Sometimes I say dumb things like that."

"Sometimes you just say dumb things," I laughed.

We laughed together for a few minutes, but I could tell Marty was serious about his decision to go to college. It seemed like he'd thought everything out and was coming to me as a notification rather than asking me what I thought. I knew him well enough to know he'd already decided; nothing I'd say or bring up as a negative would change that.

And honestly, I had no objection to him going to college. Why would I? I wanted the best for him. I wanted him to be the best version of himself that he could be. So why not college?

"I'm proud of you," I finally said. "You'll do great."

"You think so?"

"Listen, buddy. You've got a thirst for knowledge, unlike anyone I've ever known. You love to learn. You absorb it like a sponge. So why wouldn't you go to college and do amazing?"

"You think so?" he asked again.

"I do. And if I can help in any way, you know I will. Help you study? Sure. Make flashcards for an upcoming test? I've got your back."

"How'd I get so lucky to have you as my best friend?"

"How'd I get so lucky?" I asked back, smiling.

"How do I pick a college?" he asked.

"You're barking up the wrong tree, there," I said. "I have no idea." One of the reasons I never went to college was that I found the whole thing overwhelming. Picking a school, finding financial aid, looking for scholarships, actually going, and learning. All of that felt so overwhelming that I never ended up going. Do I regret it? Some days. I looked into getting a degree once, and in my analysis, the cost outweighed the benefit. It would have made more sense if I had done it in my early to mid-twenties.

"There's so many of them," he said.

"I know," I said. "And I think Massachusetts has more colleges per capita than any other state. There's a ton in the city."

"I guess I have more research to do," he said. "But I'm glad that you're supporting me."

"That's how we roll," I said, holding on to the l sound to exaggerate the word for far longer than it needed to be said.

"You're such a dork," Marty said.

"You know it!"

The Worst Diagnosis

It'd been a year since we bought the house together, and both Marty and I were doing great. Our friendship had never been stronger. Both of our jobs were going great. Marty had just met a girl that he seemed to like, Jessica. I'd just gotten a promotion at work. Things were going perfectly. Until they weren't.

"Hey, Matt, can you come here for a second?" Marty called out to me from his bedroom just down the hall. I'd been sitting in mine reading the book one of my favorite films was based on—*The Prestige*.

"Coming," I said. "Just finishing up this chapter." Call it a quirk or idiosyncrasy, but I could never stop reading in the middle of a chapter. I always have to read to a good stopping point so my brain doesn't get confused when I pick the book back up.

"Thanks. No rush," he said back.

This volley of calling back and forth to one another down the hall was something we'd done fairly often since we moved in. Was it laziness? Possibly. Was it just because we were both too comfortable in our respective rooms to get up, and either of us walk down the hall to the other's room? Probably.

When I walked into his room, he was in his bathroom. The lights were on at maximum, almost blinding from the doorway. "You okay?" I asked as I walked further into the room toward the bathroom.

"I'm trying to see down my throat," he said.

"Well, that's the weirdest thing you've ever said to me. What?"

"My throat has been hurting the last few days. I've been coughing a lot. Didn't you notice it last night when we were watching the movie?"

"I guess I didn't notice."

"Can you look? See if you see anything?"

"Sure," I said, approaching him. "Turn toward the light."

He shifted his body toward the mirror so the lights above could illuminate his throat better. I first went left, then right, trying to find the optimal place in front of him to look down his throat but not also block the light.

"Do you see anything?"

"Stay still," I said. "I can't see down your throat if you're talking."

"Gooo ooo see anyhin?" he asked, trying to do so without moving his mouth at all.

"It's pretty red," I said. "Like, really red. Looks like maybe strep throat." I stepped back a bit.

"I hope not," he said. "I just breathed all over you."

"I hope not, too, but it's really red."

His throat was the color of the red Richie's Slush I'd eaten every summer as a kid. Bright, vibrant, red, almost so red that it scared me. I'm not a doctor, obviously, but it looked pretty serious to me.

"You should probably get to a doctor," I suggested. "Best to get it looked at."

"That's a good idea," he said, walking out into the bedroom, fumbling around on this blanket, looking for his cell phone.

"I can go with you if you need," I offered.

"Thank you," he replied. "Let me call them now."

• • • • • • • • •

We were in the waiting room at Marty's doctor's office within a couple of hours. Based on the description he'd given over the phone, his doctor thought it would be best to get him in and get him seen as soon as possible.

Marty had coughed almost the whole ride there, all twenty-five minutes. "It hurts," he said on more than one occasion.

When it was his turn, the nurse came over and put her hand on his shoulder, signaling to come back into the exam room. It struck me as odd, as only two other people were waiting at the practice, presumably to see other doctors.

She led him and me in tow back to the exam room, stopping to weigh him.

Once inside, she took his vitals and swabbed his throat.

"The doctor will be in momentarily," she said. "I hope you feel better soon."

Once she'd left the room and closed the door, he said, "She doesn't know how to say my name, I think. And rather than ask, she comes and touches me to come back to the room."

"Why wouldn't she just ask you?"

"I don't know. People are strange with foreigners," he said.

"Americans. You're an American now," I said lightheartedly, trying to lighten the mood. The room felt heavy, and I knew that wasn't helping him.

"Michel, hello," the doctor said, simultaneously knocking and entering without waiting for a response.

"He gets it," Marty said, nodding toward the doctor who'd pronounced his name correctly and seemingly with little effort.

"Hello," I said. "I'm Matt, Michel's friend." It struck me that it was possibly the first time I'd ever called him anything other than Marty. Before that moment, I couldn't recall another time when I'd called him Michel.

"Pleasure," the doctor said, bushing past me in the small room to make his way over to the exam table where Marty had been waiting.

"It's my throat," Marty said.

"I know," the doctor replied quickly. "That's why Janet took a throat culture. Open."

Marty opened his mouth, leaning his head back.

"Red," the doctor said. "Very red. Been coughing a lot?"

"Non-stop," I offered, trying to be helpful, as Marty still had the tongue depressor in his mouth. "All the time."

The doctor took the tongue depressor out and placed each hand on the sides of Marty's throat. "Not tonsils," he said. "Looks too red to be strep throat."

"What else could it be?" Marty asked.

"Probably just a bacterial infection," the doctor said. "Maybe a virus of some kind. Have you been doing anything out of the norm lately?"

"Not that I can think of," Marty responded, looking past the doctor to me inquisitively.

"Jessica?" I asked.

"Who's Jessica?" the doctor asked quickly.

"She's a girl I met recently. We've been spending time together."

"Kissing?" the doctor asked. I looked away, not to embarrass him. If he and Jessica had been making out, he hadn't told me about it.

"A little," he said. "Not much."

"It only takes one time. She could have given you something. Let's wait for the lab results. In the meantime, I'd like you to go downstairs to the blood lab and have some blood drawn, and we'll do tests on that."

"Yes, sir," Marty said, hopping off the table.

I followed him out of the room, my concern growing stronger by the moment. I'd never heard a doctor say that someone's throat was *too red* to be strep throat. I always thought a red throat was a surefire indicator of strep.

The two of us walked quietly down the hall to the elevator. I lacked the right words to say to be comforting, and I assumed Marty was too nervous to say anything.

The ding of the elevator felt louder than usual. I don't know why I remembered that detail from that day, but it was the last thing I remembered until we got in the car to head back to our house.

"You'll be okay," I assured him as we pulled out of the parking lot. "I know it." But, the reality was, I didn't know it. I'd hoped, obviously. I wanted to believe my best friend would be fine. That whatever this thing was, it would be minor, and they'd give him some penicillin or whatever, and he'd be fine. I wanted to remain positive and keep him in good spirits while we waited for the results from the throat culture and the blood work.

"I hope so," he said, turning to look out the window. Much like every other time I drove us anywhere, Marty stared out the window, taking in the scenery. It'd been a long time since he was as enthralled with everything around him as he once was, but he still loved to look at anything and everything as we drove places.

He coughed a handful of times on the way home.

· · · ● · ● ● · · ·

When we got back to the house, a woman was sitting on the front steps. It was not only an uncommon thing, but I don't think it'd ever happened before.

"You expecting someone?" I asked. I seemed to have noticed her before Marty did.

He turned to look across me, through the window, to the other side of the street, to our porch.

"It's Jessica," he said. "I texted her before we left the house."

"Did you tell her to come over?"

"No. But she said she was concerned," he said.

When we got out of the car, I went around to the back of the house to go through the back door. "I'll let you guys have some time," I said.

"Thanks," Marty said. I could barely hear him greet her as I got out of earshot of their position. I saw her hug him, and it seemed like his body collapsed into her a bit.

They were closer to one another than Marty had led on when he told me about her. The quick conversation with the doctor made it seem pretty casual, too, but the level of support I saw in that quick blink of an eye made me feel like it was something more.

I didn't judge or have any concerns or thoughts other than feeling happy for him. It'd just been him and I for so many years, especially after Brooke left me. I was happy that he seemed to have found something with someone.

No sooner had I closed and locked the back door did the front door open. Marty and Jessica came in, and we stood across the house from one another. The front-to-back living room separating us. We had this brief, momentary pause of awkwardness. A silent, hanging, unsaid phrase lingered in the air. That moment of "I just left you to come in here, but here you are," hung.

"Hi," I said after a moment.

"Right, of course," Marty said. "This is Matt."

I did a sort of half-assed wave, barely moving, being completely awkward with my movements.

"Jessica," she said, waving back.

We were thirty or so feet apart, and it felt weird to stand there.

"I'll give you some time to talk," I said, going to the kitchen to grab a drink before heading upstairs to my bedroom.

"Her throat isn't red," Marty said.

"What's that?" I called back, pulling my head from the fridge.

"No redness on Jessica," he called back, loud enough for me to hear him. "She feels fine. No cough."

I walked back to the entryway to the living room and found them sitting next to one another on the couch. "Okay. Then we wait for the test results," I said. "We just wait."

A New Man

I won't pretend that the next eight months were easy. I won't sit here and tell you I didn't pray for the first time in decades. And I certainly won't lie and tell you I didn't do it every night.

And I definitely don't want to gloss over Marty being sick. It was an incredibly heavy time in our lives.

Marty's red throat was an early indicator of esophageal cancer. A type of cancer with an incredibly low survival rate. A type of cancer that kills almost everyone who gets it. A type of cancer that I was sure would take my best friend from me.

But Marty's a fighter. He's a tough son of a bitch, and he wouldn't quit. Even when his hair fell out from the treatments. Even when he lost thirty pounds, even when he didn't want to fight anymore, he kept fighting.

I vividly remember him telling me he wasn't ready to be with his father yet. That he had more things he needed to accomplish before his time was up. He insisted he'd beat the cancer.

He kept fighting, so I kept praying.

Jessica—who'd stay by his side throughout the ordeal—and I would trade off being at the hospital with him. We'd trade off hours of sitting with him when he was getting treatment or had an appointment. And, for the brief period he was hospitalized, we'd trade off in shifts of sitting with him. Sometimes, he didn't say much while I was there, but having him know one of us was with him probably felt nice for him.

It was the longest eight months of my life. Day after day, hour after hour, hoping for good news. We held our collective breath every time the doctor came in with new test results. Waiting patiently while the doctor opened the folder they were carrying and scanned over the results before giving them to us. Holding on to that hope that *this* test would be the one that we were waiting for. The one with the word every single person in the history of humankind who's been diagnosed with cancer waits for. Remission.

It was two days before my thirty-third birthday when we got that news.

Dr. Van Huasen, his primary oncologist, came into the room. He was doing something he hadn't previously done. He was smiling.

"Good morning, Michel. Good morning, Matt. Jessica," he nodded from left to right as she and I sat on opposite sides of Marty. His office was cold, literally and figuratively. There were no family photos, no decorations of any kind. Just his degrees from Boston University and Johns Hopkins University. His large oak desk separated him from the three of us as he sat down and tucked himself in.

He plopped the manilla folder on the desk, flipping open to the first page. Presumably, the test results we were there to hear.

It was uncommon for Jessica and I to be at an appointment, but, on that day, for whatever reason, we screwed up our scheduling, and we both showed up. It turned out to be, as they say, a happy coincidence.

"It's good news," he said after briefly looking down. He pulled his glasses off and placed them on the paperwork in front of him. "As of your last scan, there are no signs of cancer."

"None?" Marty asked, seemingly unassured.

"None. But that doesn't mean it can't or won't come back."

"This is wonderful," Jessica said, reaching over the armrests separating her and Marty and hugging him tightly. I placed my hand on his shoulder, showing my support while recognizing that he wanted to show her affection first.

"We need to be diligent about appointments," Dr. Van Huasen said. "You need to come in yearly to get re-tested and screened."

"Yes, sir. I will."

"I knew you'd do it," I said, mostly under my breath.

"Do what?" Marty asked, having heard my rumbling.

"Beat it."

"Well, let's not get ahead of ourselves," the doctor said. "Cancer is usually a sneaky lady and can come back quickly sometimes. She can sneak up on you when you're not paying attention. You two are pretty constant people in his life, right?"

Jessica and I both nodded in unison. "Yes," I said.

"You need to make sure he gets screened every year and takes care of himself the rest of the time."

"I'll do that," she said.

"Me too," I said.

She and I had gotten to know each other pretty well over the eight months Marty was in treatment. She'd spent quite a bit of time at the house, tending to anything Marty needed. And, since he slept a lot after treatments, she and I would talk. I got to like her and saw what he liked about her. She was kind and compassionate, two emotions I knew were important to Marty. She was helpful and fun and had a wicked sense of humor. We initially bonded over television. She entered the living room one day and asked if she could join me. I was watching *Modern Family*, which had just started airing a few years before. I'd been watching it. She'd never seen it.

Aside from Marty, I'd say Jessica became one of my closest friends. That old saying of misery loves company is true. In the darkest days, when Marty was sick, she and I were there for each other. And honestly, I don't think I could have done it alone. I can't speak for her, but I know that I would not have been able to be there for him as much as he needed, and I was beyond thankful that she helped with half of the duties.

• • • • • • • • • •

We left the doctor's office that day feeling happy, refreshed, and renewed. Marty cried a number of times throughout the day. While he never got answers to the questions he'd ask me all the time throughout the process—why me? Why is this happening? Will it happen again?—knowing that he was, at least for now, in remission meant a lot to him. To all three of us.

"I'm so happy for you," I said, getting into the car.

Marty and Jessica got into the back seat together. He scooted into the middle seat, buckled himself in, and put his head on her shoulder. She was right behind me so I could see them in the rear-view mirror.

She leaned over and kissed him on the head. A few tears fell from her eyes, and I could tell Marty was still crying a bit, but his head was nuzzled into her shoulder so I couldn't see his eyes.

Although I didn't shed any tears, I felt very emotional that day. I felt this intense welling up of it all hitting me in the chest, like the worst anxiety I've ever felt. I felt it hit me like a punch. Many times over the previous eight months, it occurred to me that my best friend could die at any moment. He could be gone at any time. And I hated that feeling. That feeling of being powerless to help. Of, sometimes, not knowing what to do or say. The only thing I was able to do for him was be there. Sometimes, carrying him up or down the stairs or to and from the car if he couldn't walk himself. Bringing him his favorite pizza and beer when he didn't want to eat. I made sure on the nights that Jessica stayed at the house that I left them to their privacy but still being available, should I be needed.

All those emotions hit me, and I sat in the parking lot, looking at them together in the backseat. She held him, and he clung to her like she was his lifeline. And although some friends would be jealous of the relationship, I was happy for him. For them. I felt love for them both, and I loved them together. I was happy they'd found each other and hoped they'd stay together.

When I finally snapped out of it, I drove out of the parking lot toward the highway. I'd hoped it would be the last time we'd ever have to go to Dana Farber Cancer Institute ever again. While I appreciated their work there and how they helped countless people over the years, I never wanted to have a reason to go back there again. Not for Marty. Not for myself. Not for anyone I knew. I'd hoped that as we literally left the building in our rearview, we were also permanently leaving it behind.

• • • • • • • • •

Marty looked like a new man when we got home. Although he was still down twenty or more pounds and had sunken eyes, he looked happy. He was smiling for the first time in a long while. He was energetic, although still visibly exhausted from his battle.

"What should we watch?" Marty asked as he flopped down on the chaise lounge end of the couch. "And when will the pizza be here?"

I laughed. I hadn't even ordered pizza, but I knew his asking for food was a good sign.

"I'll get the drinks," Jessica said, heading down the hall toward the kitchen.

"I'll call Papa Gino's," I said, grabbing my phone from my pocket.

Marty fumbled through the couch cushions, looking for the remote for the television. He'd had it on and tuned to TNT, where a rerun of *Friends* was on before I got off the phone with Papa Gino's.

"Twenty to thirty minutes," I said as Jessica returned from the kitchen. Her arm held Marty's beer, and she had a drink for herself and me in each of her hands.

"Thanks," I said, cracking open the can. "I know this is corny, but can we raise our drinks?" The three of us raised our glasses and cans. "To Marty," I said. "The strongest guy I know. A guy who kicked cancer's ass and will do it over and over again if need be."

"Hear! Hear!" Jessica said.

The three of us drank our congratulatory drinks, waiting for Marty's beloved Papa Gino's to show up. We watched hours of television that night.

"I'm glad you're okay, bud," I said during a commercial break as the delivery driver showed up.

"I'm glad I'm okay, too," he said, reaching out and grabbing my hand.

It was a good hour before I realized it was the first time Marty had felt well enough to sit on the couch with me. Every other night, he'd be up in bed with Jessica, sitting upright, watching the television in his room, or playing on his laptop. Even though he'd been feeling better for a few weeks since the last treatment, he hadn't come downstairs other than to get something to eat or to leave for an appointment.

It was one of the scariest things I've been through. It was certainly the hardest thing Marty had ever done. Not everyone is as lucky as Marty was. Not everyone gets to have that celebratory drink. Not everyone catches it early. Not everyone survives. Get screened. See your doctor regularly. It could save your life. Make your loved ones go, too. It could save their life.

2012

A Life-Changing Offer

I'd never really had a *real* career before. I'd had jobs I'd go to, put in the work, and clock out at the end of the day.

Retail. Restaurants. Customer Service. Insurance Agent. I'd run the gamut of different types of jobs. But when I had my first life-changing job, I understood what it meant to put in the effort to get ahead.

Late in 2011, a friend of mine reached out to me about a job opportunity. She'd been at a startup for a couple of years, and an enormous tech company was acquiring them. At that point, I'd been pretty happy with my job, so I wasn't necessarily looking for anything new, but the idea intrigued me.

Remember what I said about memory being weird? About the things you remember being odd, sometimes peculiar? I still remember the thing she said that got me interested. "Name your price."

She went on and on about how big the company buying the startup was and how they'd pay me whatever I wanted because she knew I'd be good at the job.

At the job I was at when this offer came in, I was paid roughly $60,000 a year. That was decent money for where I lived. The cost of living wasn't astronomical, and that money let me live a pretty comfortable life. Especially having Marty around to split the costs of things.

When she told me to name my price, I took her literally. I asked for 50% more than I was making at my job. Ninety thousand dollars. A life-changing amount of money.

After taxes, it'd be around an extra two grand a month. That was enough to cover the entire mortgage on the house, should I ever need to cover Marty's share.

It was a no-brainer. If they met that number, I'd leave my job and go work there.

They did. And, when you added in all the perks they offered and the annual bonus, I made six figures.

Me. Someone who didn't go to college. Barely finished high school. I had no formal education or training in the job I was about to take on. Making over a hundred grand a year. I couldn't believe it.

• • • • ● • ● • • •

"You're not going to believe this," I told Marty, printout of the job offer in hand.

"What's that?"

"A new job offer."

"What is it?"

"Technical support manager for a software company."

"Do you know how to do that?" Jessica asked. She'd been sitting beside Marty on the couch, watching television with him.

"Kind of. I've done customer service in the past. It's not too different from that."

"That's great," Marty said.

"They're going to pay me a literal fortune," I said, handing him the offer. I watched his eyes scan through the paper, looking for the numbers, ignoring all the other legal jargon.

"What?"

"Yes," I said. "That's the right number."

"That's twice what I make!" Jessica said, leaning over Marty's shoulder to read the offer letter.

"Me too!" Marty added.

"I'm going to take it," I said. "It requires some travel out to the office in California. But I think it'll be worth it."

"This is so exciting for you," Jessica said. "Congratulations!"

"It is a great offer," Marty added.

"When will you start?" Jessica asked.

"There's some legal stuff they have to do first: background check, references, et cetera. But I think probably in a few weeks if everything works out according to plan."

"That's so exciting," Marty said. "Are you nervous?"

"Very. Starting a new job is always stressful and causes such anxiety in me."

"I'm sure you'll do great," Jessica said. She got up and hugged me. She did this incredibly comforting thing when she hugged people; she always rubbed your back. Up and down, three times. It was like she was programmed to do it. It was such a tiny gesture, but it was so welcoming.

• • • • • • • • • •

The background check for the new mega-corporation was intensive. I'd had background checks before—at one of my customer service jobs in the past, I'd had to get government clearance to work with the FBI on something—but this was another level. They asked for personal and professional references. They asked for the names and contact information of my most recent teachers. They asked about whether I'd ever done drugs or not. They asked if I knew anyone affiliated with any known hate organizations.

They asked every possible thing you could think of.

I felt like I was applying to work at the NSA.

It didn't end with the questionnaire, either. Once I'd answered all their questions on paper, they sent me an online meeting link for the interview portion of the background check. Not an interview for the job, mind you. I'd already done those interviews and passed them. This was an interview for the background check with a third-party company. The mega-corporation contracted them to vet all the new employees coming into the company.

It was *intense*. The guy was like a drill instructor. He fired question after question, a lot of them repeating from the paper form I'd filled out prior.

He asked the typical "Are you a psychopath?" types of questions. The "there's a train on a track. Do you let it kill one person or all the people?"

"There's one lightbulb in a room and three switches outside. You can only go in once. How do you know which switch controls the lightbulb?"

Having problem-solving questions in a background check interview was odd, but we did—a handful of them.

If you're curious what the answer to that question is—I looked it up after because I got it wrong—it's simple: Turn on one switch. Wait ten to fifteen minutes. Turn that switch off and turn another one on. Go into the room and touch the light bulb. If it's on but cool to the touch, the switch you just turned on is the right one. If it's off but hot, it was the first switch you tried. If it's off and cool, it's the third switch.

What's weird is that, since then, I've been asked that same question in interviews two other times.

The other common problem-solving one I get is the one with the stones and scales. You can Google that one if you're curious.

• • • • • • • • • •

I'll never forget my first day at that job. They flew me out to California to meet the team in person—I'd only interviewed over the phone—and put me up in the Hilton. It was all very last minute since the background checks took forever to come through. It was January 9th, 2012. I remember everything about that day: what I wore, what I listened to on the walk from the hotel to the office, and what the person who let me into the office wore.

While the mega-corporation takeover was completed in August, the company hadn't moved into its offices yet. They were still in a very small office setting. It felt like a three-bedroom apartment that'd been hollowed out to become an office, but I was assured it was a legally permitted office space.

Once I got settled at a desk, they handed me a laptop, and I futzed around until the guy who would train me showed up.

Between sitting down and Ruben—the trainer—showing up, the CEO, Alex, showed up. He did something I'd never seen a CEO do before and haven't since. He ran around the office and high-fived everyone. He roused the team and pumped them up for the work week by giving everyone a high-five.

Then he stopped at my desk, introduced himself, and spent a good ten minutes talking to me. He asked me questions to get to know me. He asked about my background. He asked why I decided to join the company.

I told him all about my friend, Linh, who had introduced me to the company. When she showed up at the office around ten, he ran over and thanked her, giving her two high-fives.

It was such a surreal experience that I never thought would happen. Up until then—and, I guess now—I thought of CEOs as very strict, formal, uptight types. Up in their high offices on the 85th floor of the corporate tower, looking down on the common person. I'd never, not even once, thought I'd get a high-five from a CEO. But I did. Alex high-fived me that morning to start my career in technology. A career I would stay in. A career I was able to build upon, moving up in the world. Moving from job to job, increasing my salary and benefits, and eventually managing a team of software engineers.

It was life-changing and something I'll never forget.

Getting Over It

Our routine on the weekends had never changed. No matter how sick Marty was feeling. No matter what jobs we had. No matter who was in our lives. No matter what we needed to get done around the house. We always watched a movie on Saturday nights.

Throughout the day, we'd get whatever chores and tasks done that needed doing. We'd make sure we had groceries for the upcoming week. We'd go to the bank to do any banking business we needed to do. We'd make sure all the bills were paid.

But on Saturday night, we'd watch a movie. Marty and I had amassed an enormous collection of DVDs and Blu-rays. We'd take turns picking what movie to watch. I'd pick one week, Marty would pick the next, and Jessica would pick the third week. The only rule was "no complaining". No matter what movie was picked, you couldn't whine about it. It usually wasn't a problem, except for the few times Jessica picked some outrageous romantic comedy Marty and I had to suffer through.

The Saturday night in question was no different from any other. It was Marty's turn to pick. He picked *The Avengers*. He and I had gone to see it earlier in the year on one of the very few days when he felt up to going out in public between doctor's appointments and tests. But Jessica hadn't seen it. She wasn't the biggest superhero genre fan, but she was always willing to suck it up and follow the no-complaining rule.

We were about a third of the way through the movie when it hit me. All of a sudden, I felt this sudden overwhelming feeling. It was happiness.

I looked across the couch at my absolute best friend in the world, cuddling with the girl he was clearly in love with. I looked around at our house; not too masculine, but it was clear that two thirty-something men lived there. I glanced out the window into our neighborhood, which was full of people we liked and considered friends. People who would go out of their way to stop by and say hey because they were out for a walk in some way, shape, or form. People who checked in constantly on Marty while he was sick.

It felt so surreal—this feeling of knowing that things were good for the first time in a long time. I had a great job that was providing a new way of life that I didn't ever imagine possible. Marty and I had a stronger friendship than ever, mostly due to his cancer scare. Jessica was a very close friend of mine. Things, as they say, couldn't have been better.

It made me feel so complete. This sense of perfection. Of completion.

Then, all of a sudden, Brooke popped into my head—first, just a flash of her face. Then, I heard her voice. I heard her that night yelling at me. I felt that pain all over again.

Those weeks after she left were tough. I'd thought I had a partner for life. I thought, being my wife, she'd have stuck with me through any crisis that arose, including my friend's crisis. For whatever reason, I thought that the vows we took with one another meant the same to her as they did to me.

I felt incomplete for such a long period of time after she left. Those months of not knowing where she was or what she was doing. If she was safe or not. If she'd moved on. It felt so infuriating. To have it all end so abruptly felt horrible.

And, listen, I get it. I understand how relationships can fall apart. I understand it's not like it used to be, where couples would get married at 18 and stay married until they died. The divorce rate keeps climbing higher and higher, and that's fine. I don't fault her for leaving. I guess, on some level, I fault her for how she left.

She was just gone in the blink of an eye. Disappeared, for lack of a better word. And then went radio silent. She didn't answer calls, texts, or emails. All of her friends cut me off from Facebook immediately. They also stopped responding to texts and emails. I'll admit I never tried calling any of them.

All of this flashed before my eyes for some reason. All of a sudden, it interrupted my moment of zen, of pure happiness. Like life or karma or something reminded me that everything was not perfect. It's not all roses and rainbows and unicorns.

I zoned out from the movie for a bit. The thoughts of the past couple of years floating around in my head, reminding me of everything I'd been through. Everything that Marty had been through. Everything he'd been there for me through and vice versa.

But then, something happened that hadn't happened in a long time. I was able to snap myself out of it. I didn't wallow in my sadness. I didn't focus on the unhappiness of the past. I didn't let the small bit of depression I'd felt at the time creep in and take over my every thought. Instead, I focused on the positive things. I circled back to my best friend and his love. I circled back to our house, my job, and how great everything had been going for me lately.

I focused so intently on the feeling of pure happiness that the feelings of incompletion fell by the wayside. It just disappeared in the blink of an eye.

The happiness took over.

I couldn't help but smile.

It was a valuable life lesson. No matter how tough times can get or how difficult or trying things can seem in the moment, they usually pass. If you put your big boy (or girl) pants on, suck it up, and push through, you'll usually make it out on the other end. That, no matter what, you have to try. You have to do your best to see the positive side of things.

It's a lesson I seemingly taught myself, but one I've tried to live by since that day.

Whenever I've felt down or unhappy, I've tried focusing on that specific day. To focus on that feeling I had that day, where I could see and feel the pure joy and happiness I had in my life.

It also makes me crave Papa Gino's because, as usual, it was what we were eating that night.

THE END OF OUR ERA

It'd been a year and a half since Jessica came into Marty's life, and thus mine, when Marty came to me, perplexed.

"Hey," he said, hanging his head.

"Hey bud," I said, pausing the television. "What's up?"

"There's something I need to talk to you about."

I motioned for him to sit down on the couch. "Go for it."

"Well, as you know, Jessica and I have been pretty serious."

"Uh, huh."

"And she's been staying here a lot."

"Right. That's fine with me. I like her."

"Good, good. But..."

"But what?"

"We were thinking we might want to get our own place."

"Oh," I thought and said out loud at the same time. "I guess that makes sense, right? It's been a while since you've been together."

"It's not that I don't want to live here with you anymore."

"I know, bud. I get it. It's time to see where your next steps take you."

In my head, though, I was screaming. Not in a bad way. Not in any way that would make him feel bad if I were to scream out loud. But screaming internally, just because I was usually averse to change. Uprooting my way of living, of how I'd lived for the last couple of years, was something I wasn't prepared for.

"It won't be tomorrow. It won't be next month. But we're starting to look at our options," he said somewhat reassuringly.

"OK, so later this year?"

"Maybe. It'll depend on what happens."

"Do you want to sell the house?"

"I think that makes sense, doesn't it?"

"I guess so," I said, trying to figure out if there were any other options. "I don't have the money to buy you out."

"I didn't think you did. And if it were that easy, I'd give you my half."

"Don't be stupid, Marty. I wouldn't let you do that."

"I would, though. Or I'd try, at least."

"You really love her, huh?" I don't know where that question came from. I knew he loved Jessica, though I'd never heard him say it in my presence. I'm sure he told her in private and vice versa. They had the public-facing impression of being very much in love.

"I do," he said. "I can picture myself marrying her in the future."

"That's great, buddy," I said. "I'm happy for you."

"It's just that she's been there for me through the whole cancer thing. She seems to get me. She understands all my weird foreigner quirks. She fits, you know what I mean?"

"I get it. I felt that same way when I met Brooke. It felt like she just slotted into my life, so naturally, it felt like she'd always been there."

"That's exactly it!" he seemed excited. "I've been struggling with wording it, but that's precisely how it is. It's like she's always been there."

"That's great, man. I really am so happy for you guys."

• • • • • • • • •

Later that same night, we had a house meeting. It was something we did often over the year and a half that Jessica had been part of our lives. It was a time for us to get together, discuss house matters, vent about anything we needed to complain about, and generally work out any issues we had about the house or our living situation.

The rule for house meetings was that we didn't take things personally. We didn't get upset, either. It was just a way for us to all get together and talk.

That night's conversation was, obviously, about selling the house and us moving on with our separate lives.

"You're sure you're okay with this?" Jessica started the meeting by handing me the container of Kung Pau Chicken. Chinese food was the tradition for house meeting night. We usually ordered from Chang's, just up the road from the house.

"I am. I promise," I said.

"It's a big change," Marty added. "You know that, right?"

"Listen, guys, I'm a grown man. You don't have the pussyfoot around me with this."

"I do not know this pussyfoot," Marty said. "What is pussyfoot?"

"It means he thinks we're treating him like a little kid," Jessica replied. "Which we're not." She reached out and put her hand on my arm.

"I know, I know," I said. "You're just trying to spare my feelings, which I appreciate. But it's fine. I promise."

"Okay," Marty finally acknowledged. "It's okay. We get it now."

"So what's the plan, then?" I asked.

"Well, I think we try to sell the house first," Marty said. "We're lucky that it's worth more now than when we bought it."

"That's good. That'll make it less painful, financially," I said. "Do we know any real estate people?"

"A girl I work with does real estate on the side," Jessica said.

"Would she be willing to help us figure it all out?" I asked.

"I'm sure she would," Jessica said.

"Okay, so let's start there. I guess look at other houses and see what they've sold for?"

"I know she'll do a lot of that, too," Jessica said, motioning toward the Vegetable Lo Mein.

I handed it over to her. "I'm going to miss you. Both of you."

"We'll miss you, too," Marty said. "But we will still see each other, right?"

"I feel like I'm a teenager, and I'm getting broken up with," I said, laughing.

"You're not getting broken up with," Marty said.

"No," Jessica added. "We're just cooler than you and don't want to be your friend anymore."

We all laughed together. I'd gone into the house meeting worried and anxious. Nervous that they'd tell me they had already found a new place to live and would be moving out this weekend or something. I was nervous they'd be so eager to leave that they wouldn't consider my feelings. But, honestly, it felt the opposite. It felt like they were so accommodating of my feelings. It felt like they wanted to ensure I was okay with the whole thing before even discussing the next steps. And that made me feel loved.

"Okay, so you'll talk to your friend, and we'll see what happens next?"

"That's it," Jessica said. "Hopefully, it won't be a big deal, and the whole thing will be easy."

"I hope so," Marty said.

"Me too," I added.

2013

Moving Out & Moving In

It turns out it was a big deal. Selling the house took six months. Six long months of lowball offers. Six months of legal paperwork. Six months of open houses and private showings and buyers making ridiculous requests before putting an offer in. One couple said they'd only buy the house if we put a deck on the back. They wanted us to spend tens of thousands of dollars to build a deck so that they would buy the house.

We got a good laugh out of that.

Our realtor, Bernadette, was super helpful throughout the entire thing. She said it was common for buyers to make requests, but she'd never heard of any request that insane before.

"Fix the squeaky door? Sure. But build a deck? No," she joked.

When it was all said and done, Marty and I found new houses we could afford, using the profits from selling the house we owned together.

Initially, I lost out on the first house I wanted to buy because the timing of selling our house didn't align with when the sellers of that other house needed to sell by. It sucked to watch it fall through, but, as they say, it all worked out for the best.

Marty and I ended up with houses just three miles apart.

I know what you're thinking. That's not that far. And you're right, it's not. It is, however, farther than we've lived apart since I moved in with Brooke, and he was still living back in my mom's neighborhood with Jean Luc.

And it's not *that* far. But going from seeing your best friend every day, having breakfast and dinner together, and watching TV at night to having all of that gone virtually in the blink of an eye is a lot.

Marty had been my rock through so much of my life over the last decade. He'd been there for me through the best and worst moments, and having him be asleep out of earshot of me felt like it would be life-changing.

Honestly, it was for the first few months. But we all adjusted.

· · · · ● · ● · · · ·

"I guess this is it," I said, holding the last of my boxes, ready to go out the door to the moving truck for the last time.

"I guess so," Marty said. He still had a substantial pile of boxes for him and Jessica to move to their truck.

The neighbors probably thought we were weird. On the same day, two different moving trucks probably weren't super common.

"I don't want to make a big deal out of it," I said. The two guys I'd hired to help me move were finishing loading up my bed frame onto the truck and stood looking at me as if silently saying, "The clock's ticking, pal." They weren't the most patient people I'd ever met.

"We'll see you for dinner tonight," Jessica said from across the room.

"Your place or mine?"

It was our first time in years to think about where we'd have dinner. Usually, our discussions were around *what* to have, but not where.

"I'll probably be more unpacked by dinner time than you guys will," I said. "You've got stuff for two people, and I'm alone."

It came out of my mouth more pathetic than I'd intended, as if the words slipped out without my brain controlling them. How I said "alone" made it sound desperate, as if I was miserable in my loneliness.

The reality was that I was okay. I'd gotten used to being single since Brooke left. Well, maybe not since she left, but months after, and certainly once the divorce was finalized, I came to grips with my bachelorhood.

I'd never lived alone before, so I was looking forward to that somewhat. And owning my own place was an exciting prospect. Being able to have the freedom of being by myself excited me a bit. But, man, did I sound sad the way I said that.

Jessica ran over and gave me a big hug, rubbing my back like she always did. "Now scoot," she said. "We'll see you tonight."

Marty then took his turn hugging me. He squeezed me tight. "Thank you," he said. "Thanks for everything."

"Thank you," I said back. "I love you, buddy."

"I love you, too," he said.

Then I walked out the door of that house for the very last time. I carried the last box—full of my immediate necessities— toothbrush, shower stuff, an outfit for tomorrow, the remote for the television—down the steps. I handed it to one of the movers, who plopped it into the last waiting space on the truck and hopped down, closing the door behind him.

They didn't wait for me to get into my car. They knew where they were going and had keys, so off they went to get to my new house. My new house. Mine. It felt weird to think, but I was sure I'd get used to it.

As I buckled my seat belt, I looked back at the door. Jessica and Marty were standing at the door, waving. They looked happy, and I was genuinely happy for them. While I knew I would be alone for a while, I was happy they had each other.

· · · · •· •· · ·

"Knock knock," I heard Marty call out from the front door, through the screen, into my living room, stacked high with boxes and misplaced furniture.

"Come in," I said. "It's open."

I heard the screen door fly open and slowly close behind them as they entered. "I'm in the kitchen," I said.

"Marco," Marty called out.

"You've been here before, you doofus. You know where the kitchen is." Marty had looked at the house with me before I bought it. He'd been with me all three times I'd been there, helping me figure out where I'd put my stuff and walking through the tour with the home inspector. Everything. He'd been there.

"Oh, right," he said, chuckling to himself.

"Hey," Jessica said, kissing me on the cheek.

"You guys get everything moved out?"

"Yep. Just in time for the new owners to show up."

"Did you give them the keys?"

"I guess they didn't trust us," Jessica said.

"Huh?" I asked.

"They showed up with their own new locks. They were changing the locks when we drove away."

"Note to self," I said. "Change the locks."

It hadn't even occurred to me that the previous owners could come waltzing into my house anytime because I didn't change the locks.

"What's for dinner?" Marty asked. "Oooh. Nevermind." He'd spotted the pizza box on the counter as I fumbled with a larger-than-needed-to-be box to pull out some paper plates.

"Beer's in the fridge. I got the white wine you like, Jess."

She swung around, kissed me on the cheek again, and opened the fridge. Bachelor's life to the extreme. A six-pack of Miller Lite for Marty, a single bottle of the white wine she liked, my root beer, a half-used bottle of ketchup I brought from the other house, and the Tupperware with a meal my mom had made me and dropped by earlier. "In case you don't have time to get anything," she said, whisking through the quick tour I gave her, ending at the door to see her out. As much as I'd have loved her to stay, I needed to get her out to continue unpacking and getting enough of my life together to host my friends for dinner that night.

"You know us so well," Marty said, making himself at home at the table in my dining room. It was stacked high with boxes, both on the table and on the floor. We had to move them around a bit to make room for our plates.

"It's coming along nicely," Marty said.

"Ha," I laughed. "No, it's not. I feel like I barely did anything today."

"It'll happen. It takes time," Jessica added.

"How much did you two get done today?"

"Not much. We set up our furniture in the bedroom and unpacked our bathroom stuff, and that's about it. We were going to stop at Stop and Shop on our way home and get some groceries."

"Groceries," I said. "I should do that, too. Note to self."

"What would you do without us?" Marty asked.

"I guess we'll find out in a couple of days. Make sure to check on me." I laughed.

Although they likely knew I was joking, they exchanged glances with worrying faces.

"I'm kidding!" I said. "I'll be fine. I swear."

• • • ● • ● • • •

That first night in the new house was ... what's the word? Not terrifying. Not scary. Just, I guess, different. I wasn't used to any of the noises the house made. I wasn't used to being at the end of the street where no cars would drive by, except those coming down the road to turn around or to go to their homes. I wasn't used to how the headlights of those cars would reflect off my neighbor's mailbox sometimes and shine through my living room window, making me think someone was pulling into the driveway.

And I certainly wasn't used to the layout of the house. I bumped into more things than I could count when I turned the lights off downstairs on my way upstairs.

I fumbled for the doorknob to the bathroom at 3 a.m., in the dark, when I woke up to go pee.

Eventually, it'd all become second nature, I told myself. Just be patient, it's new.

I fell asleep to music that night. Something I never did in the other house because I was worried it would keep Marty awake, even at the lowest volume. I left the radio on until I woke up to go to the bathroom, then shut it off.

As different as everything was, I loved my new place. It wasn't huge. It wasn't modern, upgraded, or fancy. But it was mine, and I could afford it on my own. I was able to use my portion of the money from the other house as the down payment, which brought my mortgage down well within my budget.

On my way back to bed from the bathroom in the hall, there was a moment of pure serenity. I paused briefly at the top of the stairs and listened to the silence. Not a peep from anywhere. The only thing I heard was the occasional sound of the screen door on the back of the house swinging open and closing against the door. And, a few days later, the nights were completely silent once I'd fixed that.

    I thought it'd help me sleep better, but it didn't. I needed the radio on to fall asleep for the rest of the years I lived in that house. Oddly, The silence was too much for my brain to rest.

A Normal Company Party

"I met a girl," I remember saying those words over the phone to Marty for the first time just a few days after I met her. Victoria. Or Vicky, as she sometimes liked to be called. I'd met her through a co-worker. We were at an "optional" company event that just happened to be held in Boston and not San Fransisco, though I can't recall why. You know the type of party, the one where they say it's optional, but if you don't show up, you get all sorts of flak from your manager and their manager and their manager? The one where that one person *always* gets drunk and embarrasses themselves. If that person is you, I'm sorry. But stop being a sloppy drunk. It's usually for a holiday or some big event at work; your team met their numbers for the quarter, you closed a big deal that'll keep the company afloat, or something big like that.

It's usually at some swanky place that they spent too much money renting out, thus negating the revenue from the big deal you closed to warrant the party. There are free drinks and free appetizers—which are, for some reason, always shrimp cocktail, tiny meatballs, and, if you're lucky, a tiny chicken and waffles stabbed onto a toothpick—the same people always show up, and they always form their little clique. While you, the ordinary person, stand alone off to the side, waiting for the handful of people from work you actually like to show up.

This particular party was because we'd closed one of those monstrous deals that almost doubled our annual revenue for my department. It was a big win, so the company wanted to celebrate us. For the first time I could remember, they offered a plus one.

Victoria was my friend Charles' plus-one. They were friends from college, and she had just moved to the area for a new job, so he wanted to get her "out of the apartment" since she hadn't gone out much since she moved in.

I was immediately stricken, giddy, almost, upon being introduced to her. She was so far out of my league I'd have to go up two leagues, and she'd have to come down a league just for me to play the same sport she was playing. She was exactly my type: long dark hair, crystal blue eyes, not too short, not too tall.

"This is Matt," Charles had said. I don't remember what I said, but it made her laugh. The very first thing I said, and she laughed so hard she almost choked on her tiny meatball.

I don't know what famous and brilliant person said that if you can get someone you're interested in laughing, you've got a foot in the door, but I hoped so much that they were right.

"Who is she?" Marty asked. "Should I come down and talk about this?"

"No, no. Stay at your house," I said. "I'm sure Jessica is getting hungry. It's almost dinner time."

Jess was a person of routine. She got increasingly frustrated if it was 6 p.m. and she didn't have food near her or on its way. I can't say I blame her. I get hangry, too.

"So, again, I ask. Who is she?"

"I met her last week at my company party. She's a co-worker's friend and just moved to the city."

"Tell me everything."

Sometimes, albeit infrequently, we acted like teenage girls. This entire conversation was one of those times. Like we were thirteen and had our first crush crushing on us back. It was one of the dorkiest things about our friendship, but I loved it so much.

I launched into the diatribe that I just told you. How we met. How she laughed. How I felt horrible that I almost made her choke to death within sixty seconds of meeting her.

"What happened then?" he asked.

"We talked. Charles went off to try to schmooze our boss because he's one of those people who believes networking and ass-kissing is more important to getting a promotion than doing good work."

"What did you talk about?"

"Well, it started innocently enough. The typical awkward questions people ask when they first meet. Where did you go to school? What do you do for work? Where did you grow up?"

"Started innocently? Did it get less innocent?"

"Well, no. I don't know why I said that," I said. "But it got more serious. We found a table in the corner and grabbed some drinks. The conversation turned to life goals. Where do you want to go? What do you want to do? Do you want to get married? Do you want to have kids?"

"What did you tell her?"

"I felt compelled to tell her the truth," I said. "I told her I'd been married before."

"You dumb," he said. It was one of those things he'd never quite grasped, with English being a non-native language to him. Instead of insulting me in some sort of proper way, he just called me a dumb. I loved his little incorrect phrases so much.

"I know. I am. I was. But, for some reason, I felt I needed to be honest with her from the get-go."

"How did she take it?"

"She seemed okay with it. She really understood when I explained why Brooke and I split up."

"So you told her about that?"

"I did. I told her about you and Jean Luc and how you needed me."

"What did she say?"

"She said it sounded like Brooke wasn't ready for marriage and maybe was looking for a way out. 'Who doesn't want their spouse to support their best friend?' she asked. And she is right. What kind of person does that?"

"Has she been married?"

"No, she said she works and moves around a lot for work. She hopes to stay in this area for a while because her new job seems more stable than others."

"What does she do?"

"She's a lawyer. Criminal defense, I think she said."

"That sounds important."

"I thought so," I said. "And it seemed like she loves her job."

"What else?"

"It just felt so natural. I hate cliches, you know that. But it felt like I'd known her for years. Like we were old friends, catching up. Like we just hadn't seen each other for a while."

"That is amaze!" He clapped, literally. I heard it over the phone. Then, muffled, I heard him tell Jessica. "He met a girl."

"Congrats!" I heard Jessica call out from a distance. She was most assuredly in the kitchen, probably preparing a meal for the two of them.

"What else?" Marty asked.

"We spent almost the whole night talking. At one point, Gerry, my boss, came over to introduce himself. And it was this awkward moment of him thinking she was my wife."

"Your wife?"

"Yes. Not my girlfriend. Not my fiancé. He went right to wife."

"That's strange."

"I know," I said. "But the funny thing is, neither of us corrected him. We just let him think it. And I introduced her, he made pleasantries, and then went off."

"What happened then?"

"We both burst out laughing. It was funny to us, not just that he assumed we were married, for some reason, but that neither of us corrected him."

"Why do you think he made that mistake?"

"I'm not sure. Maybe we just looked so comfortable together that he assumed? I don't really know."

"So you talked all night?"

"Until the event people told us we had to leave. We stayed almost beyond our welcome."

"Did you ask her out after?"

"It was late, and you know I'm a lightweight."

"What then? How did you end it?"

"She demanded that I give her my phone. She punched her number in and saved it in my contacts. 'Now call me', she said."

"Did you?"

"I did. Right then. Then she said, 'Now I have your number, too. Call me.' Then she kissed me on the cheek and hailed a cab home. Marty, bud. Holy moly. This girl."

"Did you call her? When did you call her? Tell me you called her."

"I texted her later that night to make sure she got home safely."

"Yes! Nice guy points!"

"We made plans to go out to dinner on Friday."

"I'm so happy for you, Matty!" He only called me Matty when he was excited about something. Probably because he knew I hated it. My mom was the only person to call me Matty regularly.

"Me, too," I said. "I'm happy and anxious and scared, all simultaneously."

"Be optimistic," he said. "Be open to love!"

"I'll try. I'll do my best."

"I'm so happy. I have to go now. Jessica is coming with dinner, and you know how she gets."

"Hey!" I heard her say. I pictured her fake slapping him on the shoulder, as she usually did when they were playing around.

"Okay. I'll talk to you soon. See ya, bud."

I Fell Down & She Spilled Water

You know that feeling you get when you just know something will go wrong? It's not anxiety. It's not fear. It's not nerves. It's just this feeling in the pit of your stomach that won't subside. No matter how much you reassure yourself, no matter how much you hear positive things from other people. You know something's about to get lit on fire and fall apart miserably.

That's how I felt the entire day leading up to my first date with Victoria. We'd been texting all week, getting to know one another more, and had made plans to meet up Friday night after work to grab a bite. Casual, we said. Nothing fancy. No pressure. Just a couple of people who felt some spark when they met, getting a meal together to see where things go.

So why did my brain seem to think the sky would fall? Why was I so fixated on something going catastrophically wrong?

I didn't throw up out of anxiety, but I came close to it. The closer it got to the end of the work day, the worse I felt.

Should I cancel? No. That's ridiculous, right? I mean, I *am* technically feeling sick. Should I reschedule? No, it'd just be worse next time.

Put on your big boy pants, Matt, and just do it. What's the worst that can happen?

The hours ticked by, slowly at first, but then faster and faster, to the point where I blinked, and it was 5 p.m.

We'd agreed to meet up at a restaurant she'd already been to since she moved to town. It was downtown and only about a ten-minute train ride from my office. I decided to walk not to get there early—hello, chronically being early to everything. It was a nice enough evening, and the city wasn't too busy with tourists at that time of year.

Walking turned out to be the worst idea. The whole way there, my nerves started acting up. All that anxiety I was *sure* I didn't have before had now shown up and was eager to remind me that my brain was a giant ball of goo.

I saw her when I turned the corner to the street where the restaurant was. She was already there, waiting. Ten full minutes before the time we agreed to meet. The part of me who hated tardiness was pleasantly surprised. I don't know what it is about waiting for someone—to join a meeting, to show up for an appointment, the doctor who is perpetually running behind schedule—but I absolutely hate it. It's the fastest way to get me on edge. And, thankfully, that wasn't an issue with Victoria—at least not that first night.

"Hey," she said as I approached.

"Hey, yourself." I'm such a wordsmith.

"You hungry?"

"Famished." Famished? What the hell, dude?

I opened the door and held it open, following her inside. The restaurant was fairly popular, so many people were waiting by the hostess station. "Grab a seat," I said. "I'll get us on the list."

After a quick exchange with the host, we were on the list and began our fifteen-to-twenty-minute wait for our table.

"Shouldn't be long," I said as I joined her on the waiting-to-be-sat bench.

"Great. I'm famished, too." I couldn't tell if she was genuinely using the word or mocking my stupidity.

"How was your day?" I asked.

"Pretty good. We had a big meeting today with all the partners about a big case they just took on."

"How'd that go? Do you like being a lawyer?" Truth be told, I didn't know what a criminal defense lawyer did other than what I'd seen on television, but when she told me that's what she did earlier in the week, I didn't ask immediately and felt like a moron now if I'd asked after pretending to know what it was all week. In hindsight, I should have just Googled it.

"I love it," she said. "It pays the bills, and I get to help innocent people prove their innocence. What about you? Do you like what you do?"

"That's a loaded question," I laughed. "It depends on the day you ask me. Some days are a slog, and others, I love it."

"What kind of software do you work with?" she asked.

"It's a cloud-based customer relationship manager," I said, pausing to see if she asked what that meant.

"Oh, like Oracle? Salesforce?"

"Just like that, yes." I was impressed that she knew what it was. It wasn't a big market back then, so it surprised me.

"Were you always into technology?"

"Not really," I said. "It fell into my lap a couple of years ago. I started learning and enjoyed it, so I decided to see if I could weasel my way into the profession."

"What's your favorite thing about it?"

"Oh, wow. Favorite thing? I guess building a team and helping them grow. Helping my direct reports level up, learn more, and better themselves. I think the best manager is one that doesn't want to keep their team, you know? I want them all to be so good and graduate from my team into other areas of the company."

"That's so great," she said. "What's the worst part of the job?"

"That's easy. I get all the escalated calls. The angry people who just want to yell at someone. And I'm the boss, so I'm the one they get to yell at."

"Do you ever want to yell back?"

"At first, I did. But over the last year or so, since I figured out how to do the job, I don't. I just let them vent, scream, yell, whatever. Then I try to solve the problem they're unhappy about. Sometimes I can, and sometimes I can't. But I always try."

The host came over and motioned for us to follow him. I stood, made the universal gesture for "ladies first," and followed her to our table.

As I pulled out the chair for myself, I somehow slammed it against a spot in my shin that crippled my leg for a moment. I don't know what bone I hit or what muscle, but I immediately fell to the ground and couldn't get up. For a solid minute, I was paralyzed from the knee down on my left leg.

"I'm okay. Be right there," I semi-yelled up from the ground in her general direction.

"Are you okay?" she laughed. Not intentionally. I could tell it had just slipped out.

"Yep. Yes. I'm good. I'm fine."

Once the feeling came back in my leg, I stood up and managed to get myself seated. The host was still standing there, waiting to hand me the menu. He chuckled a bit to himself. The whole thing was moronic and didn't help set my mind at ease about how the evening would explode, and everything would go wrong.

"Thank you," I said, trying not to make eye contact or to look around the room to see what other people had seen me knock myself on my ass.

"Off to a great start," she said, still chuckling.

I was about to respond cleverly when she spilled her water all over herself. She'd just taken a sip, and when she went to put the glass down, the stem snapped off cleanly. The top part of the glass flipped over and dumped the whole glass of water across her lap.

Immediately, I jumped up, grabbing the napkins from the two extra place settings the host didn't remove from the table, rushing around to help her dry off.

By the time I got to her, she was laughing hysterically. At one point, she laughed so hard she let out a snort. Her hands immediately flew to her mouth. But it was too late. She couldn't undo the snort.

I started laughing along with her.

"I guess *we're* off to a good start," she said.

"I guess we are."

• • • ● • ● • • • •

The rest of the evening went much better than the first twenty minutes. Despite the feeling of panic never going away, we had a great conversation, great food, and a really enjoyable night together.

We had so much in common. She, too, had a severe dislike of tardiness. She loved the same movies and books as I did, and she'd even heard of my favorite band that no one ever knew. Or she was just being polite and pretended to know who they were. Either way, I appreciated the effort.

When it came time to wrap up the evening, I paid the bill. We'd had a full dinner and even shared a chocolate lava cake for dessert. Some may call it chauvinistic, some may call it old-fashioned, and, honestly, she probably made a lot more money than I did, but I was always taught that the man treats the woman on dates. You open doors. You check in to make sure they get home safely. You pay for the meal. It's just how I was raised. It's how my mom taught me to show a woman you value her.

"I had a nice time," she said as we exited to the noisy street.

"What's that?" I asked. I couldn't hear her over the city bus zipping past.

"Tonight was great," she said.

"It was. Even with my gimpy leg and your wet pants," I laughed.

"Even with that," she said. "I'm this way." She pointed down the street in the opposite direction I planned to head in.

"I'll walk you," I said. Not because I felt like I needed to protect her but because I didn't want the night to end. I didn't expect her to invite me to her apartment or anything, but I wanted more time with her. However long it took to walk from where we were to her apartment, I wanted that time with her.

"Such a gentleman," she said, doing a little curtsey.

"Don't get used to it," I joked. "I turn into a pumpkin at midnight."

"I love pumpkin seeds," she said cutely.

"Oh geez. You're going to gut me on our first date?"

"I'll wait until you're old and shriveled up." Her wit was quick. I loved it.

Throughout the evening, there was never a dull moment. No lulls in conversation. No awkward pauses. No weird or off-limits questions. I had a genuinely great time with her.

The feeling of dread didn't go away until we got to her building.

"This is me," she said. "I think." She looked left and right on the street. "They all look the same."

"208? That you?"

"Yes. 208. Apartment 4C, in case you need to send me something. I don't know why I said that. That was dumb." She turned red for a quick moment.

"4C. 208. Got it." I knew if I said it out loud, I'd be less likely to forget it.

"Well, thank you," she said, lingering momentarily.

"Thank you." What was I thanking her for? Stop being a moron, Matt. Knock it off.

"I hope this means I'll see you again?"

"I hope so," I said. "We'll make plans soon."

"Can you text me when you get home? So I know you're safe."

"Of course," I said. I leaned in and hugged her. She kissed me on the cheek and squeezed me tightly.

I waited there, on the sidewalk, for her to get inside the building and close the door behind herself before heading back toward the restaurant. I didn't mind that I walked twenty minutes in the wrong direction. Like I said, it was twenty more minutes with her.

Home safely. Good night. I texted her as soon as I got home.

Good night. She replied nearly instantly.

The panic was gone. I felt wonderful. It wasn't too late, so I contemplated calling Marty to fill him in but decided against it. Instead, I decided to grab a book from my bookshelf. Victoria had recommended it, and despite having bought it the year prior, I'd never actually read it. I dove in and read for hours, only to wake up on the couch, the book still open on my chest.

She Meets Them

Marty called me the next morning. Early. Earlier than I'd anticipated being awake. I was still on cloud nine, not only from the great date but from reading the first hundred or so pages from the book I'd picked up last night.

By the time I'd woken up fully, my phone said I'd had four missed calls from him. He'd been trying repeatedly to get me to wake up.

It was 6:13 a.m. Come on, dude. C'mon.

I was just about to call him back when the phone started vibrating for the fifth time. Buzz. Buzz. Buzz.

I flipped it open and said, "Good morning. Or, well, morning. It's early. Are you okay?"

"I couldn't wait any more. Jess and I have been up for an hour, anxiously waiting until it was late enough to call you."

"It's not late enough yet, pal. It's barely six."

"It's late enough. Spill it."

"I don't know what you're talking about," I said.

"Don't make me come over there and drag you out of bed," he said.

"Spill it, Matt!" Jessica yelled out from what sounded like not very far from Marty.

"It was awesome."

"Awesome? Say more words."

"She's lovely. She was kind and sweet, sincere and open, fun and funny."

"What did you do?"

"We met at a restaurant she'd recommended after work, had dinner, and shared a dessert, then I walked her home."

"Did you smooch her?"

"No smooching."

"But you wanted to, right?" Jessica chimed in.

"I did. Am I on speakerphone?"

"You are," she said.

"Hi, Jess. Good morning."

"So you wanted to kiss her?" Marty asked.

"I did. But it was only our first date. I didn't want to come across as too forward or pushy."

"I am so happy for you," Marty said.

"Me too," Jess added.

"Me three," I said. "That was the first date I've been on since Brooke left, and it was perfect. Like, too good to be true, fairy tale type perfect. No awkward moments, no lulls in conversation, and nothing went wrong, even though I felt like it was going to all day. It was just absolutely perfect."

"When are you going to see her again?" Marty asked. He asked when, not if. He knew me too well.

"I'm not sure. Soon, but I don't know when. It's only been like eight hours since I got home."

"Did you text her?" Jess asked. "To let her know you got home?"

"I did as soon as I got in. Then I picked up a book we'd talked about and read for a while before passing out on my couch."

Jessica squealed. An immature, giddy, happy squeal. She was just as excited for me as Marty was. It was tiny moments like that where I was reminded how happy I was that they'd found each other and even happier that she and I were as close as we were.

"You should call her today," Marty said.

"Yes. Call her today," Jessica added.

"I think I will. What are you guys doing today? Want to maybe all hang out?"

"Oh, that's a great idea. Why don't you check in and see if she's free? Then we can plan something?" Marty asked.

"Sounds good, I'll let you know."

"Great," Marty said. His voice trailed off.

"Something wrong?" I asked.

"Tell him," Jess said. "Tell him."

"Tell me what?"

I heard Marty cover the phone, and then his muffled voice said something, but I couldn't tell what it was.

"I didn't want to rain on your parade," he said. "But there's been a... development."

"Rain away, buddy. What's up?" It sounded like Jess had stepped away or left the room. Perhaps to give Marty some privacy.

"I got a phone call yesterday. Well, last night. It was from a woman who started by asking me a bunch of questions."

"About what?"

"Me. She sounded like a telemarketer at first. I was about to hang up when she said something in Dutch. 'ik ben je Moeder,' she said. I am your mother."

"What?" I was shocked. "I thought she was dead!"

"I did, too. I am still unconvinced that the woman who called me last night is my mother."

"Jean Luc told you she died in childbirth, didn't he?"

"He did. And he showed me photos of her in the hospital. Showed me how sick she got from my birth. We visited her headstone every year on my birthday."

"Okay, back up, wait." I was so confused. "What did she say, exactly?"

"She started by asking if I was Michel, son of Jean Luc. She introduced herself as Camille, pausing for a second. I think she was waiting to see if I recognized the name. I didn't at first. I didn't even know my mother's name until last night."

"How? How is that possible?"

"Papa always referred to her as Mama. At the cemetery, her headstone just had her first initial. C. None of my family ever mentioned her by name."

"Never? Not even once?"

"Maybe when I was little. But I didn't recall hearing it."

"Did she say anything to convince you she is legit?"

"What is legit? I do not know this word."

"Uhm. Sorry. It means real. Trustworthy."

"Okay. Yes. She knew all about Papa. His name, where he was born, where he grew up. How old he was. She didn't know he'd died. When I told her, she cried. Almost instantly. How would someone not *legit* cry so quickly?"

"That's a good point," I said. "What else?"

"She knew all the places I'd been, all the places I'd lived. It was like Papa had kept in touch with her," he said.

"Why would Jean Luc lie to you about your mother?"

"Why wouldn't he want me to have her in my life?" Marty added. "I don't understand why."

"And why, all of a sudden, is she showing up in your life?"

"I don't know. I didn't get any answers. She just said she was my mother and wanted to come to the States to see me. Said we had a lot to catch up on and to discuss."

"What did you tell her?"

"I didn't know what to say," he said. "I'm sorry, I'm raining on your parade much more than I thought I would."

"Don't be stupid," I said. "This is bigger than my date!"

"I was so caught off guard that I just told her to call me when she arrived."

"Did you tell her where you lived?"

"She already knew. But I don't know how. If Papa was keeping in touch with her, he's been gone for a while now. How would he have told her that I live here now? If she last spoke to Papa when he was alive, she'd still think I live back at the other house."

"Right. She'll call you when she gets here? Did you Google the phone number?"

"I did, but no results. Nothing. I Googled her name, but no results, either."

"Text her. Ask for a photo of her so you can Google that."

"I think there was a photo of her before she passed in with Papa's things that I put in the basement. I could try to see if she looks the same. Maybe she hasn't changed much in the last thirty years."

"That's a good idea," I said. "Let me know if she sends one or what she says."

"I will."

"This is wild," I said. "All of a sudden, out of the blue, she shows up. Why? Why now?"

"I hope we find out," he said. "I'm very happy about your date, Matt. But I needed to tell you what happened last night."

"Are you okay?" I asked.

"I think so. I'm still shaken, but I think I'm okay."

"How's Jess?"

"Supportive, like always. She told me that whatever I do, she'll support me."

"She's the best," I said.

"I know. I'm very lucky."

"Okay, I'll talk to you in a little while. Let me see what Victoria's up to. If she's busy, we can still get together without her. I'll let you know."

"Okay. Talk soon," he said, hanging up.

• • • • • • • • •

I must have looked at the clock every half an hour until it was a more sane time to text Victoria. I'd waited until just after nine that morning. It was a Saturday, so I figured she'd probably have slept in, and I didn't want to wake her up.

Good morning I said.

Hey you. She responded almost immediately.

Sleep well?

Very. Thank you for asking. You?

Fell asleep reading for the first time in forever.

What do you think?!

So far, so good. I really enjoyed it—about 120 pages in.

That's so great, Matt!

I know we just went out last night, but are you free today?

I am. This afternoon, anyway. I have to do some work this morning.

Do you drive? I was thinking of having Marty and Jess over.

Yes. Send me the address and time.

I grabbed a link to Google Maps directions from her door to mine and sent it to her.

Thanks. Time?

Any time is fine. I'll just be here reading.
See you later.

I texted Marty to come over whenever they wanted to, then went fishing for my book, which had snuck into the couch's cushions.

• • • • • • • • • •

They'd never met before, but it was almost like they coordinated their arrival at my house. Victoria pulled into the driveway just a moment before Marty and Jessica did. She didn't even have time to get out of her car before they pulled in.

I could see them all get out and introduce one another through the window. Jess, as she did, hugged Victoria. Marty shook her hand, then motioned toward the door. I did my best not to be a creeper, looking out the window at the three of them as they approached.

Being my best friend, Marty let himself—and the women—into the house without knocking. "Hi," he announced. "We're all here. But you knew that already."

My ploy to run over to the couch and sit with my book didn't fool anyone. They must have seen me peering out the window.

"Oh, hi," I said, trying to be casual. I got up and approached the group. "I see you've all already met."

"We met in the driveway," Victoria said. "But, like Marty said. You already knew that."

Marty fist-bumped her. "Nice one."

"Come on in," I said, leading them to the living room.

Marty and Jessica sat on one of the couches. Victoria sat down next to me.

"Meeting the best friend so soon," Jessica said. "Marty didn't let me meet Matt for months. We were dating, and I'd hear all about his best friend this and his best friend that. But I didn't get to meet him for a while."

"Why so secret?" Victoria asked. "And why do I get to meet Marty so soon?"

I felt my face turn red. I gestured toward Marty to let him explain why Jess and I hadn't met for a while.

"It wasn't that I didn't want her to meet Matt," he said. "I just wasn't ready for him to know I'd met someone."

"He was embarrassed," I added. "He thought I was going to be judgmental or something."

"Maybe a little," he said. "Maybe just a little."

"Were you?" Victoria asked, turning to face me.

"I don't think so," I said, half stating, half asking.

"He wasn't," Jessica said. "He was incredibly welcoming. We finally met when Marty was going through his cancer treatment."

"Cancer? Oh no," Victoria said. "Are you in remission now?"

"I am," Marty said, reaching out to knock on the wooden coffee table. "Thank goodness."

"So, then, why now? Why me?" Victoria asked.

"You know," I said. "I hadn't even really thought about it. It just felt like a normal thing to do. Invite you over, invite them over, and all hang out. Casual. Maybe get a meal a little later. Dinner or something."

"That's a good answer," she said. "It does feel very casual. I was a little nervous on the drive up here, to be honest."

"Nervous? Why?" Marty asked.

"Meeting his best friend after just our first date. It felt like a lot. Even though Charles had told me how great Matt was, it was still a little strange. But now that I'm here, I feel right at home. This doesn't feel weird to me at all."

"Me either," I said.

"So, to catch you up," Marty said. "My whole life, I've believed my mother died in childbirth. Or, well, shortly after I was born, I guess. Everywhere I've moved with my father, God rest his soul, he maintained the same story."

"This sounds like it's going somewhere good," Victoria said.

"Yes. Last night, a woman called me, saying she was my mother."

Victoria looked at me as if to say, "Did you know this, and if so, why didn't you tell me?"

"She had all the right things to say. She knew Papa's information and all about my life."

"Did you ask her where the hell she's been?" Victoria asked.

"I thought the same thing," I added.

"No. I was too stunned. Almost in a state of shock, to ask anything important."

"So what's next?" Victoria asked.

"She's coming to the United States. She wants to meet me, to talk."

"I told him he has to do it," Jessica said. "You can't pass up an opportunity like this. Even if it turns out to be fake, you have to try. You have to see it through."

"I know," Marty said. "I'm leaning heavily toward meeting her."

"I'll obviously go with you if you need me to," I said.

"Thanks, buddy. I know Jess will come."

"Of course," she said.

"What a wild Friday night last night was for everyone, huh?" Victoria said.

We spent the afternoon just hanging out and talking. Victoria and I got to know each other more, while Marty and Jessica got to see us together and got to know how she was and how she acted around and toward me. It all felt very natural, for lack of a better simplification. We talked about movies, music, art. We discussed everything under the sun, ending the night with a game of Settlers of Catan, an old favorite of Marty, Jessica, and me.

As the night came to an end, Marty and Jessica started heading toward the door.

"This was super fun," Jessica said, giving me one of her patented back-rubbing hugs, then moving to Victoria. "So lovely to have met you," she said. Jess always said the best things.

"Likewise," Victoria said. When Jess freed her from the hug, Victoria leaned over and hugged Marty, too. "I'm glad I got to meet the famous best friend, and so soon!"

"I don't know what you see in my dumb friend," he joked. "But I'm glad you came today. I'm glad to have met you."

"Thanks for coming, guys," I said as they descended the front steps, heading toward their car.

"You heading out, too?" I asked.

She looked at her watch. "Not yet, if that's okay? It's not too late."

I glanced behind her at the clock on the microwave. It was only 9:30. "I'd love for you to stay longer," I said. "Maybe we can watch a movie?"

"That's a great idea," she said, heading toward the kitchen.

"The living room's this way," I said.

"I know," she called back. "But I'm going to rummage through your cabinets and look for some microwave popcorn."

"Want some help?"

"No," she said. "I'll need to figure out where everything is in your kitchen eventually."

It gave me a warm feeling to hear her say that. It was, at least to me, an indication that she wanted to be around for a while. That she anticipated being at my house more than just this one time. That what I was feeling wasn't some fluke.

"How long have they been engaged?"

"Who?"

"Marty and Jess."

"They're not engaged," I said. "Just a happy couple."

I heard cabinet doors close, one after another. "She was wearing a diamond ring, Matt. Did you not notice?"

"What? Was she? I guess I didn't notice."

"Did they not tell you they got engaged?"

"Maybe it slipped their minds with everything else that had been going on?"

"Found it!" She seemed excited. "Now, a bowl." The sound of more cabinets opening and closing. "Wow, I'm good," she said a second later. Moments after that, the house filled with the sounds and smells of kernels turning to popcorn in the microwave.

She came bouncing into the living room, bowl of popcorn in one hand and drinks tucked neatly into her arm. As she sat next to me—right up against me, actually—she handed me the bottle of water she'd grabbed me, putting the soda she'd grabbed herself down on the coffee table.

"Did you pick something?" she asked.

"I was waiting for you," I said.

"Oh, okay. New rule for any other time: whoever makes the popcorn is off the hook for picking the movie. Deal?"

"That seems like a fair rule. I guess I'll pick something, then."

I got up and went over to my DVD shelf, scanning through the movies I hadn't seen, hoping to find something fun to watch. I don't remember what I picked, but I tossed it in the Blu-ray player and hit play.

No sooner did the movie start than she cuddled into my shoulder. The bowl of popcorn was on my lap, and she reached over periodically, grabbing handfuls at a time.

I put my arm around her, pulling her in a little closer, adjusting my arm to where my hand wouldn't fall asleep in an awkward position.

She nuzzled into the spot between my arm and my chest, a place she'd eventually affectionally call "the nook."

We watched the movie, snuggled up together, munching on popcorn. There was no make-out session. There was no heavy petting. There was nothing other than snuggling. And, let me tell you, it was the most comforting, natural thing in the world. It didn't feel like it was only our second time being together. It felt so perfect. It felt like the spot she was nuzzled into was designed for her, for the exact dimensions of her head and body. Like it was meant just for her.

I didn't think of anything else that night. I didn't wonder about the outside world. I didn't think of my past or my future. I only focused on that night. I only focused on how I felt there, snuggled up on my couch with Victoria. I only focused on her. Man, did she smell great.

Jessica & Marty

It seemed like everything had been a whirlwind the last six months. As I stood at the altar, staring at the back of Marty's head, waiting for Jessica to come down the aisle to marry him, it all hit me. Their engagement was low-key, so low that when it came time for them to tell Victoria and me, it was a "didn't we already tell you?" moment. I won't lie; it stung a little.

We'd been so close since we met a decade ago. We'd been through everything together, both good and bad. All the highs, all the lows. He and I had seen so much, been to so many places, and done so many things. And for him to sort of forget to tell me he got engaged was a little painful.

"We were so caught up in talking about your first date with Victoria that day and talking about my mom, I thought we'd told you. We got engaged the night before," he once had told me.

Water under the proverbial bridge, as they say. Where is this bridge, anyway? Why does the water going under it represent a good thing in that old saying? Isn't that the point of a bridge? For water to go under it.

Anyway, I'm trying to say I forgave him months ago. But color me surprised when he asked me to be his best man. The confused look on my face must have said it all. I surely felt out of the loop until he clued me in.

But of course I'd be his best man. That's obvious.

So, there we stood, waiting. Jess's sister stood across from me, just off to where Jess would be shortly. Marty was directly in front of me, a couple of people from work, two of Jess' cousins Marty had gotten close to, and a photo of Jean Luc stood behind me, making up the rest of his ... groom's party? Is that a thing? I know there's a bridal party, but is it a groom's party? Who knows? I'm so off-topic today. I'm nervous and anxious. I've never been a best man before. You'll have to forgive me.

I did the only thing I knew to do to calm my nerves. I looked over at the front row of the rapidly filling-in rows of seating and spotted Victoria. She'd arrived with me early and helped me get the rest of my tuxedo on. She also helped put the finishing touches on Marty's suit.

Much like Jessica and I had become close in the early months of their relationship—thanks cancer!—Marty and Victoria had also grown close. So, it was no surprise to him that she arrived early to help with the final touches.

"You boys look mighty handsome," she'd said. I remember the exact wording because the way she'd said it sounded southern, for some reason. Just a slight hint of a twang on "mighty." It made me chuckle then, and remember it since for some reason.

I reached out and placed my hand on Marty's right shoulder. He turned his head to look at me, and I nodded. "Deep breaths," I said. "You'll be fine."

He wasn't outright shaking, but I could tell he was nervous. He must have had that same feeling I had minutes before I'd married Brooke. That feeling of anxiety, nervousness, fright, and slight terror all balled up into one. Compounded by the fact that he—and I—didn't like being the center of attention. Standing in front of a room of people and speaking, even if those people were friends and family, was overwhelming. But, as best man, I did my job and made sure he knew he was supported. I tried to make sure he knew that he'd be able to celebrate once the public part was over. That the big party waiting in the other room was for him and for Jess. I conveyed as much of that as I could through a quick squeeze on his shoulder.

"Please rise," the priest said. Although they weren't getting married in a church, they both wanted to have a priest oversee the ceremony. "In God's eyes," Marty had said once.

The music started playing. Clair de Lune, the song Jess had picked out for sentimental reasons, started. The doors at the far end of the room opened, and there she was. Her dad was standing on her right, arm in arm, waiting for their cue from the wedding planner to start walking.

Just as the music struck a new chord, the two started making their way down the aisle.

I couldn't see his face but could tell Marty was crying. Not sobbing, not upset, but a happy cry. I won't lie; a few tears escaped my cheeks, too. It was pure happiness. For both of them. I loved Marty, obviously. He's my best friend. But I also loved Jess. More importantly, I loved them together. The two of them, as a pair, had been my most trusted humans for the last two years since Jess had shown up on our porch that day during Marty's treatment.

She'd been there through all the appointments, through all the tests, through all the follow-up scans. She'd been there just as much—if not more—than I had been. And that made me love her as a person and as Marty's partner.

· · · · ●·●·●· · ·

"Be seated," the priest requested once Jess had reached the altar.

"You look beautiful," Marty whispered to Jessica, fighting back more tears. Best man to the rescue; I handed him a couple of tissues I'd had in my pocket.

"We are gathered here today to join this man and this woman in holy matrimony. Michel and Jessica have invited you here today to witness their union. They have loved each other and are now ready to profess their love before God and you all."

There were no readings from the gospel, there were no hymns, there were no readers or speakers. The priest read a short prayer, then turned it over to Marty to say his vows.

"Jessica. Jess. Jessie Bean. My love. My heart. I don't know how I got so lucky that you came into my life, but here we are. I feel so blessed. You are my rock, my world, my truest of loves. In the darkest time of my life, you arrived like the flashlight I needed. You lit me up and lifted me up when I felt lower than I've ever felt. You helped me through the most difficult thing I've ever done. And I'm sure Matt was thankful you came along, so he didn't have to sit by my bedside all those days by himself."

I couldn't help but smile at the mention of me.

"You were and are the light of my life. I wake up daily thankful to God that you're next to me. I go to sleep every night, thankful to God that you're there. I don't know how I'd be here without you. I don't know where life would have taken me if you hadn't shown up. If you hadn't come into my life, I am sure I'd be very different right now. Matt and I would probably still be sitting in the driveway eating pizza every night."

The crowd chuckled. They all must have known about our pizza obsession. I saw my mom smile.

"I promise to love you until the end of time. Even after we're both gone from this earth, I vow to find you in the next life and continue loving you. Nothing will take me from you or you from me. I will love you for all eternity. This I promise you now. This I promise you forever."

The priest took the short pause as his cue to pass the microphone over to Jess.

"Michel. That's Marty's real name if you didn't know," she said, briefly turning to the crowd. "My warrior. My love. I, too, am so glad I found you years ago. Together, we've fought the toughest battle and won. Knowing you're in remission drives me every day. I, too, wake up thankful that you're next to me. I watch you sleep. I watch you breathing. Sometimes, I touch your face. Not hard enough to wake you up, just gentle enough that I hope it'd make me intrude into your dream. Just a quick hand on your face. Just so you know, in your sleep, that I'm there. That I'll always be there." She paused to sniffle back the tears that had started flowing during Marty's vows. "You are everything. I will love you through every lifetime. I will love you through the end of humanity. I will love you until every life we ever live ends. Nothing will stop that."

She looked past him at me. We made eye contact, and I immediately panicked, though I don't know why.

"And you. Matthew. You're his best friend. And I love you, too. Thank you for helping me take care of him when he was sick. Everyone needs a friend like you."

And the tears burst out of my eyes and down my face.

"Here, before God, I ask you to pledge your love to one another," the priest said. "Do you, Michel, take Jessica to be your lawfully wedded wife? To have and hold, in sickness and in health?"

"*ik doel.* I do," Marty said, choking back tears.

"Please place the ring on Jessica's finger," the priest said.

Marty reached back, and I handed him Jessica's wedding band.

"Do you, Jessica, take Michel to be your lawfully wedded husband? To have and to hold, in sickness and in health?"

"I do," she replied, also choking back tears.

"Please place the ring on Michel's finger," the priest said.

She reached back, taking Marty's band from her sister and sliding it onto his ring finger. He immediately adjusted it to try to make it not feel foreign on his hand.

"By the power vested in me, I now pronounce you husband and wife. You may kiss one another."

The crowd erupted into applause as they kissed. I cried some more because I'm a big baby. I couldn't help it; those tears of joy just flowed out.

I looked out at Victoria. She, too, was crying.

• • • • • • • • • •

They call it a wedding reception, though I'm not sure why. What Marty and Jess had was a straight-up party. They hired a live band specializing in covers from the '80s and '90s, the music they both loved. The caterer they hired was incredible. The filet mignon was out of this world. The venue offered an add-on of a candy bar that they'd opted into, which was amazing. Every type of candy you could imagine. Every different bar, every different bulk item, everything you could ever imagine, for the taking, by the handful.

The amount of sugar people had in their systems accounted for the amount of energy the crowd had. People were dancing up a storm the entire night. The entire dance floor was overflowing. Everyone went nuts every time a new song came on.

Jess's sister, Justine, and her boyfriend seemed to be leading the charge. They were the first ones out there; on the very first note, the band played; "Everybody Wants To Rule The World" by Tears for Fears. They did that typical "come join us" motion that the first people dancing usually did to no avail. Except this time, it worked. People, by the dozen, got up and joined in, dancing. Marty's childhood friends, who'd flown in from Belgium, friends from work, Jess' entire family, countless friends from both sides. Everyone was jumping and shaking and dancing.

Victoria and I would eventually join them, but I was too busy devouring the meal first. It'd been a long day until then, so I wanted to ensure I had something in my stomach.

"You okay?" Victoria asked between bites.

"I'm good. Why?"

"I was worried this would bring you back to your wedding."

"Oh." The thought hadn't even occurred to me except for a brief minute when we first arrived, and the venue was empty. "No, I'm good. Thank you for asking."

"I'm glad. The ceremony was beautiful, wasn't it?"

"It was! I wasn't expecting to cry so much," I said.

"Me either. It was so touching. I'm so glad they found each other." The smile on her face was genuine. She seemed sincerely happy for my friends, which meant so much to me. They all got along, which was no surprise. But it was such a nice reprieve from having to be the one everyone got along with. With Brooke, our friends never really meshed. I liked her friends; they were fine, don't get me wrong, but we were never the "hang out without Brooke" type. And I was okay with that. With Victoria, something was different. I'd often come home from running an errand or something, and Marty and Jess would have come over while I was gone. Victoria met them at my house, and they were all hanging out when I got back.

But it wasn't weird. It didn't feel forced at all. It didn't seem unnatural for the three of them to laugh when I walked into my living room. They were genuine friends, not just people who all knew Matt, which was how it had always felt with Brooke. Case in point: I didn't hear a single peep from *any* of her friends or family when she left me. No one checked in on me. No one texted me to offer their apologies. It made me wonder how she'd painted the picture from her perspective. She clearly had painted me as the bad guy.

It felt as close to being on "Friends" as I'd ever been. Everyone getting along and hanging out. The only thing we never did was meet at a coffee house during the workday.

"Come on," Victoria said, pulling on my arm just as I'd put the last bite of mashed potatoes into my mouth.

I jumped up, wiping my mouth with the napkin from my lap, tossing it onto my empty plate, and following her to the dance floor.

"And now that they're done eating," the band singer said. "Let's clear the floor for the newly married couple! Let's give them a round of applause!"

The crowd parted like traffic when an ambulance was coming through, slowly at first but urgently as they approached.

Their first dance song was a popular one that year. The band started right into Christina Perri's "A Thousand Years." The piano player happened to be a woman, so she took lead vocals to best match the original.

Marty and Jess made it to the center of the dance floor just as the first verse hit. He twirled her, and her dress furled outward. She looked like a princess.

Their eyes locked, and he pulled her in, beginning their first dance as a married couple.

Right on cue, Victoria and I joined them on the dance floor. Marty had asked us to join them quickly after they started dancing so the attention would be split between us and them. "The fewer eyes on me, the better," he'd said.

Others joined in moments later, finishing out the song to a thunderous round of applause, both for the couple and the band, I'm sure.

We then continued to party, hard. It was tough to tell why someone was acting erratic between the sugar and the open bar. Was it a sugar rush, or were they drunk? It was a fun little game I played in my head.

After dancing to a handful of songs as hard as I could, we took a break, heading directly to the candy bar.

"You know I love Snowcaps," I said, grabbing the scoop and filling a small plastic bowl.

"The fact that they put out such big bowls is clearly a mistake," Victoria said. "People are going to go nuts on this stuff."

"I think they already have," I said, pointing to Marty's childhood friends' kids. They were 9 and 11 years old. They were spinning, literally, in circles. Not dancing, just twirling one another around in circles. It made me dizzy just looking at it.

"They need to be cut off," she joked. "They're at their limit. The bar's closed. Pay your tab and get out."

I laughed, almost choking on the handful of Snowcaps I'd shoved in my mouth before moving down the line and grabbing some Hershey Kisses, M&Ms, and a handful of mini Milky Ways. I was almost instantly glad I wasn't diabetic.

Victoria grabbed a much smaller portion of M&M's, Skittles, Mike and Ikes, two Reese's Peanut Butter cups, and a few mini Kit-Kats.

"Don't make the mistake of mixing the M&M's and Skittles," I said, half joking, half serious.

"Why? What'll happen?" she seemed curious, going as far as pretending to mix them intentionally in her bowl.

"Nothing bad," I said. "It'll just be a gross combination."

"You know this from first-hand experience?" she asked.

"About two or three years ago," I began. "After Halloween, Marty and I had a bunch of leftover candy at the apartment. So, we did what any thirty-somethings would do: we opened it all, put it into plastic bags, and started eating it every day until it was gone."

"Sounds healthy," she said, poking my stomach with her free hand.

"Well, mister jokester Marty decided, one day, to mix the M&M's and Skittles. Because who would look before diving in, right? Everything was in their separate bags, so I thought I was going in for M&M's. What I got was a handful of both."

"Oh no. How bad was it?"

"It wasn't horrible," I said. "But the surprise got me. I expected to chomp into chocolate and got the squishy Skittles mixed in. My brain was like, 'What is happening?'. Marty laughed hysterically from the living room. To him, it was the funniest thing he'd ever seen."

"Obviously, it wasn't."

"Obviously," I said. "But, you know Marty. He's so, I don't know how to say it, he's just him."

"I get it, I know," she said, popping her last mini Kit-Kat into her mouth.

"I'm going to be so sick tomorrow," I said. "But I can't pass up free candy. It's against the law. I looked it up."

"Don't worry. If you break the law, I can defend you in court," she said. "And I'll be there tomorrow to take care of you if you're sick." She smiled, leaning in and kissing me gently.

Once we'd finished our way-too-large bowls of candy, I followed her back onto the dance floor.

We twisted, we thrashed, we bounced, we yelled. I had the best damn time of my life. I had even more fun than I had at my wedding all those years ago. Even knowing how that relationship would end, the memories of the day weren't sullied. It was a great day. We had a great wedding and a great reception. But Marty and Jess' wedding bash, party, reception, whatever you want to call it, was next level.

I'd love to tell you that the crowd died down as the night progressed. I'd love to tell you that the evening ended quietly, with no events, no hassles, no drama. And, save for one of Jess' coworkers getting a little too drunk and needing to be escorted out by security, the night went off without a hitch.

To say the night ended quietly would be a lie. Despite playing for almost three hours, the band still turned it up a notch.

"This is the last song of the evening, folks. The bride and groom want to thank you all for being with them today. Congratulations, Jess and Marty," the singer said. "Enjoy!"

The guitar player launched into the most recognizable first handful of notes to any song in history. The band was closing the night with Guns 'n' Roses' "Sweet Child o' Mine".

The entire place went bonkers.

People were yelling the lyrics, dancing along, swinging and twirling random people throughout the crowd, playing air guitar. The crowd was so loud I bet you could hear it outside, probably down the street.

But, wow. What a way to end the evening. What a way to end the celebration of my best friend and his new wife.

"Congratulations. I love you guys," I said, getting close enough to them to be heard over the band.

"We love you," Jess said. Marty stopped thrashing around the dance floor for a second and gave me the biggest hug he'd ever given me.

"Thanks for being my best man and my best friend," he said. "I love you."

"I love you, too, bud," I said. "This was such an amazing party!"

The guitar solo kicked in just as Marty released me from the hug.

Jess and Victoria were hugging.

"When's the honeymoon?" I heard Victoria ask.

"We leave in the morning," Jessica replied. "Cancun!"

• • • • • • • • •

The building got very quiet once the band finished their last song. People started shuffling out.

I completed my last best man duties and handed out the envelopes of cash Marty had given me to tip the various people: the organizer, the head waiter, the band, and the photographer. Everyone got a little envelope of cash, though I never looked inside to see who got what. Marty had labeled them, and I stuck with the instructions he'd given me.

Victoria and I met them in the middle of the dance floor, where they said goodbyes to people, thanking them for coming and looking at photos people had taken on their phones.

"Good night," I said. "Congrats again. I love you guys." I gave them each a hug.

"Great party," Victoria added. "Thank you for having me."

"You are family," Marty said. "Of course we'd have you."

"Now, you two get home and enjoy your night. Wink wink," Victoria said. "I don't know why I said wink wink out loud. I'm such a dork."

Sometimes, the things she did were so dorky that I found them endearing. I loved that little moment.

"We will," Jess said. "But first, we're stopping at Wendy's. I'm starving."

"Please tell me you're going in your gown, in the limo," Victoria said.

"Absolutely!" Marty said. "I'm keeping my tux on, too. And we're going in. No drive-through for my wife!"

"Your wife," I said. "I love hearing you say that."

We all crisscrossed and hugged each other, trying to avoid any collision of bodies. I looked back one last time as Victoria and I went through the exit.

The tuxedo jacket, cummerbund, and bowtie were off before we got to my car.

"You look so handsome," Victoria said. "So so handsome."

I smiled. "Thank you, gorgeous."

The drive home was exhausting. While the venue wasn't far from my house, it was much later than I'd stayed awake in quite a long time. I don't remember getting home, but I remember falling asleep.

Where I'd always fallen asleep to music or a television show, I fell asleep in complete silence that night. Only the faint sounds of Victoria breathing next to me. It brought me peace and made me feel complete.

Let's Do It

One morning, I found myself awake and upright, sitting in the reading chair in the corner of my bedroom. The clock read just after five, and the sun was just starting to come up.

At first, I had a small sense of panic. How did I end up in the chair? How long had I been there? Why was I there? I felt very confused, very jolted. Victoria was still sleeping, her back to me. Her head barely visible above the covers. No matter how warm it got, she was always buried in the blankets, claiming she was perpetually cold. Even in summer, when the nights were warm enough, but not too hot, she'd bundle up like it was the Arctic. I watched her back rise and fall with each breath.

A calmness settled over me. The panic of why I was in the chair, first thing in the morning, was gone.

I'm not sure what it was about that moment. I'm not sure why, all of a sudden, I felt such an intense feeling of love toward her. This overwhelming feeling that I wanted to wake her up and tell her I loved her. I had no doubt she knew how much I cared about her, how much I treasured her being in my life. But I hadn't told her I loved her, yes.

I don't know why. I'm pretty sure I had felt it for a while. At least since Marty and Jessica's wedding a few months ago.

She flipped over and reached out for me, as she'd done so many other nights.

"Why do you even have your apartment anymore?" I asked one night over dinner. "You are here more than there."

"It's close to the office and courts downtown," she said, brushing off my lame attempt at asking her to move in with me.

I didn't push the point, and it wasn't like it was a big deal. But what good was the apartment being close to work and the courts she went to *for* work if she was never at the apartment in the first place? I'm not crazy, right? That's silly pants.

When she couldn't find me, she scooted closer to my side of the bed. Her arm flailed around, searching for the warmth of my body.

She opened her eyes, just for a brief moment, and spotted me in the chair across the room from her. She squinted against the light from the window to my right. The sun's rays were a little too bright for her first thing in the morning, even with the blinds drawn.

"What are you doing?" she managed to mumble through a sleepy mouth.

"I'm just..." I said. "I'm just sitting. I couldn't sleep."

"Come back to bed," she said with a faux whimper. "I need your warmth."

The way she said *need* hit me right in the heart. This amazing, bad-ass, gorgeous woman needed me. She needed me more than to keep her warm; I knew it. She needed me as I needed her. She was my stability, center, and core of who I was since I'd met her. "Be right there," I said.

Slowly, I got up from the chair. I didn't feel dizzy or lightheaded. I didn't feel any different than normal. I just felt perplexed as to how I ended up in the chair in the first place. As far as I knew, I never sleepwalked. I didn't recall waking up and walking over to the chair. Why would I? It's not something I'd ever done before. I'd had that same chair for at least twenty years. It'd been my reading chair—even though I didn't read much anymore—since I was a teenager.

As I climbed back into bed, she moved over to make room for me. As soon as I lay down, she tucked herself into the nook, sliding her arm across my chest and tucking her hand under my left side.

She let out a little sigh. A small sign of comfort, of happiness.

As I always did when we fell asleep, I kissed her on the top of the head and brushed her hair out of her face.

I'm still not sure why I ended up in that chair. But what I took away from it that morning was that I needed to tell Victoria how I felt. I knew I'd fully let go of the past. I knew it was time for me to move on, be happy, and feel loved again. For the first few months of our dating, I had convinced myself that I needed to keep my guard up. That because of how Brooke just gave up on us and left, Victoria was different. That I couldn't let the pain of one experience hold me back from being in love again. That no matter how hurt I was from my marriage falling apart, this was something new. And, sure, I might get hurt again. Hell, I might even be the one to do the hurting. But that fear, that never-ending anxiety of things falling apart, couldn't stop me from trying. It couldn't stop me from feeling.

Moments before falling back asleep, I told myself I'd tell her. I'd tell her I loved her. Soon.

2015

Camille

Our Friday nights were standard for as long as I can remember. The place changed, and the people in attendance increased, but the night had been the same since Marty and I met. Pizza. Specifically, Papa Gino's pizza. We started in my mom's driveway, then the Cul-de-sac outside Marty and Jean Luc's house, then the apartment, then our house, then Marty and Jess' house or my house. We'd been alternating since Marty got married.

I think, at least on my end, who hosted depended on whose house was cleaner. Unfolded laundry in my living room? Marty's hosting this week.

Obviously, Jess had been part of our Friday night hangout for years. Victoria had joined in pretty quickly after we started dating. And, like I said before, she just fit in. They laughed together. They had inside jokes that I knew nothing about. I'm pretty sure they had a Matt-less group text, too. It was just our gang, the crew.

No sooner had Victoria and I got to their house with the pizza in hand did Marty confess a secret he'd apparently been holding from me.

"She finally came," he blurted out as I sat at the table.

I turned to my right to face him. "Sorry, who came where?"

"Camille. My mother."

"I'm sorry," Jessica said. "He didn't want me to say anything."

"She came? When? Where?" I asked.

"Who's Camille?" Victoria asked.

"I must not have told you her name when I told you about her," I said. "Marty's estranged, presumed-dead mother."

"Oh, yes. You told me about her," she said.

"She came to town. Last week," Marty said.

"Why didn't you tell me?" I asked. "I'd have gone with you."

"He didn't even tell me at first," Jess said. "When he finally told me the next morning, he told me he had to do it himself."

"I needed to go see her myself. I did. I wanted to see if she was legit or not."

"What happened?" I asked.

"Tell us everything," Victoria added.

"I met her at a pub downtown on Tuesday night after work. I didn't know what she looked like, so I couldn't pick her out of the crowd. Thankfully, she knew what I looked like and approached me when I entered. She introduced herself and asked if she could hug me."

"Did you let her?" I asked.

"No, it felt too foreign."

"Good."

"So we went to sit down, and I stared at her awkwardly, not knowing what to say. The words weren't there. She's a stranger to me."

"What did she say?" I asked.

"She apologized, immediately. She said she was sorry for leaving."

"Why did she leave?" Victoria asked.

"She said it was because of Papa's job. She didn't feel safe anymore and couldn't stay with us."

"That's suspect," I said. "Who leaves their newborn baby because all of a sudden they don't feel safe with their partner anymore?"

"I thought the same thing," Marty said. "Why would she feel unsafe for herself but not unsafe for me? Why not take me with her?"

"Did you ask her?" I asked.

"I did. She didn't have a good answer. She just kept saying how she felt unsafe."

"What did your dad do for work?" Victoria asked.

I scoffed, unintentionally. "He can't tell us. It's a secret government job, just like Marty has."

"Oh, okay."

"He dealt with bad guys," Marty said. "That's all I can say."

"I don't even know," Jess added. "And I married the guy."

"So, anyway," Marty let out a big sigh as if he was tired of answering questions about the work he does and Jean Luc did. "I peppered her with questions. I asked her every single thing I could think of."

"What did you take away from it?" I asked. "Did she seem legit?"

"She knew all the right things to say," he said. "She knew all the right answers. But something felt off."

"What do you mean?" I asked.

"It felt like she was reciting the answers like she'd been practicing exactly what to say. Which, in fairness, I haven't seen her in thirty-four years. Maybe she had been practicing. It didn't feel malicious; it just didn't feel natural. It didn't feel like she knew the answers; it felt like she'd trained to say the right thing."

"That's bizarre," Victoria said. "Do you know anything other than her name? I could run a background check on her through the law firm."

"You can do that?" I asked.

"How do you think I knew it was safe to date you?" I couldn't tell if she was joking or not.

"Just her name," Marty said. "I would guess she had the same last name as Papa and I, but I do not know for sure."

"You didn't check her identification?" I asked.

"That would be rude, wouldn't it?" Marty asked.

"No ruder than not being in your child's life for decades, no?" I quipped.

"Fair point," Jess said. "How did you feel at the end of the night?"

"Suspicious, but I can't pinpoint why," Marty said.

"Did she ask for anything? Did you get a sense she wanted money or anything?" Victoria asked.

"No. She did ask about Papa. About the home we had and what happened to it."

"That sounds like she's trying to get to whether or not you have money, to me," Victoria said.

"Me, too," I added. "You didn't tell her anything, did you?"

"I don't think so. Not intentionally, anyway. I didn't mean to if I did."

"Did you tell her where you live? That you're married?" I asked.

"I tried to tell her as little as possible. I focused on asking her about her life, our connection, and what she knew about me. Trying to figure out if she's my mother or not."

"Did she cry?" Victoria asked.

"No," Marty said.

"Why would she?" I asked.

"Well, I don't know about you, Jess, but if I saw my child for the first time in, what, thirty-four years, I'd probably shed a few tears, no?"

"I'd be crying like a baby," Jess said. "I'd hug the crap out of you, even if you said you didn't want me to."

"Exactly. Even if you have no relationship, the connection would still be there," Victoria said.

"The Dutch are different," he said. "I'm not sure she would show the same emotion as an American."

"Wouldn't she show some emotion?" I asked. "Even a little?"

"Perhaps a little," he said. "A tiny bit, perhaps."

"So, more suspicion," Jess said. "I'm not sold."

"Me either," I said.

"That makes three of us," Victoria added.

"Unanimous. I'm not sure of her, either," Marty said. "That's why I want you all to come with me the next time I see her. So you can ask the questions I didn't think of or the questions I was too afraid to ask. I didn't want to hurt her feelings. After all, she could be my mother."

"She could also be some scammer trying to see if you have money and exploiting your missing connection with your mother to get that money from you," Jess said.

"Is that a thing people do?" Marty asked.

"It happens more often than you'd think," Victoria said. "Let me do some digging through work. I've met a lot of cops since I moved here who are good at digging up dirt on people. Text me whatever info you have on her. Name, email, anything. I'll see what we can find."

"Bedankt. Thank you," he said.

We finished the night polishing off the pizza and watching *Tomorrowland* on DVD that we rented from the Red Box right outside the Papa Gino's. While we were mad that both of our houses were outside the delivery zone of the closest location, knowing we could grab a movie right outside was an upside to having to go pick the pizza up.

"Heyo," Marty said, letting himself into the front door of my house, as he'd done so many other times. I hardly locked the door, but he had a key if I had, so he'd have let himself in, anyway.

"Hey bud, where's Jess?" I asked, immediately noticing he was alone. It was uncommon for Jess to miss a Friday night hangout. I couldn't remember the last time she hadn't made it. "Everything okay?"

"Yep, all good. One of her girlfriends from work had a breakup, so a bunch of the girls from work are taking turns going over to make sure she's not alone."

"That's nice of her. How long?"

"Just for tonight."

"Oh, sorry," I said. "How long was the girl's relationship?"

"A long time. I'm not sure. But they were engaged. She caught him cheating."

"Oh man, that's terrible. I never understood the impulse to cheat."

"Nor I," Marty said. "If you're unhappy in a relationship, just be an adult and end it. It's pretty simple."

"And common courtesy. It hurts to get broken up with, but it hurts more to be cheated on."

"Speaking of missing people. Where's Victoria?"

"She had a work thing. One of the partner's wives is just about to give birth, so they're having a baby shower for her at the office. A surprise kind of thing."

"What are the chances that both of our ladies would have events on the same night that didn't require us to be there?"

I cracked open a pair of beers, handing him one and clanking mine against it. "I'm not gonna question it."

Since Marty had come to my house for dinner, he swung by Papa Gino's and picked up the pizza. He plopped it down on the counter, taking a big swig from his beer. "What a day," he said. "I feel like it's been going on for weeks."

"What's going on?"

"We went to the doctor today."

"Oh?"

"Fertility. We're talking about starting to try for a baby."

"What?" I almost yelled, mostly out of excitement but perhaps a little out of shock.

"I always wanted to be a dad," he said. "And Jess would be a great mom."

"I can see it. She's so warm and compassionate. A caring and empathetic person. She'll be a great mom. And you'll be the best dad, I know it."

"And you'll be the best uncle," he said, smiling. "Uncle Matt has a nice ring to it, doesn't it?"

It'd never crossed my mind before. Being an only child, I never thought I'd get the opportunity to be called uncle.

"It's got a great ring to it! Congratulations!" I clanked my beer against his again. "Do you want to eat on the deck?"

The back deck was one of the reasons I bought the house I did. It overlooked nothing but woods. And, due to how my house was positioned on the Cul-de-sac, you couldn't see the neighbors on either side. Both neighbors' houses were just out of sight due to the angles. To say it was peaceful would be an understatement. The only sounds were crickets, cicadas, and the occasional deer rummaging through the underbrush, looking for its next meal.

"Sounds good. I'll grab the pizza. You grab the door."

The two of us plopped down into chairs on opposite sides of the table. The sun was still high overhead, so I cranked the handle on the umbrella, spreading it to block the blinding rays. The shade was a nice reprieve from the heat of the mid-summer sun. Eventually, the sun would go behind the tall trees that lined the back of my property. Those sacred trees of the conservation land. Those trees that'd never be cut down to make room for houses to be built behind me.

"Much better," Marty said, letting out an "ahh" sound.

"How've you been?" I asked, feeling like we hadn't had time alone in a long time. Not that I minded time as a group, but it was nice to have time with just my buddy and me.

"I am okay," he said. "Victoria sent me the email today with information she found on my mother, the person, whoever. You know what I mean."

"Did she find anything good? She hadn't told me."

"I think so," he said. "Short of fingerprinting her, it's impossible to know if the woman presenting herself as my mother is, in fact, my mother. But all the information we have about her checks out."

"Everything?"

"Everything. Where she told me she lived, where she told me she went when she left, where she works. All the information is correct. It is accurate."

"So there's a good chance—"

"There's a good chance it's her," he said.

"Aren't you mad?" I asked.

"It's a, what's the word, toss-up? Sometimes I am really mad. Sometimes, I am glad that she's trying to make amends."

"Is that what she's trying to do? Make amends?"

"I think so. I'm not sure. She seemed apologetic when we met, but I don't know her end goal."

"Like you said, be an adult. Ask her."

"I hadn't thought of that," he said. "That's a good idea."

"Hi, Mom, nice to see you after thirty-five years. What do you want?"

He laughed.

"What do *you* want to get out of it?" I asked him, finishing my first beer and reaching for a second slice of pizza.

"I'm not sure. It'd be nice to get more of an explanation. To understand why she left. To grasp what she was so afraid of that she had to abandon me."

"Do you think she kept in touch with your dad after she left?"

"She must have. Well, I think so, anyway. She knew too much about me not to have kept in contact with someone."

"Weird to know that," I said. "All those years, Jean Luc had kept up the charade that she was dead."

Then it hit me. A realization that hadn't come to mind until that very moment.

"Do you think he lied to you to protect her?" I asked.

"What do you mean?"

"Well, his job was secretive, right? Were there enemies? Is it possible that someone could have wanted to hurt her, to get to him for some reason?"

"Oh. I hadn't—" he trailed off momentarily, pausing to finish his beer. "I hadn't thought of that. I could see that as possible."

"Nevermind. That's dumb. It doesn't make sense."

"Why not?" he asked.

"Why would he send her away, lie to everyone, and not send you with her? If he was trying to protect her from some work-related scary thing, why wouldn't he do the same for you?"

"Maybe he thought he could protect me better than he could protect her?"

"Possibly," I said. "That is possible."

"If she really is my mother, having a relationship with her would be nice. Get to know her. Learn about that side of my family."

"It'd be nice for your kid, kids, offspring, to have a grandparent, too."

I looked up, shielding my eyes from the ray of sun that had managed to find its way between the trees' tops and the umbrella's edge. Marty had shed a couple of tears.

"I miss him, too," I said. I made a big assumption that the tears were about his dad. The mention of a grandparent probably made him realize he missed Jean Luc.

"Papa would have been the best grandpa," he said after a moment.

"To Jean Luc," I said, raising my beer and reaching across the table to clank Marty's beer bottle.

"To Papa."

• • • • • • • • • •

"It's now or never," Marty said, opening the door to the restaurant where we were meeting "Camille." I still wasn't convinced that the woman Marty met was actually his mother. At least not based on what he had told us about their interactions.

Jessica was with the two of us. Victoria couldn't make it due to a work thing. "I'm nervous," Jess said.

"I think I'm more anxious than nervous," I said. "I just want to get this over with."

"Try to be nice," Marty asked. "If she is my mother, I don't want her first impression of you two to be negative."

"You know me, nice as pie," Jessica said with an exaggerated smile.

"I'll do my best, I promise. That's all I can offer." I laughed a little, though I'm not sure why.

We followed Marty inside and waited while he scanned the restaurant's interior, looking for her. I saw her wave from a booth in the back corner and tapped Marty on the shoulder, pointing in case he hadn't seen her.

Jess and I let Marty lead the way, assuming he'd introduce us once we got to the table, which, for whatever reason, seemed easier to me if Marty went ahead of us.

As we approached the table, she stood and outstretched her arms toward Marty, who slid into them, welcoming the hug. Her face lit up as she hugged him. She made eye contact with me, and then it looked like she did the same with Jess.

"Great to see you again," she said. "Thank you for coming."

"Camille, this is my wife, Jessica," Marty said.

"Of course, Jessica. So lovely to meet you." Her accent was faint but still present. It sounded enough like Marty's to be from the same place. Though it was so faint and almost indistinguishable, it would have been easy to fake. A rogue slip here, a phantom mispronunciation here and there, and it'd be convincing enough to trick someone not paying attention.

She let go of Marty and extended her right hand toward Jessica. She took it, shaking firmly. "Nice to meet you, as well," Jess said, ever the polite person.

"Hi, I'm Matt," I tossed out there, hoping to move the evening along.

"Yes, of course you are," she said. "Thank you for being such a good friend to Michel. He's told me all about you."

"Of course," I said, not knowing what else to say.

The four of us sat down in the booth. I gulped half the glass of water at my seat, hoping it'd calm my anxiety. Jess did the same, presumably for the same reason.

"I guess I'll dive right in," I said. "It's great you're here. After all these years, it's great you've decided to come back into Marty—sorry, Michel's life. But why now? I don't mean to come across as crass or disrespectful, but it seems suspect. We're not convinced you're his mother." It had come across as much snarkier than I had practiced it over and over in my head. The words just sort of escaped before I could make them less angry, less bitchy.

"You have every right to be concerned," she said. "I would be, too. And, honestly, I don't know why now. I want to pretend it's because Jean Luc passed that I thought Michel could use his one remaining parent. That he'd benefit from knowing the truth."

"The truth being that you didn't die?" Jess asked.

Marty sat quietly on the far side of the table from me.

"That's right," she said.

"A lie you willingly went along with for over three decades?" I added. I appreciated that Jess and I were on the same page. We planned to grill her about everything, even though Marty had asked us to be nice.

"I'm not sure how much Michel told you, but I was frightened."

"He wasn't able to tell us any specifics," I said. "Just that you were scared."

"What were you scared of?" Jess asked.

"Some of the people Jean Luc investigated," she said. "They found out."

"Investigated?" I queried, looking across at Marty, hoping he'd—finally—add some context to what Jean Luc did for work.

"Okay, look, I'm not supposed to say anything," he chimed in. "But Papa worked for the government. You knew that part. He worked in counter-terrorism. He investigated tips and leads about possible terrorism happening to Belgium."

"Oh my," I said. "Then why did you move so much?"

"Part of the job would have him go to the countries where people he was investigating lived, trying to get close to them. I'm not sure the right translation—"

"Undercover," Camille added. "He worked undercover. Infiltrating the terrorists and trying to confirm their plans so they could be shut down."

"That... wow. That's a lot," Jess said. "That seems like a legit thing to be afraid of. Is that what you do, Marty?"

"No, no," he said. "My job is similar but very different."

"It was," Camille said. "It was something I was very afraid of."

"But then why not take Marty—sorry, Michel —with you? Weren't you scared for the life of your newborn baby?" I asked, no longer caring about being nice.

"I was. I was terrified. But Jean Luc told me I was forbidden from taking Michel. That he'd track me down and bring me back."

"And you thought he would do that?" I asked.

"Very much so, yes."

"You never tried to contact Michel," Jess said. It wasn't so much of a question, but the three of us waited for her response.

"I had to keep up the charade," she said. "I had to be dead. He had to think I was dead."

"Why?" Marty asked, surprising Jess and me. "Why did I have to think you were dead?"

"You'd have tried to find me," she said. "Once you were an adult, you'd have come looking. And that could have been dangerous for both of us."

"Okay, wait. Hold up a sec," I said. "You left, when? 1980? When Marty was born?"

"Yes," she said.

"And Jean Luc was investigating a group who found out about it? In 1980?"

"Correct."

"Did he never catch them?" I asked.

"I don't understand," she said.

"Me either," Marty said.

"He'd have to have never caught this group who was threatening you. If he had caught them, the threat would be gone. You could have come home."

"I don't know," she said. She had previously been making eye contact with me but suddenly stopped.

"You said you were in contact with Jean Luc," Jess said. "Throughout Michel's entire life."

"That's right," Camille replied.

"And you never, not even one time, not even once, asked if it was safe to return?" I asked, staring directly at the side of her head. It was like she was trying to wish me away. That if she didn't look at me, I wasn't there. Proverbially burying her head in the sand.

"I suppose not," she said shyly. "I suppose I didn't think of it?"

I had just about lost it. "Come on, lady. That's bullshit. Cut it out. Who are you really?"

"I know it seems odd," she said, looking in my general direction but not at me. "It seems difficult that I did not try to come back."

"It doesn't seem difficult," I interrupted. "It seems like bullshit."

"Matt, please," Marty said, trying to capture my line of sight.

"I'm sorry, Marty. I think you're too blinded by the possibility of this woman being your mother. And maybe I'm wrong. Maybe she is your mother. But if she is, she should win an award for being the worst one in the history of mothers." Again, I felt the words fly by my lips before I could try to censor myself.

"That's not fair," Camille said.

"Yeah, Matt, take it a little easier," Jess said.

"The truth has to come out," I said. "If you're Camille, if you're his mother, prove it. Just knowing stuff doesn't prove you're his mother."

"How can I prove it?" she asked.

"You must have photos from back then? Of you and Michel, of you and Jean Luc. A birth certificate. A marriage license. A passport. Something with concrete evidence that you're who you say you are."

"I have my passport now, but it is new. I got it to come here," she said.

"From where? Where do you live now?" I asked.

"I live in Germany," she said. That's when it hit me. The accent I heard, however faint in her dialect, could have been German. The words she was mispronouncing, albeit very few, were close enough to German that I could have been getting the two accents confused.

"And you have nothing else? Nothing from when you left?" I was hounding her now. I really laid into her. If no one else was going to do it, I was.

"I left with one small suitcase. Just my clothes."

"I don't buy it," I said in Marty's direction. "I just don't buy it. It's all too suspect."

"I'm sorry I cannot convince you," she said. "I hope Marty knows the truth." She reached out and put her hand on top of his. Jessica and I both caught the movement and gave each other a look. I was fairly convinced that this woman wasn't Marty's mother. She was playing him. She was saying all the right things to him—though not to me—and working whatever angle she could to try to get him to trust her.

"I think she knows," I said. "I think she knows." I didn't know what I was talking about. I was taking a shot in the dark, hoping something stuck. Hoping that she or Marty would offer something up that could be convincing.

"What do I know?" she asked.

"Yes, what does she know?" Marty added.

That's when it hit me. If this woman were dishonest, if she weren't Marty's mother, there'd be very few reasons for motivation to try to get close to him, right? So I took a shot.

"She knows about the money," I said. Honestly, I didn't know if there was any money. Money wasn't something Marty and I talked much about, especially once he got married. "He's your problem now," I'd told Jess toward the end of the wedding party.

"What money?" she asked. I'd caught her. Her face flushed almost immediately. She retracted her hand from Marty's and put it on her lap, below the table, where I couldn't see it. If this were an action movie, she'd have been pulling her pistol from her purse, out of sight.

"Papa's money?" Marty asked. There it was. He'd finally offered a reason this woman could be trying to get close to him. A scam. "Hi, I'm your long-lost mommy. Can I have some of Papa's money?" I knew it was coming. I didn't know Jean Luc had any money, but based on those two words out of Marty's mouth, he must have.

"What money?" Jessica asked.

"Papa's," Marty said. "He had some money. He had life insurance."

"Was it a lot of money?" I asked.

"Well—" Marty started to reply.

"I'm not asking you," I interrupted. "I'm asking her."

"I don't know what you mean," she said, trying to sound innocent.

"Look, cut the nonsense," I said. "We know you're not his mother. I'm one hundred percent convinced of that now. So why are you here?"

She reached into her purse, pulling out her phone. "I have to take this. Please excuse me," she said. Marty scooted out of the booth to let her out, and she headed toward the front of the restaurant.

"Matt," Marty said. "You've been too difficult on her."

"We caught her," I said.

"Well, you caught her," Jess said. "I didn't add much."

"Okay, I caught her."

"She'll explain when she comes back," Marty said.

"She's not coming back," I replied. "She'd have left her purse if she was just excusing herself to take a call. I'm not even sure her phone rang."

Jess and Marty both stared at me with blank stares. "What?" I said. "I watch a lot of Law and Order."

She, in fact, never came back. Had we been in the movie I mentioned earlier, I imagined the phone call she took was the person she worked for. He was calling to get out of there and tell her that her cover had been blown. He must have been close, listening. We'd have chased her outside, watched her get into a cab, and then did our best to follow her. But we'd lose her.

But this isn't a movie. This is life.

And in this life, we never saw or heard from "Camille" again. Marty tried calling her phone, but the number was disconnected.

Just as quickly as she showed up, she was gone.

Vultures

"I just can't believe it," Marty said.

It'd been three weeks since the meeting with "Camille" at the restaurant. At first, he was mad at me for being so disrespectful to her and for calling her out when I knew my gut feeling was right. I knew, somehow, that the things she was saying were lies. I think Jessica knew it, too, but Marty was blinded by hope, blinded by the possibility of his mother being real or having a parent again.

It was a phrase he'd been repeating a lot since it all went down. He was, on some level, in shock. I think Jess and I were probably more relieved than anything else.

What had come out in the days after was that Marty had a substantial amount of money left to him. Now that we knew about Jean Luc's job, Marty could tell us about the insurance he'd had through the government in Belgium, just in case something happened to him. Marty didn't tell me—though I'm sure he told Jessica—how much money it was, but from the sounds of it, it was fairly substantial.

I wasn't jealous of it, given he lost his dad to get that money. Okay, maybe I was a little jealous. Victoria still hadn't officially moved in, and since she hadn't, I wasn't asking her to help with any of my bills. And honestly, I was stretched thin between the mortgage, utilities, car payments, etc. I'm sure you get it; being an adult is tough and *expensive*.

"I'm sorry it didn't work out," I said. That was a phrase I'd been saying a lot since the woman—whoever she was—walked out of the restaurant. I knew instantly that we'd never see her again.

Though, part of me had hoped her scam had continued. That we'd get to see what she was after. We'd find out if it truly was money that she was looking for. I had only guessed that's what it was, but it'd have been nice to know the truth.

Try as we might, we were never able to track down the woman. We never found out who she was. It was something that ate at me for a while before I was able to return to normal.

Jess, rubbing the back of Marty's neck, trying to console him, "It's for the best, honey."

"I know. I shouldn't be so upset because she wasn't my mother. But it feels like—"

"Like the rug was pulled out from under you?" I asked.

"I do not know this saying. What is its meaning?" he asked.

"It means you were happy with how things were going, then suddenly you're falling. You're on the ground, wondering what happened. Or something like that," I said.

"Do you... Do you think my real mother is really dead?" Marty asked.

"I think so, sweets," Jess said. "I don't think Jean Luc would have lied to you about it your whole life."

"I agree with Jess," I added. "Jean Luc, although very secretive about his job, seemed to be truthful with you, in my experience."

"That is true. He was strict about things, but I don't think he ever lied to me about things."

"And this is probably one of those things," I said. "I don't think he lied."

"But how did she know?" he asked. "How did she know so much?"

"I don't think we'll ever know," I said.

"The internet knows everything," Jess added. "Deaths are public record. So, maybe she saw something about it in the news and decided to take advantage of the opportunity."

"People are vultures," I said. "Greedy vultures."

"I just can't believe it," he said again.

The three of us hung out that Wednesday night. Victoria was at work, like usual, on Wednesdays. There was always a briefing or something she needed to finish before court Thursday morning. Best as I had tried, for weeks, to make Marty feel better, it wasn't working. His favorite pizza? He ate just one piece. Favorite movie? He didn't quote all the best lines. Bring him a puppy to play with for the day? He pet it once or twice.

    I was worried. I hadn't seen him in such a funk since Jean Luc died. For the most part, Marty was a happy guy. Always upbeat, always positive. But this whole thing had him in such a funk. It sucked knowing that I couldn't help him feel better no matter how much I tried. That killed me. And I could see the same feeling on Jess' face. The few times she and I talked about it, kind of whispery-secret conversations, she expressed the same feeling. That he just wasn't himself.

For The Rest Of Time

Victoria and I had a regular date night on Thursdays. Date night, if you will. We agreed that we would not look at our phones or take them out but also turn them completely off. We were both so tied into them, the emails, the Tweets, the messages, etc., that we knew we needed uninterrupted time, at least a couple of hours once a week.

We met at the same place we always did, right after work. A great Italian restaurant in the North End. They had fresh, handmade pasta, garlic bread that'd kill Dracula, a cozy fireplace in the corner, and cannoli to die for. Was it absurdly expensive? Yes. Was it worth it? Also yes.

"Hey beautiful," I said, spotting her sitting on the bench by the host stand, waiting for me.

"Hey, you," she said, rising to greet me. After giving me a quick kiss, she paused to hold the power button on her phone for a few seconds until the screen went dark.

"Right this way, mister and misses Gallo."

It was one of those times where we never corrected him. It was the same guy, Erik—with a K—every week when we came in. And he'd mistaken us for a married couple the first time we came in, and we rolled with it like every other time it'd happened.

Honestly, I kind of liked the sound of it. Mister and Misses Gallo. It had a nice ring to it.

Speaking of rings, I had one in my pocket. The number of times I'd stuffed my hand in my pocket on the walk from my office to the restaurant probably wore out the velvet on the ring box. I had such anxiety about losing it or having it stolen. As if some hoodlum walking by would know an expensive diamond engagement ring was sitting in my pocket, bump into me, and hurry off with it. Poof, my plans gone in an instant to someone who'd pawn the ring for a few hundred bucks.

But it was still there. I'd checked three times since walking through the door at the restaurant.

He sat us in our usual booth adjacent to the cozy fireplace, which he flicked on. It was electric, so it didn't throw off enough heat to make us uncomfortable, but it added a nice ambiance.

"Do you need the menus?" he asked, likely knowing we'd order the same thing we always did.

"The usual for me," I said, gesturing across the table to Victoria.

"Same for me," she said, grabbing her glass of water.

"I'll let your waiter know," he said before scurrying off toward the kitchen.

"How was work?" I asked.

"Oh, you know. The usual. Plenty of billable hours today. Lots of paperwork. Remember that pro-bono case I took on that I told you about with the fifteen-year-old looking to emancipate from his abusive parents?"

"Yeah."

"The judge approved the motion to disallow the parents to speak at the hearing."

"That's great, right?"

"It is," she said. "I'm not sure it'll benefit the case any since the evidence of their abuse is well documented and pretty obvious, but at least it'll prevent him from being any more traumatized by hearing them talk about or to him."

"That's great," I said, raising my water glass to toast. "Congratulations."

• • • • • • • • •

We made small talk about our days while waiting for the food to come out. Despite being a busy restaurant, the kitchen was always pretty quick.

We never had to wait too long. I don't know if being regulars benefited that process, but I'm sure it didn't hurt.

Mid-conversation about our plans for the following evening—pizza with Marty and Jess—the waiter, Jesse, brought our meals over.

Fresh-made Rigatoni with basil cream sauce and grilled chicken for me, Fettuccini Alfredo with broccoli, and chicken for Victoria.

"I can't believe it's been almost two years," she said.

"Two years?" I knew what she was talking about, but played dumb. I don't know why, but I thought it would strengthen the surprise when I proposed when dessert came. I'd pre-arranged it with the restaurant that they'd bring out her usual dessert—Tiramisu—with a special message on the plate, written in chocolate.

"Since we met," she said, looking annoyed but very happy with how her meal tasted.

"Oh," I continued with the charade. "Has it really? I guess time flies, right?"

"I guess it does. This is wonderful tonight," she said, motioning with her fork down at her plate.

"Mine too," I said. "Better than usual. Very good."

"I don't care how long it's been," she said. "I'm happy I found you that night."

"Me too. I'll have to thank Charles the next time I see him," I said. "He's the best for introducing us."

"He is the best," she said, smiling.

· · · · · • · • · • · ·

As we wrapped up our dinner, Jesse came by and scooped up our plates. "The usual?" he asked, knowing that we'd get the same desserts we always did. In addition to Victoria's special Tiramisu, I'd have the cannoli I mentioned earlier.

"Yes, thank you," I said. He and I gave each other a knowing look; hopefully, one Victoria didn't pick up on.

It meant I had ten minutes to get the timing right. I had ten minutes to tell her how much I loved her and get down on one knee before the plate came out with "Will you marry me?" in chocolate sauce written on it, potentially spoiling any surprise had I not gotten through my speech yet.

I reached across the table and took her hand. "I love you," I said. "You know that. You're my everything, and I've loved you despite being scared to love. After my marriage fell apart, I felt scared to fall back in love. I was terrified to open up and let someone in. But you made it so easy. You made me feel so comfortable, so quickly. It felt like life before you never happened."

"Oh, stop, you. You're going to make me blush."

I ignored her plea to stop. "When I look back on the past, I'm not angry. I don't regret anything I've done—however stupid some of my decisions were in my younger years—because they all led me to you. Those decisions, both good and bad, brought us to where we are today. Every decision, however small, brought us together. Had I gone ten miles an hour faster through that intersection, that could have changed the whole course of my life. Had I decided to move away to college, that could have never brought me back here. What if I had skipped the party that night? Every decision. They all brought us here."

"I love you, too," she said.

"Everyone that I love loves you." I had thought it for so long but never found the right words. "Marty, my best friend, thinks of you like his sister. Jessica, his wife, loves you like a sister. My mom already treats you like the daughter she always wanted but never had. All the people I hold most dear in this world respect and love you. And that's so important to me.

"I know it's been two years. Of course, I know. It's been 726 days, 1 hour, and roughly 32 minutes," I said, looking at my watch. "Four days from now, it will be our official second anniversary. From the day we met. I know we didn't start dating right then, but that's the day I think we both recognize as the day that our lives changed.

"Two wonderful years, full of nothing but happiness. We had one fight that entire time, and we both know it was probably my fault. You're rational and caring, loving and kind, smart and successful. You're wonderful and magnificent."

A few tears started forming in the corners of her eyes.

"What I'm trying to say is that I love you and will love you forever. I will love you through the darkest times and the brightest days. I will hold you through any sickness and not complain about all your Amazon purchases. I'll forgive you any time I'm mad at you. I'll hold every door open for you for the rest of time. I will never stray. I will never not feel for you how I feel for you right now."

With perfect timing, as if we'd rehearsed it, Jesse brought our desserts out. He stood briefly behind Victoria, waiting for me to give him a nod to put the plates down. I nodded, and he put mine down first—which he'd never done before; the lady always gets served first, he'd always say—then put hers down.

Her eyes didn't stray from mine. She wasn't sure I was done with my speech.

"I think there's a message for you on your dessert," I said, pointing. I'd distracted her enough to grab the ring box from my pocket and throw myself on the ground, landing on one knee. For whatever reason, my brain flashed back to our first date almost two years ago when I tripped and fell to the floor like some klutzy bozo.

It took her a moment to process the message, and when she looked up, I had extended my arms, ring in hand, in her direction.

"I love you now. I will love you for always. Will you do me the absolute honor of being my wife for the rest of time?"

She didn't hesitate. Not even for a fraction of a second. "Yes!" she exclaimed, jumping from her chair and meeting me on the ground on her knees. She kissed me over and over again, then wrapped her arms around my neck, squeezing tightly. "A lifetime of yeses!"

When she pulled away, I removed the ring from the box and slid it on her finger. Thankfully, it fit perfectly.

"Congratulations," Jesse said. Erik had come over to join him.

Like some sort of cheesy romantic comedy, the other patrons around us clapped.

We stood, hugging again. I couldn't help but smile.

The happiness I felt in that moment trumped every other moment of happiness I could remember having. Every part of me felt warm and safe. I hate to use cliches; I hate tropes and saying tacky things. But she completed me. She filled the empty hole in my heart that I knew was there but tried to ignore for years. She loved me in a way I'd never known before. Not through thirteen-year-old puppy dog love with Melissa. Not through grown-up love with Brooke. Not through the lust of my late teen years. Not through the false hopes of random crushes I'd develop on girls

I met. She loved me in a full, complete, and wholesome way. I was glad to have found one I didn't know I was missing.

"I love you infinity," she said.

"I love you, infinity," I said back. And I did. I do.

2016

Everything That Guy Just Said Is Bullshit

It all seemed to happen in the blink of an eye. It'd been almost a year since I proposed to Victoria, and here it was our wedding day. They say that, don't they, that as you get older, things seem to go by faster and faster? Presumably, it's because you don't have any more "firsts" to look forward to. Your first bike ride without training wheels, your first crush, kiss, and heartbreak. It all makes the time seem to go slower.

And, as you get older, those things are gone. It'll never be your first day of work again. It'll never be your first love again. It'll never be your first bike ride again. It'll never be the first time you hear that ghost story about that haunted place again. For some reason, that makes things go faster as you get older.

It's not a bad thing. Especially once you find your person. When you find the right partner, it doesn't matter how fast time goes because that person is there with you. They're always by your side.

I felt so nervous, just like the first time I'd gotten married. Like before, Marty was there for me, helping me every step of the way. He was in the back room, where we—once again—snacked on underwhelming cheese plates and assorted crackers. He, once again, assured me that I had nothing to worry about, that everything would be fine once I got out there and saw Victoria walking down the aisle with her dad.

"The difference," he said. "Is that this time, I know it's true love. I know what you and she have is real. I see things in you guys that I never saw with you and Brooke. It just wasn't there. And I'm sorry to bring her up on this special day, but I wanted you to know that this time is perfect. This time is going to be amazing. I know it."

"Thank you," I said, slightly reassured, though the anxiety in the pit of my stomach was still sitting like a concrete block at the bottom of the ocean.

I had wanted to believe everything he'd said. I kept reassuring myself that everything would be great, like he said. That Victoria was different, better, more supportive, more caring, more loving. I kept repeating those things in my head, hoping it'd stick.

And I knew it was all true. I did. It wasn't that I needed to convince myself that Victoria was wonderful. I knew she was. I think part of it, anyway, was the nerves of being out there in front of all of those people. Family, friends, distant relatives of Victoria's I'd never met. All of those people hanging on every word of mine, every word of hers. Listening as we professed our love for one another.

It didn't happen, but I felt pretty close to throwing up. You'd think someone who had previously worked in sales for a living would be a little better at public speaking than I was. But so is life, right?

Marty was right, of course. As soon as the doors opened at the far end of the aisle, I knew everything would be fine.

She shimmered and shined like a glorious princess, having come down from the high throne to be with me. She smiled as soon as she saw me, likely feeling the same anxiety I was feeling. Ear to ear, wide, causing creases to appear at both eyes. The light caught her just right, and she looked like a literal angel for a brief second.

For a second, she paused there, though I don't know why. The organizer must have caught it and restarted the entrance music so she could get to the altar at the right point in the song.

I watched her intently as if it were my first time seeing her. Like a stranger from afar, watching some woman he'd seen but didn't have the confidence to approach. And, let's be honest, had Charles not introduced us at that company party, I'd have likely never introduced myself to Victoria. There's that old saying, "In every relationship, there's a reacher and a settler." In our relationship, I was the one reaching. Victoria was—is!—way out of my league, and I'm lucky enough to have charmed her that first night, somehow.

"Who gives this woman away to be married?" the justice of the peace asked.

"I do," her father, James, replied. I reached down, shook his hand, and then took hers. "Take care of my baby."

"Yes, sir," I said, helping Victoria up to the altar. "You look incredible."

"Back atcha, handsome."

It still melted my heart when she called me handsome. It wasn't a term of endearment anyone in any of my past relationships had ever used for me. Honey, babe, cutie, sweetie, bubba, sweets. All things I'd been called. But never handsome. I loved it then as I love it now.

I won't go as far as saying I blacked out as the justice of the peace went through the rigamarole of the wedding stuff. She gave a speech we'd helped prepare about how we got together, how we fell in love, some of our quirks, our love for movies and books, and some little tidbits of our day-to-day lives.

I must have been listening for my name because I snapped back to reality as she handed me the microphone. I looked away from Victoria's eyes for the first time that afternoon for a brief moment.

"Vows, right," I started. "I've never been good with words. I've never been one to express publicly how I feel about someone. But how can I not? How can I not take this opportunity to stand here and tell you all how much I love Victoria? How can I not tell you all how much she's made me a better person? How she's fallen right into my closest group of friends." I took a brief pause to turn to Marty, then glanced over Victoria's shoulder to see Jessica, who was serving as one of the bridesmaids.

"I'd be remiss if I didn't tell the story of our first date. Of the first time I knew that Victoria was the one.

"As you can see, she's way out of my league. A solid ten to my four. I don't know what bet she lost or who she angered in a past life, but now she's stuck with me." The crowd chuckled a bit.

"I was so nervous on our first date that I tripped and fell to the floor. And, being the klutz I am, I didn't make it look graceful. I didn't have the forethought to try to cover it up with anything. No, 'Oh, I'm just tying my shoe,' or 'I thought I saw a fork under the table'. Nothing of the sort. I just fell to the ground and stayed there for a solid minute. She, as I'd have expected, laughed at me.

"I thought I'd blown it. I thought, 'There's no way this girl is ever going to forget this moment.' And, honestly, we haven't. I leaned into it. I didn't try to hide that I'm a klutz. And, yes, she laughed. I laughed, too. How could I not?

"Just as I'd gotten up and sat back down, she spilled her whole glass of water on herself. Like a waterfall off the edge of the table. And, like me, she didn't try to cover it up. She didn't jump up out of the way. She didn't make excuses or blame me for shaking the table—which I'm pretty sure I did. She just laughed at herself. We laughed at ourselves.

"And that was the day I knew I would fall in love with her. Even with my walls up and my heart guarded, I knew she'd find a way in. I knew I wanted to let her.

"There aren't enough words in the world to express to you how much I love you. There isn't enough time in forever to create enough new words. I can only promise to show you how much I cherish you today and every day. How much I cherish us. Today and forever, I promise to love you, I promise to protect you, and I promise not to be mad that you make way more money than I do." I had promised myself I'd get in that little inside joke. It was something that had come up early on in our relationship. She thought I'd be upset that she out-earned me—by a considerable amount—but, on the contrary, I loved it. I supported her career and was proud of the successful lawyer that she was.

I handed the microphone back to the justice of the peace. "And now, Victoria." She handed the microphone to Victoria.

"Everything that guy just said is bullshit," she said, completely straight-faced. The crowd gasped loud enough that I could hear them over the start of my laughter. She, obviously, wasn't serious. I'd always claimed my favorite movie was *Braveheart*. It's badass, full of violence, and it's a love story at heart. But she and I knew that my favorite movie is *My Cousin Vinny*. I could recite the entire film from memory, with all the appropriate accents and whatnot. And she knew what she'd said was one of my favorite lines. I couldn't hold back the laughter.

"That's a joke," she said, calming the anxious crowd. "It's a quote from Matt's favorite movie, but I won't say which one.

"Thank you for lifting me up. Thank you for holding me so high. Thank you for being my strength when I'm weak. Thank you for being the shoulder when I need to cry. Thank you for laughing with me when I spill water on myself. Thank you for not being mad when I laugh at you when you inexplicably fall to the ground for no apparent reason.

"You're the sky to my stars. You're the blood to my heart. You're the electricity to my car. You're the glue that holds me together, even on my roughest of days.

"Without you, I don't know how I'd survive. And, talk as you might about leagues and reachers and settlers, but the way I see it, you're the one out of my league. You're beautiful inside and out; everyone who knows you knows that.

"I will love you until the end of time, as long as you'll let me. I'll promise, here and now, in front of all of these people, to always put you first. You are my life, and I will love you for eternity."

She handed the microphone back.

The rest of the ceremony wasn't much. I remember the applause as we kissed for the first time as a married couple. I remember walking back down the aisle, Victoria's hand firmly grasping my right arm, a feeling I'll never forget.

The End & The Beginning

After we got married, we had many discussions about our living situation. We tossed around the idea of Victoria moving into my house. We toyed with the idea of selling my house and moving to the city to her apartment. We even thought about building our house somewhere, which seemed overly complicated. I know, I know, people do that every day. But it seemed like more than we were willing to bite off, at least at the time.

We settled on selling my house and buying a new house that was ours.

It made the most sense. Interest rates were reasonable. We had enough cash to put down a good down payment, and our joint income was well more than my own, so we could afford something bigger than I'd already had.

We hired the same agent Marty and I used before. Bernadette. I remember her name not because I'm good with names or because we'd hired her before but because she had the same name as a good friend from high school. She walked us through the whole process. Selling my place, buying a new place, and combining incomes. She knew everything we needed to know.

When we went to apply for the mortgage, I caught a glimpse of the form Victoria was filling out about finances. It'd never occurred to me to ask *how much* money she made. I knew she made more than I did, but not by how much.

"You make *that* much?" I couldn't help myself. I felt a little guilty for peeking, but then remembered she was my wife, and what's hers is mine and blah blah blah.

"You didn't know how much I make?"

"No. That's a lot." It was just over three-and-a-half times what I made. It was a number bigger than I'd ever imagined she'd be making. It made me, for a quick second, regret that I didn't become a lawyer.

We waited while the mortgage broker at our bank input the data and then calculated the numbers.

"This is what you can reasonably afford," she said, sliding a piece of paper across the table like we were in some sort of sitcom. Mrs. Graham was her name. I never got her first name, just Mrs. Graham from her nameplate and email signature.

"That's more than twice what my house will sell for," I said. "You're sure we can afford that much?"

"Comfortably," Mrs. Graham said. "Very comfortably. Your wife brings in quite a lot."

I turned to Victoria and smiled. She did bring in quite a bit.

• • • • • • • • •

Weeks turned into months. It felt like an endless search. We'd find the perfect house only to find out there was mold in the attic, a giant pain in the ass neighbor, or water damage in the basement. One house was beyond perfect. It had a big yard, plenty of space, and central air—the works. Then, as we were leaving the showing, the neighbor across the street showed himself. He came out in overalls, with no shirt underneath, and was gathering scrap metal in his driveway to "sell to the dump"—his words. I don't know how he existed in the Northeast, but he was a redneck. In the quick interaction with him, we knew we wouldn't enjoy living across the street from him. So we ruled out that house.

Then there was the house with the beautiful interior, incredible main suite, and two-car garage. It was beautiful. The mice living in the attic and the basement must have thought so, too.

The months felt endless. I didn't think we were perfectionists by any means, but I was starting to feel hopeless.

I could sense Bernadette getting frustrated, too. She commented on one horrid showing about how agents are supposed to warn one another about listings if they're stinkers, and the other agents weren't holding up their end of the deal. "I'm not this bad at my job," she said once. "They're misrepresenting the properties in the listings."

All the searching was worth it, though. We were greeted with a big backyard and the biggest lollipop-shaped tree I'd ever seen when we pulled into the driveway. It was perfectly round and gorgeous.

"I hope this is it," I said.

We met the seller's agent inside, and she gave us a tour. She walked us through the smart home automation, showed us the walk-in pantry, and let us sit in the magnificent stand-alone bathtub in the main bathroom. Everything was perfect, even the current paint colors on the walls.

"We wouldn't have to do anything," Victoria whispered while we were still sitting in the bathtub.

"It's literally perfect," I agreed. "Should we do it?"

She nodded, and I jumped up and out of the tub, off to find Bernadette to let her know to write up the offer.

Thankfully, the sellers accepted the offer within a couple of hours of us submitting it.

• • • • • • • • • •

We closed about a month later, scheduling moving trucks and coordinating dual moves on the same day, just like the last time I'd moved. It made sense to do both of us at once—though it was a logistical nightmare—so we could put things away at the new place together, pick where my dresser would go versus hers, decide which side of the closet was mine, pick out which drawer the silverware went in versus the cooking utensils. It was a team effort.

The living room was far too big for either of the couches we had, so we'd ordered a new one. As much as we tried to get it delivered on the day we moved in, it wouldn't come for a few days.

So, there we sat, our first night in our new house, Victoria in a folding chair, me in my rolling desk chair. Smack dab in the middle of the living room. I couldn't help but smile about the whole thing.

The doorbell rang. "Our first visitors," she said, jumping up to run to the door. "It's Marty and Jess," she called back.

"Hey guys, welcome!" I called out. "Why'd you ring the bell?"

"The door was locked. What kind of nonsense is that?" Jess joked. "It feels so out of place."

I got up and gave them both a hug, then motioned with the universal "so this is it" gesture.

"Tour?" Jess asked.

"Of course. Lead the way, Vic."

The three of us followed Victoria around the house as she talked about the plans for each room. She was excited to show them her home office, though it was just a desk, chair, and a bunch of boxes currently. She was delighted to show them the bathroom in the master.

"You could have a party in here!" Jess said.

"This is gorgeous," Marty added.

Victoria brought them downstairs, stopping briefly in the kitchen, then ended the tour in the finished basement. "We'll probably set up a big screen down here or get a pool table or something," she said. "It's still up for debate."

The basement also contained the fifth bedroom and fourth bathroom, which we knew we'd use as a guest room. Any time anyone needed to stay, we'd have the space ready for them. No pull-out couches, no sleeping on floors. A dedicated room for guests, which we'd use a bunch over the years.

"Did you grab pizzas on the way over?" I asked Marty as we headed back upstairs.

"I couldn't find a Papa Gino's anywhere near here," he said. "Why did you even buy this dump?" he poked me in the ribs, causing me to fall back on the stairs, having to grab the railing to catch my balance.

"I'm sure we'll find something," I said. "Vic, where can we get a good pizza around here?"

"I've got us covered," she called back from the kitchen.

As Marty and I entered, we saw Jess handing a square box to Victoria. "It's Papa Gino's," she said. "But frozen. You make it at home. It's not the same thing, but I'm sure it'll be pretty close."

"I've had it at work," Victoria added. "It's pretty good for frozen pizza."

Every week, when we'd go grocery shopping, we'd be sure to pick up one of those pizzas. Just in case we were hosting Friday night at our house.

And, although Marty and Jess' house was farther away than when I lived alone, we still got together every Friday night to hang out, talk about our weeks, watch movies, and enjoy each other's company.

No matter the distance, we always made the trip and put our friends at the top of our priority list.

2017

We'll Tell Them All At Once

As the great Ferris Bueller once said, "Life moves pretty fast." And, as I'm sure you likely know, the older you get, the faster life seems to move. I know, I know, I already talked about this. My point here is that life is a blur. It's zipping by at the speed of, well, life, and sometimes you don't remember the in-between moments.

You get to momentous occasions in life—getting married, buying a house, for example—but the smaller moments, the unimportant stuff, seem to go by and never make enough of a mark on you to remember it.

I know a lot of things happened between when Vic and I got married and bought a house until now. I know there were plenty of Friday nights with Marty and Jess. There were plenty of work events and parties. There were lots of ups, lots of downs, and tons of things that should have formed memories but didn't.

But I'll never forget the day Vic burst into my home office, asking if my meeting was important.

I turned off my camera and muted myself, putting up the coffee emoji, indicating, "I've stepped away; I'll be right back." I don't remember who taught me that was a thing people did, but I'd always done it on the off chance I had to step away for a while.

She pulled me out of my office and into the kitchen.

"I haven't been feeling right lately," she said. "So I took a pregnancy test."

She then pulled it from her pocket and showed it to me.

I hugged her, immediately, then pulled away. "You're sure?"

"I'm sure," she replied, pulling a handful of other tests from her purse on the counter. "I took five."

I hugged her again. I was lost for words, which was very rare. I didn't know what to say. I was excited—though immediately terrified—beyond words.

"We're going to be parents," she whispered in my ear.

It was something we'd talked about but hadn't come up with a clear timeline as to when. We knew we both wanted kids but didn't know when the timing would be right. We just knew we wanted to be parents. After seeing her with her niece and nephews over the years, I knew she'd be a great mother. She was kind and compassionate, caring, and a great listener. And she had the patience of a Pope. All qualities I knew would make her a great mom.

I, on the other hand, had concerns with myself. I'd never been around kids much. I didn't have any younger siblings. I wasn't very close with any of my cousins, who were all younger than me. The thought of holding a newborn gave me anxiety. Not because I was scared—okay, maybe a little—but because I'd never done it before. I didn't know how to do it, what to expect, or whether I'd be good at it.

"We're going to be parents," I reiterated. "Parents."

I think I was a little in shock at first. I don't think I processed it all, at least not right away.

"I love you," Victoria said. "So much."

"I love you," I said back.

"Now, go back to your meeting. We need to wait to tell people. It's bad luck to tell others too early."

"You're the boss. Yes, ma'am."

I feel like I stumbled back to my office, my feet moving themselves along with very little control by my brain, as if my body was following the motions. I have no idea how the rest of that meeting went. I don't remember who was there or what it was about. I remember getting back to my desk, sitting down, turning my video back on, and staring blankly at my screen.

MY BEST FRIEND, MARTY

• • • • • • • • • •

The timing worked out: It landed on a Friday night when it was "the right time" to tell Marty and Jess. Well, maybe not exactly on Friday night; we might have told them a few days early.

As usual, they let themselves into our house. It was our turn to host. Vic already had the frozen pizza in the oven when they arrived. Jess had texted that they were running a little behind schedule, so we anticipated everyone being hungry by the time they got to our house.

"Sorry, sorry," Jessica said as they came into the kitchen. "We had a... a thing."

"Yes, we are sorry for being tardy," Marty added.

"It's fine. Don't worry," Victoria said, pulling the oven mitt off and hugging them each.

"Everything okay?" I asked. For some reason, they both looked a little anxious. Maybe a little nervous, too.

"Yes, everything is great. I'm famished," Marty said, trying to change the subject.

"Nice try," I said, eyeing him. "I know better. What's up?"

He looked at Jessica, who gave him a slight nod. "We were at the doctor," he said, reaching into his pocket.

"The doctor?" Victoria asked. "Who's sick?"

"The OB," Jess said, waiting for Marty to pull out whatever he was reaching for.

"Who's OB is sick?" I quipped. No one laughed.

It was a sonogram.

"It's a boy," Marty said, holding the sonogram to show us.

"We're pregnant," Jess said.

"I think they got that from the sonogram," Marty joked. "We thought we wouldn't be able to have a baby naturally because of my chemo. But here we are!"

"You're pregnant?" Victoria squealed, leaping past me to hug Jessica.

"Congratulations!" I yelled. I looked over at Victoria, who had just finished wrapping her arms around Jess' neck.

She nodded.

"Well," I said. "Your son will have a friend from day one." I stepped over to the table where I'd hidden our sonogram under my placemat to show them during dinner and retrieved it.

"It's a girl," Victoria said. "We're pregnant, too!"

"Oh my gosh!" Jess yelled, pulling Victoria back in for a hug.

Marty grabbed and pulled me, squeezing me harder than I think he'd ever squeezed me. "We're going to be dads!"

"We're going to be dads!" I said, still feeling a bit uneasy with that statement. It was starting to sit right, but my brain wasn't fully on board. At least not yet.

"We must celebrate," Marty said.

I'd already bought a bottle of champagne, which felt mean since neither of the women could drink it. But Marty and I clanked glasses and made a toast to both unborn children.

"To our future children," he said. "May their mothers have healthy and easy pregnancies. May they grow in their tummies to healthy babies and be born with no complications."

"Hear, hear," I added.

The four of us clanked our champagne flutes, though Jess and Vic had sparkling cider in theirs.

"When are you due?" Jess asked as we sat down at the table.

"September," Victoria answered. "Mid-September."

"No way! We're the end of September!"

"Our kids are going to be best friends," Marty said. "Just like us."

It warmed my heart to think my daughter would have a built-in best friend right from birth. It made me happy to think that we'd go to their house on a Friday night, pick up an extra pizza for the kids, and they'd get to play in Marty's son's room while we hung out in the kitchen after dinner. They'd get into silly little kid fights about who gets to play with the Tonka truck, or she'd complain that he kicked over her block tower. They'd come down and beg for ice cream in unison until one of the four of us gave in and gave it to them. I had flashes of them having sleepovers, camping out in a pillow fort in the living room at our house. Marty and Jess anxious to leave their son overnight for the first time. Us reassuring them that it'd be fine and that they should come over for breakfast in the morning, and they'd see both kids were fine.

It made me think of my childhood. How I'd never really had a best friend until Marty came into my life. I'd had friends, and they'd come and gone. I'd had good relationships before Marty but never really had a best friend until he came along. I never felt that bond where I knew he'd be there for me, no matter what, and vice versa. And I was glad our kids would have that. With the amount of time their parents spent together, it'd be hard for them not to become friends.

Marty raised his glass again. "I'm so thankful that you two are in our lives. I'm so happy to know and love you both."

"Aww, Marty," Victoria said. "You're going to make me cry."

"Get used to that," Jess said. "I cry over everything now."

"It's true," Marty said. "Even a hint of something sad, and she's got the waterworks flowing."

"It's the hormones," she said. "Absolutely the hormones."

I was off in my little world. I'd heard what they were saying but was too busy daydreaming about the future to have contributed to the conversation. Ideas of backyard playgrounds and swing sets popped into my head. A tree fort? Maybe. Swimming pool? Probably. A big wheel in the driveway for her to ride around on when she got older? Definitely. Suddenly, I felt the anxiety fading away. The fear of not knowing what to do seemed to be easing up. The more I thought about what things I'd do for her, the less nervous I felt.

There was a hint of "I'll be the dad I never had" that popped into my head, too. I can't lie about that. Growing up with just my mom was wonderful. I'll never deny that. She was and is the best; I will fight anyone who disagrees. But knowing my daughter would have a great dad, the most amazing mom, and the best "aunt" and "uncle," she could have set my mind at ease.

"Have you told your families yet?" Jess asked.

"That's the plan for tomorrow," I said. "We're having lunch with my mom and Vic's parents, sister, and her sister's family."

"We'll tell them all at once," Victoria said. "We wanted you guys to be the first to know."

"You're the closest to us," I added. "So we wanted to share the news with you first."

"It's like we're the same people," Jess said. "We haven't told my family yet, either. We're going to call my mom and dad tomorrow. Separately, of course."

I could see a small amount of pain in Marty's eyes for a moment. He didn't have any family left. Jean Luc had been gone for almost ten years, and the woman he'd hoped would be his mother was a fraud.

I reached across the table and grabbed his hand. "Jean Luc would be so proud of you," I said. "He'd have been an excellent grandpa."

"He would have been," he replied. "I have no doubts."

The Joint Block Party

"I'm so anxious," Victoria said. It was the morning of our very first block party in our new house. We'd moved in about three months ago and had planned the party in full. Following tradition, we went around to the houses in the neighborhood, introducing ourselves and inviting people and their families to the event.

"Me too," I said, though I don't know why. I'd been doing these block parties for over a decade. Sure, the locations varied, but the core function was the same. Get a bunch of tables and chairs, invite everyone, ask everyone to bring food, and help Marty with whatever recipes of Jean Luc's he'd make. I had it pretty down pat.

But this was our first party in the new neighborhood. It was a bit of a relief that we lived on a Cul-de-sac, so we wouldn't have to block off traffic. And, instead of spreading tables out over the whole street, we could use the whole circle at the end of the road, right out in front of our house.

To make the delivery of Marty's food easier, we let him use our kitchen to do the prep. He'd already been working hard when I got up around six that morning. "I let myself in. Hope I didn't wake you," he said.

Jess was doing her best to help him where she could but needed a lot of breaks. As she neared the end of her pregnancy, she got increasingly tired when on her feet. Meanwhile, Victoria, the American Gladiator, didn't miss a beat. She didn't slow down at work. She didn't miss any deadlines or skip any chores around the house. She was a tank.

I also lent a hand where possible—ensuring I was helpful but not in the way.

"It all smells so good," Victoria said, bounding into the kitchen to grab a bottle of water before going back to her pre-natal yoga workout. "Want to join me for some yoga, Jess?"

The look on Jess' face said it all. If the puke emoji were a person, it'd have been Jess at that moment.

"Got it. See ya," Victoria said before scurrying out of the kitchen.

Marty was still working hard when I started bringing out the tables and chairs we'd rented for the event. We also, for the first time, rented some canopies and tents. In years past, we were always lucky enough to host the event somewhere that had shade: Mom's street, our joint backyard, or either of our separate houses. But the Cul-de-sac was wide open in the sun, and being August, it would be a very hot day.

Victoria had also rented an inflatable water slide for the neighborhood kids to stay cool in. Well, she described it as a water slide. When we inflated it, I found it was a miniature water theme park. It had two slides, a climbing wall, three separate pools, a ladder, monkey bars (don't ask me how inflatable monkey bars were supposed to work, but they did!), and a sprinkler system. I was sure it'd be a hit.

Our neighbors on either side of us must have seen me starting to carry stuff out of the garage and come out. John from the house on our left and Jeremy from the house on our right. It seemed like they had coordinated their efforts because they both said hi at the same time.

"Oh, hey, Jeremy," John said.

"John, good to see you." They shook hands, and then each shook mine.

"Looks like you could use a hand," John said.

"That'd be great. Grab the canopies and tents on the left there and work on getting them set up. The rental company said they should be pretty easy to erect, but let me know if you need a hand." I continued pulling stacks of chairs out, aligning them around the tables I'd already set up.

Jeremy helped John lift the bags containing the various pieces of the handful of coverings we'd rented. When I paused to take a breather from carrying all the chairs, it looked like they had made quick progress in setting up the tents. The shade was already helpful, and the sun wasn't even close to overhead yet.

"Great idea on the tents," John called out. "I was worried we'd cook in the sun."

"Not my first rodeo," I shouted from the garage. "We've been doing this a long while."

When the last of the chairs were set up, I helped get the last two tents up overhead before inflating the water theme park.

"Can you grab the hose from the side of the house?" I asked in their general direction as soon as the inflatable looked full enough to fill the various pools.

"On it," Jeremy called back.

"You guys go all out, huh?" John asked, now standing next to me.

"I think my wife went a little overboard this year," I said. "But, yeah, we do this every year, no matter where we live. It's not usually this big of an event, but we like to get everyone together to hang out, even if just for the day."

"It's a great plan," he said as Jeremy returned with the hose. A bit of water escaped through the end he'd folded to stop the flow until we were ready.

"Whoops," he said, jumping back. "I'll have to run home and change my shoes."

"Just stand in the sun for a few minutes," John said. I looked at my watch. It was already 81°. I hadn't realized how hot I was until that moment. Standing there holding the air pump, I felt the sweat dripping down the small of my back.

"When your wife came over and invited us," Jeremy said, "she mentioned something about famous Belgian food?"

"Oh, did she?" I laughed. "My best friend is from Belgium and makes so many amazing things. Your mind is going to be blown. He's in my house right now, cooking."

"I've never had anything from Belgium before. Other than a waffle, I guess," John said.

"You'll want it for the rest of your life after today," I said. "No joke."

· · · · · • · • · • · ·

I'd finished prepping everything outside and went back to my house. Not only to change but to cool off for a while. It was just after eleven, and we'd told people to start coming around one, so I had time to relax a bit and help Marty more.

"I'm ready," he said as I approached. "Just keeping things warm that need to be kept warm."

"I have all the sternos set up outside. If you want, I can light them now, and we can bring stuff out."

"That's a great plan," he said.

"I'll be sitting right here if you need me," Jess said, trying to crack a smile. It was obvious how uncomfortable she was in the summer heat.

"Almost there, my love," Marty said, kissing her on the top of her head on his way out the door.

"Hang in there, Jess," I said. "Vic, we're starting to bring the food out."

"Already?" she called back from our bedroom upstairs.

"The sternos are set up. No sense in waiting."

"Okay, I'll be down to help shortly. Just getting out of the shower. Where's Jess?"

"In the dining room," Jess shouted back.

"Be down in a bit," Victoria said.

Marty and I made twenty trips outside with armfuls of dishes, containers, platters, and Tupperware. It felt like he'd made much more than years past.

"This is a lot, isn't it?" I asked.

"Don't tell Jess," he said. "I spent way more on the food than I told her I did." He laughed, but I could tell he was serious about not telling her.

"Got it. I'll keep it between us."

"I figured there'd be a lot of people," he said. "We invited people from our neighborhood, too. Even though we live a bit away, we figured maybe people would make the drive."

"I hope so," I said. "It'd be nice to meet some new people."

On our last trip outside, we spent some time making sure everything was covered, being warmed properly, and all the little signs explaining what everything was that Jess had made were in place.

We had all of Jean Luc's favorites. So many things he'd made that very first block party we'd had twelve years prior. Marty must have spent a lot of time watching him prepare the food in years past because it all looked spot-on to me, as usual. My mouth watered just thinking about the Oliebollen, a super soft and very fresh doughnut-like dessert. If Victoria would let me, I'd eat nothing but Oliebollen the entire day. But she always asked me to eat a more balanced meal, so I'd do my best to comply.

· · · • • · • • · · ·

Mrs. Dubois from down the street was the first to show up, around twelve-thirty. "Am I too early?" her arms were filled with not one but two crock pots. Steam escaped the lid of one that jarred loose on the walk down the street.

"Mrs. Dubois, I'm so sorry. I didn't see you coming. I'd have helped you," I said. "Let me take those." I motioned for Marty to grab one from her and took the other.

"We'll set you up right over here," Marty said, placing the crock pot on one of the tables near his. "Do you need them plugged in?"

"That would be swell," she said. She was an older lady, maybe in her mid-to-late sixties, but she still had pep in her step. I struggled to balance the one crock pot I'd taken from her, and she'd carried two of them down the street problem-free.

"We hadn't anticipated power," I said. "Let me run inside and run an extension cord out here."

Thankfully, the pump for the water inflatable had a pair of outlets on it, so I didn't need to run long cords from the house. I just piggybacked off the pump.

"There we go, all plugged in," I said as I popped the two plugs into the surge protector I'd put under the table.

"What do we have in them?" Marty asked.

"One is my mother's world-famous homemade mac and cheese. The other is my own special recipe for mashed potatoes. I hope that's okay."

"Absolutely, it is," I said. "We're so glad you came! This is my friend, Marty. He's the creator of all of this other food." I gestured broadly to the two eight-foot tables behind me covered in Marty's food.

"I won't lie," she said. "I could smell it from my house. That's why I came down a little early."

Just then, Mr. and Mrs. Costello and Mr. and Mrs. Porter, with their kids, Kylie and Jackson, came walking down the road. I waved as I saw them approaching.

Cars started coming down the street, parking on either side of the road but not coming into the circle at the end.

"That's Dave and Demeter," Marty said, recognizing some people getting out of their car. He waved. "They're from my neighborhood."

"Welcome. Hi. Hello. Nice to see you." I'd gone into social auto-pilot, greeting everyone who showed up, introducing them all to Marty, and vice versa, for people from his neighborhood.

I quickly grabbed my phone and texted Jess and Victoria: *People are showing up. Come out when you're ready.*

They both thumbs-upped my message pretty quickly, and I saw the door to the house in the garage open, the two of them exiting to join us.

"This is my wife, Victoria," I said as she approached the group of people I was talking with. "And this is Jessica, Marty's wife."

Casual greetings followed.

Mr. Spurk showed up, followed by Kaitlyn, who was recently divorced and lived just up the street. Ellie and her boyfriend, Max, joined the group. Kristin and her partner, Katie, showed up.

John had excused himself back to his house and was rejoining the group, pulling his grill behind him. "I've got burgers and dogs coming," he called out to applause from the group.

"That reminds me," Jeremy said. "I've got smoked meats at my place. Back in a flash," and off he went to fetch the meats.

"Oh my god!" I heard someone exclaim from behind me. I turned around to see Marty with a huge smile on his face. Jamie and Jaimie (imagine marrying someone with the same name as you?) from the end of the road had just tasted Marty's favorite traditional dish, Belgian Waffles. He had enough whipped cream, strawberries, and blueberries to feed an army. And he wasn't selfish with handing them out with the waffles.

Without me seeing, he'd somehow set up a waffle iron and made the waffles fresh to order. It was something he'd never done in years past. He'd always made a few dozen in the house and heated them outside.

He must have seen a puzzled look on my face because he called out to me. "Jess got it for me for my birthday."

I nodded and lifted my beer to give him silent cheers from across the Cul-de-sac.

"It's so great that you arranged all of this," Kaitlyn said. "This is so much fun. And the food!"

"It's a tradition of ours," I said. "Marty and I started doing it in 2005, and we've kept with it all these years. Now, we do it in honor of his father, who passed away a while back. All the Belgian food you see is recipes his dad had passed down to him."

"We'll have to toast to him later," Ben—Mr. Porter—said.

"Great idea," I said.

More and more families showed up. It seemed like the families with kids were all arriving at the same time. A lot of the kids squealed when they saw the inflatable water playground—I can't think of a better word to describe it, so I'm going with playground. We'd prepped them for it, so most of them had bathing suits on—the couple of little boys who didn't have suits jumped in right in their clothes.

"Hey honey," Victoria said, tapping me on the shoulder.

I turned to face her. "Yes, doll?"

"This is a great success. We've got some great food from the neighbors. John's grilling up a storm. Did you try Jeremy's ribs? Wow."

"No, not yet. I haven't eaten much."

"You're not stuffing yourself with Marty's Oliebollen, are you?"

"Ha, no. Not yet, anyway."

"Mrs. Dubois' mashed potatoes are heavenly. You'll have to grab some. And Mr. Spurk, what's his name, do you know?" she didn't wait for me to respond. "He brought a cake from Davinci's Bakery, and it's incredible."

"I think we're off to a good start here," I said. I looked around and estimated at least two hundred people already in the Cul-de-sac. People who didn't know each other, had lost touch, or were old friends. All of them socializing with one another. The kids playing in the water playground often yelled loud enough to be heard throughout the neighborhood.

"They're going to expect this level of awesome every year," I said, pointing to the water playground with my bottle. "I don't even want to ask how much that thing cost to rent for the day."

"You're right," she said. "They'll expect it every year. And, no, you don't want to ask."

She kissed me on the cheek and whisked her very pregnant body away to talk to Andrew, a lawyer who lived up the street whom she'd worked on a case with once.

I stepped back a moment, halfway up my driveway, to take it all in.

It was such a small thing on its surface. Tables and chairs, some tents, people and food. It seemed so simple, but it'd always felt like so much more. We were bringing people together. Would they maintain friendships after this? I don't know. I occasionally saw people exchanging phone numbers. Some of the older kids exchanged Instagrams and TikToks. The younger kids pleaded with their parents for play dates with some of the other kids. It gave me such peace, the whole thing.

"Sorry I'm late," I heard a familiar voice calling from the crowd. It was my mom. I finally spotted her over by Marty.

She waved when she saw me looking at her. "Hi Mom, glad you're here," I thought. I smiled at her.

There was no time wasted before she had a plate full of food and stood beside me.

"Almost grand baby time," she said. "I'm so excited. How's Vicky feeling?"

"She's a tank," I said. "Aside from her stomach, you wouldn't even know she's pregnant. She goes and goes and goes."

"Mmmm," she said, sucking the barbecue sauce from her fingers. "Whichever neighbor made these ribs needs to be on a Gordon Ramsey show."

"I haven't tried them yet, but Vic said they're to die for, too."

"How's Marty?"

"He seems good. Why?"

"I think these parties are hard for him. Add in that he's about to be a dad and doesn't have either of his parents. It's a lot. You should make sure to check in on him."

"I do. I will. I'll make sure to talk to him before he leaves tonight."

"Good boy." She grabbed my face like she'd done my whole life and planted a big kiss on my cheek, leaving barbecue sauce smudges on both sides of my face. "You're a good boy."

"I'm a grown adult, Mom," I said, knowing she'd correct me. She always said the same thing and didn't disappoint.

"You'll always be my little boy." There it was. Exactly as expected, exactly on cue.

• • • • •●• • • •

The party didn't wind down until much later than I had anticipated. The street lights had just started coming on when the last kid left the playground, asking her mom for a towel.

"I guess we should get going," Jessalynn, the mom, said. "Thank you for everything. This was beyond wonderful."

"Thank you so much for coming," Victoria said. I was sitting in one of the few chairs that hadn't been brought back into the garage. Exhausted wasn't even word enough to explain how I felt. I was ready to fall asleep right there and then.

"Being social is exhausting," Victoria said, sitting beside me.

"This is why I love you," I said. "You get me. Carrying all the stuff, setting everything up, all that is easy. I'm not physically tired from that. It's being *on* for a whole day that's made me tired."

"Imagine doing all of that eight months pregnant," she said.

"Better you than me." I laughed.

"Well, I think that's the last of it," Marty said.

"Last of what?" I asked.

"Food. Tables. Chairs. Water. Everything."

"Thank God," Jess said. "I was exhausted ten hours ago. Take me home."

"You were a hit, as always, bud," I told Marty.

"Yeah, yeah, you're both great. We love you, but bye," Jess said, pulling Marty's arm toward their car.

"Good night! Love you guys," Victoria called out.

I don't know why I'd done it so much already, but I waved to them as they got into their car and headed home. I grabbed the last chair and headed in, figuring I'd deal with the water playground in the morning. I'd turned the pump off and hoped all the water would empty itself as it deflated. But that was a problem for the morning.

"I know it's only nine, but I'm ready for bed," I said.

"Me too," Victoria agreed.

We headed inside, closed the garage, and headed upstairs. I took the quickest shower known in the history of humanity and was in bed by 9:15. Asleep by 9:16.

Friends For Life

"It's happening," Marty said before I could even say hello. My phone vibrating on my nightstand had woken me up. "He's coming early."

I pulled my phone away from my face, swiped up on the phone call to view my home screen, and saw the date—September 15th.

"He's early," I said, still waking up. "Vic, wake up. It's Marty. He says the baby is coming early."

"Huh? What?" she rolled over and looked at me through sleepy eyes. "What's happening?"

"Is she in labor?" I said, switching the phone to speaker.

"Yes. Her water broke about an hour ago. We just got to the hospital. We didn't even have anything packed."

"How is she doing?" Victoria asked.

"Good. Contractions are still four minutes apart but getting closer. They put her in a private room."

"Want us to come down?" I asked.

"When you can. I know it's still early." The clock on my phone informed me it was just after six. It was a Friday, but I had no problem ducking out of work to support them.

"Ok, we'll get up and be on our way," Victoria said.

I rolled out of bed, grabbing some clothes from my dresser. "Need me to bring anything?"

"No. We're okay for now. I'll probably want some breakfast later, though."

"You got it, bud. Text me the room number."

My phone dinged before he even responded. "Text me when you get here."

"Oof," Victoria said as she stood up. "My back is killing me."

Marty's son was due on the 29th. My daughter had been due on the 8th. They were ahead of schedule, and we were behind.

"I swear, if you go into labor today, it's going to be the world trying to tell us something."

"I should be so lucky," Victoria said. "I'm done being pregnant."

If you had asked me even last month, I'd have said she enjoyed it. She was still doing yoga, still working full-time, and still enjoying life. But something changed as we crossed into the last month. The days got tougher for her. The pain got more intense. That morning sickness everyone had warned her about finally showed up. Her joints ached. The trailing days of the summer seemed to make her sweat enough to make her clothes wet almost every day. She couldn't drive anywhere anymore because her stomach was too big to reach the steering wheel. The few days she did need to go to court, I drove her or put her in an Uber. Her firm was kind enough to let her work remotely on all other days, which she'd taken comfort in and adjusted to well enough.

• • • • • • • • •

By the time we'd gotten to the hospital, Marty had texted that Jess' contractions were two minutes apart. *They'll likely bring her into the delivery room soon.*

We parked and raced inside. *We're here* I texted him.

Moments later, he came out into the emergency room waiting area and hugged us. "I'm going to be a papa!" He was so excited.

"I..." Victoria said. "I think you are, too, Matt." She stepped back to reveal the floor below her and her lower half were wet. "Either I peed myself, or my water just broke."

"Nurse!" Marty yelled. "We've got a two-for-one special." He laughed at his joke much harder than he should have.

A nurse heard his call, probably ignoring the joke he'd made, and rushed over with a wheelchair. "Are you in labor, miss?"

"Yes. I think my water just broke on your floor."

I grabbed her hand and held it through the hospital to the maternity ward. Marty in tow.

"Our children will be born on the same day!"

"They'll have a friend for life," I said.

"Jess is in the room two doors down," Marty said. "I'll go be with her now. Text me updates." He kissed Victoria on her forehead and hugged me tightly before whisking himself back to their room to check on Jess.

"Good luck," I called out behind him, but he was already jogging down the hall and likely didn't hear me.

"You ready for this?" I asked Victoria.

"As ready as I'm going to be. Are you ready?"

"I'm not," I said, honestly. "But I know with you by my side, I can do anything."

"Hi, I'm Doctor Weir. I'll be your delivery doctor today. Doctor Anders is out of town on vacation."

"She mentioned she might be gone if we didn't deliver on time," Victoria said. "Nice to meet you."

"Any pain?" she asked.

"No, not yet. My water just broke."

"Okay, we're going to get you on the monitors and give you fluids as a precaution." The nurse in the corner—different from the one who'd brought us back there—jumped to action, connecting Victoria to all sorts of monitors, and gave her an IV. She barely flinched.

And then, just as quickly as we were brought back, everyone else left the room. It was just Victoria, machines beeping and humming, and I.

I couldn't help but smile at her. The idea that we'd be parents within the next few hours was overwhelming. I knew we had everything prepared at home. The nursery was ready. The baby monitors—yes, monitors, I got two, just in case one failed—were set up. We had plenty of diapers, bottles, spit-up clothes. I thought we were ultra-prepared for everything. Spoiler: I was not. I ran to Babies-R-Us almost daily for the first few months of her life. I don't know what new parents do now that they've gone out of business. I digress.

• • • • • • • • •

In the delivery room now. Taking pictures. All good.

I relayed the message to Victoria, letting her know Jessica was doing well and that the baby would probably be along any time.

"How are your contractions?" I asked.

"Still pretty minor," she said. "No big pains yet, anyway."

It'd been four hours since we were brought back to the maternity ward. The doctor had checked on us a handful of times, pressing buttons and reading printouts from the various machines connected to Victoria. One of the monitors showed her level of contractions. Each time one hit, a little spike on the graph would pop up and then return to normal.

They averaged eight minutes apart. They hadn't gotten any closer together since the monitoring started.

"Everything looks great," Dr. Weir said, excusing herself politely to check on other patients.

"You're doing great," I said. She wasn't even breaking a sweat. The air conditioning in the room did a great job keeping the too-warm-for-mid-September heat at bay outside.

Son is here. My phone chimed. I held it up for Victoria to see.

"Marty's a dad," I said.

"Jess is a mom," Victoria added.

Congratulations, I wrote back. *Jess ok?*

Jess great. Son healthy. 9 pounds 8 ounces. 22 inches.

Big boy!

"He came out huge," I told Victoria. "Nine pounds, eight ounces. Twenty-two inches."

"Poor Jess!" She made herself laugh.

"Poor Jess, indeed."

The monitor spiked as Victoria winced a bit.

"You okay?"

"Yes," she said through the pain. "It'll... pass..." Then she let out a big exhale as the spike on the graph dropped.

It was just over seven minutes since the last contraction. They were getting closer together, but not by much.

"You okay?" A nurse popped her head in the door on her way by. "I saw the monitor at the nurse's station."

"All good," Victoria said, throwing the nurse a thumbs up.

"Great. Keep it up," she said as she left the doorway.

· · · · · • · • · · ·

Noon quickly turned to five. Then it was seven.

It was just after seven thirty—contractions just five minutes apart now—when Marty wheeled Jess down the hall to our room.

"Someone wanted to come meet his auntie and uncle," Jess said as they rolled in.

"Oh, you guys!" Victoria immediately blurted out. "He's gorgeous."

"Say hello to Lucas Matthew," Marty said.

"Lucas as a tribute to Marty's dad. And Matthew, because, well, I think you can figure that out," Jess added.

I was so touched that I literally almost fell over. I grabbed Victoria's bed to catch myself. "Wow, really?"

"Really," Jess said. "Do you want to hold him?"

"I would love to," I said, quickly grabbing some hand sanitizer from the pump on Jess' bedside table as Jess reached out, handing me their brand-new baby.

It felt surreal to hold him. Barely a few hours old, both of his parents were exhausted. But I felt a connection with him immediately. This tiny human was half and half of two of my closest friends. And, I swear, he looked at me and smiled. I know, I know, babies can't see when they're so new, but I swear he did.

Victoria's monitor beeped. Three minutes apart now.

"Do you want to hold him?" I asked her.

"Maybe when I'm done making ours," she said, seemingly trying to make light of her pain.

"He's perfect," I said before handing him back to Jessica. "He's so lucky to have you guys as parents."

"He's so lucky to have you guys as his aunt and uncle," Marty said.

It was almost ten before Marty wheeled Jess back to her room to try to get some sleep. A nurse came and took Lucas back to the nursery. Marty looked exhausted when he returned to our room.

"I'm going to go home and get Jess some stuff," he said. "Text me when your girl comes. I'll come back."

"Don't be stupid," I said. "Go home and get some sleep. You've been up since the wee hours of the morning."

"I'll come back," he said. "I don't want to miss a single minute with our kids."

It had a nice ring to it—our kids. I was so sure they'd be best friends, just like their dads.

He left just after ten thirty that night.

Victoria's monitor beeped again. Two and a half minutes since the last one.

"Getting closer," the doctor said, popping her head in. "You doing okay?"

She didn't respond but gave the doctor a hand wave, sort of a "so so" response. I could tell the contractions were getting tougher for her to get through.

"You're so strong," I said. "I know you must be hurting."

"I'm okay. I can do this." It sounded like she was trying to convince herself rather than me.

"You can. I know you can." I tried to reassure her. "She'll be here before you know it."

The monitor beeped again. Just over a minute between them.

"Why don't we call the doctor?" I asked.

She nodded. "Good idea."

I pressed the call button. I half expected a team of people to come rushing in and whisk her off to the delivery room.

But they didn't. It took them about fifteen minutes, during which the contractions got less than thirty seconds apart. Victoria was screaming in pain. It was probably loud enough to wake Jessica up down the hallway.

"Drugs! Drugs now!" She yelled as the doctor finally came in.

"Looks like it's time," she said. A nurse handed me a disposable top and pants to put on.

"Bring your phone," the nurse said. "If you want to take pictures. You do want to come in, right?"

We hadn't really discussed it, but I had assumed I'd be present in the delivery room. I looked to Vic to get her nod of approval and threw on the disposable clothes, making sure to put my phone in the breast pocket of the top.

"Off we go," the doctor said, dislodging the brakes on the bed. The nurse grabbed the headboard and pushed Victoria out of the room. The doctor and I walked out together.

"I do this all the time," she said. "Don't worry about a thing."

"Can you tell I'm nervous?"

"I don't need to. All dads are nervous. It's human nature."

"She'll be okay?"

"I can't make promises, but most of the time, everything goes off without a hitch."

I followed her down the hall to the delivery room, where a team of other men and women were waiting. Their scrubs all matched a light shade of blue.

Victoria screamed again in pain as the doctor gave her the epidural. "Give it a few minutes," she was reassured that the pain would stop soon.

Over the next eleven hours, Victoria pushed and yelled and squeezed my hands. She pummeled my chest when the pressure in her abdomen was too much to handle. She called me names and blamed me, as you'd see on a sitcom. During calm moments, we discussed names. We kicked around several ideas but hadn't settled on anything by the time she was born.

8:36 am. 6 pounds, 15 ounces. 19 and a smidge inches long.

She's here. I texted Marty and Jess.

Name? Jess replied.

"Jess wants to know her name," I told Victoria once she'd been able to catch her breath.

"Can we name her after my grandmother?"

"We can name her anything you want," I said, bringing the baby from the warmer over to the bed and giving her to Victoria, who put her on her chest and stroked her hair for the first time.

"Hello, Samantha," she said. "It's nice to meet you."

2020

An Unsuccessful Tradition

I won't lie to you, not after all this time we've spent together documenting my life here. The annual block party was a piece of cake when the kids were babies. They were both shy of a year old the first time we had one after their birth and shy of two the second year. They were easy. Toss them in a kiddie pool, plop an adult nearby, and call it a day. Put them to bed at six or six-thirty, grab a wireless baby monitor, and move on with the evening.

But when they were three, it was not so easy. They were mobile—gasp! If you have kids, you know what I mean. Once they can move on their own, all hell breaks loose. You have to lock every cabinet and drawer that contains something that could potentially hurt your kid. Imagine doing that outside, with hundreds of people, while trying to be social and maintain all the stock levels of cups and ice and everything else. Imagine your three-year-old is faster than you ever imagined a person with such short legs could be.

I won't go as far as saying it was a nightmare, but it certainly wasn't easy. And Marty felt it too, I could tell.

When he, Jess, and Lucas arrived (a few hours early to use our kitchen, like usual), Marty was already flustered. "Sorry we're late," he said, plopping down a hefty backpack and box he had in one arm. Victoria sensed his need for help and grabbed Lucas from his other arm. Jess came in shortly after that with an arm full of boxes, Tupperware, and utensils.

"Hi, hi, busy, busy," she said, brushing past Victoria into the kitchen.

"What can we help with?" I asked immediately.

"If Vic could keep Luc occupied with Sammi, that'd be very helpful," Marty said.

"I'm on it," Victoria proclaimed, whisking Lucas out of the room and into the living room, where Samantha was watching Cocomelon for the thousandth time.

"Is anyone going to even show up?" Jess asked.

It was July of 2020. I'm sure I don't have to remind you that the world was still, essentially, in lockdown. People were still elbow-bumping, double-masking, and fearful of what the world had in store. Jess, Marty, Victoria, and I (and the kids) were all within each other's bubbles, so we didn't mask around one another. And we were all extremely careful when out in public. So there was no concern there. But Jessica was right; we didn't know who would show up or if we were wasting our time with prepping the block party.

The invites we'd sent out tried to play up the "safe" aspect of it. "Block Party. Masks and Sanitizer provided." Thanks to our Costco membership, we had a surplus of safety precautions. A few neighbors had emailed or texted me to ask how many people were coming; some were still weary, even around their neighbors. The truth is, I had no idea. I'd only hoped for some semblance of normalcy. Some tiny fragment of life before the world changed.

"I prepped a lot of the food at home last night," Marty said. "Luc couldn't sleep, so he and I were up, anyway."

"Still the tooth coming in?" I asked.

"Looks like two of them," Jess said, scooting by me to put something in the fridge.

"Poor kid. Sam's got one coming in, too. It's horrible."

"And nothing you can do," Marty said. "Nothing at all, other than Motrin or Tylenol."

"And hope for it to pass quickly."

"Jess, can you get me the whisk from the bag over there?" Marty asked. Jess handed it to him and continued with what she was working on.

"What can I do?" I asked.

Marty pointed to a bag of potatoes he'd boiled and peeled the night before. "Can you mash the potatoes? Once they're mashed, add in the vegetables in the Tupperware Jess put in the fridge."

"On it, boss," I faux saluted him, which made him smile. He was more stressed than I think I'd ever seen him before.

• • • • • • • • •

Marty didn't have anything else for me to work on when I finished the task he'd given me, so I headed outside to start setting up tables and chairs. It was slightly overcast, so I didn't bother with our rented tents. Honestly, they were a pain in the ass to set up, so I was glad not to have to do it.

I sanitized between everything I touched. Not out of panic, but out of habit. It'd been about four months since the first lockdown, and it'd become part of my usual routine to grab hand sanitizer every time I touched anything. My hands were dry for months on end. You probably had the same problem back then.

As usual, I got Marty's table set up first. His offering was much more robust than anyone else's. Everyone else usually brought one, maybe two things, whereas Marty would have a dozen different dishes. Some needed heating, others needed chilling. And let's not forget the electricity needing to be run from the house for his world-famous waffle maker. I looked forward to the waffles. I think something about his homemade whipped cream put them over the top. I'd watched him make it before, and it was definitely the amount of sugar he put into it. And vanilla extract. Top-quality vanilla extract.

The kids are getting antsy. Can I bring them out? Victoria texted.

Sure. You coming out with them? Still have more to do.

Yes. Be out soon.

I heard them before I saw them. The excited screams of toddlers fleeing from the house out into the freedom of our front yard. "Careful!" I instinctively yelled, figuring they were hauling ass down the cement stairs onto the pathway.

"I'm here," I heard Victoria a second later.

"Daddy!" Samantha yelled, trying to climb up my leg.

"Hi, peanut!" I said, scooting her back a step or two, making sure to hug her and not make her feel like I was pushing her away. Which, in fairness, was exactly what I was doing.

It took another five trips to the garage to set up the tables and chairs. It seemed pointless when I took a step back and looked at everything. There were way more tables and chairs than we were going to need. I just had a feeling that there would be very little turnout.

"Hot stuff! Coming through!" Marty yelled, passing me and plopping a couple of trays into the warming pans I'd already set up. "Be back with more."

It was almost one-thirty. The same time we usually started. And not a single soul had made an appearance yet. Neither Jeremy nor John had come out to help me set up, like years past. Mrs. Dubois, who always showed up early, hadn't even looked out her window, let alone walked down the street.

"Maybe..." I said, just as Marty was getting out of earshot. "Maybe let's wait for people to show up before bringing out more food."

He must not have heard me, so I repeated myself when he came back out with the next round of trays. "Let's wait until at least someone shows up."

"Why? They'll come," he said.

"I hope you're right," I said as he went back into the house to get more trays.

• • • • • • • • •

He wasn't right. For the first time in fifteen years of hosting an annual block party, not a single person showed up.

We must have looked ridiculous to anyone who stumbled down our street. One car—who was clearly lost—pulled into the cul-de-sac to turn around and gave us this "that's a lot of chairs for the four of you" look. She wasn't wrong.

The food, as always, was delicious. Marty had mastered so many dishes that he'd learned from Jean Luc over the years. I could write a whole book about how good the waffles were. He'd prepped for the usual crowd. There was literally food for hundreds of people, if not more. And it was just the four of us and the kids. The cul-de-sac had never felt so empty before.

"Did we get the date wrong?" Jess asked.

"Even if we did, the neighbors would have seen us out their windows," Victoria said.

"No, this is a concerted effort not to come," I replied.

"I don't know about concerted," Victoria added. "But people definitely decided not to come."

"It's their loss," Jess said. "We'll eat the food ourselves. *prachtig werk, liefs*. Wonderful job, love." She clarified the Dutch for Victoria and me. Over the years, I'd picked up several Dutch phrases and sayings but never had fully grasped the language like Jessica did. I'd guess she was fluent by the time they got married.

"Thank you. I did my best," he said. His head sunk a little.

"What's wrong?" I asked.

"All this work, for nothing. I want to share Papa's great food with people," he replied.

"There'll be next year," I said.

"That's right. There'll be next year," Victoria agreed.

"Daddy. Up." Samantha said, pulling at my shorts. I scooped her up and put her on my lap. She grabbed my fork and started finishing the waffle I had stuffed myself too much to finish. She gave Marty a thumbs up, which was the highest form of praise she could give an item of food.

"Mommy. I'm hungry," Lucas said as Jess scooped him up and slid over Marty's plate with some leftover food on it.

As the kids ate, I stared off down the street at nothing in particular. "I know you love your job," I said, without looking at anyone, "but have you ever considered opening a restaurant? Making just Belgian food?"

"*Gek*," Marty responded.

"I'm not crazy! Your food is the talk of the town for a week after the party. You know, when people show up, usually."

"Opening a restaurant is hard," Victoria said.

"And expensive," Jess added.

"I'm not saying it'd be easy, but there's nothing else like it around here. And you've got built-in marketing with the block party," I said.

"I've thought about it, but not in many years," Marty responded. "I have a family to support now. I have a good job that I enjoy. It'd be foolish to stray from the safety of my current life."

"We have talked about it," Jess said. "But we would never be able to come up with the money to do it."

I looked across the table at Victoria. We had a silent conversation, using only eye twitches and facial expressions.

"I think we could help," Victoria offered. "We've been very lucky in life."

"I married rich," I joked.

"What do you mean?" Jess asked.

"If you want to consider it, seriously, we'd be willing to be involved. To help with money. Be a part of the restaurant." Victoria smiled.

"Do you have any experience running a restaurant?" Marty asked.

"No more than you," I said. "But I know how to run a business. I know how to sell things. And Victoria's a financial wizard. She has us on track to pay off the house in only five more years."

"That's amazing. Teach me," Jess said.

"I mean..." Marty started. "I guess we could give it some more thought and look into it more."

"Do our due diligence," Victoria said. "See if it's feasible."

"I worry, a little," I added. "With the pandemic happening, would it be wise? We couldn't even get people to show up to a block party. People we know."

"You're right," Victoria said.

"We could do only take-out to start. Delivery. Pick-up," Jess said.

"That's all people are doing right now, anyway," Marty said. "No one is grocery shopping. Everyone is doing Doordash and Uber Eats. Instacart."

"Okay, so let's give it some more thought and see if it makes sense," I said.

Marty smiled for only the second time that day.

• • • • • • • • •

"Are we crazy?" Victoria asked me once we'd gotten inside.

"Probably," I shrugged.

Samantha ran off to play with her toys in the living room.

"It's undeniable that his food is amazing," she said. "And people do love it, like you said."

"That's the thing I'm thinking of most, too. People walk away talking about how the food is the best food they've ever had."

"Word of mouth is the best advertising," she said.

"Exactly. And, like I said, there's already a built-in marketing plan with the block party. I'm sure by this time next year, people will attend the block party again. You're the financial person. You keep all our money. Do we have money to invest in this?"

"We do," she replied. "We have a few hundred thousand saved between cash and our investments."

I was a little surprised. As weird as it sounds, I'd never looked at our finances. I knew we were doing okay; if we weren't, she'd have told me. We'd have talked. But that never happened, so I assumed we were fine. I didn't assume we were rich.

"Okay, let me rephrase. Do we have money to invest into this, knowing we might not get any of it back?"

"I think that's a different question."

"Exactly," I said. "Are we okay losing all of our money?"

"Not all of it, no," she replied. "And I don't know if we'd lose it all. Not immediately, anyway."

"I trust your judgment," I said. "If you think we should do it, I'm on board. If you don't want to or think it's a bad idea, I will be the one to say no, so you're not the bad guy."

"Let me talk to some people at work," she said. "I think one of the partners knows someone who owns some restaurant franchises. He might have some advice or put me in touch with his friend."

"Okay, sounds good.".

The whole thing worried me. Take the pandemic out of the equation. Most new restaurants fail. It's a very competitive market, and the cost of starting a restaurant is astronomical. But, as I've said and done before, I'd do anything for Marty. And helping him spread Jean Luc's amazing food was something I believed in. I believed everyone needed to try those waffles. There were plenty of other dishes he made, but those waffles were my favorite, by a landslide.

"Mommy. Daddy." Sam called from the other room. "Come play."

I followed Victoria down the hall and found Sam sitting amongst a giant pile of Duplo blocks.

"Skyscrapers?" I asked. It was our favorite thing to build together.

"Yes, Daddy," she said as I plopped beside her. Victoria sat down on the other side, and we, for a short while, forgot about the day's events. I blocked out how sad it made me that no one showed up at the block party. I'd forgotten about all of the work that went into prepping, all the money invested in chair and table rentals, and all of the wasted food that we'd hopefully be able to donate to a shelter somewhere before it went bad. I'd forgotten about how the world was in a state of chaos. All I knew for the next hour was building the tallest skyscraper I could—but not taller than Samantha's, because you always let your kid win, no matter what.

2021

Four Jean Luc's

It took sixteen months from that first conversation about opening a restaurant to the day we opened. There were so many hoops to jump through, many decisions to make, so much money to spend. But we did it. I'm particularly proud of the name we came up with as a group: *Four Jean Luc's*.

Four was a play on the word "for," and because four of us were opening the place.

Jean Luc, as an obvious tribute to Marty's father. Though, maybe that was only obvious to us.

We opened to great success, even during the pandemic. Having worked in sales in the past, I knew we had to be prepared for all the to-go and delivery apps well before we opened. We had to have everything in place: great descriptions, good prices, amazing photos. And for months, it worked. We did very little direct business, meaning very few people called us to order or ordered directly from our website—about 4%. The rest came through Uber Eats and Doordash. A handful of walk-in orders, as well.

The neighborhood came out in droves, though. We saw so many familiar faces on opening day. We heard so many repetitious phrases: "So glad you finally did this," "Now I can have stoemp any time I want," and "Waffles are the best."

It was non-stop for Marty, me, and the handful of people we'd hired: cooks, dishwashers, and front of the house. Victoria and Jessica kept their day jobs because we needed money coming in in case things didn't work out. Marty was lucky enough to take an eight-week sabbatical to see if the restaurant would work.

I had to quit my job, but I didn't mind. I knew I could find a job anywhere if I needed to go back.

I'll never forget the end of the first week. That Friday was the first time we'd not had pizza together. In the eighteen years Marty and I had known each other, we'd gotten together every Friday night and eaten pizza together somewhere. But we were too busy at the restaurant to do it that first week.

Honestly, it came and went, and neither of us even gave it any thought. I'd only known it was Friday because the girls came in with the kids to visit. I'd never felt so guilty about not spending time with my family before we opened the restaurant. I'd never been gone "at work" for sixteen to eighteen hours a day before. It was exhausting but felt so rewarding.

We closed that first Saturday, having been open a full week.

"Thanks, guys," I said as the last two employees left out the back door. I locked up behind them and made sure the neon open sign out front was turned off.

"I'm so curious," Marty said.

"About what?" I asked, walking toward the fridge. "I'm getting a beer. You want one?"

"I want ten," he said, laughing.

"So, what are you curious about?" I asked again, returning from the fridge, beers in hand.

"It was crazy busy the whole week, right?"

"More or less, yeah. It sure felt like it was non-stop."

"So, I'm curious how much money we made."

"Oh Jesus," I said. "Don't go down that road. We're not here to get rich."

"I know, I know. It's about Papa's legacy. But I'm so curious."

The two of us sat in the office for another hour, drinking beer after beer, crunching numbers.

Just wrapping up. We're out of here soon. I texted both wives so they wouldn't worry.

Marty punched keys on the computer almost frantically, exporting numbers from the program we used to take orders, adding numbers from the various apps we sold through, and grabbing data from payroll.

It seemed like an endless barrage of very basic, yet very complicated, math.

"That can't be right," he said.

"What can't?" I asked, returning from the fridge with yet another pair of beers.

"Maybe I drank too much," he said. "The numbers seem wrong."

"How so?"

"After payroll, fees to the apps, insurance, the mortgage, the loan payment for the equipment, electricity, and all the other bills, we made three hundred and eleven dollars."

I did a spit-take with my beer. "What?"

"I must have made a mistake."

I wasn't sure whether to laugh or cry. "How much did we pay ourselves to be here?"

"I didn't," he said. "I didn't even factor that in. If we split that money, we made seventy-five cents an hour each for all the hours we were here."

I laughed. "I'm sure we made more in the tip jar than in profit."

"Oh, me. This is bad," he said. "This is very bad."

"What happened?"

"I think things were more expensive than we thought they would be. Labor and food, primarily. I thought we'd get better bulk pricing on some foods than we got."

"So what do we do?"

"We raise prices?"

"We'd have to raise a lot," I said. "Like, a lot, a lot."

"Let's talk to the wives. They're smarter than we are."

Coming from anyone else, I'd be offended by that. But he was right, and I knew he was right.

"Good idea. They'll have some ideas."

• • • • • • • • • •

They both agreed with our plan to raise prices.

"Treat the first week like a dry run," Jess said. "You are trying things out to see the right fit."

"Right, what Jess said," Victoria added. "People will understand. Plus, I think you greatly underpriced everything in the first place."

"It shouldn't cost a fortune to take your family to dinner," Marty said.

"But it also shouldn't bankrupt us," I responded.

My share of the profits from the first week, including tips, came out to around three hundred dollars, give or take. It was the least money I'd made in a week, for at least twenty years. I tried not to mind. Like Marty said, I tried to remind myself that it wasn't about the money. I was very thankful Victoria made so much money, but I still felt I needed to contribute to our household.

"So, how much more?" Marty asked.

"Twenty. Maybe thirty percent," Jess said. Victoria nodded in agreement.

"That feels like a lot," I said.

"It is," Jess responded. "But that'll align with what we found when we researched. Remember, we decided to be cheap to get people in the door."

"We did. I didn't know we'd work so hard for so little," Marty said. Jess got up and stood next to him, rubbing his neck.

"We should get you guys home," I said to Victoria. "Sam has a playdate this morning."

It was the first time we'd all been together outside the restaurant in weeks. We'd met up at Marty and Jess' house for an early breakfast before the wives went to work, and we went to the restaurant.

"I'll see you at JL's," I said. It was our shorthand for the restaurant.

"I'm on my way in a few," Marty said.

We said our goodbyes and headed to our car, ready to head home.

"You're nervous," Victoria said. "I can tell."

"I was at the restaurant for over a hundred hours. I'm thankful for tips because they basically doubled the money I made. But I made three bucks an hour."

"And you worked harder than you probably ever have," she said. "And I'm proud of you."

"Be proud of me when I don't bankrupt our whole family."

"What's bankrupt?" Sam asked from the backseat.

"Don't worry about it, peanut. We're going to be fine."

"I love you, daddy." She always knew the right thing to say at the right time.

· · · • · ● · ● · · ·

I dropped them off at the house just as Lisa, our nanny, arrived. We'd hired her a few weeks before the restaurant opened so Victoria wouldn't have to keep working from home forever. Offices had started opening up a few months back, as well as the courts. And, as lenient as her firm was, they wanted her back in the office for client meetings at least three days a week. Lisa was a godsend. She was kind and compassionate. She helped Sam learn so much and was an excellent caregiver. It also helped immensely that she'd do light cleaning around the house during nap times.

"Love you," I said as Victoria pulled Sam out of her car seat. "See you tonight, love."

"Love you," Victoria said.

"Love you, Daddy." Samantha waved vigorously over Victoria's shoulder as they walked up the pathway to the door.

I gave Lisa a slight smile and nod as I backed away.

"I'll get started raising the prices on the apps," I said as I closed the backdoor behind me. "Good morning, team," I said to the crew. I had been doing my best not to say "guys" since one of our cooks was a woman.

I got various smiles and waves back. I got a "Buenos dias" from Juan, the dishwasher, before they all resumed their prep work for the day.

They'd all been so wonderful and taken to Marty's teachings quickly. It was all food they'd never prepared, but they were all up to the challenge. "Food is food. You teach me how to make it, and I will," one of them—I forget who, maybe Raul—said during his interview.

"I'll do the boards later today," I said, hoping Marty could hear me.

It was tedious, but I went through every item on our menu in all the food apps, increasing prices across the board by thirty percent. Except on things where we already had a good profit margin. Sodas, bags of chips, pre-made cookies.

For a flash of a second, I was glad we didn't have a full sit-down restaurant. There were no menus to re-order with new pricing. Menus were expensive. We did have paper tri-fold menus people could take with them, but those were easy to remove from the counter until we were able to print new ones. The printer at Victoria's office was top-notch, and no one (at least not yet) gave her flak about using it for our menus. It probably helped that we catered any big meeting they had where they wanted to schmooze new clients. And we did it for cheap money, which I'm sure they liked, too.

The computer froze right before saving the changes to the digital menu boards mounted out front. Those were the ones that the walk-in folks used to order. I didn't prioritize it much since we had such little walk-in traffic. It frustrated me so much that I yelled loud enough for Marty to come racing into the office.

"Everything okay?"

"I'm fine," I said. "Computer just froze."

"Give it a minute," he said. "Save your work, then try rebooting."

It eventually caught up to me, and I was able to update the menus out front.

I don't know why, but I expected slower sales that day. In my mind, people would pull us up in their app of choice, look at the prices, scoff, and order food from somewhere else.

Marty quickly pointed out how wrong I was when we started taking orders. The printer went non-stop during lunch, even a little later than last week.

My job was simple: make sure the orders were right, pack them up, and hand them to the drivers when they came in. Rebecca, the girl we'd hired for the counter, helped and took any orders from walk-ins.

"Hi, Matt," I heard a familiar voice call out through the window connecting the kitchen to the counter area. I ducked down and saw it was Mrs. Dubois.

"Hey!" I called out. She was our first repeat customer. I went out to greet her. "Thanks for coming back."

"I don't mean to be rude," she said. "But wasn't it less expensive last week?"

I chuckled, trying to hide my embarrassment. "It was. We hoped the cheaper prices would work, but we needed to increase prices to make it another week."

"Of course, dear," she said. What a sweet lady. "I understand. I felt it was a little cheap last week, anyway."

Rebecca took her order, and I thanked her again for coming back before running back to the kitchen to catch up on packing orders.

"I think it's working," I said to Marty.

"Let's run numbers at the end of the day," he said, not looking up from the frying pan he was focused on.

"Keep up the good work, team," I said, trying to be reassuring. The only thing I knew about running a kitchen was from television, and if Gordon Ramsey taught me just one thing, it was that you needed your staff to be motivated. An angry staff was not a good thing.

A Christmas Break

"Shh," Victoria whispered as soon as I came in from the garage. She was sitting in the kitchen, waiting for me. The clock on the microwave read just before midnight.

"Everything okay?" I asked. She was usually well asleep before midnight and rarely waited for me to get home from the restaurant.

"Go look," she said, pointing to the living room.

I shrugged and walked down the hallway to see a fort made out of pillows and blankets. Two little heads stuck out at one end.

"That's so cute," I said as I sat beside Victoria.

"Lucas really wanted to sleep over. He loves Sammi so much," she said. "And Jess needed a break. She's basically a single mom now."

The way she said it made me feel so guilty. She couldn't possibly think that of Marty and not of me.

"I'm so sorry. I've been gone so long, for so many nights and weekends," I said.

"I know. I'm not complaining. I love our kid. And I love your motivation and drive to help the restaurant succeed."

"I think Marty's struggling," I said.

"How so?"

"I don't know. But he's been keeping to himself more lately. Really reserved. And you know that's not like him."

"Do you think it's the money?"

"I don't think so," I said. "We've been doing better the last few months since we increased prices."

"Can you guys take a day or two off for Christmas?"

I checked my watch. Christmas was in four days. I didn't even realize it was so late in the year.

"Oh my god," I said. "How is it December twenty-first already?"

"You've basically been living at the restaurant," she said. "Let's go upstairs. I have the baby monitor."

She led me upstairs, and I did my best not to pass out, knowing I needed to return to the restaurant in seven hours.

"I've taken care of all the gifts and wrapping," she said. "I just want to know you'll be home to celebrate it."

"I'll talk to Marty. I'm sure it'll be fine."

"Why don't we have them over at the house? Make dinner for them. Let Marty rest for a change," she suggested.

"That's a great idea. Did you get anything for them? For Lucas?"

"All gifted and accounted for," she said, smiling.

"You're a goddamn saint," I said, kissing her gently before passing out.

• • • • • • • • • •

"That's a great idea," Marty said when I'd suggested taking Christmas Eve and Christmas Day off.

"Two days won't kill our momentum," I replied. "Let the crew have a couple of days off, too. It'll be good for everyone to recharge. And we'll make dinner at our house."

That day was a slog. That whole week, actually. We were busier than ever, thanks to an ad I put out on our area's last remaining radio station. Well, it was less an ad and more of us sending free meals for the on-air talent for a week until one of them mentioned it to their listeners. Business was booming thanks to that.

People were starting to feel more comfortable going places, too. So our foot traffic was much higher than we anticipated. We'd gotten so busy that we needed to hire another front-of-the-house person to help Rebecca. TJ was our seventh employee and would become one of our best.

There was a lull after lunchtime, so I plopped myself down in the office to take a breather.

Marty, calling out to the crew to prep for dinner, joined me. "Busy day," he said.

"Very busy day. Hopefully, good numbers for today," I replied.

The whole thing was starting to feel worth it. It started feeling like we were making the difference we had set out to make. People quickly became repeat customers, many sticking with their favorites but often trying something new. Mrs. Dubois came in once a week, usually on Monday, for lunch. It was always nice to see a familiar face, especially in the early months.

"Hey, are you okay?" I asked. "You seem distant lately."

"I'm okay," he said. "Just trying to keep things afloat, you know?"

"I know. I get it. But you can't carry the weight of the world on your shoulders. You know that, right?"

"I need Papa to be proud," he said. "I need him to know I'm doing this for him. That we're doing this for him."

"He knows, buddy. He knows. He sees us."

"You believe that?"

"I do. I believe he's watching down on us and is so proud of you."

"He'd be proud of you, too," Marty said. "I'm sorry I've been so weird lately. Things are just weird in life."

"How so? You mentioned the restaurant. Is everything okay at home?"

"It is. It's just..." he trailed off.

"It's just what?"

"I think about when Papa and I came to America. It was almost twenty years ago. I didn't know anything. You remember the first time I used the internet?" he laughed. "It was like I was an alien or something."

"You just wanted to learn," I said. "You never got to be a kid because you moved around so much with your dad."

"His job brought us a lot of places, that's for sure. But I think back to then. Am I the same person?"

"What do you mean?" I asked.

"I feel different. I don't feel like Michel."

"You're still Michel," I said. "You're just an adult now. You have adult things that you do."

"Is that what it is? Is that what I'm feeling?"

"I think so," I said. "Sometimes I feel it, too. Remembering when we were twenty-five and could drive off into the night and see where we ended up."

"Or when we'd just sit in the middle of the road, eating pizza and looking at stars."

"We can still do those things," I said. "It's just different now. We have families."

He sighed. "And a business to run."

"And a business to run," I agreed.

"Sometimes I wish I could go back," he said.

"Me too, but I'm so happy with life now. Aren't you?"

"I am," he replied. "Don't get me wrong. I'm very happy. Jessica is amazing. Lucas is such a great kid."

"They were so cute when I got home last night," I said.

"Oh, that's right. Jess mentioned he slept at your house. How does Vic do it?"

"How does Jess do it?" I countered. "The two of them. They're superheroes."

"They really are. Why don't I feel like a good dad?"

The way he asked the question made him sound so defeated. The air just flew out of his lungs in one big exhale.

"What do you mean?" I asked, hoping he'd give me more to go off of.

"Chef?" Raul called out from the line. "You got *un momento?*"

"We'll talk more later," Marty said, scurrying back to the line to see what Raul needed.

It got me thinking. Was *I* a bad father? I was gone almost all day, every day. The only time I saw Sam was when Victoria brought her in to see me. Sometimes, they'd stay a bit, and Sam would play in the kitchen while I worked. Sometimes, it'd be during the downtime in the afternoon, so we'd all get to sit at one of the few tables we had out front, having a meal together. But, primarily, I was gone. Did Victoria think she was a single parent like she'd said about Jess? Did Jess actually feel that way, or was it something Victoria just picked up on?

I felt a ball in the pit of my stomach. It suddenly occurred to me that I had been killing myself every day, for months. Spending every waking minute at the restaurant.

Don't get me wrong, I loved it. I loved how fast-paced we were. I loved how the numbers kept increasing at the end of every week. I loved how much time I was getting to spend with Marty. We hadn't had much time since both of us started our families. Why is it so hard to juggle things in your life as you get older? Friends, families, being social, working. It all seemed like there weren't enough hours in the day or days in the week. Imagine if we had an extra day every week? I could get so much more done if there were just more time.

And I felt like I was neglecting everything in my life. My amazing wife. My kid, who was one of the best things to ever happen to me. Everything important to me suddenly seemed so much more important than handing food in brown paper bags to people.

I loved the joy I'd see on their faces, though. I can't deny that. When they'd open the door to come in and pick up their order, you'd see them take a big whiff in, really smell the place, and they'd smile. It wasn't like walking into a McDonald's or Wendy's. It was an experience just selling the food we'd made at Four Jean Luc's.

· · · · · **·** · **·** · · ·

"Hey, that thing you said earlier," I said as we were closing up. "About being a bad dad."

"Oh, don't worry about that," he said. "I was just having a moment, as you'd say."

"No. I won't not worry," I replied. "It's okay to be human."

"I don't know this saying. What does it mean?"

"It means it's okay to have feelings. To be hard on yourself. All of that is okay."

"I just feel like I'm letting everyone down," he confessed. "I need to be here all the time. I can't be at home with Jessica and Luc."

"What if you could?" I asked. "What if we tried it?"

"Tried what?"

"Take a day off. Let's see how we do without you. The crew knows all the recipes by now. And I'll be here, just in case."

"How would that work?"

"It'd work just like you're here, but you're not. I'm confident everything will be fine."

"Just one day?"

"Well, one day. We'll see how it goes. If it goes well, maybe you can cut down your hours. Not be here so much, but still be present."

"I have one stipulation," he said.

"What's that?"

"You have to do the same. You try not to be here for a day. Let TJ and Rebecca run things and see how they do."

"I'm willing to try it if you are."

"Deal," he said, extending his hand to shake on it.

"Deal." I shook his hand.

"Day after tomorrow?"

"Yes, but I think we alternate. You do the day after tomorrow," I said. "I'll do the day after that. That way, there's at least one of us here."

"I agree. I think everyone would feel more comfortable with that," he responded.

2022

Where'd All The Money Go?

"I just don't get it," Marty said, sitting at the computer in our shared office.

"What?" I asked, confused.

"It doesn't make sense."

"What doesn't?"

"The numbers," he said. "Since July 4th, we've slowly been going downhill."

"Show me," I asked, scooting closer to the monitor.

"Here, look, we spiked the weekend of July 4th but have slowly been going downhill. About five percent per week."

"So we're down about half, as we come up to our first year being open? Can we run a profit-and-loss report for the first year?" I asked him.

"Yes, I will do that now while it's quiet."

The afternoons had been our time to get things done. Mornings were for prepping for the day. Then we had a lunch rush, albeit quieter than we'd like recently. Dinner was usually crazy. Then we'd clean up and go home. So we tried—as best we could—to get any owner stuff done during the lull between lunch and dinner. It was quiet enough that we let everyone do their thing. And it just worked.

Our plan for taking a day off every week had helped. Well, with our mental health anyway. I certainly felt better, and it seemed like he did as well. I'd noticed him re-engaging in non-work conversations and laughing with the crew. He seemed to have a good time while on the line, doing what he loved.

I had also noticed Jess seeming happier when I saw her. When they'd come into the restaurant to see Marty, they all seemed happier. Lucas seemed to love coming to see his father, too. He'd run around the kitchen, waving a spatula or frying pan, yelling, "I'm daddy! I'm daddy!" It was cute beyond words.

"Forty-two thousand and change."

"What number is that?" I asked.

"That's profit for the last twelve months."

"That's it?"

"That's my thought, too," he said.

"Where'd all the money go?"

"We knew it cost a lot to run a restaurant," he said. "The bigger expenses added up."

"I knew the freezer broke. What else?"

"We needed a new fry machine. And some of the frying pans wore out, so we replaced them. Oh, and our insurance premiums went up a whole bunch after Juan's slip and fall."

"It must be a fortune now," I said, hoping he'd tell me I was wrong.

"Our unexpected costs went up over five hundred percent from what we planned for."

"Oh, Crap!" I yelled, a little louder than I'd meant to. "I don't even want to calculate how much we would make if we paid ourselves."

"I did it already. Do you want to know?" he asked.

"Hit me with it." I tightened my body as if he was going to actually hit me.

"It comes out to about five bucks an hour."

"That's worse than I thought," I said. "I thought at least ten an hour."

"Being the owner is not as much fun as being the chef," Marty said.

"I wish I were that useful," I said, feeling like a glorified cashier.

"We worked so hard," he replied. "So hard. And for what? For pennies?"

"It sure does feel like a lot of work for very little payoff."

"Why are sales declining?" he asked, almost pleading with me to have an answer that would satisfy him.

"I wish I knew," I said, knowing I'd tried every avenue of marketing I could think of. Somewhere inside, I thought perhaps that people had just had their fill of Belgian food. It was something new that people wanted to try. They tried it, and they went back to Wendy's or whatever. But I obviously wouldn't say that out loud.

"Can we cut back on staff?" he asked.

"Maybe a few hours here and then. If we let the morning crew go at one-thirty or two, you and I could do the prep for dinner. Then we're not paying six people to stand around for three hours, waiting for the dinner rush."

"That would add up," he said, seeming a little excited.

"Then the night crew can go home early, too. We'll have to work harder, you and I."

"Is that possible?" he asked. "Harder than we have been?"

"I'm in if you are," I said, immediately thinking I should have checked with Victoria. We'd gotten used to my routine of being home one full day a week and having shorter days on two other days. I'm not sure going back to super-duper-always-there time would fly. But I didn't see any other way to get costs down.

Ms. Martin Is Safe

I woke up to find a note from myself on my alarm clock. It felt a bit weird when I reached over to slap it to snooze for nine more minutes. I opened my eyes to see a piece of paper taped over it. "First day of school," it read. I'd left myself a reminder that it was the first day of kindergarten for Sammi and Lucas.

Since we lived in the same town, we'd met at Marty and Jess' house and sent both kids off on the same school bus. I suppose part of me thought they'd be better off knowing at least one person they were riding the bus with.

"Good morning," Victoria said, rolling over to give me a quick snuggle before jumping in the shower.

Sammi was already awake and had gotten herself some Poptarts downstairs.

"Good morning, Daddy," she said when she saw me.

"Good morning, peanut. Are you excited for your first day of kindergarten?"

"I am soooooo excited." The o went on for much longer than I've documented here. Let's say she was more excited than she had ever been. "But I'm sad I won't see Lisa anymore."

"I know, honey. But you'll make new friends. And Lucas will only be a few doors down." Try as I might, we couldn't get them in the same class.

"Lucas told me he's scared," she went on.

"Scared of what? Are you scared?"

"I'm not scared." She flexed her muscles to show me how strong she was. "Lucas is scared of new kids."

"He'll have you, right? And you'll make sure he's not scared?"

"I will, Daddy."

As usual, I grabbed a bagel and tossed it in the toaster, grabbing some orange juice from the fridge while waiting for the bagel to toast.

Don't forget. 8:15. Jess had texted the group thread to remind us. My memory wasn't what it used to be, so I appreciated all the reminders.

"Don't forget about the bus," Victoria yelled from the shower.

I didn't bother yelling back. I knew she wouldn't hear me over the water.

"Mommy thinks I'd forget about your first day," I said, tickling her. "I'd never forget!"

"Daddy, stop!" she squealed.

It was nice to have a normal morning where I didn't feel I needed to rush around to get to the restaurant. A morning where I could hang out with my family, eat breakfast together, and pack Sammi up for school. A morning where we could be a family, for once.

"It's good that you're home, daddy."

"Oh? Why's that?"

"So you can meet the bus driver! Duh!" I'd found that, at that age, she often said things like this as if we'd had dozens of conversations about it before. And not, like reality, that I was hearing about meeting the bus driver for the very first time.

"Of course! I have to make sure it's safe to get on a bus." It was such a contradiction. I couldn't help but think that. We spend the whole first five years of a kid's life telling them not to go with strangers, that it isn't safe. And then, on their first day of school, we send them off in a vehicle they've likely never been on before, with a person they don't know, to a whole building they've been in maybe once or twice, full of strangers. I know it'll be fine. Parents do this all the time, right? Everything will work out just fine. But, man, were my nerves at their worst. I was more nervous than Vic and Sam were combined. I'm sure of it.

"Good morning, princess," Victoria said, bounding down the stairs.

"Good morning, Your Majesty," Sammi and I responded in sync. It was our little inside joke. We both knew she was talking to Sammi, but we liked to pretend she was talking to me, so I responded in kind.

"Goofballs," she said. "Don't forget we're meeting Lucas and his mommy and daddy."

"We know," I said. "We were just discussing how I'm going to meet the bus driver."

"Of course. We'd never forget." She bopped Sam on the nose as she went into the kitchen.

The toaster dinged, and my breakfast popped up. "Can you grab that for me?" I asked, not wanting to get up from my seat.

Like the angel she is, Victoria grabbed it, buttered it, and slid it down the table to me without a word. Never a complaint from her. A true saint.

"I put your first-day outfit on your bed. Go get your new outfit and backpack and bring them down when you come back."

Sam ran off up the stairs, giddy as can be.

"You ready for this?"

"Are *you* ready for this?" I retorted.

"Not even a little," she said.

"Same. Not even a little."

· · · · · • · • · • · · ·

We pulled into Jess and Marty's driveway right as they were coming outside. Knowing Jess, they were waiting by the door for us to arrive. It wasn't just a coincidence.

"Good morning!" Lucas yelled, running across the lawn to hug Samantha.

"Schooool!" Again, the word lasted longer than it needed to. They were both jars of pure excitement.

"Morning," I said to Jess. "Where's Marty?"

"He'll be right out," she said, giving me a peck on the cheek and then hugging Victoria. "Morning, little one. Are you so excited?"

Sam tried to jump up to be at eye level with Jess. "So excited." She jumped again. "So excited." She jumped a third time. "So excited."

"I think she gets it, sweetheart," Victoria said.

Marty came out just as the bus stopped up the street, picking up a couple of the neighbor's kids.

"Now, remember, stick together, and you'll be fine," Marty said, jogging across the lawn to get to us. "Hey guys."

"That's right. You know each other, so stick together," Jess added.

"Give me a big hug," Victoria said as the bus approached. "Daddy, too!"

She squeezed me tighter than ever before. I scooped her up, patted her butt like always, and waited for the bus door to open.

"Good morning!" The bus driver yelled. "Come on!" She motioned for the kids to climb the steps, but Sam hung onto my neck.

"Check her, Daddy."

"Oh, right. Of course." I took a step closer to the open door. "This is Samantha," I said. "She wants to know your name."

"Hi, Samantha. I'm Ms. Martin. I'll be your driver. Are you ready for your first day?"

"Okay, daddy. She's safe." She jumped from my arms and ran up the stairs and down the aisle to sit next to Lucas.

The bus pulled away with the two of them waving out the window to the four of us. We stood there, not knowing what to do next. It felt rewarding, but also exhausting, to have gotten this far in their lives. Was I thankful we wouldn't have to pay for a nanny anymore? Yes. That's an expense I was happy to have gone from our budget. But everything else felt so... different.

"I don't know what I'm going to do before I go to work," Jess said. She had the luxury of working right down the street from their house.

"Oh, crap! I've gotta get going," Victoria said. "Can you catch a ride to the restaurant with Marty?"

"Fine with me," Marty said. "You want to eat first? Raul's already there prepping for the day. No rush for us to get in."

"I'm good. I ate." I kissed Victoria goodbye, and she ran off to get into her car, zipping down the street to get to the office or court; I'm not sure which she had.

Marty and I went into the house, and I followed him to the kitchen.

"You sure you're not hungry?" he asked.

"I ate at home. I had time."

I heard Jess fumbling around in the other room, getting ready for work.

"Here's hoping for a busy day today," Marty said.

"Hear, hear!"

"Okay, I'm going," Jess said, not fully stopping to kiss Marty goodbye. Just a run-by kiss on the cheek, and she was out the door and down the driveway.

Marty made himself an omelet, and it occurred to me that I had never seen him make something that wasn't Belgian before. Every time he cooked, it was something from his home country. It felt weird to see him make a Denver omelet.

I flipped through some emails on my phone while he ate, ensuring vendors' emails were replied to. I approved a time off request for Filipe, our new dishwasher.

"I'm ready when you are," he said, putting his plate in the sink.

"Off we go, then," I said, leading him out the door and standing at the top step while he set his alarm and then locked the door.

"You can never be too safe," he said.

2023

Cool & Unique

You know how I've been talking about how memory is weird and the things that stick with you the most are often weird? Well, something happened in early April of 2023. After twenty years of friendship, Marty and I had our first fight. All things considered, it was astonishing that we'd never fought before. But we'd always just clicked, always agreed on things, had the same views on most everything in life, and liked each other's wives. Even when I was married to Brooke and Marty didn't like her, we never fought.

It had been a steady decrease in business since mid-January. It'd gotten so bad that we had to let go of almost the entire staff. We were on our fourth dishwasher of the year, and he was the only person left on staff full-time. Everyone else had either been let go or chose to move on since we couldn't offer them enough hours to sustain their lifestyle. I felt terrible about it, and I'm sure Marty did, too. It was heart-wrenching watching something we put so much time, money, and effort into failing, slowly.

We were having a particularly busy Friday night dinner rush, which felt nice, for once. And it was just Marty and I working. He made all the food, and I handled the counter and to-go orders. We were very clearly both stressed out and having no one else to take it out on, we took it out on one another.

Well, that's not entirely fair. Customers (and Door Dashers and Uber Eats people) took it out on me when their food wasn't ready when they arrived. I, in turn, took it out on Marty, not really realizing that what he was doing back there was nothing short of a miracle. When times were good, we'd had a team of six prepping and cooking all the food. For Marty to do it himself was nothing short of amazing. But, at the time, I didn't realize that. I just knew I'd been yelled at for the fiftieth time that night, and I snapped at him.

"Marty, what's the holdup on order six-one-nine?" I yelled through the window.

"I'm doing the best I can," he said.

"Please do better. What few customers we have left are getting angry." I'd realized the phrasing was wrong as soon as it came out of my mouth.

"Do you want to come back here and do this?" he snapped back.

"If it'd make things go more smoothly, I will." My mouth was outrunning my brain, and when my brain caught up, it was not thrilled with how I was talking to my friend.

He threw a frying pan in the sink from a good ten feet away, startling Filipe, who jumped back. "Jesus. Christ."

I'd never seen him get so mad before. And, in fairness, it was kind of my fault.

He finished packaging the meal he'd just completed and tossed the bag through the window so hard that I had to catch it before it flew to the floor. "Chill out!" I yelled at him. I *yelled* at him. Stop it. Stop it now, mouth.

"You chill out!" He yelled back.

"We need to feed these people," I said, gesturing toward the standing-room-only counter area. Two dozen people were waiting at that point. I had angled my body away from them, through the window, so they wouldn't hear us arguing.

"I'm. Doing. The. Best. I. Can."

I tried to shift gears. "How can I help?"

"Stop nagging me and calm the riot out there."

Turning to face the crowd, I broadly announced, "Thanks for your patience, folks. We're a little busier than usual, but we're working on your orders." As much as it killed me to lose money, I went into all the apps and paused ordering. I thought getting caught up before accepting more orders made more sense. Especially orders that had so little profit—those apps take around 30% of your menu price for their fee. It's a racket.

"I shut off app orders," I told him.

"Why would you do that? You know we need the money!"

"Marty, you know I know that. But we can't keep up with the orders we have. If we catch up, we can turn them back on."

It was our forty-first day in a row of working from 8 a.m. to 10 p.m. We were both exhausted, frustrated, and overworked. Victoria and Jessica had come in here and there to help out, but they focused on ensuring our kids were taken care of and their jobs were being done. The two of them were our only source of survival for months. We hadn't made enough money to pay ourselves anything for months. You know that old saying "working to keep the lights on"? That's literally what we were doing, for months. Every penny we made had to go to the restaurant, vendors, utilities, and insurance. It all went elsewhere, other than in our own pockets.

We'd considered raising prices again, but alienating the little customer base we had left even more seemed like a bad idea.

"We're fine," he insisted. "Fine."

"We're not fine, Marty. Look at your printer; fifty more orders are waiting."

He glanced over at the long string of tickets hanging from the printer, and I could see his body shaking. It was like it gave him a small panic attack.

I wished I knew how to cook his food. I wish we still had Rebecca or TJ, or both of them, so I could go back there and at least try to help him.

"This is shit," he said. I think it was the first time I heard him swear.

"It is shit," I agreed. "Big shit." My attempt to lighten the mood failed.

"Can you turn off the open sign? No more orders." It was only seven, but I agreed. It seemed like the right idea.

"Yes." I walked around the corner and turned the sign off but left the door unlocked. Plenty of people were still coming for their orders, so I didn't want to lock them out. I also turned the phone ringer off so it'd go to voicemail with a pre-recorded message saying we were closed.

It sucked to turn down business, but we were in no place to take on more. Not without a proper staff.

• • • • ● • ● • • •

The counter area started thinning out. Marty would finish a couple of orders, and I'd hand them off, apologize for the long wait, offer a free drink or bag of chips, and watch as they left. Probably never to return after the bad experience they had.

After a handful of people left, another couple of people would come in to take their place, waiting for their orders. Once I turned the ringer back on, I'd started telling people who called orders in that it'd be an hour for their pickup, and that timing seemed to work out. They were right on time, as Marty started getting out of the weeds, as he liked to say. Gordon Ramsey had taught me that meant you were behind on orders. Thanks, *Hell's Kitchen*.

Once I'd handed out the last of the orders, I locked the door behind the customer and immediately turned off the lights out front.

I found Marty sitting on the floor, right on the line, by the oven. His head was between his knees.

"Hey, that's it. We're closed," I said.

"I can't keep doing this," he said. "I'm burning out. I'm not made for this."

"I know. I get it."

"I'm not made for fourteen-hour days. I had a nice, cushy government job, and I gave it up to work to the bone for pennies. Not even pennies lately. Fractions of pennies."

"I know. This sucks."

"It does suck. And the part that sucks the most is that it started so good. We were doing great, and then it just trailed off."

"That's the part that bugs me, too. We were doing great, and then it was like people just stopped wanting perfect waffles. Jerks."

He laughed, and I caught a glimpse of a quick smile. "Jerks."

"Hey, listen. I'm sorry I snapped at you earlier. People were really getting angry and taking it out on me. It's not fair that I took it out on you."

"It's okay. I'm sorry, too."

"On the upside, we probably made a bit of money tonight," I said, trying to keep the mood lighter.

"One day out of a hundred," he said, avoiding eye contact.

"One day is better than no days," I said.

"We have to find a way to turn this around," he said. "We have to keep this afloat."

I reached into my pocket to pull out my phone to let Victoria and Jess know we'd be home earlier than expected and to let them know how the day had gone.

"What's that?" Marty asked, pointing to the piece of cloth that'd fallen out of my pocket when I took my phone out.

I picked it up and unwrapped it, handing it to him. "It's the stone you gave me."

"Wait," he started. "The stone? The one I gave you?"

"I've carried it with me every day since."

"You've had this in your pocket for twenty years?" I could see tears welling up in his eyes. I wasn't sure if it was the gesture of my carrying the stone all those years, the stress of what we'd been through over the last handful of months, or some combination thereof.

"Every day," I reiterated. "It was important to you, and now it's important to me."

"I had no idea," he said, perking up a little.

"I guess if it meant enough for you to give it to me, it must mean enough for me to carry it with me. I still don't know what the hell it is, but I've carried it every day."

"I don't know what it is, either," he confessed. "I found it when I was four or five. I thought it was cool and unique, so I carried it. Then I met you, and you were cool and unique, so I gave it to you."

"Cool and unique?" I asked. "I'll take that."

We Tried Our Best

We did try. We tried hard. It had been about six weeks since our fight, and we had tried everything. We threw every penny we made at marketing. We even hired a marketing firm with the last of the money we were willing to invest in the restaurant. They came up with a marketing campaign and started running it—Facebook, TikTok, and Instagram Ads, sponsored posts—and we saw a small uptick in orders, on average.

Not enough to cover the marketing firm's fees, though.

Try as we might, and as good as Marty was at making the food, we weren't doing very well at the business part of the restaurant. I'd read books, I'd watched videos online, I'd learned all the software. I'd given Marty as much time as he needed to build the menu, test the market, and find the vendors. I felt like we'd done everything possible to make it successful.

We'd just finished running numbers for the week on Saturday night. Marty finished crunching them as I returned with a pair of beers from the fridge, which had become our new tradition, instead of Friday night Papa Gino's.

"We lost money again this week," he said as I sat down. "Just over four thousand dollars."

"How much more is that than last week?"

"About the same. That's five weeks in a row that we've lost money."

"How much in total?"

"About thirty grand."

Ouch. As supportive as Jess and Vic were about the whole thing, I didn't think they'd be super jazzed about the restaurant losing so much money. Especially with the marketing effort not making a difference.

"That's a lot."

"That is a lot," he said. "What do we do?"

I cracked open my beer and took a big swig from the cold bottle. "I don't know. Can we run projections for the next six months?"

"Sure, let me pull up that program."

He clicked on a few things. I did my best to follow along with what he was doing, but he knew that program better than I did.

When he finished clicking, the screen showed a line graph. It was higher on the left and lower on the right, pointing down.

"That doesn't look good," I said.

He put his finger on the left of the screen. "This is now. This is the forecast by the end of the year." He moved his finger to the right. "If this is right, we'll lose ten grand a week."

"So if business keeps trending down, we'll lose even more money."

"Yes. How much is too much?"

My head started spinning, seeing numbers flying around. But not in an "I'm smart and doing *Good Will Hunting* math" type of way. More in a "What the hell is happening" sort of way.

I got up, paced around the office, and then into the kitchen. Before I knew it, I found myself walking up and down the line, poking at things along the way. I turned a burner on, then off. I checked the oven to make sure it was off. Made sure the handle on the fridge was locked.

"What are you doing?" he'd finally come out of the office to look for me.

"I don't know. I don't know what to do."

"It kills me to say it," he said. "And we should obviously talk to Jess and Vicky first. But I think it's time."

"Time for what?"

"To throw in the towel. To give up."

"You want to shut down the restaurant?"

"No. Don't get me wrong. I don't want to. But I think it's the smart thing to do. The right thing to do."

"I don't want to either. But, you're right," I said. "We can't keep burning money like this."

"I hate to think I've let Papa down."

"Stop that right now," I said. "You did no such thing. He would be so proud of you. Proud of what we've done here. Happy to know how many people have tried his dishes. He'd probably give me flak about eating so many waffles over the last year, but he'd be proud, nonetheless."

"You have eaten a lot of waffles."

We both laughed.

I will say, on some level, I was relieved. Sure, the idea of going back to a corporate job sucked. It wasn't something I was looking forward to. But the idea of not working fourteen or fifteen hours a day, every single day, sure seemed promising. Having a normal schedule where I could see my family, put my daughter to bed? That sounded wonderful. The idea of getting a life back again seemed promising. And yes, I sure was sad to know we'd be closing the restaurant. But, like Marty said, it was for the best.

"I'm sure the women will agree," he said, opening another beer. "They're logic-minded."

"You're right. They will."

• • • • • • • • • •

They did. It didn't take much convincing, either. Once we showed them the numbers and how quickly they were falling, they agreed that it made the most sense to shut down, liquidate whatever we could to recoup some money, and return to our normal jobs.

Marty had talked to his old boss and was able to work his way back into the government job he had. A more junior role (he'd need to work his way back up), but still a job. I would look for something once we were done at the restaurant.

Our last day at the restaurant was filled with several things that made the mood feel very light. Marty had prepped every last ounce of food we'd already paid for. Enough for hundreds of people, but we didn't want it to go to waste. So we opened the door one last time, and I put a homemade "all meals free" sign on the door. We welcomed the community to get one last taste of Jean Luc's food through Marty.

And they did come. Slowly, at first, fairly skeptical of the offer of free food. But people came in, took a meal and a drink, and thanked us.

Part of me wanted to ask them why they didn't come in when we were open and selling food. Part of me wanted to yell at people for letting us down and causing our business to fail.

But I didn't. I resisted the urge to know why they let us fail.

Marty helped me out front, talking to people and thanking them. He helped explain why we were closing and that it was our last day.

Meanwhile, out back, people were coming and going, taking various equipment they'd bought from us and paid for already. It helped lessen the damage we'd felt from losing so much money in the past few months.

"It feels nice to be able not to let the food go to waste," Marty said.

"I agree."

We were both smiling for the first time in a long while. Not just casual smiles but ear-to-ear grins. We felt good about our decision and that we had the support of our wives.

"I'm looking forward to not being here tomorrow," he said. "It'll be nice to sleep in."

"When are you starting back up at the job?"

"Not for a week. I took a week off in between," he said.

"Smart choice. I'll start looking for something new next week, too."

"I'm sure you'll find something soon."

"I know. And Vic said it's fine if I want to stay home for a while and look in the fall. So I may do that."

"She's a good woman," he said.

"That she is."

The Last Block Party

Life got back to normal pretty fast once the restaurant closed. I got a job (a software company, again, big surprise there) and landed on my feet. Marty, too. He slid right back into the thick of things and seemed to be back to himself.

Samantha and Victoria loved having me home. I decided to accept Vic's offer, but only for a few weeks. I spent most of July with Sam at home while Vic went and kicked ass at work, like usual. That's when a job fell into my lap, and I couldn't turn it down.

The girls understood. I had felt so useless for so many months, not contributing to anything at home. Not bringing in any money, not spending time with them. It all felt so, I don't know, heavy.

The thought of the annual block party was exhausting. Just thinking about all that work felt like too much. But I knew we had to do it. Even if just as one last hurrah for the restaurant, a sort of farewell. A way for us to put a bow on the whole experience. And, given the pandemic was "over," it made sense to try to get everyone together. People showed up last year, but only very few.

Every time I tried to talk my way out of it, someone pulled me back in. First, it was Jess, who was very excited to have "the big party" again, in some sense of "normalcy." Marty, obviously, wanted to keep sharing Jean Luc's food with people, no matter how he got to do it. Victoria and Sam were very insistent that we do it as well.

A couple of neighbors had even stopped by while I was mowing the lawn here and there to ask if we would do it, expressing their interest.

I'd have been a jerk not to, really.

And before I knew it, I was lugging rented furniture from my garage to the cul-de-sac, like years past: tables, chairs, tents, water playgrounds. We went the whole nine yards. Against my better judgment, too. I still felt like I was a financial burden to our family, but Victoria insisted that I go "balls to the wall," as she put it. "Let's go big." So, big we were going.

Although illegal in Massachusetts, we still bought some fireworks from a place right over the state line in New Hampshire. It was only a small fine, should we get caught. And given how many people from the neighborhood would likely show up, no one would complain. At least I'd hoped not.

As I'd set up the last table, Marty backed up to it in their SUV and opened the back hatch. It was loaded with food, and the smell hit me immediately.

For the first time in almost two years, it didn't make me nauseous. Well, maybe that's not the right word. But smelling the same thing at the restaurant every day, day in and day out, made me feel gross. I thought maybe it was just me, but Marty mentioned it once, too.

"Hey pal," he said, getting out of the car and letting Lucas out of his car seat.

"Where's Jess?" I asked, noticing she wasn't with them.

"She'll be by in a bit. I wanted to get set up." He ran up to me and gave me a big hug. "Thanks for doing this."

"Thanks for wanting to make the food," I said. "I thought you'd be sick of it by now."

"Oh, I am," he laughed. "Don't get me wrong. I'm only doing this for the party. Don't expect me to cook again for another year."

"Understood," I said, grabbing some trays from the back of the SUV and plopping them into the food warmers I'd set up for him.

"Hey Luc! Sammi's inside, go on in."

"Weeee." He ran off and let himself in through the garage.

"They're getting so big," I said. "Can't believe they're going to be six next month."

"It makes me feel old," Marty said. "Really old."

"Me, too," I said.

Guests started showing up a little before one that afternoon. Well before we'd expected them. Many of them came offering their help in getting set up. Many brought more food than in years past.

At first, it felt like a funeral, of sorts. Like we were all there mourning the loss of the restaurant. "I'm so sorry about everything," Mrs. Dubois said. "It's so sad," John from next door said. And, sure, it was sad, but we were over it already. We'd moved on from it, and everything was fine. Our lives were settling back into what they used to be before it all happened. And, really, I think we were both better off for it.

I'd stopped having nightmares about whether I'd ordered enough food for a busy Saturday. I'd stopped worrying if someone who worked for us would get hurt (again). I no longer had to wake up early to get prep work done for the day. I'd only had to wake up early to get Sam off to school (or summer camp, as it were), and then I could go back to bed if I wanted to. Well, at least until I got a job again.

And I knew Marty was feeling better, even if he wouldn't ever admit it. Even if he never said the words aloud about how miserable the restaurant had been for him. How tired he was. How overworked he was. How stressed he was. He'd never mentioned it, but I knew. I could tell. Hell, I could feel it myself.

As soon as Marty pulled the tinfoil covers off the food he'd prepared and announced, "Who wants waffles?" the crowd swarmed him. With all the food options available, it was great to see people still flocking to Marty's table. Seeing them scrounge to get the last of a pan of something before he restocked, thinking it was the last of it he'd brought. Watching the line of people waiting for a fresh waffle. It made me so happy. Mostly because I had nothing to do with it. No bags, no screaming customers who were tired of waiting, no answering phones, no dealing with apps on multiple iPads. I got to stand back and watch my friend doing something that brought him joy.

I don't know who said it, but I'd heard a saying once that went, "Turning something you love into a job ruins your love of it." And I think that aptly sums up our experience with the restaurant. We went from loving something so much—making food and sharing it with people—to loathing having to go into the restaurant toward the end.

   I took a moment to look around to see the great turnout we'd had. Victoria and Jess were huddled together under a tent, along with some neighbors from both neighborhoods. Samantha and Lucas played on the water playground, where they'd been since they came out of the house an hour ago, and would stay until the sun went down. Various neighbors were having conversations, reminiscing about block parties of years past, all very happy that the pandemic and Covid were "over." Although we all knew people were still getting sick from it and dying, it sure felt like the world was as close to back to normal as it was going to get. Kids were yelling, playing lawn games, and drawing on the pavement with the chalk and paints we'd bought. Some of the teenagers were having a water balloon fight.

   But I kept coming back to Marty, who was smiling ear-to-ear the whole time. He was conversing with everyone, asking them about their lives, getting to know them all over again. And people loved it. They'd hover around his table, plate in hand, shoving his food into their mouths, while they talked with him and each other. He seemed genuinely happy for the first time in such a long time.

• • • ● • ● • • • •

Jackson, the teenage son of the Porters, offered to handle the fireworks once it got dark, and I was more than happy not to have to do it myself. Not that I was afraid of blowing myself up, but I was just exhausted from all the prepping for the day, all the setup, and socializing (I don't care who you are; being social when you're not a social person is exhausting).

   For the first time in the history of our block party, people didn't leave when the sun set. Maybe it was because they knew about the fireworks, or perhaps it was because everyone liked having the solidarity of a group. They liked being back with their friends and families, celebrating anything.

   "The food is all gone," Marty said, sitting beside me. "There's still waffle batter, but I always make too much of that."

   "Put it in my fridge," I said. "You know I'll eat it."

Samantha came and hopped up on my lap with a plate. It was nothing but whipped cream. "Uncle Marty makes yummy whipped cream," she said, shoveling a spoonful into her mouth.

"He does," I said as the first firework flew overhead and burst into a beautiful array of yellows and golds.

"I'm glad we did this," I said to Marty, looking back over my shoulder at our wives, sitting on the other side of the table, looking over us at the fireworks.

"Me too," he said, clinking his beer bottle against mine. "I'm glad, too."

Another firework flew high overhead, bursting into what would have been the shape of an American flag had it not been upside down.

"Congratulations," I heard Victoria say. "It's no longer a job but something you love, again."

"Something I love again," Marty echoed quietly to himself, but just loud enough for me to hear it.

We sat in silence, well as much silence as there can be during a fireworks show, as Jackson continued sending one after another up into the sky. They lit the neighborhood in bright and brilliant colors as they exploded. In some way, it felt like the beginning of something new. It put a nice bookend on our time as restaurant owners, but it was only a chapter in the story of our lives. The lives of Victoria, my loving wife. Samantha, my incredible daughter. Jessica, Marty's awesome wife. Lucas, Marty's son, who was so much like the grandfather he'd never met that it was uncanny. And of me and my best friend, Marty.

Love It? Hate It? Leave a Review.

It'd mean the world to me if you left a quick review with your thoughts. The QR codes below will take you to my pages on Goodreads and Amazon.

If you'd prefer to email me privately, please feel free. I'd love to chat with you! m@mjandreau.com

GOODREADS   AMAZON

Acknowledgements

My wife, Megan, who reminds me that while writing, publishing, and marketing a book is stressful and reading reviews is sometimes not good for my mental health, it's important to have a hobby that you enjoy. Thank you for being not only my best friend, but the *best* friend. To everyone.

My daughter, Samantha, who brings me joy every day.

Jill, for the reasons I outlined in the dedication of this book.

Jennifer, for being one of the best people I know. Who, in the face of some of life's toughest challenges (a lot of which are included in this book) always puts on a happy face, has positive things to say, and reminds me that there's always a bright side to everything.

My beta readers for *My Best Friend, Marty*: Samantha, Tehniat, Lorelai, Heather, Veronica, and Joanne. Thank you all for your insights, help, support, and passion for my work.

My parents, who introduced literature to me at a young age and were (mostly) supportive when I locked myself away as a teenager, typing away on my computer, writing stories that no one would ever read.

About the Author

M. Jandreau is a author known for his captivating storytelling and deeply evocative prose. With an impressive repertoire that includes acclaimed works such as "A Sour Chord," "My Last Days," and "Dudley Road," Jandreau has established himself as a masterful writer capable of immersing readers in rich and unforgettable narratives.

Hailing from the charming town of Southborough, Massachusetts, M. Jandreau draws inspiration from his life and the lives of those he knows. His works often reflect a profound understanding of human emotions, exploring themes of love, loss, and the complexities of the human experience.

Learn more about M. Jandreau at https://www.mjandreau.com

Also By

WANT ONE OF THESE BOOKS 20% OFF?

Made in the USA
Middletown, DE
02 March 2024